Tizita

The Fleur Trilogy, Book 2

by

Sharon Heath

Tizita
The Fleur Trilogy, Book 2

Copyright © 2017 Sharon Heath

This book is a work of fiction. While some of the place names may be real, characters and incidents are the product of the author's imagination and are used fictitiously. Any resemblance to events or persons living or dead is purely coincidental.

Author photograph by Marcella Kerwin.

Cover Photo: *Hamar Woman with Copper Bracelets*, David Schweitzer, Getty Images, under a Getty Images Content License Agreement.

Excerpts from *Waiting for Godot* copyright © 1954 by Grove Press, Inc.; Copyright © renewed 1982 by Samuel Beckett. Used by permission of Grove/Atlantic, Inc. Any third party use of this material, outside of this publication, is prohibited (U.S. and Canada).

Excerpts from *Waiting for Godot* copyright © Faber and Faber Ltd. by Samuel Beckett. Used by permission of Faber and Faber Ltd. Any third party use of this material, outside of this publication, is prohibited (Non-exclusive English language permission excluding U.S. and Canada).

Scriptures taken from the Holy Bible, New International Version, NIV. Copyright 1973, 1978, 1984, 2011 by Biblica, Inc. Used by permission of Zondervan. All rights reserved worldwide. www.zondervan.com. The "NIV" and "New International Version" are trademarks registered in the United States Patent and Trademark Office by Biblica, Inc.

Library of Congress Control Number: 2017936783
1. Contemporary fiction   2. Literary fiction
ISBN 10: 0-9979517-2-9
ISBN-13: 978-0-9979517-2-1

Thomas-Jacob Publishing, LLC, Deltona, Florida USA

Contact the publisher at TJPub@thomas-jacobpublishing.com.

For Eve, who pulled me through.

Tizita (pronounced tizz-i-**tah**): an Amharic word for the interplay of memory, loss and longing, sometimes conveyed in an Ethiopian or Eritrean style of music or song of the same name.

The tears of the world are a constant quantity.
For each one who begins to weep, somewhere else another stops.
(Samuel Beckett, *Waiting for Godot*)

Tizita

The Fleur Trilogy, Book 2

by

Sharon Heath

Part I

*Until the day breaks
and the shadows flee,
turn, my beloved,
and be like a gazelle
or like a young stag
on the rugged hills.*

(Song of Songs 2:17)

Chapter One
Fleur

NOTHING LASTS FOREVER. I hate to say it, but someday our dependable sun will kiss goodbye its penchant for fiery display to become first a red giant and then a white dwarf, finally shrinking into a cold clump of carbon floating through the ether. Even black holes evaporate, though a really big one can take a trillion years to die. Here on planet earth, where an organ roughly the size and shape of a clenched fist serves as gatekeeper between life and death, species as diverse as white-cheeked gibbons and black-footed ferrets manage about a billion and a half heartbeats in a lifetime. We humans do only slightly better, the healthiest of habits winning us no more than three billion beats before we succumb to the void once and for all.

Which is only one of the reasons I was having trouble with the *foie gras*. It was Adam's girlfriend, the enviably beautiful Stephanie Seidenfeld, who first introduced me to the dish not long after Adam had transformed from being my childhood tutor to, well, so many other things. I'd been sitting across from Stephanie and Adam in a red-leather booth at a bustling restaurant not too far from Caltech, nervously prattling on about my Reed Middle School classmates, who seemed to despise me for everything from my sorry social skills to my alacrity at algebraic equations and my ever-burgeoning breasts. Our waiter, who asked for our orders with one of those fake grins I associated with Little Red Riding Hood's pretend-granny, interrupted my litany of grievances. Eager to get that toothsome smile away from our table, I leapt in with a request for my standard Angel Hair Diavolo. Stephanie ordered the goose liver pâté and a small dinner salad, and Adam hemmed and hawed until Phony Granny began to show his true colors, snappishly demanding, "It's a busy night, man. Do you need another minute?"

Adam forestalled his departure with a hasty, "No, wait. I'll have the Pizza Vegetariana." I gave myself over to pure hatred toward the waiter for making Adam turn crimson with embarrassment.

Once our food arrived, I couldn't help but notice the zeal with which Stephanie dispatched her glutinous loaf, pausing a few times to dot her coral lips with her napkin while the busboy refilled our water glasses. It was only when Adam described the force-feeding of the goose killed for her pleasure that I emptied the contents of my stomach onto the white tablecloth. Not exactly what Mother would call *comme il faut*, but I suppose I might be excused, being at the time only a green girl—alas, in more ways than one—of thirteen.

Now, here I was—eight years, six months, two hours, and fifteen minutes later and twenty miles west of that Pasadena pizzeria—merely a shade less green than I'd been then and faced with the same abominable dish, this time presented with considerably more panache at a onetime drug rehabilitation center turned pricey hotel and restaurant, just a stone's throw from the Santa Monica beach pier. The occasion: an intimate celebration of my turning twenty-one on a birthday shared with Josef Stalin, Jane Fonda, Benjamin Disraeli, and Frank Zappa. And if the astrologers out there would care to explain what we five have in common, I'm listening.

My dinner companions this time were my best friend for nearly ever Sammie, her boyfriend Jacob, and my fiancé Assefa. Assefa was due to set off for Ethiopia the following day in search of his father, who'd gone missing with his childhood friend and co-researcher Zalelew Mekonin, presumably somewhere on the dusty road between Gondar and Aksum. Under the circumstances, none of us felt much like celebrating, but Assefa—nothing if not a respecter of ritual—had insisted that we had to mark my coming of age. Knowing how much anxiety he was pushing aside on my behalf, how could I say no?

The Casa del Mar's dining room was fragrant with the scent of fresh pine. We were four days away from Christmas, and the staff had gone all-out, decorating the imposing fir tree in the corner with so many colored lights and shiny ornaments that I couldn't help but secretly pinch my thigh every time I thought of the homeless veterans and sunburnt psychotics I knew were encamped on the beach only a few blocks away. There'd been a time when I hadn't understood why ample spaces like my father's old Main Line Philadelphia estate couldn't be made to accommodate those without homes of their own, but that was before I'd discovered the sacred status assigned to private property. The things people did to fend off the void were quite irrational and never failed to amaze me.

Assefa's words were slightly slurred, his capacity to hold his liquor in some kind of inverse ratio to his years spent in a tiny village near Gondar. He might have been raised by a couple of lapsed Christians, but he'd absorbed the ethos of his predominately Muslim community and was generally sparing in his alcohol consumption. Over the past several months I'd been suffused with gratitude more than a few times that he'd been brought to America before succumbing to the temptation to belong to the local majority, the price of admission a mere utterance of the words, "There is no god apart from God, and Muhammad is the Messenger of God."

In that respect, Muslims had a lot in common with my deceased Father, whose insistence that there was no god apart from God, with Jesus as his son, seemed to ignore the fact that heaven has been rather overpopulated with gods and goddesses ever since primates began walking upright. It wasn't exactly out of character that Father hadn't even begun to consider that the Egyptian baboon-headed god Thoth, the Bushman dreaming-god Mantis, the many-armed Hindu goddess of destruction Kali, or even Jesus himself, for that matter, might actually feel less passionately one-sided about abortion than he and his Cackler followers.

But Father's crusade against abortion, let alone his attempts to discredit my own small efforts to advance our knowledge of the physical world, was far from my mind as Assefa urged me on, quite unfairly I thought, with a breathtaking batting of his thick lashes, "Tayshte ... taste it. Look at *our* dishes." He gestured toward his own empty plate, which looked as if it had been licked clean. "You've got to at least try. It'll be an insult to Antoine if you don't."

Sammie, the traitor, joined in. Predictably, her original British accent was back in full swing after just one glass of Deutz Brut. She waved an expansive hand, the olive cheeks she'd inherited from her

Jewish father and Indian mother glowing a rich burnt sienna. "C'mon, Fleur Beurre, Assefa's right. How's Antoine going to be motivated to keep delivering more goodies if we send your *foie gras* back untouched? You can do this, girl." She licked her lips in search of any last little bits. "Your heart'll forgive the cholesterol just this once. Antoine's *foie gras* is brilliant."

Silently cursing Antoine, I managed a weak grin.

Antoine was the reason we were dining at the Casa del Mar in the first place. Assefa's next-door neighbor in their side-by-side duplex in Carthay Circle, he'd recently graduated from L.A.'s campus of Le Cordon Bleu with an offer of a job as sous-chef at the Casa. He'd promised Assefa he'd sneak us an assortment of yummy freebies for my coming of age party, and the *pâté* was evidently the first on his list.

I'd met Assefa himself only six months before and had been bedazzled by him from the start. We were an odd, but complementary match—he a brilliant intern with an interest in cardiology and a background in literature as sophisticated as Sammie's; me a whiz at physics, list-making, and cat quirks, and pretty hopeless at everything else.

Despite the fact that Assefa was living at that time with his parents, a mere half mile away from Caltech, we didn't cross paths until his mother Abeba came to work for my own overcommitted mother, babysitting and tutoring the orphaned Cesar Jesus de Maria Santo Domingo Marisco after the tragic death of my old nanny, who'd adopted the child when he was barely out of diapers. Mother taking on Cesar was just one instance of God's taste for irony. When I was little, my mother hadn't been able to get away fast enough from the unwanted children my father kept saving from the devil abortionists, yet here she was, on a fast jog toward forty, landed with full custodianship of one of them.

Mother had found Abeba through an employment referral list offered by Caltech. As she put it at the time, "I have to assume that anyone who advertises her services to professors at the top science university in the country has to have more on the ball than your average undereducated nanny." Looking forward with some curiosity to meeting a woman who could balance anything on a ball beyond a matchstick or a piece of lint, I felt an immediate affinity with Abeba when we were introduced, she warmly clasping my outreached hand in hers, which were surprisingly small and sealskin smooth.

In a voice like wind chimes, she'd effused, "Ah, Fleur, I've been so eager to meet you. We two share a kinship in name, you know. I am a flower in Amharic; you are a flower in French." As I saw myself bursting forth with petals somewhere in the French countryside, Abeba beckoned me toward Mother's capacious kitchen. Pouring me a cup of the best coffee I'd ever tasted, she went on to share the name of her husband Achamyalesh, which she informed me translated as *You Are Everything*, as well as that of their only son Assefa, whose name, she told me, meant *He Has Increased Our Family By Coming Into the World*. You certainly couldn't accuse the Ethiopians of minimalism.

Abeba's eyes positively glowed when she spoke of Achamyalesh. I learned soon enough that, like intelligent women the world over whose access to advanced education has been culturally constrained, she took particular pride in her husband's achievements. She seemed oblivious to her own well-developed attributes, particularly her generosity and what Mother liked to call her "pull-out-all-the-stops enthusiasm."

While I'd never regretted moving away from Mother's New York penthouse to the far humbler Pasadena cottage of my physics mentor Stanley H. Fiske and his sister Gwen halfway between my twelfth and thirteenth birthdays, I'd been touched when Mother had elected to forgo the joys of MoMA, the Met, and Mile End Deli to pack up the massive contents of her apartment and the remains of Father's estate to move to nearby San Marino to comfort me after my Nobel debacle.

Mother being Mother, always depending on one kind of group or another, it hadn't been surprising that she'd brought with her to SoCal the retinue of angels with whom I'd grown up in Father's Main Line mansion—Nana, Sister Flatulencia, Fayga, Dhani, Ignacio, as well as a decidedly seraphic No-Longer-a-Baby-Angelina and the rather devilish young Cesar.

And me being me, it had been pretty predictable that I'd found a way to continue to sleep at the Fiskes' once she arrived. The fact that Mother took it in good stride—filling her void with her Bill W. friends and her studies to become a librarian—wasn't all that surprising. Neither one of us was in the habit of much mother-daughter intimacy. I'd bet money on her feeling a bit relieved when I made my excuse that Caltech was more convenient to the Fiskes' bungalow than to her 12,000 square-foot Tudor-style home, just a hop and a skip from the Huntington Gardens. What I didn't tell her was that her new digs bore more than a passing resemblance to Father's sweeping Main Line grounds, and it would take more than a few angels to make it tolerable to live somewhere like that again.

But once she'd introduced me to Abeba, I found myself detouring almost every afternoon to Mother's on my way home from Caltech. Dispatching a noisily reluctant Cesar to his room to do his homework, Abeba would proceed to ply me with Ethiopian versions of after-school treats, regaling me all the while with stories about the remarkable Achamyalesh. Those visits were a godsend, especially on the days when my team and I had butted our heads for hours against some unyielding mathematical problem. Shoveling in handfuls of *dabo kolo*, crunchy nuggets of spice heaven that I learned to wash down with little sips of *bunna*—Ethiopia's far superior antecedent to Starbucks' finest—I couldn't help but grow *curiouser* and *curiouser* about Abeba's other half.

Who wouldn't want to meet someone named *You Are Everything*? Especially when said all-inclusive soul was an African anthropologist who, according to his wife, avidly kept up his research despite being reduced to driving a cab in the U.S.? My curiosity was rewarded soon enough, heralded on one of those typical SoCal June-gloom days that left you despairing that summer would ever come. I was mounting the Malibu-tiled steps leading up to Mother's front porch, appreciating their vibrant design as only someone who'd never lived in the house could, when Abeba dramatically flung open the front door. She clasped my elbow and excitedly tugged me so impatiently into Mother's vaulted-ceilinged living room that I almost tripped on the Persian rug in the foyer. "Oh, Fleur, it is such good news I have. The Anthropology Dean at Pasadena City College has read Achamyalesh's VITA. She is going to give him a chance in their evening public lecture series." Abeba's mood was contagious. I skipped after her into the kitchen, where she automatically reached for a pot and poured me a cup of *bunna*, nearly spilling it in her enthusiasm. "He will be speaking in just two weeks on the work he has been doing on the cultural folklore surrounding the Ark of the Covenant."

Thanks to Adam's thoroughness as a tutor, I already knew about the Ethiopian Orthodox Church's claims that the cask containing God's covenant with the Jewish people had been in their possession near the Church of Our Lady Mary of Zion at Aksum ever since the Ethiopian Menelik, son of the Queen of Sheba and the Biblical Solomon, brought the Ark back home after a visit to his wise father.

I tended to greet stories of wise fathers with a certain skepticism. Personally, I'd never met one. As for the Ark itself, I'd been fascinated by its storied contents ever since I'd learned that, according to Biblical historians, the Ten Commandments were preceded by another set of ten precepts called the Ritual Decalogue, which included such pithy prescriptions for a righteous life as "Do not cook a young goat in its mother's milk."

The controversy surrounding the whereabouts of the Ark spoke to who owned the truth, who owned a special connection with God. But I hadn't yet met a soul who actually lived by God's Commandments. Oh sure, I didn't know many murderers. (None, to be honest.) But even the smaller taboo against coveting seemed to put our species on the spot. I couldn't possibly enumerate all the physics colleagues I'd met who'd told me they envied my brilliance (read Nobel). And every time Apple released a new iPhone, the amount of coveting that went on would certainly have driven Moses to despair.

I set Mother's zebra-festooned, Hermes "Africa" espresso cup onto its saucer and asked excitedly, "Oh, Abeba, do you think Achamyalesh would mind if I attended his talk?" Little did I know I'd played right into her hands. I learned later that it was Abeba who'd persuaded Assefa to accompany his father to the lecture. The rest, as they say, was history.

Fast-forward six months, five days, and six hours and twenty-nine minutes. A champagne glass in one hand and my own pale paw in the other, Assefa nodded encouragingly toward the twin meaty mounds on my plate. But it was no use. Every time I looked down at those liverwurstian circles, I saw a doleful set of goose eyes staring back at me. Feeling myself slide toward the pit of everlasting nothingness, I had to pinch the palm Assefa wasn't holding to control the impulse to flap.

Assefa realized he was pushing me too far. "Okay, but only for you would I do this." Throwing me a conspiratorial look, he leaned in toward the center of the table and, skewing his elbow forward at an awkward angle, "accidentally" spilled his glass of Deutz into my plate while simultaneously crying out, "Oh, what a clumsy sod I am." His eyes twinkling, he pulled me toward him, his sharp collarbone pushing comfortingly against my temple. When distressed, I am always a sucker for a little pain.

A waiter appeared out of nowhere to expertly whisk away the sodden dish and rearrange the silver. I craned my neck to look up at Assefa's copper-colored face. I still hadn't gotten over my good fortune in finding a man whose heart was pure, but whose high forehead, leonine cheekbones, cushiony lips, and chin-sweeping goatee lit a host of impure flares across my belly. My only other sexual partner had been dark-skinned, too, but with Hector Hernandez it had been one brief moment of unexpected (and unwanted) penetration, subsidized by cheap beer, naiveté, and the synchronicity of multiple "Linda palomas" whispered in my ear just after I'd washed my hands with Dove soap. Carl Jung and Wolfgang Pauli would probably have turned over in their graves to learn that their notion of a-causal but meaningfully connected events (aka synchronicity) would play a role in a thirteen-year-old girl losing her virginity. But with Assefa, it was what Stanley H. Fiske liked to call "the real deal" and what Adam rather wistfully (and, as it happens, inaccurately) pronounced as "first love."

Not that concupiscence hadn't made its contribution to the mix. Just that morning, the fact of my birthday a poor competitor to the dread stirred by his father's disappearance two weeks earlier, Assefa had momentarily roused himself from his funk, convincing me to pose naked with him, hip to hip, in front of his full-length bathroom mirror. "Come, *dukula*," he'd whispered, his tongue a serpent in my ear, "let us look at one another." I hadn't needed much persuading. I liked to see the two of us together as much as he did. The contrast never failed to stir my tweeter.

I'm not a short woman, my father having bested six feet by several inches, and Assefa wasn't exactly the tallest man, so our noses were at about the same level. But the resemblance ended right there. Everything about me shouted, *American girl!* My nose was just a bit upturned, my blue eyes studded with silvery gray flecks, my eyebrows a mere shade or two darker than the sun-bleached hair concealing my slightly pointy-shaped head—a leftover of my entrance into the world from a teenaged mother's clenching tweeter. I'd been profoundly relieved a few years back when my thighs finally flared out to balance the bulbousness of my breasts, and I was extra glad of them these days, given Assefa's penchant for grasping my hips like guiderails as he drove deeper and deeper into my dark mystery, crying, "*Awon, awon!*"

"Yes, yes!" I'd moan back, trying not to pinch his skinny butt too hard as a mini-explosion sent waves of pleasure from my tweeter across every inch of my body. Assefa was as lean as a Watta hunter, his face hauntingly narrow, his hair a fine pattern of springy coils.

In the mirror, I watched my hands cup his purplish-brown balls, his member rising to a breathtaking angle. For a brief moment, I thought I saw a coffee-colored woman with wild black curls staring back at me—*who was that?*—but when I closed my eyes and reopened them the apparition was gone. I attended to the matter at hand. Assefa and I were compelled to have a nice long go at each other, with me seated on the edge of the bathroom counter, watching his glorious backside contract rhythmically in the mirror. But this time, something unusual happened. I felt a fullness inside me as Assefa came. "Oh, no!" I cried, as I heard him shout with unencumbered pleasure.

The condom had clearly not been up to its job. I felt a slow trickle of semen down my inner thigh. To my embarrassment, I began to cry until Assefa whispered, "Don't worry, *dukula*. Didn't you just finish your period last week? It will be all right." I tended to be lazy about keeping track and wasn't so sure he was accurate about the timing, but my worry faded as he held me even tighter. I've always been a sucker for a strong grip. He began to lick the tears off my cheek like a mother cat, though his tongue was much softer than Jillily's. It broke the spell. I giggled, and he laughed with me.

It had been almost physically painful to unglue ourselves and get dressed, he to pick up some last minute supplies for his trip, me to take off for Caltech. The burst condom didn't give me too much disquiet. I'd learned ages ago to shove unwanted thoughts into a seeming endless number of spare cupboards in my mind.

Actually it was precisely because of my lifelong familiarity with emptiness that I was particularly looking forward to discussing with my team certain implications of the Eridanus supervoid in an area of the universe devoid of galaxies. The void was huge: nearly a billion light-years across. It had been pretty much confirmed that supervoids were empty of all matter, including dark matter, and a few of my more imaginative colleagues were even conjecturing that Eridanus was a gateway to a parallel universe. While that sounded pretty sci-fi, serious theories of parallel universes were emerging from research into the phenomenon of quantum entanglement, famously described by Albert Einstein as "spooky action at a distance."

I was never one to dismiss seemingly outrageous ideas out of hand; if I were, I would never have gotten this far. The phenomenal world was a tantalizing gem whose facets outleapt anything the mind might conceive. Quantum entanglement was just such a phenomenon. On a quantum level, once objects have interacted with each other or come into being in a similar way, they become linked or entangled. The fact that particles of energy and matter could interact with each other and retain a predictable connection in balancing pairs despite considerable distance between them had fascinated me ever since Adam had first described it, both of us wolfing down Krispy Kremes in a combination of excitement and awe.

I'd been haunted by the void as a child. Not the common, garden variety childhood terror of disappearing down the bathtub drain, but a lurking pit of eternal emptiness that threatened me long before I taught myself to read Sister Flatulencia's *World English Bible* and Mother's *Elle* magazines when I was nearly four. It was only when Adam introduced me to Nobel physicist Stanley H. Fiske that I found a way to put that preoccupation to good use, ultimately coming up with the discovery of dark matter within all living organisms in the form of cellular black holes (I called them C-Voids), along with the potential to harness the exchange of light and dark matter to move people around with a zero carbon footprint via the Principle of Dematerialization. Those two discoveries, emerging during a feverishly insomniac contemplation of the heartache of abortion, the abominable human consumption of chimpanzees (euphemistically called "bush meat"), the self-replication of fractals, and the suspended jewels of the Hindu god Indra's web, each one of them mirroring every other jewel in the web, won me the Prize, but not even a pro-science president had been able to budge a Congress determined to outlaw any grant that would fund our application of P.D.

But now another angle on the topic was beckoning. Inspired by David Bohm's vision of entanglement as a guiding wave connecting individual interacting particles, Laura Mersini-Houghton had come up with her own model of entangled universes that was just begging to be verified. We toyed with becoming the ones to do it as we waited for my father's parting gift to me—what Gwennie Fiske called "the congressional dog and pony show to sabotage scientific progress"—to play itself out.

I'd tried out my thoughts about the Many Worlds Theory on Assefa the first time we met, explaining how one of the myriad debates in quantum physics concerns what happens to the unused possibilities when a choice is made to pursue one course of action over another. Many Worlds theorists contend that those other options actually play out in parallel worlds.

Assefa was fascinated with the idea, which proved to be a greater stimulant than the Brazilian blend I was drinking at the time. My rhapsodizing over science had been the ultimate repellent for every man Sammie had tried fixing me up with, to the point that I'd decided to forego blind dates forever. Poor Sammie had tried her hardest sell with the last one. "He looks fab, Fleur, you'll see—and super smart. Phi Beta Kappa, Law Review, the whole enchilada." She'd been at least partly right. Russell Glick had the look of a young George Clooney, but as we dined together at the fashionable Border Grill, he'd seemed more concerned about demonstrating how many Margaritas he could throw back and enumerating which T.V. shows he liked best than registering my increasing restlessness. When, finally, he seemed to recall that women tended to like it if you at least asked a few questions about them and I described to him the thrill of discovering C-Voids, he'd responded, "Yeah, but what do you do for fun?"

Delivering me to my doorstep, Russell had looked shocked that I'd averted my face as he aimed his lips at mine. I'd phoned Sammie as soon as his shiny black Mercedes sped away. "I appreciate you looking out for me, Sam, I really do, but if one more idiot tells me I need to lighten up, I'm going to spit ... or something worse." Sammie snorted, and in an instant we were giggling over how we'd repaired a major clash in our teens by shooting rice pudding out of our noses.

Russell Glick turned out to be the perfect opening act for Assefa, not that he needed one. Yakking away as we huddled together at the Coffee Club, I explained to *him* how black holes and voids had been a major part of my life since my earliest days as Mother's unwanted only child in a household full of eccentric women and cast-off children. Assefa's eyes stayed locked onto my face the whole time. One sure sign you're being listened to is that your companion actually asks relevant questions, though Assefa would have to have been more than a little crazy if he hadn't *needed* to ask questions after my meandering description of how the unpredictable variability of the Butterfly Effect had led an eleven-year-old girl to attempt to resurrect her beloved Grandfather by plumping his withering testicles with water, the failure of which had energized her then-alcoholic mother to finally wrest the two of them away from her abusive husband's Main Line estate.

"Which," I'd confessed, "was followed by my arrest for skinny dipping in someone's private New York garden, moving in with my physics mentor Stanley H. Fiske and his sister Gwennie here in Pasadena, and getting pregnant by a boy who had matching Jesus and Mary tattoos on the backs of his hands. My abortion was the last straw, as far as Father was concerned." Assefa winced, and I hastily appended, "I know, I know—it was horrifying. Even though I was just thirteen, I'll never be at peace with what I did." I felt my eyes moisten, but even the lump in my throat couldn't seem to stop my verbal Vesuvius. "I call her Baby X," I said, hastily brushing tears from my cheek. I daren't look Assefa in the eye or I'd simply implode, so I stared at his coffee cup, which had a slight nick in its Styrofoam rim in the shape of a probability distribution sign. "You'd think killing your child would ruin your life forever, but I'd tucked her into the hole in my heart, and not too long afterward I had my epiphany about C-Voids and the next thing I knew I got the call telling me I was being awarded the Nobel Prize. Really, it was a team effort. But now we're at a standstill on P.D.'s application, thanks to this lousy economy and too many members of Congress convinced my project has something to do with human cloning. Which it doesn't. You'd think they might believe me about it."

That one still irritated me. I was imperfect in more ways than I could possibly calculate, Baby X a case in point, but I wasn't a liar. At least not about anything so consequential. Contrary to the beliefs of the flat-earthers wanting to drive us back to the Stone Age, scientists generally tell the truth. The fact that I'd been the youngest scientist ever to receive a Nobel Prize seemed to be as irrelevant to certain members of Congress as had the jailed Aung San Suu Kyi's Nobel Peace Prize to the Burmese government while she still languished under house arrest.

As Assefa burst in with a series of penetrating questions, it dawned on me that I had to be either pretty nervous or something I couldn't quite put my finger on to natter on like that—especially the abortion part, which might have been in the public record after my catastrophic Nobel speech, but not something I typically talked about with anyone, let alone an attractive stranger. Looking back now, I don't think it was nerves at all, but Assefa's gift for absolute acceptance.

Once he finally managed to get some sense of what I'd been talking about, he pronounced gravely, "Enat—my mother—was right. You are quite brilliant. I do believe you've just managed to compress your whole life story into three minutes." He shook his head wonderingly. "And what a life it has been!" Without warning, he stood up, and I was afraid he was going to walk out on me, but instead he leaned forward, whispering, "Tell you what. I'll get us another couple of coffees and you can fill in the holes"—he flashed me a knowing grin—"and give me the expanded version." I watched him walk toward the busy counter, his body displaying a kind of feline grace in a tangled loop of fluidity and tension.

He came back to the table carrying two steaming cups, which he carefully set down before going back for a couple of napkins, taking the time to fold them into perfect little triangles. He pulled his chair closer to mine. I caught the faintest whiff of something—a mixture of cinnamon and Roquefort cheese?—and took a long, relaxed breath. Who wouldn't feel reassured by such interesting smells?

Unconsciously stroking his goatee, Assefa shot me a teasing look. "Now, let's start with that grandfather of yours. You didn't really think you could resurrect him, did you? By pouring water on his ... body?"

I felt myself flush. "I know it sounds ridiculous, but it made perfect sense to me at the time. The thing is, I was raised in an extremely religious household. Mother's companion was actually an ex-nun. My father was the foremost crusader against abortion in the

Senate, and the house was drenched in stories about Jesus. My mother hadn't gotten sober yet, my nanny was busy most of the time taking care of a revolving door of foster children, and my grandfather, who was mute from his stroke, was the only one who actually had any time for me." Nervously pressing the pleat in my napkin, I paused. "Well, no way around it, he was everything to me. I felt I had to bring him back to life. Somehow—well, not somehow, but that's a whole other story—I got it into my head that his balls, which went from swollen to shrunken with congestive heart failure, were somehow the key to bringing him back again, so I poured a bunch of water on him—actually, onto the crotch of his best blue suit—while he lay in his casket."

I waited for the inevitable derisive laughter, but Assefa seemed preoccupied. "Your grandfather," he said slowly, "he was a good man?"

I nodded.

"Ah." How can one word—less of a word, really, than a sound—convey so much?

That was when I sensed that there might be a connection between Assefa and me far stronger than pheromones.

He grunted, and in that moment his narrow face seemed to fold in on itself. "My grandfather Medr, my father's father, hasn't had a stroke, but the result is the same. He hasn't uttered a word since his wife—my grandmother—was raped and murdered by Eritreans when they invaded our homeland."

My mind reeled, but my mouth assumed an idiotic life of its own. "Medr. What an interesting sounding name. Does it have a particular meaning?" As soon as the words came out, I wanted to scoop them back again.

Assefa looked understandably taken aback, but responded politely, "Earth and Fertility," at which point I burst into tears. "Oh, God," I cried, "what a beautiful name!" He looked both alarmed and confused. I wanted to run out of the coffee house, but was paralyzed. "Forgive me. I've always been socially backward. What you've just told me is horrible. I am so sorry. Please forget what I just said. Believe me, it's no accident my nickname used to be Odd Duck."

God bless him, Assefa actually laughed. "Odd Duck? As in 'quack, quack?'" He put his thumbs side by side with his fingers splayed flat on the table, and, wriggling his wrists, waddled his hands toward me. But now a shadow overtook his smiling eyes. "There is nothing right to say when there is too much pain. Perhaps that is why Medr has chosen not to speak at all."

I know it goes against the grain, but I've decided that shared suffering can actually be an aphrodisiac. That night, in the back seat of his father's yellow cab, Assefa kissed my forehead, brought his soft lips to mine, and, reaching into my organic white cotton bra, fondled my breasts, which seemed to have developed a rather pushy life of their own.

I didn't know whether to laugh or cry with how much my tweeter was aching for him, but Assefa turned out to be old school. We managed to hold off moving into the mini-explosion phase until we got engaged. It was a different story as soon as a simple silver band with its hard-purchased zirconia and sapphire ring encircled my fourth finger. In his brand new double bed in his brand new duplex apartment, Assefa made up for lost time, establishing what would soon become a ritual of commenting enthusiastically on various electrified parts of my body as he nibbled at them. Surrounding my lips with his own fuller ones, he traced their shape with the tuft at his chin, pulling back to proclaim, "My little Nobelist, whose mouth is a fount of wisdom." Moving down, he licked every inch of my breasts, coming up for air to pronounce like a connoisseur, "Abundant! Delicious! Fit for a king!" As if he weren't already sending spears of fire across my belly, he tantalized me with little chicken peck kisses, inching his way down to my tweeter. Coming up once for air, he murmured, "Mmm, could this pussy be the source of all that genius?" before diving back in again.

I ended up spending every weekend I could at his apartment. Even when he dragged himself off to study all day at UCLA's Biomedical Library, I preferred curling up in his bed with a pile of physics papers to venturing out. The bed smelled of him. I brought Jillily with me most times in her dented old cage of a cat carrier, sliding her traveling litter box out from under Assefa's bathroom sink and pouring in just enough Jonny Cat to do the job. At eighteen, Jillily was a lot skinnier than she'd once been, but just as likely to stretch across the bed in her Charlotte the Harlot pose, flat on her back with her white apron exposed, giving me the look that said,

"Well, don't you want to stroke my silky belly and sniff my perfect fish breath?"

But on the morning of my birthday, it wasn't UCLA that Assefa left our bed for but a series of last-minute errands to prepare for his trip. Asking myself for the hundredth time where in the world Achamyalesh and Zalelew could have disappeared to and not getting any reassuring answers, I drove Jillily back home to the Fiskes' before my planned day at Caltech. As I launched myself up the path on Rose Villa Street, I saw Gwennie look out the kitchen window and wave. But before I could wave back, I was accosted by our next-door neighbor Fidel Marquetti. I'd always assumed Fidel to be a harmless sort of man until this past summer, when he'd taken a fierce dislike to the Korean family who'd just moved in at his other side. Well, to be fair, it wasn't the Kangs who'd offended Fidel's tender sensibilities, but their Jindo named Chin-Hwa, whose name, as Mrs. Kang had proudly informed me the first time the dog exuberantly sniffed my crotch, meant, "The Most Wealthy." Which made a kind of sense, given the fact that the success of the Kang's liquor store in South Pasadena was undoubtedly due less to the sweet potato vodka they prided themselves on purveying than the fact that they'd actually sold two winning SuperLotto Plus tickets over the past year and a half.

It was probably because of the mysterious skin condition that had Fidel feeling in flames most of the time that he developed an inordinate irritability toward Chin-Hwa. From the beginning, I couldn't help but notice that Fidel demonstrated less than an average Pasadena neighbor's tolerance for the dog's frequent escapes from the leash in Mr. Kang's frantic hand to howl at the borders of Fidel's unusual variant of a SoCal front lawn.

There was a story behind Chin-Hwa's antagonism toward Fidel's garden. In defiance of Southern California's current drought, Fidel had planted rows of tall, exotic grasses separated by neat squares of annuals, which he liked to water with one of those revolving lawn sprinklers. The thing was, the generally impeccable Jindo breed of dog had one (in this case fatal) flaw: an aversion to water and a desperate desire to avoid getting wet. Mr. Kang had attempted to resolve the situation by taking Chin-Hwa out for his walks only when Fidel's sprinkler wasn't running, but it turned out that Chin-Hwa had a second character flaw less endemic to his breed. He held a grudge. Anytime he could slip his handsome white head under the backyard fence that a desperate Mr. Kang kept unsuccessfully reinforcing, he'd make a beeline for some tidy gathering of multicolored pansies, planting a crushing dump over as many of Fidel's flowers as he could before slinking back to his own yard.

After three months of Fidel banging on the Kang door, Mr. Kang bowing his head and muttering apologies, and Mrs. Kang standing in the background wringing her hands, Fidel had finally gone over the edge, festooning his front yard with printed signs with admonitions ranging from "I Know What You're Doing" to "Curb your Dog." Though the former was the most provocative of the bunch, it was the latter that had gotten to me, only because I misread it the first time I passed by as "Curb Your God."

Which had taken me on no end of void-vanquishing mental excursions. How many world crises would simply dry up if the world's zealots would only curb their gods? Lord knew, I might have been able to make peace with my own father had he gotten past the certainty of possessing the one and only spiritual truth before he died.

But this morning it was Fidel himself, and not one of his signs, that had me nearly bursting into untimely laughter. His brown face was mottled with patches of undoubtedly painful crimson as he pointed wordlessly to what I had to admit was a pretty exuberant splash of doggie diarrhea over a plot of pink impatiens. But he found his voice in no time. "Those damn Chinks. I thought those people *ate* their dogs. These ones've gotta be spending too much time praying to that Buddha-head in their living room to even notice what that frickin' animal of theirs is doing. If I were them, I'd be spending half my days in confession. You'd think they were the ones who won the war."

I stopped myself from trying to correct him. Where would I even begin? I shrugged with what I hoped at least looked like sympathy and ran toward Gwennie, who was thankfully beckoning now from our front door. As I submitted to a giant hug, I couldn't help but think about poor Fidel, and I must have muttered out loud, "Well, *somebody's* God certainly needs a little curbing," because Gwen pushed me away and said defensively, "Huh?"

I quickly reassured Gwennie that I didn't mean *her*, but she was already walking away from me, throwing over her shoulder, "Listen, I've got some news for you. C'mon into the kitchen." I nearly laughed at how my thrifty metabolism led middle-aged women—well, middle-aged women except for my mother—to want to feed me first and talk later. Gwennie set down a plate and gestured for me to sit at the kitchen table while she sliced off a slab of banana bread, but I just stared at her. Sensing my unease, she relented. "Okay, kiddo. I got a call from your mother a few minutes ago. Abeba showed up and told her that Zalelew's daughter phoned this morning. She got a postcard from her father, postmarked Gondar." Dropping into my chair, I anxiously shoved a hunk of banana bread into my mouth. Gwennie continued, "Zalelew wrote that he and Achamyalesh bumped into a young woman from their old village when they arrived at the airport. She was accompanying three small children and the Spanish parents who were adopting them. Zalelew said she was a girl Assefa had gone to school with." I stopped chewing, but Gwennie seemed not to notice. She added, "They were going to visit the orphanage where she worked on their way to Aksum." She cocked her head hopefully. "So maybe Assefa won't have to go now?"

Reaching for my cell, I realized I hadn't turned it on yet this morning. As soon as I did, the haunting melody of the ringtone I'd assigned to Assefa, Teddy Afro's "Aydenegetim Lebie," filled the room.

Assefa's voice was trembling. "Fleur? Thank God you finally picked up. Have you heard the news?"

I began to burble about how we'd celebrate, when Assefa broke in, clearly thinking aloud, "The thing is, though, why didn't they call? Abat promised us he'd call when he landed in Gondar. Don't you think it's odd that all anyone got was a postcard? My family always phones when we arrive at our destination. It's what we do. And why haven't they called since?"

"Gondar's a pretty small city. Maybe the phone service has been down," I ventured hopefully. "Maybe the cellphone he rented was a dud. Maybe he figured a postcard would do the trick."

"And make us wait for two weeks? The postcard wasn't even from him."

"Maybe you'll get one tomorrow. Sometimes mail travels at different rates. It is Ethiopia, after all."

He snapped, "What's that supposed to mean?"

I got a little short myself. "Oh, come on, it's an underdeveloped country. For God's sake, even the U.S. Postal Service screws up half the time."

Assefa paused, then conceded grudgingly, "Yes, of course, of course, you're right."

Gwennie shot me a look and crossed the room to load the dishwasher, flinging in plates and cups a bit more forcefully than usual.

I knew my argument made sense, but Assefa's voice, though calmer now, was no less determined. "Nothing has changed, really. Something's not right."

"So …?"

Assefa asked defensively, "What can I do? What if it were *your* father?"

I felt like I'd been struck. I could hear the stiffness in my voice as I reminded him, "If it were my father, things like phone calls wouldn't have been an issue."

Gwennie twisted around to frown meaningfully at me, anxiously stroking her Physicists are Spacier apron, the one with the "a" in Spacier x-ed out and replaced by an "i."

Assefa was contrite now. "Ah, *dukula*. I have been insensitive. And on your birthday, too. But you do see, don't you, that I must go? My mother is still very worried."

"I suppose," I muttered ungraciously.

But just as I ventured the question that was niggling at me, "Oh, by the way, who's the girl they bumped into," Assefa said, "Damn. My cell's breaking up. I'll see you tonight at—"

That was it. We'd lost the connection.

I tried talking it over with Gwennie, she sitting on my left so she could hear me with her good ear. "You're being ridiculous, child. I don't know what I was thinking. Of course, he has to go. It's not like his father to skip the call. He would have found a pay phone or called from the hotel. Something."

I was too ashamed to share the real source of my disquiet, telling myself not to be an idiot. Besides, Gwennie—ever the political animal—was already taking the conversation in a new direction. Muttering something about orphans, she pulled her eyeglasses down from the top of her head and wandered over to the wicker basket of the week's worth of newspapers she kept at the corner of the kitchen.

Pushing aside my plate, she spread a marmalade-stained page across the table.

"Look at this," she said, pointing to a headline that announced, "Ethiopian Ministry of Health Acknowledges More than a Million AIDS Orphans.'"

She flung out her arms for emphasis. "One fucking million!" The last time I'd seen her like this was when Father's Cacklers—otherwise known as Campaign America to Crush C-Voids—had joined with Big Oil to mount their campaign against my research. Pulling up a chair, she began reading aloud. "'UNICEF predicts that the number of street children will only increase, with teenage girls ending up as prostitutes. The number of orphans may top two million by 2015.'" Gwennie pounded the table hard enough for my plate to jump. "Who's going to care for all those children?"

Her face had gone red enough to make me worry about her blood pressure. She wasn't getting any younger, and after Nana's sudden death last year, I couldn't afford losing anyone else I loved. In an attempt at diversion, I broke in with my Fidel story, ticking off on my fingers his multiple feats of historical revisionism.

At first, she looked annoyed. Nobody likes to be interrupted in the middle of a political rant. But when I got to the part about the "Chinks" thinking they'd won the war, she was bending over with laughter. Then the hiccups began. They were the worst kind, climaxing in wet burps that ominously suggested something worse might not be far behind.

Laughing apologetically, she hurriedly grabbed a glass from the cupboard, filled it with filtered water, and drank it upside down over the sink. She wiped the drool from her chin, waited a moment, then pronounced, "There. That's better." Trying to control her tittering this time, she shook her head. "Poor man." Then she proceeded to pack up the rest of the banana bread for me to take to school.

As it turned out, wild bathroom sex wasn't my only overindulgence that morning. In my nervousness, I'd pigged out on more banana bread than I'd realized—there was only half a loaf left to bring to my team at Caltech. Thrusting the tin-foiled care package into my book bag, I squinted out the living room window to make sure Fidel had gone in. Dashing outside, I started up the dented green Prius I'd inherited from Gwennie. As I glided past Fidel's yard, I saw that he'd tacked up one more sign. This one was clearly an impromptu job. You had to give Fidel credit for pride of place; all the others had been made up professionally at the local stationer's. This newest effort was hand lettered in a downward slant, and despite being brief had a couple of misspellings: "Buda Hades go home." Given that Fidel's whole family had taken advantage of one of the surges of amnesty following their emigration from Cuba on an illegal fishing boat, the message packed more than a little irony.

My short drive to school was filled with long thoughts, including the AIDS crisis in Africa, which I generally managed to shove into a dusty storage cupboard at the back of my mind. Normally, any mention that the cradle of our species had two out of every ten people prematurely dying was as unbearable as pictures of polar bears and penguins stranded by melting ice caps. I tried remembering who it was who'd said that the loss of one human being was the loss of a whole universe. If that were the case, how could we even fathom the loss of a million? If it were a question of a million pet dogs or cats being felled by a preventable disease, red states and blue states would come together at last and the whole country would be clamoring to send in the marines.

Still fuming, I pulled into the parking lot, slid out, and slammed the car door. Despite its impact on the world of science, I was thankful Caltech wasn't a huge campus. I got halfway to Lauritsen before realizing that I might have my purse and laptop with me, but I'd forgotten the banana bread and had to leg it all the way back again.

When I finally entered the lab, the whole team—except, of course, Adam—was there. Stanley stood at the blackboard, while Gunther leaned his tall-glass-of-milk body against the back wall, thoughtfully rubbing his blond-stubbled chin. Amir, Tom, and Katrina were huddled together, doing some computations at a long table. Adam's replacement, Bob Ballantine, sat at a student's desk in the middle of the room, turning quickly when I opened the door. Bob was becoming something of a problem. From the moment we'd met, it was clear he was going to have a crush on me, while all I could think of was Uncle Bob, the imaginary shrinking relative who spent half his time in my pocket and the other half skipping by my side during some of my more memorable childhood adventures.

Before I knew it, Bob rose from his chair, struggling to tuck his blue Oxford shirt into khakis that were just this side of being honest-to-God floods. Within seconds he was close enough for me to detect a hint of smoked fish and orange juice. On the whole, not an unpleasant combination. His signature eye tic more pronounced than usual, he thrust a manuscript into my hand with the air of a dog presenting his favorite throw toy to his master. Or a cat triumphantly delivering a dead hummingbird to her mistress' bed, which Jillily had done just a few weeks before.

"I know we're supposed to be sticking to the supervoid," he said, "but look at this paper. By one of my best undergrads. He's taken an unusual twist, connecting Pribram and Bohm's holographic models with C-Voids."

I wanted to push him aside and head straight for Stanley, but everything I'd read so far about the possibility of a holographic universe stopped me dead in my tracks. "Why, thank you, Bob." He grinned broadly, and I tried not to notice what looked like a sliver of lox fat snagged between his left front tooth and lateral incisor. Running my eyes down the first page of the manuscript, I commented, "Actually, Jack Ng just published a piece suggesting that quantum foam is holographic. I think your guy might be on to something."

Passing him Gwennie's banana loaf, which he eyed with the kind of suspicion one greets an unexploded bomb, I hurried up to the blackboard, waving the paper at Stanley before I was treated to one of his class-A hugs. Though age might have taken a half-inch or so off his height, Stanley was still a lot taller than I. He managed to extract a quarter from the scrunchy atop my head, which gave me as much of a thrill as the first time he'd performed that particular magic trick when I was an eleven-year-old girl. Then he croaked to the rest of the room, as if they couldn't see for themselves, "Here's our Fleur," before sweeping the paper from my hand. I don't think I've mentioned that, despite being a man of great distinction and unquestionably the most brilliant person I'd ever met, Stanley had the face and, well, hop-ability of a frog. His brilliant head was squished rather flatly onto his unusually long neck, and his bottle-cap glasses magnified his already buggish eyes. When excited, he was prone to jump around the room, and in our early days proved to be as skip-happy as Uncle Bob himself. And that's just what he did: a hop and a skip in front of the blackboard for old times' sake. I saw Gunther stifle a snort from the corner and gave him a little wave.

I shot a conspiratorial look toward where Amir, Tom, and Katrina had been, but they'd disappeared. How had I missed that?

Just as I was about to ask Stanley where they'd gone, he seemed to realize he was holding the manuscript. Peering down at it, he worked his rather pronounced Adam's apple and asked, "So, what's this when it's at home?"

I laughed. "I don't know about home, but when it's here, it's from Bob."

As if on cue, up trotted Bob himself, brushing banana bread crumbs from his shirt. A brown triangle of banana bread crust had moved in next door to the lox fat, so I assumed Gwen's package had been promoted from object of suspicious derivation to the highly valuable item it actually was.

Bob grinned and scratched his head. I noticed that he'd actually styled his chestnut hair in spikes and put some kind of product on it that called attention to its generous dusting of dandruff. "Jaime Gomez," he offered enthusiastically. "Great paper. 'The Holographic Argument for C-Voids.'"

Without a word, Stanley nodded, walked to one of the front row desks and, crouching on its chair as if it were a toadstool, lost himself in Jaime Gomez's paper. Bob and I exchanged an unusually accordant look. With Stanley reading the paper, we knew we were invisible to him, consigned to the black hole into which all human relationships descend when even the kindliest of scientists gets grabbed by an idea.

I bore Stanley no hard feelings for this, since I'd once been one of that law's more egregious examples. I'd had no end of grief as a young adolescent trying to repair my relationship with Sammie after the call of C-Voids and P.D. temporarily blinded me to the justifiable demands of true friendship. Since then, I'd taken great care to let Sammie know how much she meant to me.

Which is why, when my cellphone went off to the tune of Duffy's "Warwick Avenue"—the ringtone I'd assigned to Sammie—I hastened out of the room to take the call.

As soon as I stepped out, I saw Katrina coming down the hall, Tom and Amir grinning behind her. Her ponytail bobbing, she carried a Petri dish with a large pale-colored muffin on it. A small, lit candle protruded upwards from its center like an erect nipple. Breast on a platter, I thought. That was what I got for having wild sex first thing in the morning.

The phone was still ringing. I took the call. "Sam, love, I think I'm in the middle of a birthday surprise."

I heard that infectious giggle on the other end. "No worries. Just rang to sing you happy birthday." Which she proceeded to do, at least the first six words—terribly out of tune, as usual. Laughing at herself, she gave up. "Oh, hell. What a waste of Mum's genes." Her mother Aadita's voice was exquisitely elastic; it was almost indistinguishable from one of my favorite singers, India's famed fusion artist Nine Virdee, with whom Aadita had familiarized me. "Anyway, call me later. Many happy returns of the day, girl."

I walked beside my birthday muffin back to the lab, letting my kindly colleagues assume that the wide grin on my face was for them alone, and not the girl who, sitting with me on a front porch in the pouring rain, had taught me everything I needed to know about friendship.

Not that Stanley and Amir and Tom and Katrina and Gunther and even Bob Ballantine were chopped liver in that department. Actually, they weren't chopped liver in any department, they had hearts and kidneys and brains and bladders, too, but I've long since learned that most people aren't as intrigued as I that some words have both literal and idiomatic meanings and that chopped liver is as good a metaphor for insignificance as *piss-ant* or *small potatoes*.

Anyway, getting back to my physics pals, I soon discovered they'd chipped in for half a year's worth of yoga classes at Golden Bridge as a birthday gift. Better still, they indulged me while I ran through my ideas about the applicability to P.D. of Gerardus 't Hooft's speculations about holographic theory. My fellow Nobelist had suggested that the whole universe could be understood as two-dimensional, our perception of three dimensions being a function of an information structure "painted" on the cosmological horizon.

"Hang on a mo," I added, my enthusiasm building. I ran over to my laptop and brought up an article in *Scientific American*. "Here it is. Jacob Bekenstein making the argument that the physical world is comprised of matter and energy, yes, but also information. Information tells matter and energy what to do with themselves, like a robot in a factory that needs instructions telling it which bits of metal and plastic to weld."

I flipped my laptop closed and threw a meaningful look at Stanley. "Same with a ribosome in a cell, which can't synthesize proteins and get power without information brought from the DNA in its nucleus." I grinned. "Don't you just love it? That's where P.D. comes in, just as soon as we perfect getting the information to the cell to trigger the shift from light to dark matter."

Gunther looked pretty excited himself. His wandering eye added a slight air of lunacy to his demeanor as he broke in, "I like it. Simplifies our job. Makes me think of Wheeler's insistence that information, not energy and matter, is the basic building block of life."

I could tell Bob was itching to take part. "Wheeler's from Princeton, right?" he asked, left eye twitching madly.

I couldn't help but wonder how many ocular anomalies one physics team could display. "Right," I said. "You know, don't you, that he was the first one to publicly refer to black holes?" But my mind was already racing ahead. I went up to the blackboard and tentatively chalked out what I saw as the problem. "I'm not so sure, Gunther, that it's all that simple. How're we going to send the message to dematerialize and rematerialize without catastrophically altering the mass and energy of our subject?"

Gunther broke in excitedly, his untethered eye wandering even more wildly. "Well, if the team at Max Planck can actually create an optical cavity with two laser beams for a water bear, they might be able to adjust the frequency of the beams so that the laser photons absorb the vibration energy of the water bear around its mass center, slowing it to a ground state and allowing it to both appear and disappear into a void state."

Tom frowned. "You're assuming the void state awaits it somewhere outside the water bear, but Fleur's idea is to harness the water bear's cellular voids and create an internal energy exchange between dark and light matter."

I nodded, wondering whether the application of dematerialization would rest on Gunther's water bears, science's more recent superstars, prized for their relative indestructibility. Tiny little creatures—most of them no longer than a millimeter—they're sometimes called moss piglets, which is my favorite name for them, since they move their chunky little bodies across moss and lichens in slow motion, supported by eight tiny, pudgy feet.

Stanley gave a happy little hop. He liked nothing more than group riffing on a mind-stretching theme. Amir made him even happier by offering, "But maybe that's where Eridanus comes in. If Mersini-Houghton's right, we just instruct our object to shift itself into one of its parallel universes."

"But, wait," interjected Katrina, nervously tapping her pencil against the arm of her chair. "You're assuming that the other universe has similar physical properties, which it can't. At least, I don't think so. Unless …." She scratched her scalp just below her shiny ponytail, in the process pulling pretty little wisps free. "Unless it's all part of some larger guiding wave."

Stanley smiled slyly and clapped his magician's hands. "Looks like we've got lots to think about, boys and girls." He gave a froggish croak. "Fleur, didn't Gwen tell me she and I were taking you out to Rose Cottage for a birthday lunch?" God, banana bread for breakfast, English tea for lunch, dinner that night at Casa del Mar. My birthday was guaranteeing my hips would be more grabbable than ever when Assefa returned.

But thoughts of Assefa returning, no matter how deliciously erotic, meant Assefa had to go away first, which sounded like a dangerous stretching of an invisible cord between us. That night, as I struggled to slither my butt into my best black dress, I struggled even harder with a serious case of dread. I had to force myself to muster a cheery grin as a silk-suit-clad Assefa greeted me forty minutes later when I approached his Commodore Sloat Drive door, though fake melted into for-real once he brushed his generous lips against my cheek and nibbled at the diamond stud in my ear.

But the lively spirits that marked the beginning of our dinner began to fade as alcohol coursed through our bloodstreams and our tummies expanded—mine, of course, minus the *foie gras* lumping up inside the other three. The conversation at the table got looser, which is, I suppose, why Sammie spoke aloud the question we'd all been secretly asking ourselves. "How can two men disappear on a road only 217 miles long without anyone noticing anything?"

"Well," I countered, "it's not like some straight throughway. Isn't a lot of it wild mountain land?" I darted a look at Assefa, who I could see retreating into himself.

He responded glumly, "I know so little of my homeland. I hate it. All I remember are little bits of life—isolated scenes—mostly inside our compound. My cousins—they're still there, you know? Bekele and Iskinder. They were older. Iskinder taught me to play Kelelebosh with rocks. It is a little like your jacks." Your, I thought. He's already distancing himself. "A school chum or two would visit sometimes. There was a girl …." He caught me staring at him and seemed to shake free from a memory. "For all I know, my father going missing is calling me back to my roots."

Sammie laughed, "Roots? I'm a Jew living in diaspora. Jacob, too. Jews have no roots except for some land we stole from a group of other now-displaced souls."

Jacob lashed out, "Didn't steal. It was all down to you Brits. They raised expectations with the Balfour Declaration. It was only a matter of time until the U.N. passed the Partition Plan." Which got everyone going on one of those impossible arguments about who the true underdogs were, the Palestinians or the Israelis.

I barely kept track of the points my dinner mates were attempting to score. All this talk about roots was making me nervous. I told myself to relax. Sammie had gone back to England several times since we'd made friends when she was twelve and I thirteen, and more recently she'd traveled to India for her grandmother's funeral. Dhani had taken Angelina back with her for a visit to her parents in Delhi. Mother had even accompanied Cesar to Guatemala to visit the town where his *coca*-addicted mother had been born. They'd all returned safe and sound and just as before. But I found myself saying, "Don't go!"

Everyone looked taken aback by the non sequitur. Shifting gears the quickest, Sammie jumped in indignantly. "Fleur, that's not fair! He's got to find his dad." Having lost her own father as a child, she was a sucker for people connecting with their fathers and had cut me off for a while after I refused to attend my own father's funeral.

"You're right, you're right." I didn't repeat my request, but I meant it—meant it as our cab took us back to his duplex, meant it when Assefa bent down to kiss my forehead goodbye at the crack of dawn the next morning. It didn't help my peace of mind that he was adamant about wanting to go to the airport alone.

"I can't stand teary goodbyes," he repeated, nuzzling my neck.

As soon as his cab turned the corner from Commodore Sloat to Schumacher Drive, I fled to Stanley and Gwennie's, where I found my mentor seated at the kitchen table in his pajamas, absentmindedly petting Jillily while he pored over the paper Bob had given me the previous day. When I flopped down beside him, he immediately proceeded to speculate on its implications until he finally threw up his hands and asked irritably, "Why do you keep looking at your watch? You're not bored, are you?" He had a salt and pepper beard now, which—combined with a slightly bent frame that resembled an old TV antenna—made it difficult to forget that he wasn't getting any younger.

I wanted to say, "Bored? Who could be bored by the idea of a holographic universe?"

Instead, I burst into tears.

I hadn't lived with Stanley and Gwennie for the past decade without Stanley learning how best to comfort me. He scooted over, and his arms encircled me with the kind of confident firmness that only two other humans had ever known how to execute. The second was Adam, but Nana had been the first. She'd been gone for nearly a year, but she'd left her heavy imprint on my heart and across the landscape of my skin, which retained a cellular memory of her chicken peck kisses and Mack truck grip.

I was pleased to get a whiff of Stanley's sunflower-seed breath while we hugged.

"It's Assefa," I sniffed. "What if I never see him again?"

He pulled away and skewed his head at me. "But that's ridiculous, child. No matter what happens, he'll surely come back to you."

Just then, as if we both had a sixth sense, we turned to see a bird crash into one of the kitchen windows. My heart sank. It was a young crow. Corvids were ubiquitous in SoCal. This one balanced on the window apron for a moment, visibly stunned, then gathered itself and took off again, a survivor, joining a cackling trio of others on our next door neighbors' oak.

"What the hell?" Stanley muttered.

Then we turned to each other and burst out simultaneously, both of us laughing—though mine was definitely more of the nervous variety—"A murder of crows!"

Chapter Two
Fleur

WHAT I HADN'T told Stanley was that I'd been awake since 3:00 a.m., the hour my yoga teacher Siri Sajan called the *Amrit Vela*, or Time of Deathless Consciousness, the best hour to meditate. Except I wasn't meditating. I was imagining Assefa on his long journey away from SoCal. Waiting with him in a chaotic line at LAX's international terminal to check in for his Emirates flight. Glued to his side as he fought his way to the Great Hall—past women in *serapes* and *burkas* and *saris*, men in *kurta* pajamas, African print vests, *shemaghs* and *kufiyas*. I fantasized nursing Coronas with him at a crowded bar between a wrinkled-suited Dallas businessman bound for Russia and a pair of German newlyweds who couldn't keep their hands off each other.

Would he think of me then, or merely feel inside his leather bag for his passport and ticket, wondering if he should take his Ambien before or after his meal, worrying whether he'd managed to sleep for at least a few hours at the Holiday-Inn-like-no-other during his layover in Dubai?

I prayed the rental car would be waiting for him once he arrived at Bole Airport. And, even if it were, then what? Would the son of émigrés have any clout with the alleged laissez-faire local police or the more feared Federals? Without their help he'd be pretty much consigned to trying to follow the trail his father and Zalelew would have taken. Or—far worse, from my perspective—he would see if he could locate the young woman the men had bumped into at the airport. Her name was Makeda. I'd gotten that much out of Assefa as he was dropping off to sleep.

"What's her name?" I'd whispered in his perfect, shell-shaped ear.

"Who?" he'd answered drowsily, a tiny bubble of spittle moving toward the edge of his goatee.

"The girl in Zalelew's postcard. The one they saw at the airport."

"Makeda," he'd mumbled. And—again—"Makeda," before a little snore escaped him. I knew it was my own fault, but still: my lover had fallen asleep on my birthday with another woman's name on his lips.

You'd think that, as a scientist, I wouldn't be so superstitious. But what I began to think of as "the Makeda episode" continued to haunt me during what ended up being a late-nighter at the lab. Despite my exhaustion, I found myself detouring past Abeba and Achamyalesh's house on my way home. It looked as if all the lights in the house were on. Abeba would be anxious to hear her son had safely arrived.

I pulled my Prius to the curb and hesitantly walked up the concrete path. Abeba flung open her front door before I could even ring the bell.

"Come," she cried, grabbing my elbow. "I thought you were the doctor. I am waiting for him. He promised me he would come right away."

"Why—what is it? Are you okay?" I cried, as she installed me on the faded gold velvet sofa, my tailbone making uncomfortable contact with a gimpy spring.

Glancing at her watch, Abeba responded, "It's Medr. I heard a terrible groaning coming from his room as soon as I hung up from Assefa's call."

God help me, but for all my love of the old man, my instantaneous response had nothing to do with Medr. "His call? Assefa called?"

Was it a look of disappointment that Abeba shot me from under those thick Assefa-like lashes before she lifted her wrist again to see what time it was. "Yes. It was after Assefa assured me he'd arrived safely in Dubai that I went to Medr's room." She glanced back down the poorly lit hall. "He's sleeping now. I just checked. But I am worried. It is so hard when he does not speak." It finally struck home that Abeba would never have called for a doctor if she didn't have serious cause for worry. I was overcome with shame. *Oh, God, let him be okay.*

The doorbell rang, and Abeba and I both sprang to the front door. The formally attired doctor who stood there looked startled by the force with which Abeba had flung it open. He recovered himself and gave her a quick hug, his face nearly as dark as the burnished leather bag he carried. Gently letting go, he asked, "How is he doing?" I saw a flash of curiosity in his eyes as they lit upon me. I automatically smiled, then felt like a fool. Who smiled at a moment like this?

"He was asleep the last time I looked," Abeba said, already halfway down the hall. The doctor nodded briefly as he brushed passed me.

As soon as they were out of the room, I reached for my purse and dug a hand into it, my fingers crawling around brush, wallet, keys, errant scraps of paper bearing various quantum computations, a cosmetic bag, and a crackly container of chewing gum, until I managed to wrestle out my iPhone. "Fuck me," I muttered, uselessly punching buttons. Who let her battery go dead when her fiancé was traveling halfway around the world?

Disgustedly flinging the bag onto Achamyalesh's favorite easy chair, I tiptoed up the hall, unsure whether I'd be welcome. I stood in the doorway, watching Abeba try to help the doctor lift Medr to a sitting position. The room was saturated with the sharp smell of *bunna*. Had Abeba tried to revive her father-in-law with a cup of strong coffee earlier? I debated whether or not to step inside and offer my help, but Medr seemed to come to, pushing away his daughter-in-law's hands and cautiously settling his skinny frame at the edge of the bed. The doctor said something I couldn't hear, and Medr began to loosen the top button of his pajamas, evidently responding to the doctor's request. When Dr. Sitota lifted his stethoscope to Medr's chest, I averted my eyes, taking in the photos of Assefa's USC graduation on the opposite wall.

I'd been in this room just once. Assefa had insisted on introducing me to his grandfather the day we got engaged. That time, Medr had been sitting in a straight-backed latticed chair in the corner of the room, a footstool pulled close to the chair for his long, leather-slippered feet. He'd looked as though he might have dressed up for my visit, wearing stunning turquoise, silk V-necked pajamas with red and yellow trim. He didn't smile when we were introduced, merely stared at me like a dark ghost. Loss had mapped his face like a rugged continent. He was speechless, of course. But he'd surprised both Assefa and me by reaching up to cup my chin in his sculptured hand. After that, you couldn't have dragged me away. I asked Assefa to bring me a chair from the kitchen, which he did, lingering for a moment while I settled myself beside the old man.

We sat silently together. I closed my eyes awhile. The dim little room was a far cry from the airy bedroom whose wide windows had afforded my grandfather and me a perfect view of every bird landing on our tree. That sycamore was long gone, chopped down by my unnatural excuse for a father in a fit of revenge. But the tree had survived in its own way, along with Grandfather and the bird on the lawn and Baby X—all of them lodged securely in the hole at the center of my heart. I'd learned over the years that sometimes memories filled the void as no scientific discovery could. I confided some of this to Medr, not knowing if he understood English well enough to fathom my words.

He understood *something*. He nodded, and I saw that he had a halo of gray hairs at the crown of his still plentiful head of tight black coils. I held my hand out to him, and he stroked the back of it, his ancient, calloused hand hairless and bony. His movements were hesitant, as if he hadn't touched any skin but his own in quite a while. But in that moment I knew he was one of my angels, his kindness reflecting Grandfather's as surely as a jeweled mirror in Indra's Web.

As if from a great distance I watched Medr's hands trace my knuckles and the birdlike bones leading to my wrist. His dusky hue was so different from my own nearly translucent skin. Yet after watching a particularly pronounced vein on his hand pulse insistently, I put my right hand to my neck and found my own blood coursing in the same rhythm. I knew we were all said to descend from Mitochondrial Eve, the most recent matrilineal ancestor for every living human. Geneticists had gone so far as to claim that human beings spread out from what we now call Addis Ababa a hundred thousand years ago, which was why it seemed fitting that the fossilized skeleton of a very early hominid, Lucy—called Dinkinish, or *You Are Beautiful* in Amharic—was on display at the Ethiopian National Museum in Addis Ababa. So why not imagine Medr as my third grandfather?

But now Dr. Sitota's formal voice broke into my reverie. "Medr, Medr, I know you can't speak, but will you stick out your tongue and move it from left to right?" I stared curiously. Medr looked as though he felt insulted at such a foolish request, but, shooting me a conspiratorial look—I hadn't even known he'd registered my presence—he stuck out his tongue and, not only moved it slowly from side to side, but stuck his thumbs in his ears and wiggled his fingers.

For a brief moment, the doctor looked affronted, but then he began to chuckle. As relief flooded through my veins, I snorted, "Hah!"

Abeba, though, was not convinced, ripples of worry constricting her forehead. "He is okay?"

The doctor rubbed his chin. "Well, I doubt it's a stroke, anyway. And the humor is a good sign, wouldn't you say?"

Which didn't stop the doctor from arranging to have Medr immediately admitted to Huntington Memorial Hospital for tests.

Racing back home once I'd seen Abeba installed in a little cot by her father-in-law's hospital bed, I reached Assefa from the Fiskes' landline.

He answered the phone with his mouth full. "Asheffa hew."

"What?"

"Way-min." A pause, then a laugh. "Fleur, my love. Sorry. I had a mouthful of chips to get down. Do you believe I'm sitting in a bloody Irish Pub in the middle of Dubai Airport? Positively surreal." Then, when there was no quick response from me, "How are you, *dukula*? I tried to reach you, but it went straight to voicemail." He lowered his voice. "Did you get my message? About how that spectacular body of yours would be the hit of Burka-land? And what I'd do to every inch of it if you were here with me?"

I felt a little flutter in my tweeter, but this was no time for phone sex. "I didn't get your message. I'm an idiot. My damned phone battery was dead. I heard you'd arrived from your mother."

"Enat?" A slight tinge of anxiety in his voice.

There was no other way to say it. "Listen, he's fine, but your grandfather had a little episode this evening."

33

"Episode? What—"

"Wait. It's not as bad as it sounds. Really, I think he's fine. Your mom thought he was coming down with the flu or something, but the doctor—actually, Doctor Sitota; your mother said he's a friend of the family? He said he didn't exhibit any of the symptoms. He actually came to the house. I was there. He examined your grandfather pretty thoroughly. Medr actually made silly faces at me. That's got to be a good sign."

Assefa machine gunned questions at me. "What's Sitota's thinking? Any signs of stroke or heart attack? Chest congestion? Fever?"

"Assefa, I don't know. That's why they've got him at the hospital. Dr. Sitota said he didn't think he'd had a stroke, at least."

For a moment I worried I'd lost the connection, but then I realized I could hear faint crowd sounds coming from the phone. I knew that, as a medical intern, Assefa must be running through the possibilities. Finally, he heaved an audible sigh. "Christ. It seems like nothing's gone right since my father disappeared. You've got to keep me posted. I don't want to be bothering my mother. Look, I'll call you when I land in Addis Ababa. I have a brief layover there before my flight to Gondar." Before hanging up, he said in an unusually astringent tone, "Charge your cellphone, will you?"

The dial tone joined the fridge hum in Gwennie's otherwise silent kitchen. I stared at the receiver until I became aware of Jillily brushing against my ankles. I dropped the phone into its cradle and lifted the cat to my chest. She proceeded to clean my face with long rasping licks. When I opened my mouth to complain, "Well that was a side of Assefa I didn't know about," my cat's tongue made contact with my own. "Ew, Jillily. That's disgusting. Don't do that!"

Her eyes grew wide and I contritely chicken peck kissed her sleek head. "Your mama's so mean," I whispered. She wrapped her front paws around my neck as I spirited her off to my room, where I fell asleep with her warm back spooned solidly against my belly.

Despite having slept like an angel, I woke feeling devilishly voidish the next morning. Heading out for the lab with a dark, obsessive loop playing in my head, I nearly ran over Chin-Hwa as I backed out of the driveway. I slowed to make sure the Kangs were aware that their dog had broken loose again. Sure enough, Mrs. Kang came barreling out their front door as I shifted into drive, her black hair in curlers—who wore curlers anymore?—and her short legs in comical leaping ballerina mode as she cleared her lawn just as her Jindo crouched to do his business on one of Fidel's particularly vivid young cyclamens.

As soon as I came to the stop sign at the corner of Rose Villa and Sierra Bonita, I instructed my Bluetooth to call Sammie.

"Sam, you're not going to believe this."

"What's happened?"

"Oh, just everything."

"Are you okay?"

"Do I sound like it?"

"Where are you?"

"Just left home."

"Where are you going?"

"I thought I'd swing over to school. Drown my sorrows in the Eridanus Void." I slammed my head against the steering wheel. She must have heard me.

"Come on over. Sounds like a Grade One."

Sammie and I had a system of grading our personal emergencies. We'd devised it after not even four calls in a row had gotten her to answer her phone when Nana was killed. Not that Sammie could have known. She'd been racing to finish her master's show at Otis and had convinced herself that no distracting *Bohemian Rhapsody* ringtone was worth making a whole year's worth of work and a multitude of sleepless nights go to waste. I'd actually had to drive over to her house, bang on the door, and fall into a fetal curl on the front porch to get her attention.

Of course, once she wrested from me the fact of Nana's shocking death, she'd come through like a champ, pulling me to her chest tightly enough for me to feel the quick drumming of her heart. As always, she'd been a veritable fountain of words. "Oh, my luvvie, my sweet, my Fleur Beurre. She loved you so much. What a shock. What a loss. But thank God she went quickly. I know, I know, you didn't get to say goodbye, but she didn't suffer. That's worth something. You'll make it through this. I know you will. We both know how to do it. But first you have to get through this awful shock. And to think that the only one of the three to survive was Sister F. She must feel wretched. And guilty, I'll bet. Survivor's guilt, you know. We won't even think of the kind of karma that bag of shit earned for himself. I'm sorry, but I'm actually quite glad that he died, too."

She was referring to the drunk driver who'd careened through a red light and veered across to Fayga's lane as she was driving Nana and Sister Flatulencia to Toys 'R' Us to pick out presents for Cesar's twelfth birthday. The fact that the latest record label wunderkind had been driving a Range Rover while the three older women were huddled in a cramped two-door Civic hadn't improved my friends' odds. Sammie tried reminding me that Siri Sajan had told us just the past week that 'death is union with the divine,' but her words were no competition for images of Nana's bountiful bosom crushed by the Rover's blunt nose, nor of Fayga's big frame sliding under the dash. Ironically, it was Sister Flatulencia's gas that saved her, her Beano having been less effective than usual that morning. Not wanting to constrict her bloated belly with a seat belt, she'd flown through the sunroof and landed well away from the meld of hot metal that became the other three's coffin.

Sammie's consoling words might have helped—and ultimately would help once the immediacy of the crisis passed—but when I'm falling at breathtaking velocity down the bottomless pit of everlasting emptiness, only the solid feel of someone else's body compressing my own brings me back to ground level again. Which was something I'd learned as an infant from Nana's Mack truckish grip.

I can't say how many times afterward I reflected on the ambiguous properties of physical pressure, which seemed to be a kind of second cousin to nuclear power, with capacities for good and evil wrapped in one potent package. I ended up conveying those thoughts to my physics team, and for a time we even played with the possibility of physical force as one component of the cellular exchange we sought in dematerialization.

But on the evening of Nana's death, tucked tightly with Sammie under her winter comforter, taking little sips of hot chocolate brewed by Aadita and purposely not wiping off our twin melted marshmallow moustaches, such thoughts were far from my mind. Sammie, clever girl, managed to keep me just this side of despair—it was nearly impossible to imagine the world without a force like Nana in it.

Afterward, Sammie proposed a system to ensure that neither of us would ever let the other down again. We ended up designating emergencies like that day's as Grade One. On my side, Grade One was to be reserved for deaths, public humiliation, and the temptation to flap, twirl, and head bang. For her, it boiled down to death, abandonment, and, as she liked to put it, "making a right balls-up of a perfectly good painting by not having the sense to leave well enough alone."

We each had our own versions of Grade Two. For me, it mostly had to do with states of voidishness that would have sent me into Nana's closet in the old days, my back pressed against the nails in the cedar paneling. Sammie's own symptom of a Grade Two event would be talking so fast that not even her mother Aadita could follow her—typically occasioned by an argument with Jacob, who she had the habit of claiming was really a sweet guy despite his need to be right all the time and his verbally well-aimed temper.

Recalling that day with the kind of hollowness that always tormented me when I remembered that Nana was no more, I made a quick U-turn and was soon parked in front of Sammie's Craftsman-style house. I'd never stopped feeling grateful for the summer day when she and her mother had moved in right across the street from where I lived with the Fiskes.

Flicking a quick glance at the daddy-longleg sprinklers drenching Fidel's front yard, I slunk out of my car and took Sammie's front steps two at a time. A dirty-blond rug spread across the banister moved of its own accord, lifting a tail from its rear section as if to spray me. Midget was still alive and, unlike Jillily, just as fat as in the old days. I put my nose to his, then gave him a vigorous chin scratch. His purr was loud enough to wake the dead.

Sammie opened the door and grinned. Unable to resist, she came closer and joined in, rubbing the fur leading to her cat's tail just long enough for him to lift up his backside welcomingly, revealing the slightly soiled starburst of his butt. We exclaimed simultaneously, "Gross!" before she took my arm and led me into the house.

Aadita peeked a head out from her office into the hall. "Hello, love. Haven't seen you for a bit." Her hair had gone an elegant, shiny silver. With her figure still compact and trim and her big brown eyes taking up nearly half her face, no wonder she'd landed a new boyfriend fifteen years her junior.

I'd worried about Sammie when I first heard that Aadita was dating her young yoga teacher. She and her mum had the kind of mother-daughter relationship I would have severed a few fingers for. But no—if anything, it was better for Sammie that her mother had found someone who couldn't even pretend to be a replacement for her father, who'd regularly danced his daughter around their Primrose Hill flat, her feet on his, until he'd lost his life to tetanus on a humanitarian aid trip to Indonesia.

I kissed Aadita's cheeks, then caught up with Sammie in her room. Its Oriental-carpeted floor was still the dense jungle of paintings and books it had always been, though her original Liberty comforter had given way to a minimalist blue-gray duvet that was lent a slightly rosy hue by cherry blossom paper lanterns on the bedside tables. Since visiting Japan with Jacob the previous summer, Sammie had entered an Asian phase. A few calligraphed scrolls were the sole decorations on her walls.

The two of us flopped onto the bed. "Right," she said, kicking off her embroidered Chinese slippers, one of which landed beside a framed picture of Gwennie holding a "C The Big Picture" picket sign in front of the White House, a bunch of Father's Cacklers making angry faces at her in the background. Sammie leaned over to light a half-burnt stick of incense that had already spilled a puddle of soft ash onto its black stone holder. "What exactly did he say?"

I felt my eyes well up. "Well, it was more his tone than what he said. Honestly, I've never heard Assefa sound so ... peremptory."

"Meaning?"

"Imperious. Arrogant."

Sammie waved an impatient hand. "I know what the word means. I was trying to get a sense of what he was being bossy *about*."

I swept a hand over my forehead, then felt my bangs fall right back. "Right—of course. Well, it was when I told him about Medr."

Sammie frowned, and I realized I hadn't even told her what had happened to Assefa's grandfather. As I described Dr. Sitota's examination of him, I saw her shoulders lift an inch or two, a definite tell that she was anxious.

"Honestly, Sam, I really think he's going to be okay. Listen, I've got to pee."

As I sat on the toilet, I reflected, not for the first time, how Sammie and I had such different ways of coping with worry. Hers

38

was more forthright. She made no apologies for it. She admitted as much, claiming it came from having had a Jewish father.

I, on the other hand, favored distraction and tended to go up into my head. I'm not bragging about it. It's just that I'll do almost anything to avoid falling back into flapping and whirling. "Stimming," as Mother once put it, "is so undignified."

When I came out of the bathroom, I saw that Midge had joined us. He was perched at the top of Sammie's dresser, making throaty, "I-want-to-eat-you" sounds at an Anna's Hummingbird outside the window. Midge looked so excited, I imagined his heart was beating way faster than its typical hundred and fifty beats per minute, but it still wouldn't come close to the twelve hundred the tiny hummingbird could claim. I began explaining this to Sammie, who cut through my compulsive verbiage with an impatient wave.

"No, wait," she interjected. "You haven't finished about Medr. Is he or isn't he going to be okay?" With her hands on her hips, she reminded me a little of Father, and I took a few steps back, catching my quarter-inch heel on a pictureless frame on the floor. I steadied myself by leaning a hand on the dresser, which startled Midge, who catapulted across the room in one long arc, landing hard enough on Sammie's bedside table for Sam's dental night guard to bounce up. Midge caught it as fiercely as if it were the hummingbird itself. Just before escaping with it down the hall, he shot us an exultant look, the mouthpiece covering his teeth like a set of fake lips.

Sammie cried, "Did you see that?"

She and I fell to the floor in hysterics.

Aadita poked her head into the room. We tried explaining, but the story lost something in translation. She left us to our slowly de-escalating hilarity, shaking her head.

When we finally fell silent, not unexpectedly we both felt a bit depressed. Sammie asked me with considerably less aggression to reassure her that Medr was okay. To satisfy us both, I called Huntington Hospital from my cell. I was put through to Medr's room before I could explain to the operator that I needed to talk with a nurse, since Medr was mute. But a man's voice came onto the line. "Yes?" For a brief moment I thought that Medr had found his voice again. That is, until I heard, "Doctor Sitota here."

Those were the words, anyway. The tone said something different: "Don't you know I'm a busy man? Hurry up!"

So I did. "Doctor Sitota, this is Fleur Robins. We met last night? I'm sorry to bother you, but I was hoping to find out how Medr is doing."

"Ah, yes. Miss Robins." He paused, and I imagined him rolling his eyes at the ceiling. "All our tests have been negative, which is good. I'm pretty confident that this is a case of simple dehydration. It turns out that his digestion has been a little active lately. So we are administering fluids and he seems to be responding quite well. With any luck, he'll be discharged tomorrow."

"Oh, thank you, thank you. Thank you so much," I gushed, then felt more than a little voidish at the protracted silence at the other end of the line.

He saved me from pinching by replying, finally, "Sorry, the nurse was asking me something." I thought I detected a slight softening of his tone in his parting words, "I don't think you need to worry, Miss Robins. I'm afraid I really must ring off now."

"Well?" Sammie said. She was sitting cross-legged on her bed. Having swept her hair into a careless black knot at the nape of her neck, she was nervously picking a corn on her little toe.

"He's going to be okay. It was dehydration. Sounds like he had diarrhea."

Sammie fell back onto her pillow, stretching out her legs. Little black hairs poked out like baby cactus needles from her brown skin. The fact that she hadn't bothered to shave signaled she wasn't planning on seeing Jacob today.

"I hate it when that happens," Sammie sighed. "The runs're probably even worse when you're old. Poor man." She patted the space next to her. "C'mon, then. We never really got to Assefa."

I settled myself in next to her, readjusting the pillow behind my head, and took a breath before describing Assefa's impatience with me. I held back, though, from mentioning the mysterious Makeda, half-convinced I was making something out of a great big nothing. I realized Iago was right: the Green-Eyed Monster was most tormenting if you weren't quite certain your suspicions were true.

Sammie rubbed her forehead. "Yeah, that seems to be the deal with guys. Romance and sweetness in the beginning, then once they know they've got you in their pockets, all the ugly bits come parading out."

Uh oh. It sounded like Jacob's temper had made another appearance. I knew it was starting to grind away at her. She was probably still steaming over the zinger he'd let fly at my birthday dinner.

To be fair, she'd provoked him a bit with her castigation of "those one-track-mind Zionists who think the Holocaust entitles our people to make everyone get out of our way. What's a million-and-a-half stateless Palestinians, anyway?"

But his shouted response, "You're a fucking self-hating Jew, that's what you are," had shocked the whole table.

I felt defensive about Assefa. "No, wait. That's not it. Can you imagine what it's like for him? Halfway across the world, his father gone missing, not knowing how in the hell he's going to find him? Then I tell him his grandfather's in the hospital? He must feel like everyone he counts on is in danger. You remember what he said—he's already been feeling a little rootless."

In some ways, I could be describing Sammie's life of a decade ago—the death of her father preceding her emigration with her south Asian mother to the British Commonwealth's most xenophobic spawn, right on the heels of a terrorist attack that made anyone with brown skin and an unfamiliar accent host to an invisible neon sign on their forehead, proclaiming, "Suicide Bomber." The two of them had even been detained on their arrival at JFK because Aadita's name matched someone on the No Fly List.

Sammie had managed to create a whole new life for herself in the years since then, ultimately popping out paintings like hotcakes and finding a boyfriend who was smart and funny and shared her passion for travel. But who knew how heavily those earlier losses sat inside her? As close as we can be with another person, we're still encased within our own distinct worlds. For now, Sammie sat bathed in stillness, and my own unspoken thoughts growled from my belly like indigestible pieces of gristle.

My cell pinged and I jumped off the bed to fish it out of my purse. It was a text from Katrina: *where are u??? we're going nuts over the multiverse issue.* I knew exactly what she was referring to. We couldn't figure out whether David Bohm's idea of the universe as a unified whole—what he liked to call "the implicate order"—helped or hindered the Multiple Universe theory. I mean, really, if entangled particles don't even require instant communication, since they are in fact one and same, what does that say about information being the basic building block of the universe?

Small emergency, I texted back, *but no worries. C U soon.*

As I stuffed my cell back in my bag, Sammie shot me a wry smile. "Let me guess. Lord knows, they can't wipe their arses without you." I started to apologize, but she merely teased, "It's okay. I know when I've been used. Your geeky pals'll distract you better than I ever could." She walked me down the hall, made me promise I wouldn't take any more shit from Assefa, listened to me prattle on about him not really being a shit giver, and gave me a warm hug before sending me on my way.

I drove off wondering if Sammie was right. Was Assefa already taking me for granted? And where was he now? By my own reckoning, he should have arrived in Addis Ababa a while ago, his four-hour flight having transported him from one of the world's wealthiest countries to one of its poorest. Would an alien landing at the luxurious Dubai waterfront recognize the tin shacks of Addis Ababa as part of the same planet? And would Assefa even bother to call me to tell me he'd arrived?

As if on cue, my phone rang. Heartened, I accepted the call on my Bluetooth, but Assefa sounded like someone who needed a crash course at charm school. "Fleur, it's me. How's Medr?"

I responded as if on automatic pilot, pinching the inside of my thigh while I kept my other hand on the wheel. "He's fine. I just spoke with Dr. Sitota. It was probably just dehydration from diarrhea."

"Yes, but did they test him for ...."

That was it. I broke in, barely controlling myself. "They tested him for everything. Dr. Sitota has him at Huntington, for God's sake. It's not exactly a third world hospital." (Okay, that was a low blow, but I wasn't sure I cared.) "Why won't you trust me when I say he's fine?"

A longish pause. "Sorry," he said. Though his voice didn't sound sorry at all. It sounded strained. Clipped.

I silently counted to ten as Adam had taught me to do in the old days, when a minor frustration would send me to Nana's closet, her cave-scented robe thrust halfway up my nose. "I know you've been worried. But ... how *are* you? *Where* are you?"

"Where do you think I am? Far enough that I can't check on Medr myself."

I didn't trust myself to respond.

It took him a few seconds. "Fleur Buerre." He never called me that. It was Sammie and Aadita's name for me. I said nothing. "Dammit, Fleur, why won't you talk? Are you going me make me beg like a dog?"

The words shot out in spite of me. "No, just apologize like a human." Then I started to cry. I didn't want to, but I couldn't help myself. It was that or bang and flap, and I could hardly do that while I was driving.

Finally, he came back to me. The Assefa I knew. The Assefa I loved. "Ah, *dukula*. I've hurt you."

"You have," I wailed.

He waited for my sobbing to subside, then offered contritely, "I just … can't explain … this journey … my father … Medr …."

"I know," I sniffed. And I did. Or thought I did. "But it's hard for me, too. You're so far away. It's different … when I can't feel you against my skin."

A quick intake of breath on the other end. "You make me hard, Fleur." He laughed. "Hard in this shabby little hotel room with cracks everywhere, bugs like you've never seen in your life, and not a hint of hot water."

"Is it bad?"

"The room or the hardness?"

"Both!"

"Good!"

We both laughed. It took so little to restore the connection. But where had the harsh-voiced man who'd spoken only a few moments ago gone? Into some alternate universe? If so, it was one I wanted nothing to do with.

Chapter Three
Assefa

FLEUR WAS RIGHT to be angry with me. Of that much I was certain. I knew it during our first phone conversation, knew it during our second, knew it in between, when, feigning interest in the tedious monologue of the Anglican priest at my side on the four hour Air Emirates trip from Dubai to Addis Ababa, I saw myself for what I was: a hanging man, suspended between what I wished I could be and what I actually was—a monster of hiddenness and secrecy.

The shame of such falseness was unbearable. The girl I had asked to be my wife had a heart as soft as that silken wrist of hers that I liked to circle with my thumb and forefinger. Her gift for happiness as sweet as a ripe apricot. When she was sad, her tears freely flowed. Frustrate her, and she'd bang her head. But I—I had to be … complicated. My own heart a warren of abrupt twists and jagged angles. My *washela* standing at attention for the enticements of pale gold hair, a crooked smile, shy thighs bursting open like the petals of a white rose. The same *washela* a sword of ecstasy rising to the memory of a *bunna*-skinned girl with ancient eyes and a *krar* player's long fingers, her smell an intoxicating blend of rich earth, *tej*, *mitmita*.

No one had warned me how love reshapes your world. The delicate turn of a falling leaf resembles the sweep of your lover's hand. You wonder what she is doing when you are pulling on your socks. Her concerns become your concerns. You begin to feel annoyed by those little traits of others she cannot stand. Her skin and smell become your touchstones. The song that she can't help but move her hips to becomes your favorite, even if you'd detested its mediocrity the week before. Details that once comprised the impersonal wallpaper of modern life become animated and shaded with particular meaning.

The landmarks of Fleur's life had become my own. A pro-life rally reported in the news filled my belly with acid at Senator Robins' betrayal of his daughter when, little more than a child, she'd fallen pregnant. Medical school discussions of the debunked relationship between vaccines and autism were reminders of her continual questioning whether her quirks put her on the spectrum. Every cat I encountered was a harbinger of the pain my lover would endure when she inevitably lost her aging Jillily. Suddenly references to black holes were everywhere: newspapers, gossip magazines, popular songs.

But there was still the matter of the invisible companion I'd brought with me as a boy to this bleached continent. *That one*, Enat called her, not liking to see what came over my face when anyone uttered the name *Makeda*.

Makeda, who, like Fleur, also bent and shaped my world, even as her actual features faded into ghostly glimpses of flashing black eyes and the sweet promise of generous lips. In some moments, the two of them, Makeda and Fleur, formed an uneasy mandorla leaving a bare minority of me to think my own thoughts, the majority swinging to and fro between Assefa-Makeda and Assefa-Fleur.

Assefa-Makeda had been born in the time before memory. Makeda herself had been the constant playmate of my earliest days and refused to leave me—or to be left, even when, clad in the crisp white shirt and short blue trousers of my primary school, I'd slid into the backseat of my uncle Getachew's Corolla for my first, and last, journey out of the Amhara region of Ethiopia. Tucked in tightly between Enat and Medr—the two bulging suitcases on the floor of the car forcing our knees to our chins—I'd felt nothing but a gathering gloom. Even my boyish shoulder-shoving goodbyes to Bekele and Iskinder could not compete with the image of Makeda, standing in front of the only home I'd ever known, her *café au lait* palm waving like a windblown flag, "*Sälam, Sälam.*"

That moment had fastened itself onto my mind with the force of a leaping kudu, like the one who'd failed to run fast enough from the spear of Demissie after he'd insisted on teaching me and his grandson, my best friend Girma, to hunt in the old way. I ended up telling the kudu story to the Anglican priest on the flight to Addis Ababa. The man insisted I call him Bertie, which sounded a ridiculous sort of name. Hadn't he the dignity to call himself Albert? I could barely stand to look at him, my eyes immediately straying to what looked like an incipient goiter pushing against his dog collar. I knew I had to keep talking, if only to forestall his pitying tone when I told him about my missing father. I didn't like, either, the too bright light that shone from his eyes when he described his calling to work with AIDS orphans. As a literature major turned pre-med student, I knew what it was to want to be useful, but there was a touch too much zeal in how the man spoke of the appalling conditions in the country of my birth.

I launched into my story as soon as a stewardess swept away our packages of curry-flavored crisps. "It was like this," I said, watching Bertie settle in like a child for a bedtime tale. "My friend's grandfather was a hunter. He was a highly respected elder of his village, and physically large—his hands as wide as a dog's head—with a personality to match."

I hadn't thought about that day for years. Demissie's voice had been intimidatingly deep, his gaze pitiless. I felt he could see into the weakest corners of my soul. The first time Girma and I paid him a visit, Demissie had insisted it was his duty to teach us boys what it was to be a man. "Not some weak city version," he said, spitting on the ground, "with all the force leeched from your bones by Western music, the fumes of automobiles, the comfort of indoor toilets." As if to drive home his point, he spat again.

As I spun my tale for the wide-eyed Bertie, the vividness of our hunt was borne back to me like an evil wind. I remembered how we'd spent half the morning looking for the herd. It had been hot and dry, and I was unspeakably tired before our hunt even began.

I had not mentioned to Girma or his grandfather that I had brought a disability of sorts with me to our journey. I had a sore anus from a miserable episode of constipation I'd suffered the previous week. "Too much spiced cheese," Enat had muttered, shaking her head at my greediness. It wasn't as if she hadn't warned me.

I have to admit to a streak of cruelty. I found myself describing in infinite detail to my goitered companion how my bum had chafed like the devil with every step I took. I asked him, "How could Demissie have suspected that my mind was as far as could be from that dusty forest we traveled, inhabiting instead a world about an inch or two wide, where I was sure blood was beginning to erupt from a tiny volcano that made up in intensity what it lacked in size?"

Bertie the Anglican didn't know whether to look away in embarrassment or make a sympathetic nod; he compromised with a sort of a twitch, his goiter making a little dimple in his white collar, which by now was damp with perspiration.

I didn't mind one bit that I was making the man uncomfortable. If anything, it made my memory even sharper. I could almost smell the bitter sack of fear thrown back and forth between Girma and me all those years ago.

I took a long draught of iced tea before continuing. "At last, Demissie relented and indicated we could take a break, motioning us to drink from our water pouches. He deftly slit open a papaya for us with a sharp knife he'd extracted from his goatskin bag. I lay awkwardly on my side, while Girma sat up tall and straight, mimicking his grandfather. Demissie said nothing to me about my odd posture, but the look he gave me signaled his contempt for my presumed laziness."

"But I didn't care. Anything to ease the acute stabbing sensation at my bottom caused by movement, though in truth the throbbing I felt while lying there wasn't much better. All too soon, Demissie waved us to our feet. I nearly tripped as I struggled to stand, and my friend disloyally snickered, shooting a quick sycophantic look at his father's father."

"In the end, it wasn't a herd that we found but a female and her calf, the white stripes across their flanks looking almost painted onto their brown hides. The terror in the mother's eyes put all thoughts away of my own pain. But Demissie was a swift hunter, and he reacted automatically. Mother and baby fell without sound, the baby's front hoof crossing its mother's stunned eyes like a blindfold. I could not stop myself. I ran to the fallen pair and dropped onto my knees beside them, putting my hand under the cheek of the dying baby, which gave three great quivers before its heartbeat ceased."

But now I stopped. There was something I did not wish to reveal to Bertie the Anglican: only Makeda knew, and even she I had confided in with considerable hesitation, "I know, Makeda, that the calf's spirit came into me in that moment. I just don't know what I'm supposed to do with it."

Tears streaming down cheeks the color of *weira* bark, she'd nodded in comprehension. "You don't have to worry. You will know—the spirit of the calf will tell you—when the time is right."

Ah, Makeda. A sudden pang of longing for her was making me feel increasingly antagonistic to the man sitting beside me, the man who couldn't begin to comprehend the land he was heading for. I wanted to rub into his mind every detail of Demissie efficiently ripping off the skins of the still-warm animals. But as I watched Bertie the Anglican gag, I sensed that the time Makeda had referred to was fast approaching.

It occurred to me then that there was a strange similarity to flying in a plane and sitting in a hospital waiting room: the stale air, the sense of being captive, sharing intimacies with total strangers. I must have fallen asleep on that thought, though it couldn't have been for long. My conversation with the Anglican had taken the better part of three and a half hours. But it was time enough to dream the dream I'd been dreaming since my voice became a man's voice, tufts of hair springing up like dense forests under my arms and below my belly. The dream began as always, with me inserting my *washela* between the welcoming thighs of a now-grown and laughing-eyed Makeda. This time, though, I became aware of an Eritrean soldier to my right, his camouflage trousers pooled at his ankles as he plunged his *washela* again and again into my *sayt ayat*, the wife of my now-mute grandfather. Horrified, I looked back to the face of Makeda, whose expression had taken on a sense of urgency, and I found myself unstoppably thrusting my *washela* into some nameless mound of death and disease.

I came to with a start. I must have cried out, for I woke to the alarmed face of a dark-eyed stewardess. "Sir? Sir?" As I straightened myself from my cramped position, I saw Bertie the Anglican leaning well away from me, as if he wished to push his back through the wall of the plane, anything to get away from this mad African, who told stories of vulgar brutality and didn't even know how to dream a dreamless sleep.

Chapter Four
Fleur

I HAD TO LAUGH. Modern technology had made it possible to live multiple incarnations in one fifteen-minute ride to work. As soon as I got off the phone with Assefa, I saw Mother's number on Caller ID. She was phoning from her limo ride back to San Marino after arriving at Burbank Airport via a red eye from D.C., where she'd been lobbying for the inclusion of alcoholism treatment centers in the health care amendment bills currently up before Congress. Though her hair was already greying here and there and her glamorous persona somewhat dimmed by the thickening of her waist, Mother was still a bundle of energy. Her demanding day job didn't keep her from devoting astonishing chunks of time to the sobriety community. She was full of an excitement that I initially took as indicative that she'd won over a Blue Dog vote or two. But no, it was about me.

"I may have missed your actual birthday, Fleur, but I'll be damned if I let your celebration blend in with Christmas this year. The great news is that everyone can come. Dhani—gem that she is—has put together a fabulous menu for such short notice. We're lucky Ignacio's a good sport; he'll probably have to make do with a Honey Baked Ham tomorrow night for Christmas Eve."

"But Mother, you've got to be exhausted."

I heard her take a deep drag on her cigarette. "Not a bit. Besides, I can take a nice nap as soon as I get home. Abeba's got everything in order."

"But—"

"No buts. She swears her father-in-law is fine now, and he's quite comfortable at Huntington—they actually found another Ethiopian patient to assign to his room. Besides, it'll do her good to take her mind off worrying about Achamyalesh." Without skipping a beat, she pivoted, "Now let's see, I don't think I've left anyone out. Dhani's coming, of course, and Ignacio and Angelina. By the way, have I told you how nicely Angelina and Cesar are getting on these days? I swear, that Ritalin is a godsend. I hate to say it, but that boy was going to drive me out of my mind. When a sweet girl like Angelina doesn't like someone, you know she's got some really good reasons." She paused just long enough to take another drag on her Sherman, no doubt telling herself I couldn't hear the faint rasp of her inhaling. But now I could just see her ticking off the names on her fingers. "Sammie, Jacob, Aadita and that boy of hers ... who knew Aadita was such a cougar?"

It was more than a little jarring to hear the gracious Aadita referred to in that way. Besides, Mother calling Aadita a cougar definitely belonged in the Pot-Calling-the-Kettle-Black Department. "Mother! He's not a boy. He's forty years old. And his name's Arturo."

"Okay, then, that cute forty-year-old boyfriend of hers, Arturo." It occurred to me that Mother must've cleared her head from her overnight flight with a massive dose of caffeine. She rushed on, "Not to mention Sister Flatulencia, Katrina, Tom, Gunther, Amir, Stanley, and Gwen. Let's see, that looks like seventeen, counting you and me."

I stifled a groan. I really didn't do well with that sort of attention. It tended to remind me of being pierced by the King of Sweden's perfect blue eyes while I prattled on about Grandfather's balls.

"Mother, really? Seventeen people? You're going to have to haul the leaves out of the storage closet. They're too heavy. Don't let Abeba do it by herself. I'll come early and help."

"Nonsense! Ignacio's already said he'd do it. He promised to shave a few doors, while he's at it. Nobody warned me about that one. Every time there's a little earthquake in this town, everything in the house shifts. Oh—and a chap named Bob. Stanley said you'd want him, too. Is he on your team now?"

Bob? Damn. "Mm hmm, yes, sure …."

Mother fell silent, and I sensed she was waiting for more of a response. She and I hadn't forged anything close to a normal mother-child bond until my Nobel crisis, when I beat out previous odd ducks like Phillip Lenard, who attacked Einstein as "the Jewish fraud," and Harold Pinter, whose videotaped speech was a fulminating rant against American crimes against humanity, for world's most outrageous Nobel acceptance speech. Who else would stand before an audience that included the King of Sweden and ascribe her scientific breakthrough to a failed attempt to save a dying baby bird on the lawn, an equally abysmal effort to effect a modern day resurrection by pouring a vaseful of water onto a dead man's balls, and having to get an abortion at thirteen merely because some ignorant hunk of a teenage boy kept whispering, "*Linda paloma, linda paloma,*" in her ear? If there was anything to Father's public accusations that whatever came out of my mind was a product of mental disturbance or autism, my Nobel speech veered awfully close to proving his point. Which was why I'd especially appreciated Mother standing by my side when the media had its field day with me.

I knew it hadn't been easy for her. Our pattern had been set early on: she, way too young and fragile, far more comfortable holding her wine glass than her unwanted baby; me, prone to whirling and flapping, finding comfort only when being squeezed within an inch of my life. A pretty unlikely pair. Add to that my more recent choice to continue living with the Fiskes after she moved her whole crew to SoCal to be near me, and it was a miracle Mother hadn't given up on me for good.

"Mother, you don't have to do this."

I could feel the smile lifting her voice. "Nonsense. It's my pleasure, darling. You've always been the sweetest rose in my garden."

We both choked up over that one. Mother had first cultivated her David Austins—peony-like in pattern, ambrosial in scent—on Father's vast grounds. The expanse of what I used to call their invisible beds was so beautiful, they could have given the Seven Wonders of the World a run for their money. As soon as Mother moved to San Marino, she'd immediately installed as many Austin bushes as she could fit into her considerably more confined backyard. Her comparing me to those cabbage-petaled treasures might be a bit—dare I say it?—flowery, but I knew the sentiment was sincere. It had taken years of elbowing my way out of the darkest black hole to actually understand that.

Mother blew her nose loudly before adding, "I just wish that fiancé of yours could be here. Any promising leads? I hope you hear something good soon."

As it turned out, what I *hoped* to hear and what I actually heard turned out to be two different things. Assefa's call came early that evening, as I sat with my improbable extended family at Father's old banquet table, chowing down a series of some of Dhani's most scrumptious Indian dishes, presented with panache on Mother's "Africa" china, festooned with cheetahs, elephants, giraffes, and monkeys so idealized they would undoubtedly make Amir's rescued lab chimp Lord Hanuman throw a poop ball or two.

What I heard was that the aesthetics of upper class SoCal didn't hold a candle to the charms of poor-as-Job's-turkey Ethiopia. Or at least that was what I extrapolated from the enthusiastic paean pouring into my ear despite a lousy cellphone connection.

"Wait, Assefa, I can barely hear you; let me try another room," I said, pushing back my chair and angling out of it, avoiding the curious eyes of half the table.

Settling myself upstairs onto the quilted covers in Mother's spare bedroom and purposely positioning my neck against the sharp-ish corner of a copy of *The Big Book* Mother had flung onto the bed, I asked him, "Where are you, anyway? Addis Ababa?"

"It's amazing, Fleur. No, I've left Addis Ababa. Which is a great city, by the way—a lot more elegant than either of us would have imagined. And dizzying. I'd forgotten about the altitude. But I'm over it now. No, I'm in my hometown, Fleur! Tikil Dingay. I never thought I'd see it again. Do you believe it? My home is gone, and I haven't been able to track down Bekele and Iskinder, but so much feels familiar. The smells. The sounds. The crickets are *insane* here, and I know you probably won't believe, but our ibises are much louder than your crows. I'm like a buried man, coming back to life again …."

I dug my fingernails into my arm. *Our* ibises, *your* crows? *Like a buried man?* I'd realized early on that we each have multiple incarnations within one lifetime—such different ways of experiencing ourselves that we're nearly completely different people at each stage of our lives. But *buried? Really?* Who'd been pouring his seed into me, licking my breasts, telling me how amazing I was—*a dead man?*

But I have to confess that scientists can be pretty cold blooded. Despite my hurt and fear, the physicist in me was having a field day. I wondered whether I could use Assefa's image of a buried self to expedite the application of my Principle of Dematerialization. If our pasts were like multiple universes, each previous incarnation a road in an alternate terrain, how might we move that process forward intentionally, cellularly? And might we also move it backwards and alter history? A part of me wanted to drop the phone and run downstairs to pose the question to Stanley and Amir and Katrina and Gunther and Tom. Even to Bob, who'd walked into Mother's house wearing a broad grin and trailing a cloud of the world's most cloying aftershave behind him.

But that particular state of dissociation lasted less than a couple of heartbeats. Altering the past was, at best, a dubious proposition. If Mother hadn't left Father, I might never have met Stanley H. Fiske. If Nana hadn't been in the middle of an intersection just as an entitled Brentwood brat burst through a red light, she might have lived another thirty years, with Abeba going to work for some other family. If Assefa hadn't come to the U.S., he might have married the girl who I just knew had brought him back to his village. Oh, he didn't mention her, and I didn't ask, but I knew. I could smell her otherness, her other-than-*me*-ness, in what Assefa *wasn't* saying.

A nasty little voice uncoiled from the bottom of my belly. "What about your father," I asked, all innocence. "Have you found your father?"

I'd achieved my goal. Assefa's voice caught guiltily and his tone dropped to a whisper. "Well, no, not yet, but—"

"Actually, I think I might be able to help. I'll be meeting with an expert on the Ark tomorrow. I'm going with—"

Assefa broke in with a non sequitur-ish, "Can you believe it, the orphanage Zalelew wrote about in his postcard is actually in the town where I was born." And then I heard another voice, feminine in timbre, piping up in the background, "*Yike'rt*, Assefa," which Assefa interrupted with a hurried, "Listen, Fleur, my cell is breaking up. Reception is crap here. I'll email you as soon as I can. Tell my mother—" It really did break up then. I was left with nothing but static. I flung my phone onto the bed and felt myself begin to slide down the side of a slick, funnel-shaped pit.

It wasn't much later that Mother entered the room, catching my hands up in hers to stop the flapping. Pulling them, and me, to her breast, she said, "Assefa?" I nodded. She tugged me even tighter, as if Nana had been giving her lessons from the other side. "Tell me," she murmured into my hair. Her breath smelled of garlic, cumin, and cardamom, which did no end of good in helping me surrender to her embrace. Dhani's spicy *jimikand* and *chatpate Baingan* would no doubt turn my poo into fiery red bullets in the next twenty-four hours, but for now, transmitted to my nostrils via Mother's whispered, "What is it, love?" the aroma was rather settling.

I gently loosened myself from Mother's grip and edged backwards to sit cross-legged on the bed, rocking just a bit as I crossed my hands below my breasts. "He's supposed to be looking for his father, but he's out in the middle of nowhere with some girl."

Mother sat down beside me, hip to hip, adjusting to my rocking motion. She clasped her hands tightly in her lap, like Sister Flatulencia in prayer. "What do you mean, in the middle of nowhere? What girl?"

"Well, not really nowhere. He's in his hometown. Tikil Dingay. Where I always imagined visiting with him someday. But he's with her."

"Who's *her*?"

"I only know her name's Makeda. She's the one Achamyalesh and Zalelew bumped into at the airport."

Mother's face relaxed. "Well, then, it makes sense he'd look her up, sweetie. She might know where his father is."

I stared at her. We rarely sat so close. Her chiseled, almost austere features had spread and softened with age. The pores on her nose were larger than I ever remembered. The last traces of maroon lipstick feathered a bit around her smoker's lips. Here was a woman who'd been to hell and back several times over—losing her own mother as a young child, falling captive to alcohol when a teenage pregnancy pushed her into a loveless marriage, watching her remaining parent rendered mute and powerless by a stroke, having to endure her abusive husband being revered by every whack job in the nation. The fact that she'd been able to haul herself out of those layers of hell wasn't solely thanks to the intervention of her companion Sister Flatulencia and the ongoing support of the twelve-step community. No, she'd been fortified from birth by a keen mind, a kind heart, and a thirst for learning that ultimately sent her back to school in her early thirties. Mother becoming a librarian at L.A.'s stunning Art Deco Central Library might strike anyone who'd known her during her out-of-control adolescence as more than a little ironic, but Stanley wasn't the first to assure me that no one should be held too much to account for the idiocies of youth.

I was well aware that Mother knew a thing or two about the opposite sex. She hadn't wasted much time once she shook herself free from Father's pincer grip. AA was the primary supplier of a stream of (generally younger) men who were all-too-willing to bed the winsome ex-wife of the infamous Senator Robins, though she tended to collect suitors *wherever* she went, including the Swedish wedding she and I crashed on the night of my Nobel debacle.

But in the end, she'd seemed to decide that celibacy suited her best. Having survived devastating loss, addiction, and an odd duck of a daughter who would never fit into a white-picket-fence mold, she wore about her an aura of humorous serenity steeped in a firsthand knowledge that, as the Buddhists say, life is suffering.

So I grasped at the straw she proffered. "You're right," I sighed. "Adam always warned me not to get too carried away by the Green-Eyed Monster."

Mother shot me a quick look, as if checking to see if I was faking it. Which was a joke in itself. With a few notable exceptions involving my failed status as a resurrector, I was about as good at fakery as Jillily casually waltzing into the house with hummingbird feathers spilling from her mouth. Mother gestured toward the door. "Shall we?" Which I translated as, "We're being rude. We need to go back downstairs."

As we stood up, Mother smoothing the wrinkles in her rose-patterned linen dress, it occurred to me that falling in love is like learning a new language. I had mastered the argot of physics and had worked even harder to grasp the crude idioms of our time, but cracking the code of Assefa was proving to be the most difficult challenge of all.

By the time the two of us reached the bottom stair, Abeba and Sister Flatulencia had just finished clearing the table, and everyone seemed to be talking at once as they awaited Dhani's dessert. I rushed toward the kitchen to give Abeba the latest Assefa bulletin. Entering the room, I saw Dhani and Sister Flatulencia make a quick, conspiratorial exit into the pantry. I couldn't help but notice the cloud crossing Abeba's forehead when I told her that Assefa hadn't yet found his father. Her frown deepened when I added, "He was calling from Tikil Dingay. He said he couldn't find your house. It was gone."

"But why is he *there?*" she said, gesturing plaintively. "Does he think Achamyalesh and Zalelew stopped there on their way to Aksum?"

"I don't know, Abeba. His cell cut out in the middle of our conversation." Then I slyly slid in, "Didn't Zalelew's postcard mention bumping into some girl from your village?"

Abeba's lips clamped tighter than a ziplock bag. Seeing I wasn't going to leave the room without some sort of response, she offered an uncharitable, "I can't imagine what *she* would have to offer."

While I found her tone extremely satisfying, I had to admit that her comment lacked logic. I knew why *I* didn't trust Makeda, but I couldn't fathom why Abeba would be holding a grudge against someone who had, after all, been only a child when she'd last seen her. Abeba abruptly turned her back on me to resolutely stuff leftovers into plastic containers, and before I knew it, Dhani and Sister Flatulencia had joined us, Sister F. carefully closing the door to the pantry.

I gave Dhani a quick hug, enjoying the sensation of her rounded belly against me. "You are so sweet to do this for me," I declared, to which she responded with a self-deprecating little wave.

Abeba removed a stack of dessert plates from the cupboard and hurriedly ferried them out to the dining room, as if she'd been looking for an opportunity to escape. Sister Flatulencia, wearing what looked to be a new lavender pantsuit, her now-white kinky curls struggling to escape her signature bandana, leaned her tall, skinny frame against the fridge and watched me and Dhani with a pleased grin. It was good to see her smile. She'd been understandably subdued ever since the tragedy. When I'd mentioned it to Adam in our most recent phone call, he'd pronounced, "Survivor guilt. How would you feel if you were the only one to make it through such a terrible accident with only a broken wrist to show you'd been there at all? Give her time, Fleur. She's a strong woman. She'll come back." Maybe he was right. I knew that moving in with Dhani and Ignacio after the death of her two closest friends had to be helpful; babysitting for the adorable Angelina while Dhani taught at her cooking school would be healing for anyone.

Dhani threw me a moist-eyed look, speaking in that lilting way of hers, still tinged with the Hindi-British accent of her youth. "Ah, my dear girl," she said, though of course her *girl* came out sounding like *gull*. "I simply can't believe it was ten years ago that I first cooked you an Indian dish."

"Yes," I replied, "and my butt's never gotten over it." Sister Flatulencia frowned, which was pretty hypocritical of her, considering what hell her digestion had wrought on the rest of us before she discovered Beano.

Dhani giggled, reminding me of the comely young woman Father had hired to replace Cook, whom he'd fired in a fit of scapegoating after the media had actually deigned to give his pro-choice rival (and Adam's father), Senator Manus, equal air time.

Time does many things to people, but rarely alters their essence. Though Dhani's round black eyes were now creased at the corners and her waist had widened in the nine years since Angelina was born, her heart was still as generously full as the lips that I'd once, in horror, watched Father nibble.

"No, really," I said in earnest, worried that she'd mistake my wisecrack for ingratitude, "it's all delicious. I don't know how you do it. I just hope you're teaching it all to Miss Beauty out there."

Dhani eyes lit up in maternal pleasure. "Yes, she is that. And yes, I am teaching her, slowly, which my *naniji* said was the best way." I knew Dhani had learned to cook from her grandmother, her communist mother being too busy with the cause to bother much with the kitchen. Now her expression became mischievous and she gave me a mock-slap on my butt. "Now, off with you, my girl. Your guests are going to feel ignored."

Re-entering the dining room, I sat down next to Sammie, realizing soon enough that hostilities had just broken out. Sammie replied with a testy, "No, and I wish you wouldn't remind me," to

Aadita's question, "So, did you manage to get a meeting with the gallery owner?"

I saw Jacob shoot Sammie a sideways glance.

Even in normal families, mothers inevitably seem to reach a point where they fail to understand their daughters—whether because the daughters grow past them or veer into their mothers' blind spots or fall victim to blind spots of their own. In Sammie's case, I knew it was her frustration that Jacob didn't want to have children that was making her so irritable lately—and who better to take it out on than her eternally adoring and reliably forgiving mother?

Actually, it wasn't so much that Jacob didn't want kids. He was one of those guys born to be good fathers. I'd seen him enough times goofing around with his young nephews to know he was playful and enthusiastic, with reams of patience for playing the same game over and over with a child who insists repeatedly, "Again!" But he was anxious he wouldn't be able to support a child. Money wasn't exactly one of the major perks for a comparative religion student, whose best-case scenario would consist in getting hired for a university position, which, given the state of the economy, was about as likely as an ethical politician getting elected.

Sammie's interests were hardly conventional—her art, ecstatic dancing, Kundalini yoga, Jungian analysis, old foreign films, the more *noir* the better. But her personal dreams were pretty white picket fence-ish. She wanted to get married, buy a quasi-reasonably-priced house somewhere on the Westside, and have two children, ideally a girl and a boy, and preferably without the aid of fertility drugs or the latest hotshot Chinese acupuncturist.

Sammie was convinced they'd be able to get by, especially if she applied her own M.F.A. degree toward becoming a museum curator. Lord knew, she had the brains for it. But, to everyone's surprise, Jacob was out-picket-fencing her, insisting that he couldn't possibly have kids until he could comfortably support both kids *and* mother. Having been a latchkey boy himself, the thought of his own progeny being partially raised by a nanny was simply beyond his tolerance level.

The whole thing confused me. If everyone decided not to have kids for fear of replicating whatever they'd had to endure as children, the human race might as well pack it up once and for all.

Which, come to think of, might be pretty much what we were doing, anyway.

It was at that point in my ruminations that Sammie threw down her napkin and left the room. Aadita looked around the table with palms raised, as if to say, "What did I do?"

Jacob slid over to Sammie's chair, took my hand in his, and gave it a courtly kiss.

"How's tricks, kid? Was that Our Man in Ethiopia you left the table for? It's all us Jews' fault. If it weren't for the Ark of the Covenant, Achamyalesh would be sitting right here with us, and Assefa would be the lucky dude holding this pretty hand of yours."

I gave him a grateful grin. Sammie had once said that Jacob's hands were as smooth as butter, and she was right; the sensation was quite comforting. But then I caught sight of Aadita conferring anxiously with Mother and Arturo, and I slipped my hand out of Jacob's, telling him, "You'd better go get her, or she'll be mortified tomorrow that she spoiled my party."

Jacob made a face, instantly pushing back his chair. "Damn. You're right. Lemme go find her."

I could just spy Sister Flatulencia, Dhani, and Abeba hovering through the crack in the dining room door. No doubt they'd already lit the candles on my cake and were waiting for the guests to get their collective act together and be seated.

The fact was, the dinner party had become more than a little chaotic. Ignacio was lurking outside the plate-glass-walled dining room on the back deck, a cigar clamped in his lips while he inspected the stylish MoMA birdfeeder he'd installed for Mother earlier in the day. Cesar and Angelina were sitting across from me, laughing noisily over some game on Cesar's iPhone, and my physics team was huddled together at the other end of Father's long table, no doubt mashing up the latest thinking on the Eridanus supervoid. Who was missing?

Just then, I felt a tug at my sleeve. I turned, and there was Bob Ballantine's face, just inches from my own. I knew he was nervous, because his left eye was twitching faster than usual. He gave an anemic little cough before murmuring, "Nice party, what?"

Was he kidding? *Nice party, what?* Poor Bob had been watching too much *Masterpiece Theater.* But who was I to judge? I'd only acquired the few social graces I had because Adam had taken me under his wing when he was a physics wonder boy and I a feral creature of twelve.

I laughed. "Let's be honest, Bob. It's all a little bonkers, which is what you'd expect at a party for an odd duck like me, don't you think?"

But Bob was nothing if not earnest. His brown eyes got bigger and rounder and he actually clapped a dramatic hand to his forehead. "Don't. You shouldn't. You ...."

I felt ashamed then. If I was an odd duck, then what was Bob? Crazy as a hoot owl? Nuttier than a fruitcake? Probably. But it wouldn't do to rub it in.

"Sorry, Bob. I'm awful. It is nice. Definitely nice for all of you to show up for me. And I'm glad you're having a nice time."

And then Bob said something I never would have imagined. In a voice I never would have imagined. In a tone about two timbres lower than the one he generally spoke in. He said, "Nice? This has to be the happiest moment I can remember. Actually, it's the happiest time in my life, period. I mean, landing on a team headed up by you, after what you did ... not just your brilliance, but also your courage. Letting it all hang out and not giving a damn. The Nobel Committee. The media. All those assholes mouthing off on Fox News. And you just telling it like it is. That science doesn't just exist in a vacuum. People's lives get changed because somebody, somewhere, had the balls"—he blushed, remembering just why my Nobel speech had been so controversial in the first place—"to go with her gut instinct and say out loud things that other people don't even dare let themselves think."

By the time he'd finished, I'm sure my mouth was hanging open.

I was saved from having to respond by Sister Flatulencia, Dhani, Abeba, and a reassuringly handholding Sammie and Jacob bursting into the dining room, singing, "Happy birthday to you ...." Bob looked disoriented for a moment, but then, he, too joined in. Letting my eyes travel around the table, I saw everyone looking at me, and then their faces started to blur. I wanted to clap my hands in gratitude, but instead found them covering my eyes.

I realized I was crying. I noticed another thing, too. This was starting to become a habit.

Chapter Five
Assefa

I KNEW IT was wrong. It wasn't as if I had forgotten Fleur. Hardly. Her crooked smile was a guilty punctuation mark to my thoughts. Her constant heart thrummed close to my chest. The earnest single line lightly bisecting her brows was like a Mnemosynian thread tied around my little finger.

But a hanging man cannot hold still, and Makeda had pulled me toward her like a powerful gravitational force. It was shocking to realize that only yesterday I had walked for miles in the hot sun, lightheaded with the altitude and jetlag, increasingly worried that I had misunderstood the directions I'd been given to the place where I might find her. Stopping to remove my shoe and empty it of three tiny, but vexing, pebbles, I had nearly decided to turn back, but then made a deal with myself that I'd follow the winding, scrubby road for one more turn. Sure enough, there it stood, the orphanage where I had been told Makeda worked, its whitewashed *chikka* walls bearing a simple, hand-lettered sign, "*As-Salāmu `Alaykum*," below a weather-beaten ornate Ethiopian Orthodox cross.

A rusty iron gate hung beside the sign at a slightly skewed angle. I pushed it open, cringing at the loud screech of metal against metal. Scanning a wide dirt yard where a score of noisy children played, I spotted her immediately, repositioning the sun-burnished toddler on her hip as she turned to see who'd come. Despite the fact that her proportions had elongated, her graceful *habesha kemis* dress revealing hips and breasts flaring from her lithe torso, she was exactly as I had dreamed her. My loins nearly exploded. With an exultant shout of recognition, she broke into a near-run across the dusty, uneven ground, a chaotic crowd of children falling in behind her. As she came closer, I saw an expression pass momentarily across her face of mysterious indwelling, reminding me of pictures Abat had shown me of Aksum's renowned black Madonna, St. Maryum Sion.

Reaching a mid-point between us, she halted and looked down, issuing a sharp, "*Tew!*"—stop it!—to a child at her feet who'd dared hit another with a stick. Despite that momentary fierceness, the impression she created was soft and welcoming. Her shapely arms made a sweet sling for the lucky baby suspended above the high-pitched, scrabbling crowd below. I sensed she must be, for many of these orphaned children, a living buffer zone against the abyss.

All this I saw in those few, brief moments, and more.

Wretched man that I was, I couldn't help but contrast this woman and the one I'd left behind only two days ago, but several light-years before. Fleur looked a child compared with this imperiously postured, kink-haired goddess hurrying towards me, her white *shama* nearly falling off one shoulder. Her gaze never once left my face, her moist black eyes claiming the old intimacy, an ageless twinship of the soul.

Each sway of her hips awoke in me a world of cellular familiarity. In America, I was the Ethiopian boy, the one with a taxi driver for a father, bound by the good fortune of intelligence and physical charm to rise up in the world. I never mentioned it to Fleur, but something in me never quite forgot that my mother worked for her mother. Oh, I knew it was not fair to blame the daughter for the mother's social class. And lord knew, my mother needed the work.

But the truth was that, while Margaret Robins called my mother her friend, she was still her employer, the one who guaranteed that, even on one of my father's low-volume days, we would still have *wat* to ladle across our *injera* on our dinner table. My father had once remarked how odd it was that the same Angelenos who installed locks and deadbolts and alarm systems in their houses simultaneously offered beloved pets and children to the care of virtual strangers, women whose addresses they often didn't know, with backgrounds they didn't check and phone numbers that changed with some regularity. "Think of it!" he'd said wonderingly. "They entrust them with their jewelry, credit cards, silver, favorite articles of clothing ...." He stopped abruptly, and it occurred to me that he might as well have finished his sentence with "their stained underwear."

The gap between our visceral assumptions was so vast that Fleur and I might as well have come from entirely different universes.

I had found my way back to this village with Makeda my true north, telling myself she would be the clue to my Father's whereabouts, but secretly hoping she would cut the rope and let this hanging man down. Dropped off in Tikil Dingay's dilapidated version of a main street district by the driver of a blue and white taxi far worse for wear than Father's yellow version back in Pasadena, I had aimed for the closest shop and had been informed by its clearly curious proprietor that Makeda's home was long gone, as was mine, burned to the ground.

The mantis-thin man lowered his heavily lashed eyes and made a dismissive gesture before finally spitting out that the torching had been committed by the PFDJ, which I knew to be Eritrea's Peoples Front for Democracy and Justice. But my informant didn't waste another minute, hastily directing me to the orphanage where Makeda worked, nearly pushing me out the door as I clutched my just-purchased, but nonetheless creased and worn map of Amara and a bottle of Coke. I suspected that this spear of a man, purveyor of *bunna*, unguents, brightly-colored textiles, and probably—given his racing speech and nervy demeanor—*khat* to a small community that rarely saw a stranger, couldn't wait to inform anyone who'd listen that an American was asking after Makeda Geteye—youngest daughter of the Geteye family, the very same Geteyes whom my mother and father refused to speak of once we emigrated, though I was never able to learn why.

I would worry about that later. For now, my sole challenge was to contain myself as Makeda bypassed my slight bow by leaning forward to kiss my cheek three times. The sensations of her plump, dry lips against my skin and the sweet and sour smell of the scalp of the baby in her arms, whose moist forehead gently butted against my neck with each of her kisses, were nearly intolerable. I wanted her to let that wide-eyed child onto the ground, encircle me with her arms, and bring back the boy I once was, the one who'd known this brown earth as a Mother for whom he was but a natural extension, a bush from a branch, a toe from a foot, a rush of blood from a rhythmically pumping heart.

But I didn't have long to linger in that fantasy. At the very moment that Makeda stepped achingly back onto her own separate patch of ground, laughing just a little and brushing the child's forehead with what I fancied was a sudden shyness, a voice broke in. "*Sälam neshway?*"

The sea of children surrounding us parted to make room for a quick-footed man, small and wiry and wearing a rather soiled *netela* over his long jodhpur-type trousers. He grabbed my hand and pumped it up and down enthusiastically. "You are surely Assefa Berhanu, yes? Son of Abeba and Achamyalesh Berhanu?" I nodded, disconcerted. "Father Wendimu."

He noticed my surprise and added quickly, "Sorry. Still go by the old appellation. The Church and I parted company a few years ago— the good Lord had His own ideas for me—but nobody in this town seems to want to pay that any attention. Power of habit, I guess. Anyway, lad, it's so good to see you after all this time. My God, it has been … how long? Eighteen years?" He stopped, still holding my hand, which he now clasped with both of his. I was all-too aware of Makeda grinning at my confusion. "Forgive me. Your father was my friend. Does he ever mention me? Used to beat me regularly at chess." He gave a short, barking laugh and scratched what looked, under his *netela*, to be a nearly bald head. "Don't worry. I'm not psychic, but I would have known you anywhere. You have his same forehead and … the famous smile. He was always a one for the ladies. He is alive, Makeda tells me, and on his way to Aksum."

Makeda nodded. "They should be there by now."

Father Wendimu went on. "So you've come to join your father."

I opened my mouth to explain, but he was already on to another question. "And your mother, blessed woman, how is she?"

"She's well," I replied. Father Wendimu's voice had summoned an unfamiliar, but insistent memory. My father and another man bent over a chessboard in the corner of a narrow room. A large window behind them framed a darkening sky that looked as if the entire universe was contracting. Thunder crackled and suddenly the whole world—the sky, the ochre walls surrounding the house, our little room—was brilliantly alight. The white of the two men's eyes looked exaggerated and frightening. I clutched at the folds of Enat's green and red apron, feeling shame as I saw both of the men throw back their heads and laugh. I buried my head in my mother's skirts, ashamed to be the butt of their amusement.

But now I realized that they'd been laughing at their own surprise and terror—unmanly, perhaps, but unavoidable, automatic.

I loosened my hand from Father Wendimu's and turned to Makeda. She was staring at me quizzically, as if aware that my attention had wavered for a moment. "Actually," I said, "I'm not here so much to join my father as to locate him. We haven't heard from him since he left Pasadena."

She shot me an uncomprehending look. "I am more happy to see you than I can say, but is that really why you are here, Assefa? Because your father has not contacted you?" She shrugged, and her *shama* slid down to reveal a generous half-moon of breast. "You know how it is. Everything here moves slower than a forty-year-old camel. You send two pieces of mail on the same day and one gets to its destination in thirty-six hours, the other shows up thirty-six years later. Buses break down, so you try to hunt down a hire car. Phones work, and then they don't work. The PFDJ blocks a road and as soon as they get a little *khat*, they forget they were supposed to be blocking it, but meanwhile there's a burnt out car blocking the way. And then you decide to take a little detour, visit an auntie who knew you as a child, take a little nap that turns into a series of naps, and as soon as you get going again, your hired car breaks down and you need to wait for someone in the closest village to track down the friend of a friend of a friend who might be able to fix it."

Laughing a little, she reached out a hand to my cheek, then seemed to think better of it. "Don't worry, Assefa. Your father and Galelew were well and full of excitement when I met them. I was going to bring them here, but your father thought better of it and decided to hire a private taxi to take them to Aksum. I know the driver." She turned to Father Wendimu with an informative, "It is Negasi." Then back to me, "We both know him well. He sometimes brings adoptive parents here. He is a good man. Your father is safe, my friend." She made a circle on her abdomen with her free hand and the baby in her other arm made a mimicking circle on his own. "Please don't worry." Despite the fact that I knew nothing more of my father's whereabouts than I had on Fleur's birthday, something in me relaxed a little. I found myself smiling.

Father Wendimu, too, beamed at her, then turned to me. "I think you can trust her instinct, young man. Rubbing that belly of hers like that, I've never known her to be wrong." He immediately stooped to swoop up one of the children and turn him upside down, making little clucking sounds to accompany the boy's delighted laughter. The other children shouted to be given a turn, and he complied with a few of them. Putting the last one down, he felt around his back, groaning overdramatically.

"*Mintifeligialesh*?" What do you want? "Can't you see I am an old man? My back is breaking. You should be carrying *me*!"

The children laughed as if they had never heard anything so funny. I found myself feeling sorry for my erstwhile traveling partner Bertie the Episcopalian. It would take him years, if ever, to achieve the ease with such fate-trampled children that came as naturally as shitting to Father Wendimu. I marveled at the man's seemingly endless fund of good cheer.

But then I saw him shoot a look of what seemed to be raw grief at Makeda, and more stinging still, saw her return it. For a brief moment, the sky went blacker than that cloud-stricken expanse of my boyhood, but I was still waiting for the thunder.

It would not come for several hours. When it did, I would wish I had never returned to the land of my birth.

But fate had to soften me up for the blow. Until then, there was a feast to take part in, sitting in the middle of the cluster of children who clung to Makeda and Father Wendimu like a cloud of buzzing bees.

I'd followed them all past a thatch-roofed *tukul* smelling strongly of goat into the largest of the trio of rough dwellings on the property. There seemed to be no other adults here besides the one woman who emerged from a room to the left with a copper pot and basin. I introduced myself, and she mumbled something that sounded like "Adey Gatimo" before slipping past me. I noted that she wore her *shama medegdeg*-style, with her shawl's shiny tassels hanging down, which I knew meant she'd recently lost someone close to her. The day now coming to a lingering close had been hot and humid, and my mouth began to water as the smells of onion, cloves, cinnamon and a host of other spices widened my nostrils. There was a wild rush to the score of stools around the worn *mesab*, whose hourglass wicker design was a far cry from the tall, rectangular pine dining table my parents had purchased at the Rose Bowl swap meet not long after we made the move to Pasadena; Enat had polished it to a shiny patina that Fleur's mother had groaned to see, claiming, "But, my dear, it's meant to look *rustic!*"

But after we all said a simple grace and cleaned our hands under Adey Gatimo's poured water, the *injera* and rich red *wat* and vegetable-crammed *alecha* made me feel entirely at home. Father Wendimu gestured toward the *injera*, indicating that, as host, he was forgoing his prerogative to serve himself first. I tugged off a square of the gray flatbread and scooped up some *wat* that I figured had probably been made freshly from a relative of one of the scores of chickens roaming free outside. I assumed that the larger portion of food was a milder *alecha* for the children.

As a blast of red chili burst open on my tongue, I wasted not another moment before tugging another piece from the pancake of the edible tablecloth. I was starving. It dawned on me that I'd only had a Coke to sustain me for most of the day. But then I noticed that Makeda and Father Wendimu hadn't yet touched food to lip, tending instead to the younger children, making sure they had their own portions, straightening limbs so they didn't fall off their stools or lean too close to their partners. Father Wendimu took a moment to tenderly wipe the rather unappetizing drippy nose of one of the smaller boys across the table with a handkerchief he'd whipped out with the ease of familiarity from his trouser pocket. I saw the serving woman step in again with her jug and an expression of forbearance, as if she'd had to do this mid-meal a million times before.

It was a lively gathering, the children jabbering so quickly in Amharic I had to struggle to keep up with them, especially after downing a bottle of Hakim Stout to soothe my burning mouth. Our native tongue was one I rarely spoke myself, having learned early on that my parents preferred to use it with each other when they wanted to keep something from me. You'd think I would have been nosier, but I was a boy eager to fit into his new world, and being burdened by the accent of my heritage was the last thing I needed. Or so I'd thought then.

As the supper wound down, with me surreptitiously loosening the top button of my slacks to accommodate the results of my gluttony, the old woman took the now quiescent children away, presumably for their baths and bed, the older ones leading or actually carrying the littler ones in the age-old way of large families.

Father Wendimu motioned for me to follow him, while Makeda stood to clear the table. I offered to help, but she held up a hand. "No, please. I've got to tuck them in. You go on ahead. I won't be long." It was hard to leave her. I would have been quite happy to watch her sing those babies to sleep.

Suddenly I was overcome with a memory so real that I lost sense of where I was, narrowly averting stepping on Father Wendimu's heels. I was seeing Makeda's mother Genet tucking Makeda and me into my friend's stone-hard bed, softened only by Makeda herself and a layering of flannel blankets, one mulberry, one copper, one gold. We were quite young. And very mischievous. As soon as Genet sang us into what she thought was sleep with her slightly off-key version of *Ehsururu*, Makeda whipped out a piece of *injera* she'd plucked earlier from the table and hidden in her pajama pocket. She tore off a ragged half of it for me, and we proceeded with an old game, rolling little teff pancakes into peas that we stuck into our ears and nostrils.

It just so happened that I had spied my parents performing intriguing acrobatics on their bed the previous week, so I suggested we see where else we could stick our rolled dough. I instructed her what to do. Obediently, she pushed away the covers and completely unselfconsciously spread her spindly brown legs. My observation of my parents had stimulated something strangely compelling in me, and I sensed that we were about to cross into a whole new territory. So, too, the ancient Adam must have felt when Eve dangled before him her vernal, nectarous fruit. Makeda put her fingers to the small cleft between her thighs and stretched it wide enough for me to lodge several small teff balls inside. Maybe it was the tightness of the fit, or perhaps she was reacting to my breathing, which had become quicker than usual, and my unusual silence, because she made a nervous little face, and I wasn't sure if she liked it.

We heard a sound coming from the corridor and, suddenly frantic, Makeda hissed, "Take them out." So I scraped away at the hallway just inside the tiny, purplish doors of hers, my gaze traveling back and forth between those odd little lips and an unreadable cast to her familiar face.

It occurred to me now that her face had borne, all those years ago, the same mysterious St. Maryum Sion expression she'd displayed today out in the yard. I shook my head to push away the provocative memory. Father Wendimu had stopped and was gesturing for me to join him at the entry to a second building. "Not proper etiquette for a man in this country," he explained, "to sleep so close to the women and girls." We walked past a goat and her kid, who actually put its forelegs up on my chest until the priest admonished sharply, "Menelik!" I shot him a look of surprise before he motioned me to follow him through a shallow doorway to a small room with a single bed made up with a white cotton sheet and a few colorful pillows, a dresser, and a straight-backed chair, to which he motioned me.

There was a small, yellowed basin in the corner. If the priest had taken me by surprise with his goat's name, I was gobsmacked when he offered me a pinch of *khat*. I shook my head. Only slightly sheepishly did he mumble, "Just use it for special occasions, you know. Truth be told, this batch is less strong than *bunna*. Buy it from the shopkeeper down the road. The man's got five kids and a sister with AIDS to feed. You probably bought that old used map from him." I looked down at my shirt pocket, where the mangled edge of my map was sticking up. "Remind me to give you a more current one before you hit the road."

I did accept his offer of a Nyala cigarette, something Fleur would never forgive me for if she'd known. Thinking of her, I felt a pang all the way from my heart to the groin that I couldn't begin to convince myself was heartburn. It was as if someone had given the hanging man a shove. He dangled precariously over a vast chasm.

"I suppose you think all this is odd from an ex-priest. You're probably wondering how I came to be a priest at all. Perhaps you'll be less surprised if I tell you that it was the only guarantee as a child that I'd eat, and my mother had put great thought into which of her children was worth offering to the church. Since I was the resident bleeding heart of our family, I drew the short or long straw, depending on your point of view. Being an ugly man with two undescended testicles, it turned out to be a good match. Celibacy was the least of my sacrifices. It wasn't why I left the priesthood, by the way." He squinted at me, then laughed as he stuffed another small leaf into his mouth. "I figure God will forgive me a little mood-lifter, given what Makeda and I have to witness each day." He shook his head. "These children have been through much, deserve more, but our resources are very limited. I can't tell you how infrequently we manage to get a doctor out here. And some of our AIDS orphans are HIV-positive themselves."

I winced. "That's terrible. But if you've got your *khat*, what's Makeda's comfort, then?"

He laughed, leaning back against a small yellow and green embroidered pillow on the bed. "Comfort? Ah, my young man, you may be well on your way to becoming a doctor, but you clearly don't know much about women. This work is Makeda's flowing breast, the smile of a child her full reward."

"Yes, but what about *her* sacrifice? She could have her own children to nourish and watch grow. And," I added wistfully, "a man to help her do it."

But at this moment Makeda glided into the room. She and I both caught the look the priest shot her. She looked away. Father Wendimu stood up.

"There's something I ..." he mumbled, fishing around the top of his dresser. "Where did I? The iPod that last set of adoptive parents gave me. I can't seem to find it."

Makeda gave him a long-suffering grin and shook a finger. "Father, if you can't remember to hide your iPod away, I can't help you. It's probably Dawit. Mark my words, that boy will be a seasoned thief long before his eighteenth birthday." She made a half-turn. "Let me go see."

"No, no," Father Wendimu rose suddenly to head her off. "The boy has so much trouble sleeping. Don't bother him. We can deal with it tomorrow."

Makeda's eyes flashed. "He has trouble sleeping because he also knows how to 'liberate' pinches of that *khat* of yours."

Father Wendimu shifted his posture guiltily, nearly falling against the iPod player on his dresser.

Makeda sighed. "Forget it. I shouldn't put you in the position of lying about your *khat* habit. Who would you confess to?" She swept her hand across a nonexistent wrinkle on the bed. "This place is a bottomless pit of need. Why should I begrudge you a little relief?" I had the distinct impression that, of the two of them, Father Wendimu wasn't exactly the one in charge. "So what did you want to play?" she asked him, wrists pressed winsomely against her hipbones.

Father Wendimu revealed a slight dimple in his cheek with his sideways grin. "*Tizita?*"

She threw back her head and had a nice, long laugh. "You are spreading it a bit thick, aren't you? If I didn't know better, I'd think you were trying to tempt poor Assefa into working with us."

"I don't know what you mean," Father Wendimu replied in a falsely affronted tone.

"Now you're being dishonest again. Didn't you say just yesterday that you'd give anything to have someone on staff with real medical knowledge? Then along comes our old neighbor Assefa, intern now at one of the best medical schools in the U.S., and you mean to tell me the thought hadn't crossed your mind?"

She turned on her heels and walked out.

Father Wendimu looked up at me in appeal and lifted his shoulders. "What did I do?"

But Makeda was back in no time with the device. A faint line of perspiration called even greater attention to her cushiony lips. I had to look away.

I was disconcerted to recognize the version of *Tizita* that she played. I had a couple of Teddy Afro CDs myself, purchased with Fleur on a shabby stretch of Pico Boulevard. We had discovered the hole-in-the-wall reggae record store when we took her mother's high-end vacuum to a Miele repair shop improbably located on a corner of a rundown African American neighborhood.

The melody was intoxicating, as was the very fact of listening to it on an iPod speaker here in my native land. Ironically, it felt like a message from an alternate universe. Fleur and I had made love to the song. She had gotten so carried away by it that she'd made me lie still on my back so that she could trail her silky hair up and down my chest, belly, and thighs before circling her lips around my member. She made me play it all over again while I licked her little man until she climaxed, releasing a long wail like an orphaned dik-dik.

It was no accident that *tizita* was regularly compared to the American blues. I'd explained to Fleur as we'd lain in bed after our lovemaking that *Tizita* wasn't just the title of a song, but referred, as well, to any Ethiopian or Eritrean song with a particularly distinctive musical style or *qenet*. When I added that the word *tizita* roughly translated into English as a cross between memory and longing, she'd murmured languorously, "I think it sounds like a cross between sorrow and ecstasy."

My reverie was interrupted by Father Wendimu's dismissive grunt, "He's out of jail now, isn't he, Teddy Afro?"

I saw Makeda's eyes flash. "Yes. I know you disagree, but he never should have been sent there in the first place. The whole thing was a sham. His real crime was taking a stand for peace and unity."

The hanging man could relate to *that*. He could use a little unity himself.

Father Wendimu scratched his armpit and yawned. "Well, I don't know if he's a good man or a bad man. But I can tell you that nobody sings *Tizita* like Seyfou Yohannes." He beckoned me with his fingers, reminding me of nothing but England's queen waving to the crowd from her car, and I followed him into a decent-sized closet, which seemed to contain fewer articles of clothing than stacks of L.P.'s. A rather battered old record player assumed pride of place atop what looked to be a tall plant stand. Father Wendimu had to stand on tiptoe to drop the needle onto the record that was already in place. I felt Makeda crowd in behind me.

The three of us swayed together in that cramped closet, listening to a scratchy recording of Ethiopian blues by one of its masters. Seyfou's version had a decidedly Arabic, undulating rhythm—like something sung on a camel, or to an unwinding snake. I could smell Makeda, her perfume a lush mélange of sweat, frankincense from the charcoal stove, dish soap, and something else—something like desire. Or dread. Father Wendimu seemed to sense the shift in energy. He pulled up the needle as soon as the last notes sounded. Nodding somberly, he gestured for us to return to the larger room.

"I'll leave you two children to talk. I know you have much to reminisce about." He flicked a glance over to Makeda. "But don't forget, our Assefa here didn't come here for a vacation. Your intuitive belly or not, he's going to want to locate that father of his." He paused. "Besides, it's clinic tomorrow morning." I couldn't escape the suspicion that his words were code for, "Don't go too far, Makeda." He was like a father to her. I could tell. But what had happened to her *own* father? And mother, for that matter?

I hoped she hadn't become an orphan herself.

Chapter Six
Fleur

"OW!"

"What is it, Fleuricita?" Ignacio shot me a solicitous glance from the striking array of Abraham Darbies he was tending.

"Thorn." I licked my thumb, then eyeballed it in dismay. "I think I managed to push it in pretty far."

Tossing down his shears so he could remove his mud-caked glove, he crossed the lawn toward the Claire Austin I'd been pruning, murmuring, "*Pobrecita.* Let me see."

I let him have his way with my hand. While he turned it this way and that, I gave Claire Austin's last few delicate white blooms a forgiving smile. Only under the gathering cloud of climate change would we be enduring such an unbelievable heat wave the day before Christmas. The previous summer had stayed June gloomish through October, and now the city was threatening rolling blackouts thanks to a million air conditioners whistling away at full speed.

Ignacio sighed in exasperation. "You should have worn the gloves."

Embarrassed, I looked down at Mother's perfectly manicured rye lawn, where I'd discarded the floral gardening gloves he'd brought out for me. They'd landed with fingertips pointing toward each other, as if in prayer. "I know, I know. Assefa tells me all the time how stubborn I am. But I like to actually feel what I'm touching. With the gloves on, I feel like I have too little control."

I, of all people, should have known that there are things over which we have no control. Rose thorns were probably somewhere near the top of the list. Affairs of the heart had to be pretty high up there, too. I'd tried telling myself that Assefa could no more forget the girl he'd grown up with in his first incarnation than I could my grandfather or Nana. Like the rhythm of our mother's heartbeat, our earliest connections are root systems that nourish and define us.

"Stay here," Ignacio ordered. "I've got some tweezers in the truck." Before I could stop him, he bounded down the driveway. I hated to think I was interrupting his work. He was probably dying to get home to the Christmas curry Dhani was preparing and a nice, cold bottle of Negra Modelo. Really, I didn't know what was wrong with Mother. Why was he working at all today?

I wandered toward the pool, looking for bees. Sure enough, one was flailing near the spillover from the Jacuzzi. I ran to fetch the turquoise pool net to scoop it out, gratified that it was still moving its antennae and not wearing that water-logged, give-up-the-ghost look. Poor bees. So many of them dove in, thinking they could get a little sip until a surge of water from the Jacuzzi got the best of them. I'd been on a mission to save everyone I could once I'd learned the devastation that neoconid insecticides were wreaking on their worldwide numbers. And I'd been thrilled the previous spring to see a swarm of them moving over the pool like a solid, buzzing organism to establish a new colony because the original one had gotten too crowded. I took it as a good sign.

I waited till this one flew away, inspected the pool one more time, and saved a yellow jacket, who thanked me by aiming straight for my nose. "Get away from me," I shouted, ducking and darting just as Ignacio reappeared.

"What now, Fleuricita?"

"Oh, don't bother about me," I laughed, relieved that the wasp had lost interest. "I'm just your local backyard basket case. First thorns, now wasps."

He shot me a look. "Sting you?"

"Not this time. Probably thought I'd be bland meat."

Chuckling, he motioned me to hold out my hand.

He took such care, sweet man. As big as a bear—especially with the gut he'd put on since marrying Dhani—with hands the size of baseball gloves and just as leathery. But his touch was as deft as a surgeon's as he coaxed away several layers of pale skin to extract the narrow brown sliver. Once he'd gotten it out, I marveled that something so small could cause so much pain.

Ignacio fished a little packet of rubbing alcohol from his pocket. I asked him about it.

"Best thing I've found for cleaning my tools. It does a great job on mold."

"You're an angel," I declared. And I meant it. Guardian spirits had graced my life ever since I'd been born: Grandfather, Nana, Cook, Fayga, Sister Flatulencia, Ignacio, Dhani, Adam, Stanley and Gwennie Fiske. How ironic that I'd been moved at the age of twelve to the angels' very own city.

If a nut-brown man could blush, he would have. "What're you up to the rest of the day, *muchacha?*"

"Actually, I'm going to temple with Sammie and Jacob."

"In that?"

I laughed. I was wearing Mother's baggy, faded garden trousers and an old paint-spattered tank top.

"No," I said, giving his chest a playful shove. "I've got my nice clothes waiting for me upstairs. Wouldn't dream of shaming Sammie in front of her new rabbi. Even if Sam's really a Hindu-Jewdist-Sikh in sheep's clothing."

Ignacio, a lapsed Catholic from San Luis Potosi who'd married a woman born in Delhi, snorted and fell back a step or two, pretending I'd actually managed to shove him off balance. His dark eyes danced. Beer belly or not, he was still a handsome man in a careworn, Benicio del Toro sort of way. I was so grateful that, over the years, Angelina had increasingly grown to resemble him. While I wouldn't have minded being related to her, I couldn't bear having had that kinship purchased by a liaison between Dhani and my father.

When I was younger, I could never understand why Dhani had carried on with Father and Ignacio at the same time. I knew now how love could get the best of you and was just beginning to comprehend how lust could, too. It was just about impossible to think of my father as sexy, but he'd knocked up more than a few women in his day. I guessed the holier-than-thou veneer was attractive to some.

Ignacio was still grinning cheekily at me. "Wise guy," I said. "As for dress codes, I don't know how you manage to stay so neat when you've been working twice as hard as I have." It was true, his garden greens—shirt tucked tidily into his pants—were pressed to perfection, presumably by Dhani, and the only signs of our faux summer were two half-moons of perspiration under his arms.

I was sweating like a pig myself by the time Sammie and Jacob arrived an hour later. Sammie raced up Mother's walkway to throw me such an enthusiastic hug, you wouldn't have suspected we'd seen each other the day before. She kissed each cheek, clinging onto me so fiercely I wondered if she and Jacob had been having another row. As we disentangled, she gave me an appreciative once over and whistled. "Love the dress. BCBG? Why couldn't I have gotten breasts like those?"

I snickered. "Because they're a matched set with a big butt. Don't be so ungrateful. You've got the perfect gym ass without ever having set foot in a gym." Leading the way down Mother's Saltillo tiled steps, I said, "I can't believe we're going to synagogue on Christmas Eve."

"Why not?" she retorted. "Mary was the archetypal Jewish mother, and Jesus her nice, Jewish boy." Then she squeaked, "Wait," pointing to my shoulder. I looked over it, but she said, "No, no," turning me toward her and pressing a finger against my right shoulder blade. I could smell coffee on her breath.

I was getting the heebie-jeebs. "What are you doing?"

A horn honked.

"That'll be Jacob," she muttered, then, "Gotcha." She joined my side and held out her index finger. "Look who was taking a ride on your T-shirt."

It was a ladybug. Or as she put it, "ladybird."

I grinned. "Back garden?" She nodded. We ran back onto the porch and followed it around toward the back stairs, rolling our eyes at each other when Jacob impatiently honked a second time.

I led her toward the lavender bushes. Mother had planted three species of them—French, English, and Goodwin Creek Gray—to alternate with low trailing rosemary bushes behind the navy blue lounge chairs surrounding the pool. It was always a treat to brush a sun-baked hand against any one of them and release a hint of olfactory bliss. Sammie carefully tipped her finger toward a furry French lavender flower, and the ladybug toddled obediently off her finger. It choo-chooed assiduously over the top of the flower and down the other side.

We simultaneously sighed, and I imagined a congratulatory hoot from the fake owl standing guard on the garage roof, but our reverie was interrupted instead by a very long blast from Jacob's horn.

I gave a little jump, and Sammie swore. "For fuck's sake!" But by the time we reached Jacob's gray Prius, she was all contrition. She flung open the passenger door and poked her head inside, oozing the rest of her body towards Jacob in a serpentine slither that allowed her to plant a kiss on his frowning forehead. I heard her say, "I'm sorry, sweetie. Fleur had a ladybird on her back, and we could hardly take it out of its environment all the way to temple. It would've felt completely lost."

Which was exactly how I felt when we entered Temple Isaiah on Pico Boulevard. I'd never before entered a Jewish house of worship, but I *had* prepared for today by pestering Jacob about this particular one. He'd told me that its senior rabbi was a woman and that she was also a novelist and poet. He said that the membership were advocates of *tikkun olam*, a Hebrew idea that roughly translated as "repair of the world," rooted in the Kabbalistic teachings of Isaac Luria.

I'd already heard of Luria, thanks to the catholic-with-a-small-c tutoring I'd received from Adam, who'd been determined to balance the punitive theological views of my Catholic-with-a-capital-C father with the myriad ways we humans have imagined the divine, from Zeus (Friend of Strangers and Thunder God) to the dreaming mantis god of the Bushmen of the Kalahari to piquant Ungud (aboriginal God of both rainbows and erections). I remember feeling a little stunned to learn that the Jesus whom my father all but claimed as his personal friend was not the only God in the deck. But when Adam pulled out the Luria card—with its science-smelling God contracting His light to make room for the creation of the world, storing excess God-light in containers, some of which broke and became shards of dark matter that threatened us all—I felt myself edging toward a particularly steep precipice. Seeing I was on the verge of a serious bang and pinch fest, Adam had hastened to explain Luria's notion that the repair of our wounded world could be achieved by each of us doing good works.

Always one to expand my knowledge, I set out to do some research on *tikkun olam*. I discovered that Luria thought that God Himself had been fractured into shards in making our world and that it was our job to heal Him. When I'd shared my mental meanderings on the topic with Stanley, he'd given a casual shrug, commenting, "Sounds like Jung and the gnostics," as if he were tossing out the name of a rock band. Stanley's lack of perturbation over the image of a broken God was one more clue that other people's black pits weren't nearly as bottomless as mine.

Maybe that was why the concept of multiple gods and goddesses grew on me. If two heads are better than one, then what might a thousand godheads accomplish? Then again, what if all those deities were broken, too? What would it take to repair them? And what did it portend for *us*? I pictured all the diverse worshippings going on in our world as a kind of mockingbird symphony, urging the broken gods not to forsake the wounded creatures of this world. Mockingbirds had always been my favorites, their glorious, layered mimicry guaranteed to vanquish the most dismal of voids.

I could use one of them right now. I felt like the founding member of the Odd Duck Society sitting in the Temple Isaiah sanctuary next to Rabbi Goldenrod, who'd led us there because some repair work was being done in her office. My little joke to her about God not being the only one needing repairing had gone over like a lead balloon, and being invited to sit here with her, Sammie, and Jacob in a row facing a massive, modernistic altar didn't exactly feel conducive to easy conversation.

But trust Sammie to sense what was required. My endless descriptions of Nana's Mack truck grip hadn't been for nothing. Sam had motioned Jacob to sidestep his way into the curved upholstered bench first, then the rabbi, then me. She'd plunked herself down close enough to my other side that we might as well have been conjoined twins.

Sammie revved up the motor with, "So, Rabbi Goldenrod, what can you tell us about the Ark of the Covenant? I know Jacob's already filled you in about how Fleur's fiancé's father has gone missing somewhere in Ethiopia. Since he's there researching the folklore surrounding the Ark, we thought you might have some sort of clue as to where he might be."

Rabbi Goldenrod ran an impatient hand through her abundant, tight blond ringlets. She'd seemed distracted from the moment we were introduced, and I felt guilty for taking up her time. But she shot me such a sympathetic look right then that I felt my muscles relax. I understood why Sammie had formed such an affection for Jacob's mentor.

"You're very kind to meet with us, Rabbi Goldenrod," I chimed in.

"Please," said the rabbi, shaking her head. "Call me Miriam. I'm more than happy to meet with you, but, as I told Jacob, I'm not sure I can help. I've certainly read that the Ethiopians claim to be housing the Ark in their church in Aksum, but—"

"Aksum, yes!" I blurted out. "That's where Achamyalesh and his friend Zalelew were supposed to be going. It's fascinating, really—they say the Ark's guarded by a single priest who's given the job from age seven until death. Sort of like the Dalai Lama." Sammie shot me a look. "Well," I conceded, "not exactly. But you know what I mean."

Rabbi Goldenrod responded with a polite, "Mmm." Choosing her words with care, she continued, "I don't mean to disappoint you, but to be honest the whole idea of the Ark being housed at Aksum sounds far-fetched to me. The only possible biblical connection is that some interpretations of the *Song of Solomon* equate the Queen of Sheba with an Ethiopian queen." Her expression bespoke her lack of enthusiasm for the notion. "I don't know if you realize how many people say they have the Ark. These claims come from all over the world—England, Ireland, France. Some Mormons actually think it's buried in Utah." Did I detect a flicker of a sly grin? "The latest claimant is an archaeologist who's said he's found a section of bedrock on the Temple Mount in the exact dimensions of the Ark as described in Exodus, but he can't verify it because neither the Israeli nor Muslim authorities will allow the site to be excavated. Personally, I'm satisfied that the Ark is no longer on this earth, which is what's suggested in both the *Second Book of the Maccabees* and the *Book of Revelation.* The truth is, it's a mystery. It's more valuable as a symbol than a concrete physical object. Which is as it should be, don't you think?"

The truth was, I didn't know what to think. Organized religions were as liable as governments to be rather literal about what they valued. Why else the endless war over that portion of the world dubbed the Holy Land? But it would have been rude to pose the question now, particularly since the rabbi was obviously taking time she didn't have to speak with me.

My discomfort only increased when she added, "I have a confession to make. I'm a big fan of yours. I've been a very amateur student of physics most of my adult life, so I couldn't resist a chance to meet you." She gave a little self-deprecating laugh. "Actually, I'm pretty lousy at understanding most of it, but I can't seem to leave it alone. Quantum physics really does seem to speak the language of the ineffable."

I slipped that one into a corner of my mind to consider later. I was an expert on what a terrific void killer physics could be, but I'd never considered that others might find in it a bridge to the gods. Right then, I knew only that I felt unaccountably grateful to Rabbi Goldenrod—though there was no way I was going to call her Miriam.

The rabbi paused a moment to stare up at the abstract planes on the polished wood ceiling. This modernistic sanctuary was hardly what I'd expect for worshippers of a 4,000-year-old god. It was certainly a far cry from my old stomping grounds at Saint Monica's, where I attended services with Mother and Father until Eric Tanner, nearly a year older than my four years and thirty-three days, unhinged me with a particularly graphic imitation of Christ's agony on the cross. Much to Father's tight-lipped displeasure, my whirling and screaming got me banned forever from Sunday school class and from St. Monica's itself. From that day forward, it was Sister Flatulencia who took responsibility for my catechism, delivering her own version of God's truths along with little dolings-out of extraordinarily pungent gas, which were accompanied by no end of penitential "Forgive mes," as if I were her pint-sized confessor. But I still remembered the church where I'd been baptized and its confusing references to a God fragmented into three pieces: Father, Son, and Holy Ghost. (Though it occurred to me now that the trinity might be a second or third cousin to Luria's broken God, with the Christian God redeeming us, rather than the other way around.)

Anyway, I could tell you with dead certainty exactly where Saint Monica's nativity crèche would be displayed today, nestled on a layering of straw atop a quilted, if slightly wrinkled, gold tablecloth beneath a stained glass window depicting Christ standing beneath a distinctly feminine-faced, fiery-plumed sun.

I glanced over at Miriam Goldenrod, her spiral curls a bright cloud around her face. She nodded, seeming to make up her mind about something. She gave me a little wink. "But, listen. As a rabbi, what I do know is stories, and we never know where a story can lead us. Shall I tell you a few of my favorite ones about the Ark?"

All three of us eagerly assented. I noticed that Jacob had been unusually quiet the whole time. Was he intimidated by his livewire of a mentor?

The rabbi broke into my reverie. "Fleur, have you ever read the Bible?"

I made a face. My earliest memories involved sitting on my pastel yellow potty seat in the prettiest bathroom of our family's wing of Father's house, reading *Vogue* and *Elle* magazines, but mostly Sister Flatulencia's Holy Bible.

Drawing entirely the wrong conclusion, Rabbi Miriam put a hand on my knee and soothed, "Don't worry. We Jews aren't big on conversion. I just wanted to know if we shared a frame of reference. Basically, the Ark is said to contain what we call in Hebrew *Luchot HaBrit*, the Tablets of the Covenant that were inscribed on two pieces of stone when Moses ascended Mount Sinai. We learn this from the Book of Exodus, which refers to the Tablets of Testimony that give insight into the nature of God. It's said that the Tablets were made of blue sapphire, a reminder of God's throne in the heavenly sky. The first set were said to have been inscribed by God Himself—or Herself, as I sometimes like to say." She waited for an objection, but in our little group, none was forthcoming. "But they were smashed by Moses in a rage over his people worshipping the Golden Calf. Moses inscribed the second at God's instruction as atonement. Both the shattered and the unbroken set are said to be contained in the Ark." *More shattering? Was everything sacred doomed to be broken?* "But never mind. It's better to begin at the beginning, anyway. As a storyteller, I should know that."

She tugged her sweater over her thin shoulders, pulled a stray corn-colored curl out of her eye, and began, "The stories about the

Ark are abundant. And they always involve a kind of charged energy. Our neighbors up the street at the Jung Institute"—she shot a little smile at Sammie—"like to call such energy 'numinous.' I call it 'holy.'"

"There is a saying that Palestine is the center of the world, with Jerusalem the center of Palestine, the Temple the center of Jerusalem, the Tabernacle—or Holy of Holies—the center of the Temple, and the Ark the center of the Holy of Holies. In front of the Ark itself was a stone called the foundation stone of the world."

Her mention of Holies brought an entirely different image to mind: Dhani throwing Easter egg dye at me as I whirled and twirled in our own impromptu enactment of the Hindu holiday Holi, which was rudely interrupted by Father coming out of the house to chew on Dhani's lips and trace his rubbery hand over her bulging belly, terrifying me by teasing her that he wanted to eat her baby.

Except he'd called it "our baby."

I reminded myself that he'd been wrong about that one, as he'd been wrong about so much else. I felt a little guilty recalling what a creep Father had been, especially since we were here to learn more about the container of the tablet that enjoined the whole world to honor its mothers and fathers. But there was no way around it. Outside of the few months following Father's loss of his mind and before he'd regained it—seeming for a time to like nothing better than to play horsies with me in his living room and make silly jokes about Sister Flatulencia's farts—he hadn't behaved particularly honorably. It wasn't just the shady transactions between him and baby clothes' wholesaler Leland Du Ray when he was senator (causing him, ultimately, to be ousted from office), nor the hypocrisy of him hating having children underfoot when he was always parading before the press all the unwanted babies he'd saved, nor his pincer grips and disownings when he didn't like what I was doing. No, what sealed the dishonorable deal was Father's using my declining grandfather's name in such a humiliating way in his "pro-life" speeches. Not to mention his attacks on C-Voids and P.D. as the products of what he liked to call his daughter's "twisted, autistic mind."

Sammie gave me a barely perceptible jab with her elbow, and I pulled my mind away from what I'd already known could be a particularly circular set of ruminations. Hatred is like that—a hostage-taker of perfectly good mental energy.

I could see that Rabbi Goldenrod was warming to her story. Her almost Asian-cast, dark brown eyes were luminous, and two daubs of pink had sprung up on her pale cheeks. She gestured toward the head of the room, with its broad blue and green pillars like giant candles on either side of the altar. "Actually, it's a little synchronistic that we ended up in this Sanctuary, since the Ark was used as a kind of moveable sanctuary that miraculously provided safety to our people, particularly during the Exodus, when it was carried into the bed of the River Jordan and opened the path to freedom."

I was used to religious lectures. In Father's house, they were a daily event. But Rabbi Goldenrod's obvious enthusiasm for her topic was coupled with an endearing humility. She gave me a little smile, as if she knew exactly what I was thinking, and put a hand to her heart. "Forgive me. I do get carried away. But when I think about what it takes to win freedom—in any time, for any people—when the powers-that-be are dead set on holding what they've got, the image of the Ark as a container of hope and action for the human spirit just takes my breath away."

I found myself holding my own breath, too, realizing I was sitting next to a truly religious person. Everyone I'd ever met who'd announced themselves as believers had seemed a little off-kilter, all too happy to dismiss those who thought differently as either clueless or evil. I didn't count Sister Flatulencia, who'd become disaffected from the Roman Catholic Church after her nervous breakdown, or Aadita, who'd reminded me more than once that Buddhism wasn't a religion in the common sense of the word.

Rabbi Goldenrod was a believer. Yet somehow, when she expressed the tenets of her faith, I didn't feel like some worm, liable to spoil the perfect roundness of her apple.

Confirming my suspicion that she was psychic, she remarked, "I like to let my mind flow over the images like a meditation. Wherever your thoughts take you is where God wants you to go." Maybe Rabbi Goldenrod was secretly a Jewdist, like Sammie. "Most people think of the Ark as a container for Mosaic Law—the basis of all law, you know, in the western world. But the Ark was also said to contain Aaron's rod."

Sammie and I exchanged a glance, and I had to work to stifle an incipient snort. We'd discovered Lawrence's *Lady Chatterley's Lover* when she was twelve and I thirteen and, while Lawrence's quaint reference to Mellors' and Connie's genitals as John Thomas and Lady Jane made us giggle at the time, I think we shared a similar hunger for an eroticism sweeter and more personal than our era's Internet porn and sexting. I'd ended up using my own inner images of the wedding of John Thomas and Lady Jane to set off innumerable mini-explosions in my tweeter, so I wasn't too surprised when Sammie excitedly brought over a copy of *Aaron's Rod* a few weeks later on the assumption that the title referred to a plethora of phallic scenes. Disappointed, we were forced to make up our own, ones that were informed by images from Internet porn, but the thrill was never the same as when Connie fashioned a garland of flowers for Mellors' bulging member.

This time, I was the one to jab Sammie with an elbow before turning back to listen to the rabbi.

"Aaron's rod is an example of the power of the Large Force, which is how I personally think of God. In the story of the exodus of my people from the oppression they endured in Egypt, God instructed Aaron and Moses to use their magical rods to persuade the pharaoh to free them. The pharaoh was so set on holding onto his own power that he didn't even budge after Aaron's rod made snakes of his guards, then became an even larger snake that swallowed all those smaller ones. So, what does God do? He visits ten plagues upon Egypt. Not so nice, but there it is. Ten of them, each worse than the one before." She started ticking them off on her fingers: "Blood, frogs, flies, livestock death, boils, hail, locusts, darkness …. Wait, that should be nine. What have I forgotten?"

We sat for a moment. I sensed some shifting movement down the row and saw Jacob open his mouth and then close it.

The colored pillars at the head of the sanctuary reminded me of the blue and green striped shirt I'd bought for Assefa before he'd left for Addis Ababa. He'd objected to me spending unnecessary money on him when he could hardly return the favor on his meager intern fellowship, but I didn't care. I would have been happy to dress him in a brand new wardrobe every day.

My reverie was broken by a sudden exclamation by Rabbi Goldenrod. "Lice! Of course I'd forget lice. Between you and me, we had a lousy bout of it this past season in the nursery school. It's been making the rounds on the Westside for over a year, and we thought we'd escaped it, but it got us in the end. All of us, including the adults. Frankly, it is a bit of a plague. Have you ever had to comb a head of frizzy hair like mine with a nit comb?"

Within seconds, I was back in Father's house in Main Line. After shampooing my hair in the worst-smelling soap known to mankind, Nana had sat me down between her voluminous thighs at the edge of my bed, where she jerked a comb again and again through my tangled hair, whistling the opening tune to *I Dream of Jeannie* and snatching my hand away from my belly every time it tried to sidle down for a pinch or two. I'd tried concentrating on my Laura Ashley wallpaper, with its floral pompoms in soothing tones of duck egg and cream. I kept attempting to count the number of flowers on the wall, but each time Nana gave a particularly hard yank, I'd lose track and have to start all over again. Being a sort of aficionado of pain, it wasn't the pulling that made me want to pinch, but the noxious smell the shampoo left in my nostrils. It was worse than Jillily's sickly-sweet diarrhea poops, worse than Sister Flatulencia's silent but deadlies, worse than anything I could remember to this day, save perhaps the poison gun Ignacio had aimed, just before we became friends, at my favorite weed.

I sneaked a quick glance at the rabbi's hair, its light honey color anomalous for someone with such dark eyes. Though a good deal finer than Assefa's coarse coils, her curls were pretty tight. I couldn't imagine what it would feel like to try to comb through hair like that, when even my own straight locks had been no picnic for Nana. Though I'm sure it hadn't helped that I had such an oddly shaped head.

"No," I said to Rabbi Goldenrod, "I never did."

She made what Jacob liked to refer to as an *oy oy oy* face. "I hope you never do. But what are lice compared to the tenth plague? Killing all the Egyptians' first born—every one of them—from livestock to the pharaoh's own child?" She gave a little shudder.

Which must have been my cue to display my own abominable lack of tact. "Don't you think that was a little severe? Making so many innocent babies suffer? No wonder we have terrorists, if God's like that." As soon as the words came out, I blushed. I suppose it could have been worse. I could have cited other religiously motivated atrocities, such as the destruction of the Twin Towers or even the Israelis' bombing of Gaza. *That* would have gone over with a bang. But I was actually thinking of the Ethiopians—in particular, of Medr, whose wife was brutally murdered in one of the myriad miseries his country had been subjected to. No wonder his countrymen and women wanted to keep their hands on the Ark. Maybe they figured that God owed them.

But the rabbi had leapt ahead. "I know how you feel, Fleur. Actually I've always thought of Aaron's rod as epitomizing the two sides of life, which is really what God is about, isn't it? Life. Sprouting sweet almonds on one side and bitter ones on the other."

That didn't settle me down much, but I was grateful for her lack of defensiveness. "The other thing about the Ark," she continued,— "and this is why I admire your fiancé's father for attempting to chronicle one of its many stories—is that it's been shrouded, quite literally, in mystery. It was always supposed to be wrapped in a veil and blue cloth—remember how the tablets themselves were made of blue stone?—and any approach to it would have to be accompanied by protective rituals."

If that were true, what to make of the stories Achamyalesh had told of the Ethiopian Orthodox Church parading the Ark through the streets of Aksum from time to time? How would they be able to do it without being stricken dead, or at least have some godawful plague visited upon them?

Then again, maybe they had.

I wasn't much surprised when Sammie and Jacob had one of their humdingers right after we said our thank yous to Rabbi Goldenrod. The rabbi had apologized for not having much to add to what we already knew, but that hadn't kept Sammie from commenting as soon as we crossed the street to our parking spot in front of the Jung Institute, "Well, you know I like her a lot, but that really was a waste of time."

Buckling my seat belt, I saw Jacob look at her as if she'd decreed the death of his people's first born.

"What?" she demanded, defensive.

He didn't bother to reply. The black turn of his mood was palpable. He turned on the engine, and our car pulled away from the curb with a screech. An Audi coming up along our left side swerved to avoid a collision and blasted us with its horn. Sammie gasped, and shouted, "What the fuck do you think you're doing, Jacob?"

Jacob bested her one, pounding the steering wheel as his eyes shot bullets. "Who the fuck do you think you are, Sammie? Miriam Goldenrod took time for us. She's one of the busiest women in the city. She's an authentically great human being—rabbi of a major congregation, writer, organizer of three different social outreach programs, member of a national task force on earth-justice, working on a documentary about the commonalities between Jews and Muslims."

"You don't have to quote me her fucking *vita*. I respect the woman already. I bloody well like her. All I'm saying is that she didn't tell us anything we didn't already know."

If they kept this up, I was going to have to keep a new journal listing all the times they uttered the word "fuck" during their arguments. Jacob pulled over to the curb as soon as he came to Overland. Cars started piling up behind us on the narrow street.

His shouting was actually louder than their honking. "What she told us is that this trip of Achamyalesh's is bogus. There's no Ark in Ethiopia. There's just a bunch of fucked-over, impoverished people trying to salve their self-respect by pretending they own the greatest treasure of the world. Sort of like a cab driver creating no end of havoc by tootling off to no-man's-land and getting himself lost on a fool's errand."

I must say, Sammie wasn't the only one who was offended by Jacob's diatribe. Adam had taught me that people said things when they were angry that they didn't really mean. Which had helped a little with Father when he started his Cackler group to undermine my discovery of C-Voids. Until I realized that Father really did mean all the nasty things he'd said about me.

If I felt angry on behalf of Achamyalesh, I felt awful for Sammie. All I could see was the back of her head, her dark hair caught up in two silver butterfly clips peeking over the tops of her ears. Her hair was so shiny. She sat, silent and immobile, and I could only imagine what was going on in her head.

The clamor of the cars behind us increased and even a homeless man on the sidewalk shouted for us to get moving—what he actually said was, "How'm I s'posed to get my cart across this street with you fucking up traffic, assholes?" I guess it finally got through to Jacob. He started up the car again.

But before he could pick up speed, Sammie undid her seatbelt, opened her door, and jumped out, thank God without a stumble. I'd broken out in a sweat. "Thank you, Jesus," I muttered under my breath.

I caught a quick glimpse of her standing on the sidewalk, her face ashen, her eyes unseeing, before we moved beyond her—the car door still open—and up toward Olympic Boulevard.

"Let me out," I demanded. Jacob didn't bother to respond. The backs of his ears were as red as a Darcey Bussell rose. What to do? The car was moving just a bit faster now, and I didn't fancy making a leap myself.

Jacob kept going. Had he even heard me? But then he signaled, made a right turn onto Olympic in front of a barreling line of traffic, and stopped the car. Again, we were treated to a cacophony of horns. The guy was becoming a one-man traffic jam. I slid out without a word.

Rushing back on Pelham Avenue in the direction of the spot where we'd left Sammie, I pulled out my cell, but she wasn't answering. Trying to run in this heat was hell, and me wearing my two-inch black pumps made me feel and—I was sure—look ridiculous.

I stopped to pull off the shoes and stuff them into my purse. Just ahead was a group of people in front of a well-groomed Spanish-style house. They'd spread out a Pendleton style blanket on the lawn, and a woman was bouncing a pink-pajamaed baby on her shoulder with such enthusiasm that she didn't seem to notice that her efforts were only exacerbating the infant's unhappy squealing. One of the young men in the group said to the others, "Don't ever offer to babysit your own child," and they all burst into laughter.

"I don't get it," I muttered to myself as I ran, my bare feet registering every dry leaf, every crack in the sidewalk. Each pebble and twig felt like broken glass.

When I finally reached Sammie I was completely out of breath. She fell into my arms and wept. Really, there wasn't much to be said. Only she could determine whether Jacob's intelligence and wit were sufficient compensation for these rages that seemed to be part of his package deal.

We called a cab, and when we arrived at Rose Villa I insisted on paying the exorbitant fare, knowing that the particular cabbie Jacob had defamed would never have charged fifty-five dollars to deliver a palpably distraught woman and her friend home.

Chapter Seven
Fleur

I LEFT SAMMIE crying on her bed. I hated going, but I knew she'd reached the point where it was no longer useful to be comforted. She needed to fall into her misery, roll around with it in her bed, mine each vein of self-blame for having put up with Jacob's rage, probably throwing in for good measure some extra grief over the loss of her father and a little disgust for her willingness to trade her precious fine art for art history to make things work with this kind of a man.

It had taken me two decades to recognize that falling into hell was actually necessary from time to time. Its scorched-earth policy seemed to clear the way for new incarnations of ourselves. I had to leave my friend to her abyss.

Besides, Mother would kill me if I weren't home in time for our Christmas Eve dinner. Even after her impromptu birthday bash for me, it was still our ritual. This would be our first Christmas Eve without Nana and Fayga. I couldn't afford to dwell on the fact too long lest I disappear into the void once and for all, but homage had to be paid to the woman whose fierce attentions had kept me going in the early years when Father seemed like he wanted to squash me like a bug.

When Mother, Sister Flatulencia, Cesar, and I sat down at Mother's perfectly laid table, Nana's absence was a haunting presence. But we tried. Inspired by Gwennie, Mother had prepared a nut roast all by herself, and I have to say it was pretty good, despite the fact that Cesar claimed she was ruining Christmas by feeding us birdseed. He ran to his room, slamming the door as dramatically as a thirteen-year-old girl. Mother wrung her hands, muttering, "Oh, dear, and I thought the Ritalin was working."

Muttering, "It's not the Ritalin, the child's suffering from loss," Sister Flatulencia hurried from the room to calm him. Ever since the accident, it seemed as though she was coping with her own grief by trying to fill Nana's clomping, triple-C-width shoes. Mother and I both breathed audible sighs of relief when she was able to persuade the boy to return with the promise of an extra slice of Vanille Bakery's sinful *Bouche de Noel*.

Despite it all, it was sweet spending time with Mother at Christmas. I imagined that what I saw in her sparkly-eyed enthusiasm over her ten-foot tree (done up this year like a fairy princess, with white ornaments, silver bubble lights, and perfect white and silver satin bows) was the innocent little girl she'd once been, much loved by my grandfather and the grandmother who'd died before I was born. I'd seen glimpses of that girl from time to time, like when she tended her Austins or spoke of a particularly moving children's book—her favorite (and mine) still being Madeleine L'Engle's *A Wrinkle in Time*.

But mostly what she let show of herself was the post-apocalyptic woman, the one who'd endured the constant shaming of a sadistic husband following her unwanted conception of yours truly at the age of sixteen. Not to mention what she now called her "lost years," which pretty much coincided with my own childhood, where she languished in a bewildering (for me, anyway) intermittency of alcoholic stupor. She'd come out of her prison eventually, left Father, become an active member of AA, supported her odd duck of a daughter after the Nobel debacle, tolerated the intolerable loss of Nana, taken on the challenge of raising Cesar, gotten well-deserved promotions at the library, and become the unofficial Washington lobbyist for the recovery community. But rarely did the wide-open wonder of the child she'd once been find its way to peek through.

Which was why I felt guilty packing up my things for home at the crack of dawn the next morning. (How ironic that Stanley Fiske, the world's premier genius of the quantum world, could barely wait to open his presents from Gwen and me in one wild tornado of torn wrapping paper. Talk about the inner child peeking through. In his case, the bug-eyed boy—crazy for presents and magic tricks—and the prizewinning physicist were one.)

I'd been going through guilty mornings like this one ever since Mother had moved out to SoCal to be near me after my Nobel debacle. I was like the child of divorce twice over, divvying up Christmastime between Mother—who got me on Christmas Eve— and the Fiskes, who on the actual day hosted Sammie and Aadita and the physics gang in all its geeky glory.

Mother stood in the doorway, watching me pack. Spotting the telltale moisture well up in her eyes, I approached her. She was wearing the cozy, recycled poly robe I'd given her last night. I put a hand on her cheek, marveling at how her skin had softened even more with age. "Are you sure you're okay with me going?"

She nuzzled my tangly head. "Don't be a goose." Her nose still buried in my hair, she gave a dramatic sniff. "Mmm. You smell good. Jo Malone Orange Blossom?"

I grinned. It was a little joke between us. She bought me a bottle of it, with a matching-scented candle, every birthday. "You know it is. But really ...."

Mother stepped back and regarded me appraisingly. Never comfortable with being stared at, I focused on tugging my nightie out of my butt crack.

"Sweetheart, I'm grateful for what I get. You're a complicated young woman with a complicated life, and, actually, I'm quite happy for you about that. At your age, I was still pickled in wine and going nowhere." She looked off into the distance, and I wondered if she was seeing what I saw: a house divided both literally and figuratively between a wing devoted to lively little fruits of Father's anti-abortion crusade—with Nana, Sister Flatulencia, and Fayga working themselves to the bone for that revolving door of foster children— and a wing containing the pesky lone fruit of his most public dalliance, flapping and whirling so frequently she drove her mother straight to the bottle. I was well aware that I wasn't supposed to think such thoughts anymore. Adam and a host of angels since then had worked very hard to persuade me that it hadn't been my odd-duckishness that had created my mother's misery, that, if anything, her youthful inability to be a proper mother may have contributed to my own troubles with the void. But as much as I understood all that on a rational level, I couldn't rid myself of the suspicion that she might have been just a tad less tempted by demon alcohol if she'd given birth to a more normal, albeit less scientifically gifted, child.

Of course, I was also aware that if that had been the case, I would never have met the Fiskes. Which I simply could not imagine. For if Mother were Mother, then Stanley and Gwennie were the godparents to the person I was fated to become. Sammie liked to talk about what her analyst told her was "the challenge of holding the tension of the opposites." By which I understood her to mean honoring life's predilection for paradox. The awareness of which Niels Bohr had purportedly contended was a precondition for progress. I suppose both Jung and Bohr would have judged it a good thing that I simultaneously hated leaving Mother and couldn't wait to get home to the Fiskes.

But one thing was certain when I arrived back at Rose Villa: holding the tension of the opposites might be fine for humans, but cats have no patience for it. As soon as I tiptoed into Stanley and Gwennie's living room, Jillily took a flying leap toward my gift-laden arms, only to fall when her nails found no purchase. As always, she'd been waiting at the front door, seemingly intent on confirming biochemist Rupert Sheldrake's ideas about animals knowing when their owners were about to come home.

Stanley wasn't much better. As soon as I set down the packages and concentrated on scratching Jillily's thrumming throat, I spied my mentor excitedly shuffling up the hallway in his Nick and Nora skiing dog pajamas. Sixty-four going on six. Or four.

"Merry Christmas," he croaked froggishly, bending over to extract a quarter from Jillily's ear. My cat favored him with a long-suffering stare.

I managed to talk Stanley out of waking Gwennie by offering to scramble him some eggs with chervil and mushroom. I knew he would have loved to have a slice or two of Parma ham thrown in there, or even some cheap bacon bits, but there was no way Gwen would have tolerated meat in her kitchen.

Only after Stanley had contentedly smeared his lips with his napkin and put his feet up onto the only other chair onto which the *New York Times* wasn't piled did the topic arise that I'd been trying to duck for the past twenty-four hours.

"So how's that man of yours?"

"Huh?" I extemporized, admittedly poorly.

"What's wrong, Fleur?"

Damn. I tried to keep my voice level, but instead it came out like Alvin the Chipmunk. "Who says anything's wrong? Actually, we talked last night."

"And?"

"And nothing. He hasn't found his father yet, if that's what you want to know." I couldn't help but add dryly, "Which is why he went there."

"Yeeess. Of course, that's why he went there." He squinted his bulgy eyes and licked his lips, which made him look like he was about to leap after a fly. Except the leap was mental. "What's the man gone and done? It's not another woman, is it? Oh, don't give me that surprised look. You're about as transparent as glass."

"Why do you think that's what's going on?"

"Because in my own limited experience—and don't start on me, please, with that feminist crap of my sister's—women are particularly susceptible to jealousy. I lost a perfectly good marriage because Doris got it into her head that I was in love with one of my students. Never mind that the girl had a very bright young man waiting for her back in Massachusetts and that she had absolutely no sense of humor."

That *would* have been a decided black mark in Stanley's book. Jillily jumped onto my lap just then, circling awkwardly a few times before settling her bony body down in a way that jutted satisfyingly against my femur. I stroked her absentmindedly while I considered Stanley's words. I tended to forget that Stanley had once been married. It was hard to imagine, since I'd always known him as a part of a duo with his sister Gwen. It wasn't that there was anything incestuous about it, but the two were like a comfortable pair of shoes. Gwennie complained incessantly about his sunflower seeds and the stain he made on the back of the couch with his oily hair. On his side, Stanley could be counted on to grumble rather incessantly about Gwennie's cooking—not that it was bad; it wasn't, but it didn't include sugar or meat. How many times had our physics team gorged on donuts in Stanley's Caltech lab because our mentor was being subjected to corn syrup deprivation at home?

I thought I was saved from having to answer Stanley's question by Gwennie popping her gray head into the kitchen, faux-complaining, "Why'd you let me sleep so late?" But then she frowned. "Is something wrong?"

Stanley grunted. "Fleur thinks Assefa's cheating on her."

"No, I don't! Stop. Please. It's Christmas morning." Hoping to head them off at the pass, I got up and pulled out the tea drawer. "Morning Thunder?" Gwennie nodded. "You want some, too, Stanley? We really should get to those gifts, don't you think?"

Stanley clapped his hands gleefully and bounded off toward the living room. Gwennie shot me a considering look before she hurried after him, shouting, "Don't you dare start before Fleur can join us."

It wasn't the first time I fantasized doing a chemistry experiment, comparing the caffeine content of Morning Thunder and Starbuck's House Blend. We went through our gift opening like a house afire, tossing our torn wrapping paper to Jillily, who quickly turned it into red and green and gold confetti. Gwen had purchased Stanley a super-soft, frog-green cashmere sweater, which I didn't have the heart to point out he might never have occasion to wear if this winter's testimony to global warming had anything to say about it. For me, she'd artfully concealed in a handmade gift bag a generous gift certificate to our local Aveda hair salon. Downing the last of my Morning Thunder, I fetched my own present to her from under the tree and was delighted to hear her little squeal of pleasure at the Vitamix juicer I'd bought her, which still couldn't compete with Stanley's roar of appreciative laughter at my double gift of *How to Teach Physics to Your Dog* and Taschen's *Magic: 1400s to 1950s*. I was just absorbing Stanley's present to me—a plane ticket accompanying a breathtaking written request from Guy Wilkinson to visit and consult for his team at the Large Hadron Collider in Geneva next fall—when my cell vibrated.

I sneaked a quick glance at my watch and tried to instantly compute what time it was in Ethiopia. Finding my phone, I hurried up the hall to my room and pushed the door closed with my butt.

"Hello, handsome. Merry Christmas! I love you so much," I gushed, losing any cool I might have pretended to have.

The voice on the other end gave a confused little laugh. "Am I missing something? I mean, you know I love you, too, Fleur, but I feel a little like that character in *The Truth About Cats and Dogs*."

Now I was the one who was confused. Confused and, despite how much I adored Adam, disappointed. "Huh?

"You know—'you can love your pet, but you can't *love* your pet.'"

"Oh, right."

We were both a little dense. It took a moment for Adam to get it. "Ah," he said, in what I could have sworn was a rather pained voice. "You thought I was Assefa."

Jillily wound around my ankle, still licking her lips from her Christmas Greenies. "Mmm hmm."

"Okay, what's wrong?"

Oh for heaven's sake. I burst into tears.

"Christ, Fleur, what's happened?"

"No, no," I managed to muster. "He's okay. It's just ... he didn't remember to wish me Merry Christmas, and I think ... well, I'm almost certain he's located a girl he knew when he lived in Ethiopia. Her name's Makeda. After the Queen of Sheba. I looked it up. It means 'beautiful.'" I heard a light knock. The door opened a crack. Gwennie peeked in and raised an eyebrow. I shook my head. She put a hand on her heart, blew me a kiss, and then withdrew.

Adam's voice was subdued. "My poor Fleur. It's really gotten to you, hasn't it? The Green-Eyed Monster."

"Don't," I pleaded. "Anyone would feel the way I do. He flies all the way to Ethiopia. Supposedly to look for his father. His *missing* father. And what does he do? Looks up his old childhood friend in the town where he was born. His *female* friend. And he hasn't called since last night."

"Fleur, you don't even know whether he has regular access to phone service. He could've been trying to call you ever since."

I paused and reached across my bed for a Kleenex. "Well, his phone did cut out when we were talking ...."

"See? Anyway, how do you know about this Makeda? Did he tell you?"

"Not exactly. But that makes it worse."

"What do you mean, 'Not exactly'?"

"I asked him about her when he was falling asleep. Actually, he may have actually been asleep."

"Fleur."

"What?"

"You're bad."

"I'm not."

"You are. You're cooking up something in that imaginative head of yours that may bear no relation to reality."

"You sound like my father."

"And now you're being silly. You know what I mean."

And I did. If I were one of my physics students, I'd tell myself to stop letting my imagination run ahead of the evidence and put it, instead, to a test.

"What do you think I should do? His phone cut out before I could ... oh, Adam, do you think he's okay?" Why hadn't it occurred to me that something might have happened to Assefa? His father and Zalelew had disappeared, hadn't they? What did I know about Ethiopian crime? About natural hazards? The countryside was rugged and mountainous. His car could have run off a cliff. I found myself wishing the reason he hadn't called was Makeda. I said a silent prayer. *Please God, let him be okay.*

"Fleur. Sweet Fleur. I know this is scary. He's far away, this is your first separation, and he's your first love." At least in this, Adam was dead wrong. I blushed to think how many times I'd given myself mini-explosions while imagining Adam's thoughtful green eyes, his tender smile, his tight hugs and slight limp, his armpits smelling perfectly of Campbell's Chicken Soup and B.O. "What about a little Kundalini?" Adam suggested. "You're always telling me how much meditation relaxes you." I felt a stab of guilt. Here was Adam, taking time from his own Christmas celebration with his new fiancée, and I'd made our conversation all about me.

I took a couple of deep breaths, rolled my eyes up to my brow center, and, releasing the effects of caffeine and anxiety, felt my heartbeat slow down. "I love you, Adam," I said.

He sighed audibly. "This is how we started. I'm going to assume you mean that you just love me and not 'love' me."

I was considerably calmer by the time we got off the phone. He'd described the beauty of the snowscape outside his window, and I told myself with only the palest green tinge how great it was that he'd found a woman smart enough to appreciate his gentle strength and loyalty.

Thankfully, helping Gwennie get the house cleaned up from its chaos of wrapping paper and sunflower seeds ended up being a welcome distraction from obsessing about Assefa. We worked side by side on a new recipe she'd discovered for a carrot and cashew fan with orange and cardamom sauce, served with lentil and dill salad. I found the slicing tedious, but singing along to this year's version of Stanley's eclectic Christmas music collection filled the void quite nicely. Who wouldn't laugh to see stout Gwen's mimed striptease to Eartha Kitt's "Santa Baby," climaxed by whipping off her Physicists are Spicier apron and flinging it on the floor? As for six-foot Stanley's bizarre, stylized strut to Louis Armstrong's "'Zat You, Santa Claus," popping cashews and orange segments into his mouth as he circled the kitchen—it was a miracle we didn't pee ourselves.

At five minutes to five, the three of us subjected our nervous systems to another jolt of caffeine, this time via some face-squinchingly bitter espresso one of Stanley's students had brought back from Italy. We did a superficial tidy up and turned on the air conditioner just in time for the doorbell to ring, with the Caltech crew arriving en masse. They burst into the house so noisily that Jillily immediately retreated under my bed, where not even a catnip mouse from Amir could coax her out.

When Sammie and Jacob arrived, I was relieved to see that she, at least, was in good spirits. She confided in me during a quick bathroom break that they'd had a truce in which he'd actually— miracle of miracles—apologized for his appalling behavior. She stood up from the toilet, pulled her skinny red skirt back down her hips, gave herself a quick glance in the mirror, and confided in a low tone, "He even hinted that he might be open to me working part time if my mum would be willing to shift to teaching three days instead of five so she could help us with a baby." The lord giveth and the lord could just as easily taketh away, I thought cynically, doubting Jacob's sudden conversion to sanity.

And sure enough, I couldn't help but notice that Sammie's mood was markedly different from her lover's. Jacob was sitting at the end of the table, next to Aadita's boyfriend Arturo, whose valiant attempts at small talk were met with clipped responses and condescending stares. I began to suspect that Sammie's mood had a hint of the manic when she summoned more than her usual forced politeness as the scientists amongst us (Stanley, Aadita, Amir, Katrina, Tom, Gunther, Bob Ballantine, me) did our damnedest to bore the rest of the table (Sammie, Jacob, Arturo, Gwennie) with talk of string theory, multiple worlds, the Large Hadron Collider, and Chile's Very Big Telescope.

Alas, Isaac Newton's famous "What goes up must come down" applied to more than just gravity. I shared with the group what Stanley had given me for Christmas, along with Wilkinson's invitation, which was received with gratifying *oohs* and *aahs* until Sammie broke in. "You're joking, right? Very Big Telescope? Large Collider? That's what they're actually called? I can't fathom why you scientists can't exercise a little more imagination in naming your machines. I mean, what's the next one going to be, the Ridiculously Huge Thingamabob?"

Her olive skin uncharacteristically flushed, undoubtedly in sudden recognition of how rude she'd sounded, Sammie pivoted to mentioning a couple of films about Facebook that had recently been released. "Jacob and I were both left less than impressed by that new documentary about Facebook, weren't we, hon?" Jacob, seemingly staring at a Chagall print on the opposite wall, didn't even bother to look at her.

"Oh, Facebook," Bob muttered, inadvertently spitting a cardamom seed across the table onto Aadita's cheek. Aadita quickly brushed it away and kept her eyes on her plate as if to spare him discomfort.

But Bob was oblivious. "I want to tell my students who yatter on and on about Facebook to get a life." I stifled a snort by coughing into my napkin.

"Wait, no," Sammie insisted. "I wouldn't have met Jacob if it weren't for Facebook."

The room went silent, as if we all had a single thought: and that would have been so bad?

"We were both tagged in a post about those weird predictions about twenty-twelve. You know, the end of the world crap. I don't mean we're not in trouble. I know we are. Here we all are, sweating in our short sleeves at Christmas dinner. But the twenty-twelve thing was more airy-fairy than that. You know, the Nostradamus predictions. The Mayan calendar. The sort of thing that used to be reserved for New Agers and Tea Baggers. Well, maybe not Tea Baggers, but their forebears. The Evangelicals. The ones who root for Israel just so they can get raptured. Anyway, when I commented something along those lines on a post by someone I knew from the Analytical Psychology Club, someone tagged Jacob in her response.

What was her name, luvvie?" She leaned toward Jacob, sloshing her wine dangerously close to the rim of her glass.

"Esther Samowitz," Jacob replied, abruptly pushing back his chair and stalking from the room. Oh hell.

But Sammie merely turned back toward us and said, "Right. Esther Samowitz. I was really impressed by how Jacob methodically countered the evangelicals' distortions of the books of Daniel and Ezekiel, even though I didn't really understand much of it, not having read either the Old or New Testament. Which Jacob tells me isn't exactly something I should brag about."

The smiles of the rest of the table were looking stretched increasingly thin. Giving it the college try, Gwen mumbled, "Time for dessert, then?" She stood up and began to clear plates.

But Sammie wasn't to be stopped. She was speaking so fast, even I had a hard time keeping up with her: a dead giveaway for a Grade Two emergency. "I don't know about you, but I find the amount of knowledge out there a little overwhelming. Well, more than a little. A lot. I mean, there's so much *information*. And then you have to decide the right attitude to take to it. Red states, blue states, left-wingers, libertarians, people who think Obama's a socialist, people who think he's a sellout, Jews, Christians, East, West, Black, White, Muslims, and everybody else, atheists thinking religion's a pathetic attempt to rationalize death." Sammie took another swig of wine, and I was tempted to move the glass away from her. Her voice got still louder. And more shrill. "My mum says physics teaches that we alter reality as soon as we observe it. Fleur tells me we're actually living amid invisible, other worlds. I mean, how crazy-making is that?"

There was a loud series of sounds and we all jumped in unison. I assumed Jacob had slammed a door. But six times in a row?

Stanley leapt from his chair, shouting, "Shit! That's a gun."

"Stanley," Gwen screamed from the kitchen door. "Don't you go out there!'

But he did. And we did, too. So much for the rationality of scientists. I ran outside right on the heels of Gwen and Amir. A blast of hot air hit us as soon as we hit the porch. It was the time of day when the SoCal sky glowed a garish pink and purple with the sun's imminent setting.

Other neighbors across the street had already come out, cautiously peering around, much as we were. But now a few of them were pointing toward Fidel Marquetti's yard, where the lawn genie was going full blast. Not too far from where it spouted its rotating arc, Chin-Hwa was lying on his back, his light red coat darkened to mahogany by the water he hated so much. His intelligent eyes stared unseeing at the brilliant sky. A pool of blood under his tail signified that this dog had been curbed once and for all. At least one "Buda Hade" had gone home.

Pained, I looked away from him to see Mr. and Mrs. Kang standing nearby, their heads bowed. The sprinkler had soaked their clothing through to the skin, so that you could make out the exact shapes of their bodies. Mr. Kang's surprisingly protruding ribs. Mrs. Kang's tiny little breasts, her Y of a pubic mound revealed under her bedraggled butterscotch-colored skirt.

Only then did I register the screaming. My eyes sought the sound. Fidel Marquetti was running in circles in his driveway, making such a racket I couldn't imagine why I hadn't heard him before. He was clutching his buttocks, which, unlike the Kangs', was not soaked in water. But his jeans were torn, and his hands looked bloodied.

It wasn't too hard to reconstruct the story. Chin-Hwa had sunk his teeth into Fidel's butt, and Fidel had retaliated in humanity's age-old favorite fashion—not an eye for an eye (or in this case, a butt for a butt), but by upping the ante. You've encroached on my airspace? Fine then, I'll just let loose a few bombs on you.

A neighbor whose name I didn't know wandered over, a green, paper party crown on his head and, in his hand, a wine goblet. He spoke with a British accent, and I noticed Sammie and Aadita exchange a look. A *lantsman* on the block they didn't even know about. The man saw us eye his head and whipped off the paper hat. "Sorry. Hardly appropriate, under the circumstances."

For someone clearly beyond middle age, he had an unusually thick head of black hair. It almost looked as if he had a small animal perched on his head. I shot another glance at Chin-Hwa, then darted a quick look back at our front door. Thank God it was closed. I didn't know what I'd do if Jillily got out.

What if it had been Jillily on that lawn? I might not love my pet in the way that Adam joked about, but I was definitely an ailurophiliac.

A whimper escaped me, and I felt a hand reach for my own. It was Bob Ballantine's. He was looking at me with an expression of such dismay that I burst into tears.

A blare of sirens got louder and louder until an ambulance and several police cars screeched to the curb. Three paramedics raced to Fidel's side and busied themselves. The policemen emerged from their cars, scanning the crowd. Stanley and Gwen had joined the Kangs.

Stanley towered over Mr. Kang, who seemed to be speaking quite calmly to him. As if he was not soaked with water. As if his dog was not lying dead just a few feet away. Gwennie had managed to wrap Mrs. Kang in her arms. Strangulated cries came from where they rocked together.

The black-haired neighbor was talkative. "We all knew something like this was coming, didn't we?" he declared. If so, why hadn't I?

I thought of something Sammie had said earlier at the dinner table about it being laughable that people were so worried about a cataclysmic amount of dark energy being released by the Hadron collider, when the largest colliders resided within the human heart.

Chapter Eight
Assefa

MAKEDA AND I fell asleep far later—and far closer—than Father Wendimu would have wished. I don't know where he himself slept that night, as we two ended up talking for hours, wedged together feet to head on his rather narrow bed, with Makeda's plump toes close enough for me to have to censor the impulse to nibble them, and my legs slightly overshooting her wild puff of black hair, spread gloriously across Father Wendimu's small pillow. As the night air grew biting, Makeda got up to fetch a few thin green and yellow blankets to cover us, and it struck me that my bare feet with their thick calloused heels looked slightly ridiculous poking out of the covers to brace themselves against the back wall. We spoke as ceaselessly as we had in the old days, with only the barking laugh of hyenas, the high-pitched sawing of fruit bats, and an occasional child crying out from a nightmare punctuating our whispered conversation. Why we whispered, I don't know, except that was how we'd talked long ago, two children sharing jokes and secrets in an innocent disregard of being opposite genders, let alone two separate beings. In those days, it was as if we were but one soul tricked into inhabiting two separate bodies—the ease of our laughter, the familiarity of our mingled smells, the finishing of each other's sentences clues to our true unitary identity.

Needless to say, I was hardly heedless of our separate genders now. The heat from Makeda's body could have lifted the chill of an Arctic winter. It lifted something else entirely in me. I borrowed Fleur's penchant for pinching to try to keep my *washela* from pushing up the bedclothes, then sidestepped any further thought of my fiancée lest the hanging man spoil this dreamlike moment.

For the first hour, it was just old friends reconnecting. We caught each other up on our current lives, which for Makeda was almost entirely about the children. She explained the intricate bureaucratic hoops she and Father Wendimu had to jump through to make the adoptions of their young charges possible, how they had to prove over and over again that they weren't part of the regrettable wholesale practice of impoverished parents selling their babies to unsavory adoption agencies. She told me that the three children she'd been shepherding to meet their adoptive Spanish parents when she bumped into my father and Zalelew at Bole Airport had nearly been turned back due to a last-minute slashing of quotas by Ethiopia's Ministry of Women, Children, and Youth Affairs.

I was sufficiently in awe of Makeda's dedication that I hesitated when she asked me about my own life. I had no such humanitarian enterprises to impress her with, but she beamed with gratifying pride when I told her I was planning on continuing on at UCLA for a residency in cardiology. When she asked after my family, I took care not to mention Fleur in my recitation of how happy Enat was to have a full-time job despite the temper tantrums of her young charge Cesar, how Medr was recovering from a bout of dehydration, how thrilled Abat was to break free from driving his cab to join Zalelew on this mission.

"A cab!" Makeda hissed, shaking her head in disbelief. "What kind of a country lets a brilliant man like your father drive a cab?" Noting my defensive shrug, she said, "I'm sorry. But which is the backward country, then? At least here, it is a blessing for Negasi, who never learned to read and write, to have such a job."

Negasi was the driver who had ferried my father and Zalelew to Aksum, and she promised to track him down to have him take me to where he'd dropped them off. Which left my mind free to listen fully as she began to describe her life since Getachew's dusty Corolla had taken me away from her all those years ago, her hand waving like a flag that ended up planting itself permanently in my heart.

"At first, I pretended you'd just gone off for a family holiday," she said, so faintly I had to lift myself onto my elbows to read her lips in the dim light of Father Wendimu's little lamp. I snickered, and she favored me with a wry grin. No one we knew took holidays in those days; the war with Eritrea had sacked the treasury and depleted the country's rudimentary infrastructure to the breaking point.

But now her expression grew more serious, the steep triangle of a frown line appearing as if from nowhere to intersect her winged brows. "Eventually I started pestering my mother about when you were coming home. Each time, she managed to avoid me, until the morning my father returned from peace talks between the People's Revolutionary Democratic Front and the Derg. Failed as usual. I thought I'd never seen him look sadder in my life." She bit her lip, her voice raising several octaves, reverting to the girl-voice I recognized from long ago. "This time, I got up a bit more nerve, raising the question with both of them as the three of us sat at the dinner table, scooping up a particularly spicy *kitfo* that my mother had marinated in *mitmita* for a day."

She paused. "Do you believe it?" she said wonderingly. "I even remember what we were eating! I told them how much I was missing you and demanded to know when I would see you again. As soon as the words were out of my mouth, Abat spilled his glass of Harrar into his lap, and looked down at it like a boy who'd wet his bed. My mother behaved just as strangely. She didn't move, merely flicked anxious eyes at him, like a kudu alert to a stalking panther, until she finally wagged a finger at me. 'Hush, child,' she said. 'The boy will never come back.' And then she fetched a towel for my father to wipe himself, adding, 'Not any of them will be back here again.' And all this time, my parents didn't look at each other, and my father never uttered a word.

"And so,"—she smiled apologetically—"I have to confess it to you. I was a girl, preoccupied with all sorts of foolish things. I put you out of my mind. Not to excuse myself, but life was also changing so quickly. Other people in the village were leaving, too. Men were disappearing from their families in the middle of the night. The war was heating up." She shot me a look of sheer misery. "What is it with our people, Assefa, always at war?"

It took me a moment to register what she was saying. I was distracted by her story of her parents' mysterious behavior, which so mimicked my own parents when I'd brought up her name. My delayed response was to mutter dryly, "Ethiopians are hardly the only ones."

She clapped a hand to her forehead. "*Dedabe*! I am an idiot. Have you fought in your war with Iraq? Afghanistan?"

I heard my voice rising. "It's not *my* war!" I made what I realized even then was an overdramatic gesture, like a circus shill. "Step right up, folks, take your number. Eritreans, Ethiopians, Marxists, Nationalists, Muslims, Christians. All of them up for a fight. Oh, and don't forget the Jews, their treasure locked up in an Ethiopian church, whose priests had to borrow their chosenness because they didn't feel they were good enough on their own. Believe me, Ethiopia holds no patent on war." I thought of Medr, a world away from where his wife had been brutalized beyond comprehension, speechless in his hospital bed in a new land whose soldiers had posed for pictures flaunting its enemies' body parts.

She sat up in dismay, putting a hand on my knee. Embarrassed now, I put my own lightly on top of hers. "Don't worry, Makeda, no one fights in America if they don't want to. We don't even know we're at war. Instead, we walk around like crazy people speaking to the air—well, really, into our cellphones, and we've got twenty brands of toilet paper to choose from when we go to the market to keep us distracted."

"You're teasing me, yes?" I shook my head. It gave me such pleasure to see the arc of her neck as she threw back her head in laughter. But my relief was to be short-lived. She withdrew her hand from mine. The shout of a lone jackal sliced through the night, and it occurred to me I could probably identify the cries of nearly every creature out there. Moving to a new land layers but the thinnest of skins over bone and heart.

Makeda turned onto her side. I shifted to accommodate her, wanting to lay my head against her leg, but forcing myself not to. "Oh, Assefa. It's as if you've come back to us from another universe. I can't imagine so much toilet paper, especially when we made do for so long with no books." She shook her head, disheartened. "They actually closed the school, you know, not all that long after you left. Before the next spring the soldiers were advancing. We didn't even know if they were theirs or ours. The Derg were bad enough." She looked at me with assessing eyes, and for one moment I felt terribly exposed. And small. "Do you really want to hear this?"

Something about her tone prompted my muscles to tense. But still I nodded. I wanted to know everything about this woman now that I was here with her in the flesh. Hadn't I been dreaming of this moment forever? She shifted onto her back and stared up at the ceiling, her voice growing huskier. "We heard stories of houses being torched. Oddly enough, that didn't worry me too much. I couldn't really take it in. But Enat and Abat became irritable with me, and I spent long nights wondering what I'd done wrong. Very early one morning—really, it was still dark—I woke to shouting. It was as if the whole world was howling. I ran outside without thinking. The sky was on fire. I thought it must have been more of the lightning that had killed dozens of people that winter. And then a big boom! I looked around, and there was Abat, on his hands and knees in the dirt, flames reflected in the tears running down his face. Then, and only then, did it dawn on me that your house was on fire."

She was speaking of burning, but her voice was chilling. I felt the hairs rise on my arms and had an impulse to put a hand across her mouth, to stop her from whatever she was about to say. But she was relentless now, and I remembered an old saying of Enat's, "When spider webs unite, they can tie up a lion."

I was in a net and Makeda's words were tightening it around me. "That was the last I saw of him. The next thing I knew, I'd been grabbed from behind, my hands tied behind my back—even now, I can feel how the rope bit into my skin. Some kind of heavy cloth was thrown over me. I couldn't see. Could barely breathe. I was dumped onto something and felt the vibrations of a vehicle starting up. It was moving very fast. My body was tossed around by every turn. I could tell we were ascending. I knew Enat was somewhere nearby—I could hear her shouting and shouting until they must have cracked her across the face with something very hard because I could hear the sound of metal against bone, bone splitting, really, and then I heard her no more." Her voice went flat. "I never saw either of my parents again."

I hadn't yet had my psychiatric rotation, but I'd heard about the dissociation that comes of trauma. I detected it in Makeda now. She was speaking with as little emotion as if she'd been quoting the price of yams. I, on the other hand, was trembling all over. My upright

111

washela was history. I was just slightly aware that I was shielding a shriveled version of it with two hands tucked between my thighs. Makeda must have sensed my distress—on that bed, we were, after all, fitting together like two interlocked pieces of a jigsaw puzzle. But in that moment, she had no pity.

"I was sent to a place for war orphans, somewhere outside of Tigray, but as unlike this place as night and day. There was no Father Wendimu to put a stop to the madness. They were all women there." She laughed harshly. "The first thing they did, those Tigretes, when I arrived, nearly out of my mind with terror and thirst, was to determine I was still a virgin. They wouldn't take my word for it. An old woman with all her front teeth missing took it upon herself to check first hand. She spat on the ground when she saw I still had my clitoris." A long tear spilled from the corner of Makeda's right eye and made a tortuous journey down her glistening cheek. "She took care of that on the spot. She said they couldn't have anyone unclean amongst the younger children to pollute them." Suddenly, Makeda pushed her body away from me and out of the bed. She disappeared into Father Wendimu's closet, and soon I heard the strains of Seyfou Yohannes' *Tezita* coming from the little room.

And then Makeda was standing by the bed, completely unclothed but for a rolled up cloth between her legs. My eyes widened and my *washela* rose like a kudu's ear, but my belly was as tight as a *kebero* drum. She had something in her hand. She stuck it inside her mouth and then came over and handed me some. I didn't know what to do with it. Though green, it smelled of bananas. I learned later that *khat* is often packed in banana leaves. "Unclean," she said wonderingly, sitting on the bed and then sliding next to me again under the covers as if I were not even there. "She cut with me a knife so rusty I was picking little bits of rust out of my wound for weeks."

I myself dissociated right then. I registered her words, but could not find the feelings that should have accompanied them. She was speaking much more quickly now, the *khat* doing its work. "It was only once the orphanage was raided and I was brought back here to this village, to the church, only after Father Wendimu got hold of some antibiotics—lord knows what he sold of his own possessions to obtain them—that my body had a chance to heal. I'd become a wild animal by then. Even when my body began to hurt less, I was useless." She made a fierce face, and I saw chewed bits of leaf covering her teeth. "Until the other children began to arrive. In the beginning, they were war orphans like me, but then the AIDS babies came, younger and younger, dropped off outside our gates in the middle of the night, brought by nurses from one of the makeshift hospitals. More than a few had just been set down by the sides of their dead mothers, howling to the point that they were hoarse for days afterward."

Now Makeda sat up suddenly, and I shrank back a little from her heedlessly displayed breasts. A shaft of moonlight entering through an ill-fitting window illuminated her face, and I had the fantasy she was actually a ghost. She smiled then. Actually smiled. "It was the children who saved me. Father Wendimu knew exactly what he was doing. He made sure I was assigned the worst cases, the ones closest to death. I had to mobilize. And he—he begged, borrowed, and stole whatever he could to get me supplies. As soon as books became available again, he found me books for beginning nurses—I don't know how. Over time I became something resembling a human again. I began to think of them as my children. Even when I knew they would leave me. *Hoped* that they would leave me. *Igzee'abihier*, the Lord of the Universe had made them mine, and I knew that some essential part of them would be mine forever."

I, too, had stayed hers forever. Witch! What force was it that this woman possessed? And now the moon had found a way to insert as much of its glow as possible into this little room, as if the two of us were spot lit on a stage. Makeda looked me full in the face. "That raging infection would prevent me from having a child, and my disfigurement and my shame took care of any desire I might have had to make one." She looked at me with something akin to pity. "Pain, Assefa. All I know here"—she touched a hand between her thighs, as if for emphasis—"is pain." And now she touched her naked breast. "But *here*, what I know is love."

I knew this was not dissociation. This was truth. This was an uncanny form of grace. For the face of my old friend Makeda was now identical with Ethiopia's own dark virgin, Maryam of Sion. And she was asking me, "So, tell me, what is the name of the girl you have left behind?"

Chapter Nine
Fleur

I SUPPOSE IT MADE its own kind of cockamamie sense that it was Serena McKenna I turned to after we all bade a miserably useless set of goodnights to Fidel Marquetti and the Kangs. I went to bed with the small comfort that the police hadn't taken in either Fidel or the Kangs, leaving the Kangs to retreat into their home in stoic silence as the paramedics swept a still ranting Fidel off to Huntington Hospital. Only then did Animal Control load Chin-Hwa's bullet-ridden body into a van to be tested for rabies. Did I mention I felt useless?

Serena was one of the wisest people I knew, even if she shared with her employer Jane Goodall the inability to recognize human faces. Their malady, by the way, is called Prosagnosia, and they shared it with one of my favorite actors, the endearingly loopy Stephen Fry, as well as the renowned neuroscientist Oliver Sacks, who could escape the London blitz, teach at multiple major universities, write ten ground-breaking books, but couldn't tell his brothers apart. In the six years I'd known her, Serena had mistaken me for her old Cambridge classmate Stanley H. Fiske and my physics team member Gunther Anderten, whose own affliction of vision, strabismus, made you wonder if he was looking at you at all. I'd never gotten around to asking Serena if she and Jane recognized chimp faces, but I suppose it didn't really matter, since they had the primates' naked bodies, idiosyncratic sounds, and distinctive odors to give them clues.

Before composing my email, I checked the time in Tanzania, where the Jane Goodall Institute is based. We were ten hours behind, which I should have known since we were also ten hours behind Ethiopia. Which made me stop in my tracks with an alarmingly accelerated heartbeat. I recited a couple of Ra-Ma-Da-Sas and stroked a soothingly motoring Jillily before commencing my message.

"Dear Serena," I wrote, "I hope you and the chimps are fine. Please send my regards to Lord Hanuman and tell him that my team talks about him all the time." Which was true, particularly whenever we needed a little comic relief from our enforced hiatus from dematerialization research. What better reprieve from our frustration than recalling how a rescued lab chimp helped move our mathematical computations forward by flinging poop bullets at a blackboard, one of them just happening to attach a much-needed numeral seven?

I chewed at a tiny flap of cuticle before continuing, "Serena, I hate to bother you, but something terrible has happened. An animal has been murdered right next door, and I don't know if I can go outside again without ..." Mumps-like balls forming just below my ears, I flung myself out of my desk chair onto the carpet, where I rolled into a fetal ball, rocking and quietly moaning and sneaking in a little upper arm pinch now and again to prevent myself from alerting Stanley and Gwennie that a pity party was taking place down the hall. How ironic to have reached my supposed age of maturity just in time to throw a tantrum like a toddler over the death of dog I didn't even particularly like. As for Fidel, he'd evaded sharks and the Coast Guard to come to this country from Cuba; why hadn't he been able to take a little doggy doo in stride? The stupid signs he stuck up everywhere spoiled the symmetry of his garden more than a few turds, which, after all, pretty much blended in with the soil. As for the Kangs, why hadn't they kept the dog they supposedly loved safely inside their house and just walked him like other people did their pets? And what was wrong with Chin-Hwa that he failed to pick up that a dangerous human lived next door?

If there were situations where nobody and nothing is right, which god should be blamed for such inefficiency? Cydoimus, the Greek god of din, battle, confusion, and uproar? The Egyptian god of chaos Seth? Or, better yet, the Hindu Akhilandeshvari, otherwise known as She-Who-Is-Never-Not-Broken?

I laughed harshly enough for Jillily's ears to prick up like hypervigilant antennae. I scooted her toward me and pressed my nose against her belly, feeling her heartbeat decelerate as she purred.

"The Never Not Broken Goddess," I murmured into her motoring ribs. "She's the one, isn't she, girl? Silly me. I should have been worshipping her all along."

Chapter Ten
Fleur

IT WAS MY half-Jewish friend Sammie who'd first called my attention to the Buddhist notion of mindfulness, but it took a pale-skinned, blue-eyed Sikh to offer me practical guidance on making the body-mind connection. Which is why I was driving like a maniac to Siri Sajan's home studio, skidding precariously close to the butterfly-tattooed ankle of a preoccupied cellphone gabbing teenager as I swerved into a hasty right turn. I'd already detoured back home to grab my purple yoga mat, for once unbothered by its embarrassing Etch-A-Sketch of Jillily fur. I vaguely recognized the irony of driving too fast to a yoga class, but took a dark pleasure in blaming my carelessness on a series of bewildering conversations with Assefa.

Siri Sajan, as good as her name—which translates from Punjabi as *friend*—had offered me a private session as soon as I'd babbled into her phone, "It was either call nine-one-one or you, but I think I'm too young for this to be a heart attack." Who better than a master of Kundalini to realize I was at risk of falling into the everlasting pit of eternal emptiness?

Did I say bewildering? Make that unsettling. Better yet, let's call the spade what it was. Actually, that's not the most accurate image, since the actual Greek expression, mistranslated by Erasmus, was to "call a fig a fig and a trough a trough." I personally didn't give a fig what to call what I was feeling. I only knew I couldn't bear it alone.

I'd been climbing out of the tub when my phone rang the first time, and it had taken me a few minutes to register that it wasn't Jillily I was hearing, but the new meowing cat ringtone programmed into my phone as a Christmas present by Amir. Amir himself had his own new ringtone comprised of escalating Lord Hanuman grunts recorded especially for him by Serena, and he was only too happy to install a feline counterpart for me.

I'd grabbed my cellphone with one hand and swiped my plush, orange bath towel from the closed toilet seat with the other. I managed to set the cell on speaker and began to hurriedly swab my breasts and belly until I heard the faint "Fleur? Fleur? Are you there?" At the sound of Assefa's voice, fire streaked upwards from my tweeter. I envisioned the soft tuft of hair below his lower lip, his dark and liquid eyes. The whole time he'd been away, I'd been aching for the breathless unity of lying with him after our mini-explosions, our hearts beating in unison.

I hastily clapped the phone to my ear. "It's me, Assefa. I'm having a hard time hearing you. God, I've missed you. Can you speak up?"

Assefa's voice got louder for a few seconds then faded again. "Fleur, I need to talk to you. I want to explain ...." The line crackled. "It's not easy ... so sorry .... Oh, hell, this connection's terrible. Let me call you on another ..." And then he was gone. I tried to star sixty-nine him until I realized it would hardly work with a call from Africa.

I stared balefully at my image in the heavily misted bathroom mirror. With most of my face obscured by steam, I looked like a headless ghost. Was it my imagination, or was it more than the lousy connection that made Assefa sound so far away?

As I replayed the few words in my mind that I'd managed to hear, Jillily pushed open the bathroom door. Scratching her under her chin, I muttered, "It's all right, Jillily, isn't it?" But instead of rubbing her head against me for more, she turned her back, arched, and commenced the lurching strains of "I'm going to toss my breakfast all over the floor." Which she did. And it was bad. It looked like she'd gotten hold of some of last night's cauliflower curry. As soon as she relieved herself, she seemed perfectly fine, exiting the room with her question mark tail insouciantly aloft.

Usually, I mop up Jillily's messes without a thought. It's simply a part of having a cat. But this time I swabbed up the saffron-colored gook haunted by a gloomy felidomancy, which, in case you're curious, is a method of divination that interprets cats' movements as omens of future events.

I knew I was being ridiculous. Surely I was reading more into this than the occasion warranted, but I set off for Caltech with a vague unease that mounted into full-fledged alarm as soon as I took another abortive call from Assefa on my car's Bluetooth. This time, he sounded less troubled than irritated when the static set in. I heard him mutter, "Damn it, Fleur! Maybe it's you," before the connection fizzled out again.

That was when panic—and acid reflux—set in. Which I tried to explain to Siri Sajan when she opened her door. But my yoga teacher wasn't having any of it. She put a finger to her lips, guided me into her Persian-carpet-strewn living room, and gestured for me to unroll my mat. I couldn't help but reflect that my purple yoga mat looked garish against her faded burgundy and green rugs, but I tried to let the thought go as I sat cross-legged opposite her. We sang together, "*Ong Namo, Guru Dev Namo.*" *I bow to the Creative Wisdom, I bow to the Divine Teacher.*

Siri Sajan was definitely divine herself. The session she offered me was more restorative than taxing. By the time we got to the sweet final refrain of Kundalini meditation—borrowed from The Incredible String Band's "May the Long Time Sun Shine Upon You"—and exchanged *Sat Nams*, I was feeling fit for human company. I drove to Caltech with the assurance I'd been making a tempest in a teapot. (And if you're wondering—as I did when I first heard it from Father's thinly repulsed lips—about the derivation of that phrase, you might be interested to know that it has counterparts in Arabic, Bulgarian, Tamil, and Portuguese, with my favorite being the Greek variant that translates as *drowning in a spoon of water.*)

Anyway, by the time I finally poked a head into Stanley's classroom, the crew was already breaking up for the afternoon. Stanley had a dental appointment, and the rest of the team had errands to do. All but Bob, that is. Which was how I ended up joining him for a meal at the Broad Café. It would have been just plain rude to turn him down.

The Broad is Caltech's answer to New York delis, a California hybrid offering ridiculously caloric processed meat sandwiches coupled with organic produce. We were still debating what to order when Bob reached into his briefcase and said shyly, "Maybe when we find a table, you'd like to take a gander at this."

I looked down and laughed. "What, more? Bob, I swear you must be the messenger of the God of Physics, doling out the secrets of the universe, article by article."

If Bob was blushing before, he'd now attained the bright crimson of one of mother's Tess of the d'Urbervilles roses. He looked even more embarrassed when I slid a thumb under my jeans waistband with exaggerated difficulty and confessed, "My heart longs for the Reuben, but the scale says I'd better stay with the Caesar." I turned to the nose-ringed girl at the counter and asked, "Can you put a little chicken in it?" before muttering a quick aside to Bob, "Gwennie would kill me, but I've got to have a little animal protein once in awhile."

Seeing that Bob was still a rather spectacular shade of red, I tried taking the focus away from myself, asking, "What's looking good to you?" before I realized what I'd done. I added a hasty, "What do you have an appetite for?" *Oh dear.* I really did suffer from foot-in-mouth disease.

Bob made a visible effort to gather himself. "I'm going back and forth between the Lumber Jack and the Herder." I snorted, and he darted a paranoid look at me before Nose Ring Girl turned her attention back to us and asked him, "Have you decided yet?" She actually sneezed into her hands as he replied, "Okay. Make it a Lumber Jack. But just the roast beef and turkey. No ham."

"Is that all?" she asked, her dark eyes wandering between the two of us.

Bob looked tense. He turned to me. "Do you want anything to drink?" I shook my head. "No, that'll be all, but"—he paused—"would you mind washing your hands?"

The girl shot him an incredulous look, gave a curt nod, and then pivoted toward the back. She wasn't the only one who was shocked.

I beamed at Bob. "Bob, you're not just a messenger of God, but my personal hero. I would never have had the guts to say that, but it needed to be said."

Grinning, Bob led the way to a pine-topped table, and as soon as our food was ready we chowed down like there was no tomorrow.

Finishing my salad first, I turned to the article Bob had handed me. It was a contribution to the journal *Physics Letters B* written by Indiana University physicist Nikodem Poplawski. My heart skipped a few beats as it dawned on me where Poplawski was going. I didn't even mind Bob pulling his chair around so that our thighs were nearly touching. He read the final page along with me, though he obviously knew what it said.

I smiled up at him gratefully. "All kidding aside, you sure do come up with the good stuff, Bob. First Jaime Gomez, now this." And I meant it. Bob seemed to have an unerring eye for work that would be helpful once we got our green light on P.D. The fact that Poplawski had developed mathematical models of the spiraling motion of matter falling into black holes opened all sorts of possibilities. He was proposing that a black hole wasn't made up of matter collapsed into a single point, but was instead a kind of wormhole or tunnel into which matter was sucked before it gushed out of a white hole at the other end to form an alternate universe.

Which, as Bob excitedly pointed out, suggested that the cellular black holes I'd postulated in the human body were just as I'd predicted, bridges to alternate realities into which we might disappear and reappear according to the Principle of Dematerialization. And while Congress had virtually decreed that we couldn't yet go forward on testing P.D., we could certainly follow up Poplawski's ideas when the time came.

Nodding encouragingly, I said, "I think you're onto something, Bob." His face lit up like neon, and the foot of his crossed leg jiggled like Jillily beset by fleas. I was right there with him. "This opens up no end of —"

My cellphone erupted with a series of meows. As much I wanted to continue our conversation, my heart leapt at the thought that it might be Assefa. With a quick nod at Bob, I rose from my seat and moved to a quiet corner of the café.

There was static on the line again, but it didn't get in the way of Assefa's "Fleur, can you hear me?"

"I can! I can hear you!" I could barely contain myself.

"Listen," he said. "Something's come up."

I pressed the phone more tightly to my ear. "Is it your father?"

"No. No. Abat is fine. He's actually on his way back. The government expelled him. It's absurd. They say he and Zalelew wanted to steal the Ark of the Covenant. As if they could even if they wanted to." He gave a sardonic laugh. "As if it was there in the first place, and not just a fiction of my people's inferiority complex."

His use of the phrase "my people" gave me a moment's pause. "Mmm, yes, sounds pretty outrageous. But why aren't you on the plane with them?"

"That's why I'm calling, Fleur. I've got a bit of sorting to do."

"Sorting?"

For a moment the line went silent. Despite my earnest attempt not to, I began to spin, which was how I discovered that Bob had come up behind me. As I swung past him, he mouthed, "Is anything wrong," but I just kept turning. I had to hand it to Bob. Rather than politely averting his gaze, he observed my whirling with an air of mild curiosity.

But on my next turn, I saw he'd given up. He was heading toward the curving food counter, undoubtedly seeking another multi-grained something to add to the lonely seed between his teeth.

Now Assefa was speaking again, albeit haltingly. "Well, here's the thing, Fleur. I've been visiting this orphanage. You wouldn't believe what this country has been through. Really, for more years than anyone could possibly count. And these children—so many orphans. War, AIDS, well, it's ridiculous. There aren't nearly enough doctors to begin to address their needs. It's shaken up everything I thought was settled. I don't know if I can go about my plans as if I hadn't seen this. I need a little time to think."

I don't recall how I'd got there, but I found myself sitting with my legs stretched before me on the checkered linoleum floor, a catsup-streaked napkin and a few withered French fries just to the right of my knee. I responded in a mortifyingly whiny voice, "But why can't you come back and think here?"

"Well, that's the thing, Fleur. There's so much more I need to find out. It would be foolish to leave and then to have to come back again to get all the data."

"All the data on what, Assefa?" And why did he keep referring to "the thing?"

"On what it would take to transfer my studies here."

124

I could barely breathe. "Why in the world would you do that? You're interning at one of the best university hospitals in the world. Surely, if you wanted to volunteer some time in Ethiopia, it would be so much better to finish your education here first."

"Yes, but here's the thing," he interjected. "What if it isn't actually volunteering I'm thinking about but something more … permanent?"

I have to admit, that one caught me up short. It was as though he'd just turned my head upside down and given its contents a serious shake. I fought to regain equilibrium. "Assefa, what are you talking about? What about your life here? What about us?" My head was beginning to pound. "What about *me*?"

I'd never heard Assefa's voice so stiff. "Fleur, I know this is a shock. I'm a bit shocked myself. But maybe there was a meaning to my father going on his wild goose chase. Maybe he was called to do this on my behalf. Something that was never resolved. Well, anyway. You have to understand, everything's under the microscope right now. I can't just leave all this as if it were a bad dream."

Why not? This was fast turning into *my* worst nightmare.

Anyone with any sense would have gotten the message by now, but I can be dense at the best of times. "Assefa, you didn't answer my question."

"Fleur," he pled, "please. I need a little space to think."

Space? Think? He who only a week before had told me that he couldn't imagine life without me? Who liked to call me his little lamb? *His dukula?* A vast pit opened up inside me, and, unable to find purchase, I was tumbling down. Eight days after toasting my birthday at Casa del Mar, Assefa had evidently excised me from his heart as casually as a host in a crowded restaurant crossing a name off his list. I knew now what "the thing" was. The thing was *me*.

Before the void enveloped me completely, I pushed up from the floor and brushed off my jeans, looking across the room to see that Bob had evidently decided to order a second lunch. He was stuffing a sandwich into his mouth with hippopotamic gusto.

I felt something nasty and reptilian climb up the back of my neck as I switched my cell to the other ear. "Thanks so much, Assefa," I hissed, "for asking how I am. And your grandfather. Last time we talked, he was being treated for dehydration. Thanks for asking about Medr, too."

"Ah. I've already phoned Enat. She's reassured me that he's fine. And she is so relieved that my father is coming home." The feeling of betrayal nearly gagged me. "But you're right. I should have asked about you, Fleur. I really am very sorry. Very. I know this must be hard for you. I can't tell you how terrible I feel for—"

"Oh, don't worry about *me*, Assefa. I'm just fine. You know what they say. It's all good." I turned off my cellphone and stared at it, full of wonder that a tiny gadget with a circuit board at its heart could so effectively sever meaning from a life.

Somehow I made it back to the table and sat down. I have to hand it to Bob. He might have been a bit dim at times, but right now his eyes telegraphed nothing but concern. "Is there anything I can do?"

I couldn't possibly recount my phone conversation to Bob. On the night of Chin-Hwa's murder, he'd finally confessed his crush on me, at least in a Bob-ish sort of way, but completely unlike his namesake Uncle Bob, who'd been an utter chicken during the traumatic episode with the Boy Who'd Called Me Beautiful. That shrinkable imaginary uncle of mine had disappeared into my pocket as soon as the young stranger had dared me to remove my clothes and immerse my body in the pond near Sleeping Beauty Castle, resulting in me having a police gun stuck in my face and being put in a jail cell nearly as proportionally confining as Jillily's cat carrier. And if you're wondering, as I have, why cowardliness is called being chicken, you'll have to content yourself with the fact that William Shakespeare first coined the phrase in his play *Cymbeline*, which happens to be about jealousy. Into whose pallid landscape I'd pretty much been thrown, for I knew quite well that the orphanage where everything was needing to get re-thought was the one presided over by Makeda, whose name muttered under my lover's breath had been an omen I'd been foolishly trying to ignore.

So when Bob asked again if he could do anything, I eyed his plate appraisingly and responded. "Yes. Yes, you definitely can." I held out a hand. "Will you let me have the rest of your Herder?"

It was Bob's idea to take me to the beach. I'd broken down in the midst of stuffing the remainder of his oversized sandwich into my mouth, tears and snot drizzling down my face to make the taste of corned beef, pastrami, turkey, salami, cheese, and Russian dressing even saltier. Bob helplessly watched me cry for several minutes, finally thinking to reach into his shirt pocket for an unrealistic shred of Kleenex before I retrieved a more intact version from my purse.

As I swabbed my cheeks and chin, I could almost see a light bulb go off in his head. "I know," he offered, "we should go to the beach." He stood, gathering Poplawski's paper and stuffing it into his briefcase. It didn't seem to occur to him that I hadn't agreed to go. But before I knew it, I was rising out of my chair like a zombie and following him out of the café.

He was talking the whole time. "It's where I go when I don't like what's happening in my life. Nothing feels as bad when I'm near the ocean. Must be something about all life coming from there. It's like Dorothy from *The Wizard of Oz*."

I shot him a confused look. "You know," he prompted. "'There's no place like home.' Actually, she said it a few times, didn't she? Clicking those shiny shoes of hers. I'm addicted to that movie." He scratched the top of his head with an air of mild embarrassment, sending an avalanche of dandruff onto the shoulders of his navy T-shirt. "Actually, I watched it a few days ago and couldn't help but wonder if the writer wasn't secretly suggesting Dorothy had dissolved into a wormhole that took her right where she needed to go. That wouldn't be too far from what we're aiming for with dematerialization, would it?"

So, our Bob was a closet philosopher. If I'd been in a state to laugh, I would have. Here I was, the archetypal jilted lover, current president of the Red Nose and Wet Booger Club, and Bob was zipping along the cosmic highway.

Bob shot me a paranoid look. "What?"

"Oh, Bob, I don't know, but anybody who could actually make me smile right now deserves his own Academy Award for kindness."

Bob blushed so intensely I imagined his toes turning bright red.

"Actually," he replied, managing to skirt my praise, "they lost the award to *Gone with the Wind*."

I have to admit, the diversion momentarily rescued me from my apocalyptic loss. "You can't be serious. That piece of revisionist crap?" Bob looked taken aback. "Sorry," I pleaded, embarrassed. "I do believe I just channeled Gwennie Fiske. You know how she likes to rant about the insidious impact of racism in books and films." I paused. "But, you know, it was Sammie who first taught me about racism. I'd never imagined such a thing could exist. You met her, so you know that beautiful olive skin of hers. One time we spent a week with her grandparents in Orange County, and her dark skin prompted a disgusting volley of nasty racial slurs from a mischief of mall rats at the South Coast Plaza."

Bob flushed with anger. "Assholes!" But then he cocked his head quizzically. "A mischief of …?"

I laughed. "Never heard the expression a 'mischief of rats'? How about a 'murder of crows'?" He shook his head. "How about a 'shrewdness of apes' or—actually, I hate this one—'a nuisance of cats'?"

By the time I'd described to Bob the running contest Stanley H. Fiske and I had over who knew the most elusive group names, we'd arrived at Bob's car, a bird-poop-bedecked dark blue hatchback that proclaimed itself a Festiva.

Now, we physicists might just be ranked as royalty in the realm of absentmindedness. Which is why I wasn't insulted when Bob proceeded to unlock the back door with a click of his key, throw his briefcase onto the back seat and shut the door, open the driver's door to slide inside, and glance into his rearview mirror as he started up the motor. Only when he heard me tapping on the passenger side window did he peer over at me, still standing outside the locked passenger door. Mouthing his mortification, he hurriedly exited the car to open my door for me, fussing around to make sure I was belted in and inadvertently brushing his hand across my breast, which made me reflect upon how readily Bob's complexion transmuted from pale pink to neon red.

Returning to the driver's seat, he shot me a look that said something like, I'm hopeless, aren't I? and then valiantly started up the car again, exuberantly breaking into the familiar tune, "We're off to see the wizard, the wonderful Wizard of Oz."

Who could be depressed around a guy like this?

Under the circumstances I certainly could, but since he was being so kind at a time that Assefa most definitely was not, I felt I owed it to him to tie my misery to the mast. I resolved to keep myself from jumping overboard until I got home.

Bob wasn't a freeway kind of guy, so I had a lot of opportunities to distract myself on the way to Santa Monica Beach. Since Adam and the gang had taken me to the beach numerous times during my first summer in SoCal, this drive was like being in a time warp, tracking bits and pieces of my history. Here are some of the more memorable neighborhoods we passed through:

1. Griffith Park. Actually, as soon as Bob's car neared the vicinity it occurred to me that the last time I'd been there was with Assefa. My heart rate accelerated as I recalled dragging Assefa to the park's world-class observatory on a Friday night for a book signing by Harvard's Lisa Randall, who'd responded to a question about multiple universes that our own universe might be merely "a three-dimensional 'sinkhole.'" Which made a heck of a lot of sense to me now.

2. West Hollywood. The first time I'd seen it was when I was twelve years old. I'd been in the car with Adam, who was driving me to my first interview with a local paper about my discovery of C-Voids. We'd passed two blue-jeaned men with John Edwards hair walking down the street with a hand in each other's pockets. I'd started screaming, and Adam had to explain to me that the men weren't trying to pick each other's pockets, but were actually demonstrating affection.

3. Beverly Hills. The only people out on the sidewalks fronting rows of imposing Spanish, Tudor, and Mid-Century Modern homes were brown-skinned gardeners, brown-skinned nannies pushing fancy prams with white-skinned babies, and two alarmingly skinny, sunburnt female runners—one who looked to be older than Mother, wearing a canary yellow tracksuit and a sequined baseball cap, and the other with the biggest mouth I'd ever seen outside of a *National Geographic* issue that featured the plate-like adornment fashioned for the lips of Mobali women of Northern Congo. Which, when I pointed it out to Bob, elicited from him an excited, "Yeah, but have you seen pictures of what the Mursi and Suri women do to themselves? Their lips get stretched so far from their faces that you could serve drinks on them!"

Frowning, I felt around inside my mind to see if I recalled any knowledge of the Mursi and Suri tribes. Failing, I asked Bob what country they inhabited.

Clearly pleased to know something I didn't, Bob shot back an exultant, "Ethiopia." At which point, despite my best efforts, I burst into tears all over again, Bob pulled to the side of the road and, looking like a lost dog, muttered pathetically, "I'm sorry. I'm so sorry. How dumb can I be?"

It took seven minutes and thirty-five seconds for me to calm down. I knew, because I'd been staring at the digital clock on the dashboard to avoid Bob's eyes, which were full of enough pity to fuel a day's worth of non-stop tears.

By now, I'd given up on finding enough tissues to do the trick and pulled up the bottom of my T-shirt to wipe my face. Unsurprisingly, Bob forgot to politely turn his head, and when my eyes caught his staring at the lacy bra barely containing my breasts, he merely shrugged with the hint of a not-overly-guilty grin.

"Bob!" I chided.

But Bob was clearly getting more comfortable with me. "You didn't ask me not to look," he said. And he was right. I hadn't. Bob turned on the ignition, I backed away from the void, and we darted into traffic to the sounds of the Shins' "It's Only Life," which should have been depressing, but somehow wasn't.

I should probably mention that riding in Bob's car was a singular experience, and not just because it was being driven by Bob. When I'd first flung my purse into the back seat, I saw it was jammed with books, what looked to be about a hundred loose physics articles, and scores of folded brown paper bags. Unsurprisingly, it smelled of smoked fish, which made me wonder how Bob would respond to the idea of ferrying Jillily and me to the vet the next time she needed to go. The smell might be a comfort to her while she was trapped in her pink jail cell of a cat carrier.

But the corker was that Bob had hung on his rearview mirror a miniature mobile of Mobius strips made of rainbow-hued satin ribbon that danced to the beat of the music on his CD player. He claimed he wasn't distracted by it, but I myself found it mesmerizing as Bob and I sang along with James Mercer about going down the rabbit hole.

After deciding that it might be interesting to park near the palisade and cross the bridge over Pacific Coast Highway to get to the beach, Bob led me through an obstacle course of homeless humanity toward the urine-reeking concrete steps leading to the bridge. We passed several people minus teeth, others minus company, still others clearly minus their minds. Which took my own mind back to the (very) few days when Father and I had actually enjoyed each other. It had been after he'd lost his original mind in his nervous breakdown and before he'd taken refuge in the old one—the one that hated me enough to crusade relentlessly against my scientific research.

When we'd exited the car, Bob had grabbed a few paper bags from the back seat, and now he let them carelessly dangle from his hand, as if he'd done this a million times before. By this time, realizing I was fighting a losing battle, I'd given up worrying about hurting Bob's feelings and was so carried away with telling him about Assefa's call that I didn't even ask what the bags were for. Instead, I took poor Bob with me on every repetitive spin of my mental wheel.

But crossing the pedestrian bridge over the Pacific Coast Highway put an end to my chattering. For a void-fearer, it was terrifying. The wind was brisk and whipped my hair across my eyes and around my chin with gusty slaps. Bob's paper bags became low-slung kites flapping from his fingers. Traffic surged beneath us like a herd of steel beasts. A vagrant strain of music reached my ears from the beach below. I made out Jackson Browne's mournful, "Fly away, *linda paloma!*" as I set foot on a bottom step layered in hieroglyphs of sand. The words *"linda paloma"* led, as words will do, to a host of memories: the painful penetration of my virginal tweeter by Hector Hernandez's bulging member, followed by the murder of Baby X, which in turn handed me right over to the realization that Assefa and I would never conceive the brilliant child I knew we were meant to create. That was, unless our recent condom collapse had proferred its own fateful vote.

That possibility caused my eyes to release another burst of tears. Looking by now a little wary of my emotionality, Bob shot me a sideways look, but kept on walking, so I did, too, noticing that his bags were brushing against his jeans with a kind of 'shhh shhh, ba da shhh' in time to our synchronized steps. Now that we'd shifted from cement to sand, our stride slowed, and the omnipresent roar of the ocean drowned out all other sound. By the time we reached the shore, my monkey mind had pretty much chattered itself out.

Reaching the shoreline, we removed our shoes to walk on the wet sand. Bob held out one of his bags for my tennies, depositing his own loafers inside. "You know," he ventured, "my dad always told me I didn't need to stick around people who treated me badly. He said there were way too many human beings in the world to waste my time with people who weren't worth it." Bob squinted up at the sky. "At that point, it was probably somewhere around five-point-three billion." He shrugged. "Of course, he wasn't reckoning on the fact that most people didn't find *my* company particularly appealing, so I had plenty of practice assessing my worth on my own."

I'm afraid I didn't pay much attention to the melancholy turn of Bob's last remark. Instead, I fixed on his father's message. Bob was implying that Assefa was one of those time wasters. Could that be true? Everything my lover had said and done before now had proclaimed he was decent down to his long and perfect ebony toes. Hadn't he listened to my lengthy, multiple-alleyed stories without a hint of impatience? Accepted the presence of Jillily's litter box in his own home without complaint? Worried constantly about his parents, his grandfather? Had as his passion in life the repair of people's hearts? But then it occurred to me that perhaps it was his goodness that was causing my current problem. He was worrying about those orphans more than he was worrying about me.

But a more cynical voice balked at my rationalization. What if Assefa was what Sammie liked to call a dog? At first, I'd assumed the term was a compliment. If men could be referred to as cats—in my book the highest praise possible—and given that Sammie herself used to call the two of us birds, and since dogs were generally thought of as good-natured (though I wouldn't exactly have applied that to Chin-Hwa or one particularly sharp-toothed creature who'd lunged at me rather terrifyingly when I was a child), then why was "dog" such a dismissive epithet? Sammie had sorted me out on that one with a certain savage intensity, no doubt attributable to the two men she'd dated before Jacob, each of whom had cheated on her with far inferior partners.

But now a stranger's face was suddenly sticking itself just a few inches from my own. The woman's long straight hair was being swept dervishly around by a sudden gust of wind. "You're Fleur Robins, aren't you? I hope those right wing bastards get thrown out and you can start up your project again." I actually felt her spit splatter my cheek with the word "bastards."

Though I agreed with her sentiment, there was something in her eyes that scared me, and when Bob pulled me away, he said, "Don't pay her any attention. Fame brings out the roaches of every stripe."

Before I knew it he'd shoved a Ralphs's bag into my hand. Actually, as soon as he got the bag into one of my hands, he took my other hand in his own and tugged me toward a spot where a frothy wave was being sucked back out to sea. He knelt, and since he had my hand, I knelt with him, our knees knocking against each other on the ground, which was surprisingly firm given the fine dusting of sand—soft as powdered sugar—layered at the top.

Within seconds, he'd scooped out a little crater of sand to reveal a spread of tiny shells—most of them broken, but some decidedly not: delicately crafted little exoskeletons whose twists and whorls had been crafted by an unseen hand into something as precise and perfect as a baby's lips. He reached into one of his bags and pulled out a pair of crimson faux-velvet pouches, handing me one and pantomiming what I needed to do. The ocean was making conversation an unrealistic option. I deposited my first beige-and-white-patterned shell inside its soft new home with solemn care and placed the pouch at the bottom of my Ralph's bag as I saw him do with his own. A sudden shaft of sunlight speared the horizon, giving the brown grocery bag a golden hue and illuminating the letters L-P-H like an ancient manuscript.

So this was what Bob did with his bags. I didn't want to move. The sound of the sea was mesmerizing. If we could find such gems right here, why go anywhere else? Ever. We could inhabit this moment eternally, impermeable to anything outside this sun-kissed spot, never again bothered by worthless friends or faithless lovers.

But words like *never* are folly in this incarnate world. In this case, the change agent was Bob himself, who insisted we'd find more of such beauties, and larger ones, if we walked north, past the crowds of families and kids hugging the shore.

"Besides," he shouted against the roar of a breaking wave, pointing to an admittedly stinky pile of seaweed-wrapped jellyfish drawing more flies than the largest of Chin-Hwa's pansy bombs. I nodded and followed him.

I was sweating profusely by the time we reached Will Rogers State Beach. It was hotter than hell. So much for the climate change mumpsimusses. It had taken us about an hour's walk to get there.

We'd long passed the last family crowded near the Santa Monica pier with their broad umbrellas, broader smiles, and ice chests packed with Coronas and Cokes, and were now in the land of bikini-clad girls and surfer boys whose toned, athletic bodies brought me right back to dark thoughts of Assefa. But Bob was intent on getting me safely seated on a large rock jutting onto the sand so we could show and tell about the stashes of shells we'd each accumulated on the way.

"May I?" Bob asked, reaching into my bag to select a small spiral shell with a dark circle on the outside. "You know what this is, don't you?" I shook my head. "It's a moon snail. Also known as a Shark's Eye." Well, that made sense. The black center was surrounded by a milky aura that looked uncannily like a staring eye. "Actually, its real name is *neverita reclusianus*, and it dates back to the Oligocene. Can you imagine this fragile-looking home of a tiny carnivore surviving at least twenty-three million years?" Of course, I couldn't. Not when we comparative giants barely made it to a hundred.

The soft creature who'd inhabited this dainty home had undoubtedly been protected by the intimidating ocular image on its outside. I wondered how many heartbeats the ferocious shark eye façade had bought the shell's inhabitant. A billion? I asked Bob, who seemed to know everything there was to know about aquatic life forms.

He frowned and enthusiastically took up the question. "Well, let's see. I think your average mollusk lives at least five years. They're about as slow moving as you get, so I'd guess they have a heartbeat of about ten a minute. So, what does that work out to?"

"Something like twenty billion beats. That can't be right."

Bob nodded in agreement. "Sounds like a lot." I knew this one was going to drive me nuts until I tracked it down.

We resumed sorting through our haul. Bob pulled out a couple of spectacular specimens, including a couple of perfect *turtella ocayas*, long spiraling cones without a single chip. After *oohing* and *aahing* enough to turn his skin just the side of fuscia, I marveled at the floral design on the outside of the one sand dollar I'd found. I speculated whether it was a fossilized imprint of a flower that the sand dollar had been lodged against. Bob smiled indulgently. "Actually, what you see as a flower is actually the fivefold radial pattern of its exoskeleton, which we call a 'test.'"

I felt more than a little humbled as Bob revealed the scope of his knowledge. Back at Caltech, he'd come in (and come across) as the acolyte, and I admitted to myself I'd looked down at him a bit. Well, actually, a lot. But in the open air Bob actually looked an inch or two taller, as if here at the beach he was one of its natural denizens. Which, I was soon to discover, had its dark side, too. On our walk back, we came upon a largish piece of plastic with indistinct blue lettering wrapped in and out of the ribcage of a rotting dead pelican. The bird had undoubtedly ingested the plastic before it died. Without warning, Bob sunk to his knees and pounded the sand, shouting, "I hate humanity!"

I had to resist the temptation to flap, but I knew what he meant. The implications of the corpse were disgusting and all too familiar, signs of our species' utter lack of concern for our biosphere. It stirred my own utter frustration at the standstill forced upon my P.D. team by a body of 379 men and 93 women blindly committed to an ecologically disastrous status quo. My team and I had discovered a potentially revolutionary means of getting from one place to another that might obviate the most egregious uses of fossil fuels, and Congress was blocking our research as a sin comparable to human cloning. Which it wasn't.

But I was yanked out of that familiar internal rant by Bob's visibly heaving chest. I hesitantly put a hand on his shoulder. "You're right. It's awful. With all our vaunted intellect, we're a short-sighted species."

He shrugged me off, his face twisted. "No, Fleur. That's too kind. We're the suicide bombers of the planet, willing to take down more than eight million other species with us." So this was Bob's void. I stepped back, but Bob grabbed my hand, putting it against his chest, saying, "No, no. Listen, I'm sorry. It's just that it gets me so fucking mad." I didn't have the heart to pull away, but was more than a little relieved when he finally let go of my hand. He seemed to be staring at something behind me. The slight smile playing at his lips took me by surprise.

I turned to see. Why was he grinning? The bird carcass really was awful, as was the enthusiasm of the flies encircling it. I heard Bob say, "You know what they are, don't you?"

I looked back at him. It took me a minute. "The flies?" He nodded.

"A swarm."

"What else?"

"A cloud."

He motioned, "More," with his hand. I grimaced, frantically scouring my mind, but I didn't have it. I sighed. "Okay, I give."

His expression was victorious. "A business!"

Damn! I *had* read it somewhere. Ages ago. "You're right," I said with a grudging groan. "A business of flies."

Bob rewarded me with a sly expression I wouldn't have imagined he was capable of. "I think that entitles me to cook you some dinner. Why don't you come back to my apartment and hang out?"

Chapter Eleven
Assefa

WHEN OUR BEGINNINGS are marked by extraordinary cruelty, whatever comes afterward either confirms our mistrust or threatens the wariness we employ to ensure we'll never be that vulnerable again.

So powerful was the force of Makeda's love for her orphans that it completely disarmed them. When I woke the next morning, it was to the same laughter, singing, and exultant shouting that had greeted me upon my arrival less than a week before.

On my second night here an exasperated Father Wendimu had asked Adey to make up a cot for me next to the goats. As the younger man, I'd adamantly refused to take his bed and so had fallen asleep in the shed to the not altogether unpleasant sensation of a kid's wet nose pressed against my neck. There was a reckoning the next morning. Struggling to rise from a wooden plank covered with two colorful but thin blankets, my knees and back chastised me and I cursed myself for my politeness. But now I reminded myself that stiff joints were a small price to pay for having finally committed myself wholly to one course and one course alone.

The sweet smell of jasmine greeted me when I stumbled out of the thatch-roofed tukul. Inhaling appreciatively, it occurred to me that, despite all my washing under the surprisingly efficient outdoor showerhead at the back of the property, I must stink of goat.

I scanned the yard and saw a rooster strut unconcerned past the orphanage's lone cat, a ginger-colored creature that looked malnourished compared to Sammie's similarly colored feline back in Pasadena. A small group of orphans clustered around a sun-faded, painted wooden table. I approached closely enough to see Makeda preparing to give the HIV positive children their antiretroviral meds. I held back for a moment. She was making it into a game, singing, "*Ete emete yelome sheta ….*" The children's rousing accompaniment was punctuated by a certain amount of sputtering and coughing as diminutive young throats struggled with large capsules and pills.

By now I'd learned that over 80,000 Ethiopian children were living with HIV. It was partly why I'd decided to stay. Despite advances spurred by Ethiopia's Ministry of Health and its Office of General HIV Prevention and Control in reducing HIV infection of mothers and children, those 80,000 who'd already been infected were doomed to short, miserable lives without the kind of consistent care Father Wendimu's charges were getting. Back in the U.S., these kinds of statistics would have remained just that for me: statistics. But now?

Last night, I'd washed the worryingly thin limbs of six-month-old Eldana in a battered tin bath and sung a hyperactive Kanchi to sleep with *Ehsurusuru*. Earlier in the day, I'd played Kelelebosh with two limber, dimpled twins named Hagos and Girma and a boy called Lebna, who laughed off what I knew was a painfully mangled hand to beat us all. We'd finished up with a game I'd never heard of that involved a small bean bag, a pile of Pepsi bottle caps, and lots of triumphant running. The thought of children who could be my own distant kin dying for lack of medical care was intolerable.

As Makeda registered my presence, her lips widened in slow motion to reveal her perfect teeth like the sensuous peeling of a luscious fruit. My *washela* rose in Pavlovian enthusiasm until I remembered. I still could not grasp how women who held each other in the moist, warm earth of their own wombs would want to cut away from their daughters the source of one of life's sweetest pleasures.

I walked over to help, aware of sharp pebbles already in my shoes, but not caring. She wrinkled her nose, undoubtedly at my goat smell, and reluctantly handed me a couple of pill bottles, tapping the heads of a few of the children in front of her, their black coils already glistening in the morning sun.

While Father Wendimu had actually danced a little jig when I proposed shifting my studies to Addis Ababa University, Makeda herself was far less encouraging. She'd argued, "You need to go back to your woman, get your fine education. Devote yourself to helping HIV children, if you must, but do it where you belong."

Stung—who was she to decide where home was for this hanging man?—I'd argued that there were plenty of doctors in the States eager to do just that, but very few willing to commit to the children of Africa, which was, after all, as much my home continent as hers. That silenced her, but it didn't stop her from compressing her lips later in the day when she walked into Father Wendimu's room as the two of us were talking about the practicalities of making the shift from UCLA to Addis Ababa University.

Nor did it stop *me* from ruminating on her implication that I belonged with the materially pampered back in the U.S. If anything, I was savoring life's preciousness in this place where it was constantly under threat. Only last night, having finally soothed young Kanchi to sleep, I'd tiptoed out to see the stars, and Father Wendimu had come out to sit beside me on the rough ground, commenting quietly, "You know, she's tightly wound for a reason, is Kanchi. We buried her little cousin Afeworki only days before your arrival. The two of them were inseparable. Two years ago we woke to find the two of them curled around each other at our gate, and we never got quite clear on what their story was, except that they were related and spoke to each other in a secret language, which is more common, as I'm sure you know, in twins. I don't know how the child is going to manage now." What he didn't mention was that his own struggle to manage was constant. He and his tiny staff were all that stood between these children and the abyss.

I had grown very fond of this Khat-chewing infidel, so I was more than pleased when he caught me on my way to the shower this morning. He looked me up and down, for a brief second inserting a forefinger between my bare chest and the thick, wrap-around blue and white-fringed towel that Fleur's mother would have died for.

He grinned. "We may be poor, but our people weave the best towels in the world." He squinted up at the sun. "I wish the same benefactor who supplied our towels would subsidize the appetites of children recovering from starvation. The cost of *enset* and *injera* alone are criminal." He shook his head, and I noticed for the first time that he had a thin vertical scar running from his hairline to his jaw. How had he gotten it?

"But enough of my complaining," he continued. "I'm going in to town. Would you care to help me pick up some provisions? I'm sure that was one thing you didn't do as a boy." He grinned. "We can get you some stronger soap while we're there."

I was mortified. Even though I knew he was waiting for me, I showered for longer than usual, actually until the water ran out, and once I was back in my hut, I shoved away the normally endearing Menelik the goat.

Sniffing my arms and hands several times for reassurance, I went looking for Father Wendimu, noting in passing that Kanchi was sitting on the far side of the yard, her sticklike legs spayed out like a wishbone from her too-large turquoise and orange dress, her arms wrapped tightly around little Eldana in her lap.

I found Father Wendimu poking his head into Adey's corrugated-tin-roof hut. Stopping just behind him, I peeked in to see Makeda inside, busily sewing nearly knee-to-knee with Adey. Adey shot us her usual somber look and Makeda barely raised her eyes when Father Wendimu announced, "We're going now. Can you handle lunch on your own? We'll be back before dinnertime."

I ambled out to the yard while Father Wendimu ran back to his room for his car key. I held the rusty gate open for him as he passed through, but I struggled to close it behind me, muttering under my breath, "My kingdom for a can of WD-Forty."

"Here," called Father Wendimu, stepping back to deftly perform a little twist of the spring latch that made a terrible screech, but did the trick. Rubbing together his wide hands, he grinned. "Takes a little convincing, but easier than budging the hard head of a woman who thinks she knows what's best for you."

I laughed. So he knew. But there were more obstacles to be navigated that morning. One was the motor of Father Wendimu's battered blue Corolla. As I slid in onto the stained and frayed gray cloth seat, Father Wendimu shot me a smile, gave a little flourish with his hand, and turned the key to absolutely no effect. The motor didn't even bother trying to turn over. Not even a cough. The only sounds we heard were the *wra wra* of a couple of chickens and, in the distance, a wailing child. That is, until Father Wendimu slammed the dashboard and let loose a joltingly loud, *"Dikala!"* With a guilty look, he mumbled, "Sorry." He sighed and opened the driver's side door. "I guess it really is good I asked you to help me. Care to take a little walk, son?"

Joining him at the dented front bumper, I asked, "Is there really no way?"

I offered to open the hood, but he said with some asperity, "No. Don't bother. It was just like this the last time I tried." He reached into his pocket for a wrinkled handkerchief and swabbed his forehead. "Somehow I was hoping you might have brought some American luck with you. I know I should be more grateful for this old bus. It's gotten me into town more times than I can remember. But now"—he stuffed the handkerchief away again and kicked the already mangled bumper with one last flare of anger, muttering, "It is like me—barely fit for the junkyard. I will have to ask Yohannes to fix it the next time he comes for a cup of *bunna* and a game of chess. And then I will owe him." He shrugged. "But that is Ethiopia."

Our strides automatically adjusted themselves into an easy unison as we set out on the dusty road. Unsurprisingly, there wasn't a vehicle in sight, though we passed an occasional whitewashed chikka-walled house and even a couple of tan-colored villas hiding behind bright explosions of orange bougainvillea. I marveled that a shabby town like Tikil Dingay could house at least a few families that had managed to lift up from the heavy gravity of poverty.

Sadness washed over me that I hadn't been able to find Bekele and Iskinder. Father Wendimu had assured me they were probably alive—possibly in Addis Ababa, to which war had driven most of Tikil Dingay's version of a middle class. I'd reflected at the time that it said much that he and Makeda had chosen to stay.

I saw Father Wendimu fetch his handkerchief from his pocket and mop his forehead. The day was becoming as hot as the one on which I'd first arrived. I began to ask, "Why does she—" but he interrupted, waving his cloth to the left of us, where a shower of brilliant purple flowers spilled from a stand of handsome trees at the top of the hillside.

"Hagenia," he pronounced. "We use it sometimes when we can't get our hands on Prazinquantel. Damned tapeworms are the bane of my existence. Well, one of them, anyway." He made a wry face.

141

"Distillation of hagenia is only partially effective, but we do what we can. Sometimes it's barely better than nothing. On the plus side, though, I've never had it kill a child. What is your oath? 'First, do no harm'?"

We continued on awhile in silence, except for the sounds of our shoes scraping pebbles and dry bark, the buzz of bush crickets, and the piercing trill of starlings flying in formation overhead. This was something I'd never get over. The sounds of the Ethiopian countryside were a universe away from the leaf blowers, humming traffic, and screaming sirens of Southern California. I imagined Fleur by my side, inhaling the scents of burning frankincense and fruity-smelling leaves crushed by our sandals. The cheap-soapy smell of hyena dung would surely drive her mad with delight. But then I caught myself, my heart as leaden as a sack of teff flour. Fleur would never join me here in my homeland. And even though we would not be together again at all, my notion that I had cut down my hanging man was the height of absurdity.

I tried to summon interest in what Father Wendimu was saying. He was speaking about Yohannes, the cab driver who'd brought Abat to us on the third day I was here. Not only had Yohannes turned out to be the cousin of the man who'd driven me to Tikil Dingay, but was, according to my father, the nephew of Jerusalem, the woman who'd helped Enat care for our home in my first years of life. I remembered nothing of her, but her name caused me to reflect on the many ways my people had colonized themselves with Jewish mythology. After Abat had spoken of her, I'd reminded myself to say something about this to Sammie's Jacob when my father and I got back to the States.

That was when I was still imagining I'd be returning to Southern California. I had been so overjoyed that Abat and Zalelew were safe that nothing else mattered, not even the disappointment written across Father's face that his project of a lifetime had been thwarted by politics—lord only knew, Fleur would commiserate with that— nor his obvious discomfort whenever Makeda came into the room. I had tried to draw him out about that, tried right up to the eve of our planned drive back to Bole Airport for our hastily booked flight. We'd been sitting outside after the others had gone to bed, the high-pitched cry of a distant cheetah sending chills up and down my arms.

I asked him with a fake casualness: "Do you remember Makeda when she was little?"

"No," he said, his shoulder twitching almost imperceptibly. "Not so much." How could that be true?

"Do you know what happened to her parents?" I sought his eyes. "To her?" He shook his head. There was such terror in his expression that I could not bear to tell him, but that didn't stop me from wondering what terrible thing had stopped my father from asking what had happened to Demeke and Shewa Geteye. Why was he treating the daughter of his best friend like a stranger?

What a couple of tap dancers we were, eventually distracting ourselves with a conversation about Ethiopia's sorry relations with Somalia and Eritrea under a star-filled canopy that cared nothing of nations. All the while, I carried on my own rant, but internally, deciding right then that I would not return to the U.S. with Abat. If I could travel all this way to find my father, only to be met with such palpable dissembling, then I would be damned if I'd be guided by a need to satisfy his expatriate dreams.

I stood and told him so on the spot. Except, with my anger curbed by a self-betraying cowardice, I put it that I wanted to take advantage of being here to soak in a bit more of the country of my birth. I could see that he was shocked.

"But what of your school?"

"I'll deal with it when I get back." Heat rising in my face, I'd added, "As far as they know, I'm still looking for my father."

He looked as though I'd slapped him. "Your mother will not like this. You will have to tell her yourself."

I promised him I would call her before his plane touched down in L.A. But I still hadn't been able to bring myself to do it. Instead, here I was walking into town with the bonhomic Father Wendimu, who hummed under his breath as we continued along the pebbly road. We reached a bend and found ourselves approaching what looked like an Ethiopian version of the farmers markets of Pasadena and West Hollywood, though far more rough and enticing. Flanking the humble row of salmon, green, and cream painted shops where I'd first gotten my directions to the orphanage, *netela*-clad men and boys and women wearing colorfully embroidered *kemis* displayed a vast variety of goods overflowing from large wooden flats supported by wheelbarrows.

Many of the men had flung off their *Plakkies*, which were strewn like a dance-step diagram on the dusty ground beneath the flats. Faded floral umbrellas stretched to a suddenly cloud-scudding sky, protecting vendors and perishables. Which didn't stop the flies from making an incessant buzzing accompaniment to the lively patter of good-natured bargaining. After I was offered a slice of honeyed *dabo* from a young boy's colorful flat *ukhaat moot* basket, I was tempted to taste everyone's wares—my mouth watering at the fragrant ripe bananas, soft *lab* cheese wrapped in banana leaves, the spiced beef jerky that was called *Quwanta*.

But Father Wendimu wanted to introduce me to everyone, and before I knew it, we'd had our goods bundled in plastic bags and I was rushing to catch up with him as he pushed forward into the store where I had purchased my Coke and map of Amara. The screen door, rent by holes large enough to admit swarms of mosquitos, banged behind me just as I saw the skinny man behind the counter pass a white packet to Father Wendimu. Both of them glanced over at me, exchanged a meaningful look, and then Father Wendimu cleared his throat rather formally before asking for a couple of five pound bags of teff flour. I knew I had just witnessed an illegal transaction, and the wide-eyed shopkeeper had no way of knowing that I'd never tell. He looked only too relieved when Father Wendimu reached across the counter, clapped him on the shoulder, hefted up the two bags, and told him that, since we wouldn't be able to carry much more on this trip, he'd probably be back again in a day or two. I caught him winking at the man just before I led the way out the door.

Our conversation on the way back was far more serious. There is something sobering about carrying a heavy load. The sun had reached its zenith, and we kept stopping to swipe the sweat from our eyes. Father Wendimu suggested we take shelter under a stand of *dobera glabra* trees and make a little picnic of Coca-Cola and the *kolo* he'd bought, wrapped in paper cones. I was only too happy to take a rest, but wasn't so thrilled when Father Wendimu mentioned that the wife of the man who'd sold us the teff flour had recently lost her oldest sister to AIDS.

"It's the anal sex, you know. That and the damned clitorectomies and Pharaoinic circumcisions."

"What's a Pharaonic circumcision?" I laid down my *kolo* on top of one of the plastic bags.

"You're not familiar with it? You're lucky. The fools remove the clitoris and labia, stretch the remaining skin across the vagina from each side, and stitch them together so it's nice and tight for the women's husbands. Of course, they have to keep doing it over and over again each time they have sex. You can imagine what a fertile fuel that's provided for the conflagration of HIV throughout Africa." He sighed. "It's what happened to Makeda, but she managed to avoid the sex."

I stood and staggered to a nearby bush, vomiting up my *dabo* and *kolo*.

When I returned, Father Wendimu looked abject. "What an idiot I am."

This was more information than Makeda had shared. If I'd thought the Hanging Man was intolerable, what of these millions of women whose chances died on crosses of ignorance and cruelty?

When we got back, it was dark. I looked in on Makeda's room, but her bedclothes were unwrinkled. She had to be with one of the children. I knew that many of them regularly suffered nightmares.

That night, I had nightmares of my own. Fleur was a pale ghost haunting me through a disjointed series of images: back in Carthay Circle, clutching my sheets to her generous breasts, her eyes pooling with tears of hurt and accusation; skipping with Stanley across the one of Caltech's manicured lawns, something I'd actually seen her do; shoving her back against a rusty protruding nail in her Nana's closet. I'd not seen her do that myself, but I'd shuddered when she'd described to me this childhood practice of hers. It was this that made me wonder if she truly was an Asperger's girl. Autistic or not, the professor on my psych rotation would definitely classify it as masochistic.

I got up from my straw bed, nearly tripping over the protruding leg of Menelik as I exited the hut. His goat smell competed with the scent of jasmine. I felt impelled to light a cigarette. I'd resumed my adolescent habit in the past few days, this time smoking Nyalas rather than Marlboros. Enat would kill me if she knew.

The acrid taste of smoke defeated the scents of jasmine, myrrh, even goat. I poked a finger through a smoke ring as a shooting star sped by. Who was the masochist, Fleur or me? My love of two women of an unusual fate kept me strung up on my own painful cross. Fleur, twice exceptional, condemned to be an outsider by birth and upbringing. Makeda, condemned to estrangement from her instincts, the swift slashes of an old woman's knife guaranteeing she'd never know the carnal pleasure I'd imagined in all my foolish fantasies.

Really, each of them was superior to me. Makeda, a flaming, sturdy Erythrina tree; Fleur, like one of her namesakes, a delicately nuanced rose, vulnerable to the vagaries of the wind. The harshest wind of all had been my phone call to her. I had been ice. I had not known how to announce my betrayal in any other way.

I don't know what time I returned to the hut and fell asleep, but I woke far too early, shooting up from my makeshift bed. The sun was just beginning to rise. It was way too early for such screaming. I ran outside.

For a moment, I thought they were doing some odd dance. Hand to hand, moving in an ancient ritual. But my senses came to me, and I realized that Father Wendimu was struggling with a green-shirted boy who brandished something that glittered in the dawning sun. My body knew it was a knife before my mind fully realized it. With a life of their own, my legs propelled me forward, my ears ringing with the shouts of women.

I saw the young man slash the neck of Father Wendimu, saw the blood spring up against his ebony skin like a crimson necklace. I leapt to grab the boy's wrist and struggled to wrest the knife from him. For someone so skinny, he was surprisingly strong. I felt something caress my left hand. It took a moment for me to register the pain, which nearly bent me double. I pulled back my right hand and slammed his face with my fist, feeling satisfaction at the sound of bone shattering. The boy dropped to his knees. In my confusion, I wondered, *Is he praying?*

But the knife was still in his hand. I kicked so hard that it literally flew through the air. The boy collapsed onto his side, and for a moment I didn't care if I'd killed him. I turned anxiously toward Father Wendimu, but Adey had already reached him and was pressing her *shama* against his neck. I motioned to her and whipped off my shirt and held it firmly against a point between his carotid artery and his jugular vein. The blood was still springing up from my own wound, and Adey now pressed a pleat of her shama against my hand as I put full pressure on Father Wendimu's neck. I realized I was shouting. "Don't die on us! Don't you dare die!" I was still too close to terror to trust my clinical assessment, but the wound seemed superficial enough. If he got stitched up and we could avoid infection, he might actually live.

Makeda knelt beside me. I smelled the fear emanating from her pores. A quick glance confirmed she held the boy's knife. Returning my gaze to Father Wendimu—who was blinking in confusion, as if he literally didn't know what had hit him—I said, "We need to get him to a hospital." The two women stared at me, and it occurred to me there was no hospital in Tikil Dingay.

Adey cried mournfully, "A hospital is only in Assela."

I tried to reassure her, "I believe he will live." I struggled to subdue my trembling. "But I will need your help."

I gestured with my head toward the boy, who lay curled in on himself just a few feet away.

"I'm afraid *he* will live, too," muttered Makeda, "but with a crooked nose. I warned Father Wendimu that his *khat* habit would attract danger like flies to shit."

I understood her rage, but hadn't we chewed *khat* together only a few nights before? Despite the distraction, my critical care training kicked in. Showing Adey where to press, I rose and ran through the options. There was one. Only one. "Okay, then, we'll start with Father Wendimu. Where's the best place to clean this wound? I'll need your help getting him up. I hope to God you have a decent suture pack."

That evening, after we'd seen to the children—who'd stayed frozen in their beds while chaos reigned in the yard—and with Father Wendimu in his bed attended by Adey and a chastened young Dawit stretched out on the floor, Makeda and I sat outside together and shared a Nyala. The moon was full and bright, and I could see every nuance of her features. She looked beautiful, even with her hair in a lopsided nap and deep circles under her eyes. There was a little streak of teff flour on her cheek, and I gently brushed it away with two fingers. She gave me a faint smile and gently took my bandaged hand in her own. It throbbed with pain, but I didn't care.

Looking up at the sky, she said in a voice just slightly above a whisper, "Your courage. It was the spirit of the kudu." I started in recognition. I knew it was true. I saw the eyes of the kudu—as brown as the earth—fog over and close. It was one of the few times in my life where a moment from the past was as alive as the present, as if two universes had merged. Still holding my hand, Makeda twisted around to face me. "You have redeemed the calf and done what God sent you here to do." She let go of my hand. "And now you have to go."

I rose up to my feet, stumbling a little, my voice simultaneously angry and pleading. "Go? There is no way I'm going to go! Can't you see that you need me?"

She laughed harshly. "Do you think I need you?" She thumped her chest. "I have you forever. You are written on the inside of my skin."

"No! This is crazy. This place is falling apart all around you. You are two women and an old man. What would you have done without me today?"

She pushed herself up from the ground, brushing the dirt from her *habesha kemis*. "Yes. We needed you today, and we will never forget you for what you have done. The children will tell stories about you. They will tell others who come afterward what you did." Her face was somber as she locked her eyes into mine. "And now you must go so that I do not suffer every day with a longing for something I will never experience. You will go to spare me the pain of never bearing your child."

She began to walk away, but then she turned back, clearly struggling to express something she hadn't thought through. "Assefa, you will go as a kindness to me. Out of your love for me. But you must leave that love behind as you left that kudu. I have learned from my own suffering that love has a life of its own, that we cannot possess it like a jewel, like a medal. Sometimes love must be released so that something else can be lived. My *enat* and *abat* have gone from my life forever so that I can serve as many children as possible. You must not even think of me when you are gone, you must not hold me with your spirit. If you do, we are so connected that I will feel it, and I will not be free for the particular joy God has allotted to me. Now you must find what God wants to allot to you."

And with those words, I was flung onto the sorrowful road of learning how to say goodbye to Miryam Makeda.

Chapter Twelve
Fleur

LET'S FACE IT. I'm a weakling. After all he'd done to try to rescue me from the void, I didn't have the heart to say no to Bob. When he invited me for dinner, all I wanted was to get home as soon as possible, put on my pink flannel PJs, sneak a gallon of Ben & Jerry's Chunky Monkey, slither under the covers with Jillily, pig out, and die. I think I was as surprised as Bob was when I opened my mouth and heard myself utter a traitorous, "Sure."

How could I have predicted what would happen that night? Of all people, I'm more than familiar with the power of the sensitive dependence on initial conditions, known commonly as the Butterfly Effect, a phrase coined by mathematician Edward Lorenz to describe the impact of small events on much larger ones in our interdependent universe. According to chaos theory, the flap of a butterfly's wings in Brazil might lead to a tornado in, say, New York. The trouble is that, though we may take from that image the awareness that our choices really do matter, we never know exactly how.

All I knew when I entered Bob's apartment was that it was even more Bob-ish than his car, smelling comfortingly of spaghetti sauce, musk, and the heavy product he wore in his hair. The place was a warren of unmatched furniture, two-foot-tall mountains of books, only slightly shorter stacks of academic journals and papers, and Ikea-style shelving displaying carefully arrayed seashells of all sorts grouped by type, color, and size.

I was aware of Bob silently watching me, as if daring me to make fun of his eccentric collection, but I was more interested in how he'd arranged his shells in patterns. I knew about patterns. At certain points in my life, they were all there was to give me a sense of cohesion and meaning, a perfect antidote to the void. Reflections of light in the waves of a pool, birds hopping in and out of branches, fractals, the Fibonacci Sequence playing itself out across the natural world. The possibility of a pattern in my own life was another story. If I could ever manage to discern that one, I might actually deserve my Nobel.

But now a cluster of conch shells grabbed me from the edge of the abyss. I walked over and put one of the larger ones to my ear and heard the roar of the ocean. I commented on it to Bob, who favored me with a tolerant smile. "You know," he said patiently, "my friends in middle school—not that I had many—used to make fun of people who thought they could hear the ocean in a conch shell, when in fact it's captured ambient noise around them resonating inside the shell. But that's never stopped me from sticking one to my ear when I'm stuck at home and missing the sound of the sea."

Mumbling, "Of course," I felt mortified at my ignorance.

But Bob was moving away toward a narrow hallway. He looked back at me. "Speaking of shells and sound, take a look at this." I followed him obediently, noticing several Lakers pennants and a few framed science fair awards pinned up on the dimly lit wall. I turned after him into his bedroom. The effect was even more claustrophobic. There were more shelves here, one of them looming rather precariously over a single bed covered by—I blushed for him—a Star Wars-themed bedspread. He followed my eyes and shrugged without an ounce of embarrassment. "Never thought to get rid of it. Still crazy about those movies. Especially the first one. Thought it was the most amazing thing I'd ever seen. What about you? Did you like it?"

Who didn't? My feelings about Bob changed forever right there and then. A man who didn't dissolve in shame at a moment like this was either very stupid (he wasn't), very naïve (well, not that much), or supremely comfortable in his own skin. I envied him.

Bob took a large brown and cream conch from the second to top shelf, and as he lifted it to his lips, I saw a tassel dangling from the other end. He blew into what I now realized was a hole at the tight end of the shell. It made a long, reverberating vibrato. Bob smiled at my obvious surprise. He rubbed the blowhole with the bottom of his T-shirt before handing me the instrument. As I put my lips to the shell, he remarked, "It's called a *nagak*. Korean. They play it in rituals. The shell's from a large sea snail, *Charonia Tritonis*. Triton's trumpet."

I knew about Triton from the days I'd been tutored by Adam, knew he was half man and half fish, the son of Poseidon, or, as the Romans called him, Neptune. As Adam had remarked at the time, a little moist-eyed, "So it's kind of poetic that we call the largest moon of Neptune Triton." I'd learned by then that Adam had pretty much been deserted by his own senator father, and if I wasn't already a little in love with him then, his teary eyes had sealed the deal. God, I thought with a pang, how I'd love to fall into Adam's arms now, comforted by his Campbell's Chicken Soup B.O.

I found myself blowing harder than I'd intended into the *nagak*. "Wow!" Bob exclaimed. "You've got some serious chops." I made him explain the expression, promising myself to enter it into my *Diary of Patois, Cant, and Jargon* when I got home.

Returning the *nagak* to its place, Bob retrieved another shell from a lower shelf. I resisted the temptation to diagram the design of the dandruff on the top of his head. "Look at this beauty," he murmured, passing it to me.

I'd never seen anything quite like it. It was apricot in hue, with little tendrils of turquoise and a multitude of ornate figures carved into it. I looked up, "What?"

"It's from India. They call it a *sankha*. They use it in religious ceremonies." He placed a finger on one of its delicate images. "This one's Vishnu." He slid his finger down. "And this one here's Lakshmi." He passed it to me. "The person I bought it from told me she's a symbol of female fertility." The sound of Assefa's snapping condom in my ears, I blanched and passed the shell back to Bob with unseemly haste.

He frowned. "Am I boring you?"

I shook my head, spitting out a vehement "No!" Itching to get out of the room, I said, "You know, I'm a little thirsty."

Bob clapped his hand to his forehead, nearly blinding himself with the tip of the *sankha*. He set it back on the shelf. "Jeez, what a jerk I am. Definitely not a good host." He hurried toward the doorway, then turned. "Red or white?"

I looked at him blankly.

"Wine."

"Oh. Well, since you ask … red, please."

"Merlot?"

"Great." I followed him out of the room.

His kitchen was a humble affair, more suited to a railway coach than an apartment. A few cereal boxes, a giant cellophane bag of popcorn, and a quartet of canisters containing various shapes of dried pasta lined a Formica counter of a particularly odious shade of chartreuse.

He caught me staring. "Fifties. Lousiest period on the planet for interior design. It's really a disturbing color, isn't it?"

I smiled, lying, "Oh, it's not so bad. Just … unusual."

"You think? They had it everywhere when I was a kid. Not in your home?"

Thinking back to father's modernistic, granite and chrome-heavy kitchen, expanded to feed all the babies he'd saved from the devil abortionists, I shook my head. And hurriedly changed the subject. "Seems like a lot of those conches are used for religious purposes. Are you religious yourself?"

"Ha!" Bob pulled out the cork with surprising savoir-faire. Retrieving a couple of water-stained wine glasses and carefully pouring, he said, "I was the only child of a pair of Jewish atheists." He gave a short laugh and passed my glass to me, clinking it so hard with his own that they both spilled onto an olive green linoleum floor embellished with haphazard flecks of baby-poop yellow. I grabbed a paper towel from its standing dispenser and knelt to wipe our spills, with Bob muttering, "You don't have to do that." He took the soggy paper from me, squashed it into a ball, and tossed it across the room into a wastebasket. "Not bad," he crowed, then nodded toward the living room. "Shall we?" I took a nice long sip as we walked, deciding that Bob had surprisingly good taste in wine.

As we settled onto a tattered but cozy slipcovered sofa, Bob clicked glasses with me again, this time intoning quite seriously, "Here's to friendship." I took what I realized too late was an indecorously long swig of wine. Bob raised an eyebrow and set down his glass on the pine coffee table. Running his finger around the glass's rim, he said, "Now where were we? Oh, yeah. Religion. What I learned as a kid about the religion of my ancestors would easily pass through the eye of a needle." He paused to make sure I got the joke. I smiled obediently, using the occasion to throw back another overzealous swig of wine. "Oh, I knew that Jews as a group laid claim to the moral basis of Western Civilization. You know, the Ten Commandments and all. One of my favorite movies"—he grinned— "besides *Star Wars*, was *Raiders of the Lost Ark*. I learned from that about the stone tablets inscribed with the commandments being supposedly hidden in the Ark of the Covenant."

You can imagine where that took me. If only Assefa's father hadn't gone off to research the Ethiopian version of where that Ark was housed, I might be in my lover's arms right now. But he wasn't my lover anymore, was he?

As if sensing my sadness, Bob rose abruptly and turned on a laptop sitting on a small brown side chair. He looked back at me. "Ryan Adams?" I nodded and took advantage of the moment to finish the rest of my glass. It really was good.

When he sat down again, he seemed a few inches closer. He gave a little laugh. "My parents used to joke that I was breaking the commandment to honor your father and mother whenever I objected to the unfairness of their rules. They'd inevitably come back with something like, 'Life isn't fair,' or as my dad liked to paraphrase his fellow Columbia grad, William Goldman, 'Life's not fair, but at least it's fairer than death.'"

I knew that was a cue to laugh, but I couldn't. My heart felt like drying concrete. We sat for a long while without speaking, music filling the silence. Bob roused himself to retrieve the wine bottle from the kitchen. As he refilled our glasses, it occurred to me that he was keeping pace with me.

Ryan Adams had reached his second refrain of "Damn, Sam, I love a woman that rains," when I suddenly realized I had to use the toilet. Excusing myself hastily, I ran up the hall and pulled down my panties just in time to release a veritable flood and one tiny puce-ish poop that would fit in perfectly with Bob's kitchen décor. I felt grateful for his fragrant green tea hand wash and poured a little into the toilet bowl after I dried my hands.

Walking a little shakily back to the living room, I inadvertently plopped down an inch or two closer to Bob than before. He asked in a tone of concern, "Everything okay?"

I assured him that it was, hazily aware that, right now, the word "Okay" had absolutely no meaning. The last time I'd investigated the word's origins, I'd found multiple possibilities ranging from the French *aux Cayes* (referring to good rum from the Haitian port Cayes) to *orl korrekt*, a humorous misspelling of the "all correct" used in the U.S. in the seventeenth century. Tightening my lips with Germanic precision, I let slip a "*But vich vun is korrekt, mein herr?*" accompanied by a sardonic little laugh. Which seemed to send Bob on a defensive tear.

"Listen," he said, "just so you don't think my family was gloomy all the time, you should know that we went snorkeling together at least once a year, sometimes in Baja or Hawaii, but more often in La Jolla or San Diego. That's how I fell in love with the sea." The tenderness with which his lips wrapped themselves around the word "sea" had the effect of softening my leaden heart. I gave him an encouraging smile. He cocked his head at me, perhaps not quite sure whether to trust me, but continued anyway, "We weren't exactly rich. The take-home pay of a couple of high school science teachers is pretty pathetic. But my folks knew how to have fun. Almost every weekend, they'd have dinner parties. Mostly potluck dinners for other science teachers, whose kids were just as dorky as I was." Bob leaned back and closed his eyes, as if summoning up a memory. "Benjamin Hurley was the most pathetic of the group; he actually let my pet parakeet Teddy out the window to see if he'd fly back again. He didn't."

I was aware of Bob's loss traveling on some invisible railroad from his heart to mine. I put my hand on his shoulder and he took it and held it against his chest. I could feel his heart under his navy blue shirt. Just as I registered that it was beating rather quickly, Bob opened his eyes, leaned forward, and kissed me on the lips. I was so stunned that I didn't stop him. If anything, I felt like a neutral observer watching him fold his torso across mine, his hand slowly traveling from my hand to my neck, pulling me toward him. I let his tongue discover my tongue. Our mouths tasted of Merlot. Bob pulled away for a moment. He looked stunned. I said nothing, but reached toward the table and drained my glass. Bob followed suit and sent me a hopeful looking smile. I barely recognized him. In unison, we rose from the couch. I followed him to his room.

I'd forgotten about the bedspread. I threw him a sideways look. He was close to my age, but so much younger. I sat on the edge of the bed and motioned him to me. I cupped my hand over the bulge in his jeans, then undid the button and tried to pull down the zipper, hampered by what I fuzzily thought must be the world's biggest erection.

Bob was breathing so heavily I thought he might have a heart attack. We fumbled together until we got the zipper down. I reached toward his member, painfully aware that it was nothing like Assefa's, but he pushed me back onto the bed, and, stronger than I would have thought, lifted me up so that he could get me further up on the bed.

He kissed my neck. Then my eyelids. They fluttered like shy butterflies at the touch of his lips. He inserted his tongue into my mouth. Pawing at my blouse, he managed with my own assistance to remove all my clothes. He put his finger in my tweeter. On a cloud of melt, I asked him to suck my little man.

"What do you mean?" he asked thickly.

I realized I'd used Assefa's word for it, but at that point lust trumped everything. "My clitoris," I responded, rather loudly.

"Ohhh," he breathed. And complied.

Things moved rather quickly after that. He moved back up my body, his fingers pinching my nipple and his eyes locked into mine. "Condom!" I cried, as he came.

As the sticky wetness trickled out of me, I thought, with some astonishment, *This is getting to be a habit*. With a shudder, it occurred to me that I might be inhabiting parallel universes in which the same things happen. The same unwanted things. I pushed that one to the farthest corner of my mind.

From the other room, the sultry sounds of the Chromatics' *Cherry* slinked in. Bob rolled off me, and I felt around for his T-shirt, which had come off somehow in the heat of things. I couldn't remember him removing it, but also knew it would be close by. I lifted up my bottom, noting that Bob's semen had spread like a Rorschach across the nose of Chewbacca the Wookie. I shoved the shirt over it before I let my bottom down again.

Bob was lying on his side, his head propped up by his hand, his thick eyebrows furrowed with worry. "Was that okay? I mean, I know I ...."

I rolled toward him and put a hand on his mouth. "Don't," I said. I put my lips against his damp forehead and left them there long enough to feel him relax.

Before I knew it, I'd begun to cry. Bob, who'd been on the whole a gentle lover, was kind enough not to say anything. He stroked my arm. His tenderness had the effect of drawing my hurt and longing for Assefa to the surface like a phlebotomist's needle. But there was something about Bob's actual touch that reminded me of Grandfather. Grandfather, whose lined and pop-veined hand could soothe me in the most troubling of times. As my tears subsided, Bob traced a slow circle around my belly button with one finger and softly said, "Once upon a time, oh, maybe about fourteen billion years ago, the void got so weary of itself that it erupted into a giant explosion. The eruption took so much energy that it was followed by a dark and quiet state that took ages and ages, at least a couple of hundreds of millions to years, to cool into forces and matter that would coalesce into all kinds of new possibilities ...."

I reflected for probably the zillionth time how much our scientific understanding of the origin of the universe was echoed by the Biblical myth of creation.

Bob burst into my bubble. "You don't regret it?"

Momentarily disoriented, I thought he was referring to the birth of the cosmos. But then I realized he was talking about our having had sex. I shook my head. "Not really, but maybe I should. I saw this movie once—I can't remember what it was called or even the name of the actor who said it. He said he had no regrets. I remember thinking, 'What kind of asshole has no regrets?'" I stared at Bob, who lifted himself onto his elbows and stared back at me. "Maybe I've become that asshole." I shrugged. "Oh, I don't know. Aadita tells Sammie and me all the time that the key to tranquility lies in the capacity to let go."

It was as if I'd set off a land mine. Bob exploded. "Let go? I hate that shit!" He jumped off the bed and stood with his arms akimbo, his penis shriveling as if in fear of his rage. "As a scientist you should know better. The crisis of global warming is spinning out of control precisely because people have decided it's too much of a giant bummer to do anything about, anyway, so let's just ignore it. No worries. It's all good. Great. Let's achieve personal serenity while thousands of species, including our own, slip through our fingers. We *need* to feel regret if we're going to stop this slide into disaster. And if we don't change, all the Buddhists, Christians, and Voodoo Hoodoos are gonna regret it."

As Bob ranted, I could feel myself split into two Fleurs. I knew he was shouting out of a deep hurt, one that had nothing to do with what we'd just been up to, and it was almost funny, but not really, not when you considered what he was upset about. Of course, he was right, but his timing was, well, I guess you could call it Geek Timing. It was hard to believe that this shouting, naked giant was the same Bob who, only a week ago, was an object of mildly annoyed amusement in my eyes. At the same time, the raised voice, the male presence looming over me brought back with unwelcome vividness the voidish terror kicked up with some regularity by Father in his I-hate-children-underfoot moods. I wrestled free from the harness of politeness and flung myself off the bed and down the hall to the bathroom. Locking the door, I noticed that Bob's clearly deficient plumbing had conspired to leave a vagrant portion of my previous little poop in the bowl. I resisted the temptation to lay strips of toilet paper across the seat, reminding myself that it was my own bottom that had been the last one to press against it.

Bob knocked softly at the door as I peed. The heat had clearly left him. "Fleur, I'm so sorry. Can you forgive me? I can't think what came over me."

I didn't reply immediately, but carefully wiped as much of Bob's semen as I could away from my tweeter, praying that I had some terrible congenital malady that rendered me infertile until I remembered Baby X languishing in the hole in my heart. I reached for what looked to be a relatively clean washcloth hanging off an uneven plastic towel rack, wetted it in the sink, and completed the job, rubbing my vaginal lips rather cruelly as if I could retroactively crush any sperm that might be lurking in the dark of my folds, biding its time before creeping toward its glistening goal. I contemplated stepping into Bob's bathtub, but seeing its hair-carpeted, rust-streaked state, opted instead to open Bob's tiny excuse for a vanity. I found a comb there, and it looked just as I might have imagined. I rinsed the dandruff specks from its black teeth, then painstakingly tugged it through my matted blond hair. My lips, still slightly plump from kissing, were stained a deep shade of plum by the Merlot. Baring white fangs, I hissed at myself like a wild cat, thinking the previously un-thought thought. *Assefa.* What in God's name had I done?

I closed the toilet lid and sat down. If Assefa only knew. But what was I worrying about? He wouldn't even care. I should be grateful to Bob for taking pity on me. The fact was, he'd shown more courage than I would ever have imagined. I was the head of our physics pack, and he'd idolized me like a teenager, achingly, impossibly. Making a move on me had been a hell of a risk. Then again, I'd caved in pretty quickly. *No, Fleur, be honest. Instantly.* I felt my cheeks go red with shame.

Bob had clearly given up now. I heard him padding around the apartment. The music stopped. Clinking sounds. He must be clearing up. Now footsteps re-approached. Another knock. This one less hesitant. "Fleur. Do you like to tie?"

Really? Having had me once, the guy was getting brazen. I fumbled with the lock and flung open the door. "Bob Ballantine, I am *not* interested in bondage!"

He was dressed. Me: naked. His eyes looking determinedly in mine, he laughed a little nervously. "Fleur, please. I feel terrible. Taking advantage of you like …. Anyway, I was wondering. Thai food. I asked if you liked Thai food."

I was mortified. Head down, I hurried past him and swung into the bedroom. The bed was made, the Wookie looking none the worse for wear, and my clothes were folded carefully in a pile, right across the chest of Princess Leah. I had to hand it to Bob. He gave me time to compose myself. I heard the toilet flush, then Bob calling out from what might be the living room, "If you don't hate me forever, I thought I could at least offer the dinner you thought you were coming here for." Straightening my chin, I walked down the hall. He shrugged as I entered the room. "I know I'm an asshole, but …."

"Bob," I said, dropping onto the couch, "We're undoubtedly both assholes. And I really don't want to do that again. Ever. Not because it wasn't nice, but for a whole lot of reasons, most of them having to do with the fact that I clearly don't know how to do relationships. But we're colleagues. And I'd like to be your friend. Shake?"

I extended a hand to him and he gave it a shake that seemed a bit more confident than it would have a few hours ago. It was all a little surreal. I knew we were both thinking about where these hands had just been. I shook my head. "Oh God, what a day." I got up and walked over to his computer, clicking on Pandora. My heart was heavier than lead. But I knew there'd be plenty of time for that. Too much time. The Foals were singing "My Number." I turned around to face Bob, who looked as though he was holding his breath.

"You know," I said, "I really am kind of partial to Thai."

Chapter Thirteen
Fleur

EVEN THOUGH IT barely took ten minutes, the drive home from Caltech after Bob dropped me off felt interminable. I still couldn't believe I'd slept with Bob Ballantine! But my mortification paled in comparison with my continued state of shock that Assefa had discarded me like some used plastic bag.

Thanks to Bob, I now knew where those bags ended up—in toxic swirls like the 270,000 square miles worth of horror called the Great Pacific Garbage Patch, located midway between Hawaii and California. And in the stomachs of marine birds and animals. The image was so voidishly nauseating that when I arrived back at the Fiskes', for one brief second I thought that the smell assaulting my nostrils was my imagination.

"Hello? Is anybody home?" No Stanley. No Gwennie. No Jillily—bad girl, she was undoubtedly hiding. The previous year, on my way to giving a talk on the Higgs Boson at Paris Descartes University, I'd passed an ancient urinal on Boulevard Arago whose stench was unbelievable. This was worse. Who knew that female cats could spray at all? It had happened the first time back in November, when we babysat Sammie's Midge here at the house for a week while Sammie and Aadita flew to Delhi for Aadita's mother's funeral.

The name Midget was the ultimate misnomer. These past years, the butter-colored creature had put on even more weight, and as soon as we brought him home with us, he put paid to our delusion that he and Jillily would get along by actually lumbering over to sit on top of her. Jillily had barely managed to ooze out from under Midge's rump like a slow-moving black turd.

Since then, I'd been trying to explain to Jillily that lifting her tail to let loose a great arc of foul-smelling liquid was no longer necessary to persuade us to evict the uncouth intruder from the house. But alas, spraying turned out to be an attraction that, once discovered, had an atavistic life of its own.

The thing was: the stench was so pervasive that we had no idea where it was actually coming from. Closing the front door, I flung my backpack onto Stanley's favorite leather chair and—not for the first time—dropped to my knees, sniffing my way from the book-cluttered living room to the book-cluttered den to each of the three book-cluttered bedrooms. The good news was that Jillily didn't seem to have sprayed the books. The bad news was that I (a) banged my head as I came up from a knot of old Christmas ribbon and a ratty catnip ball under my bedside table, (b) managed to snag my favorite jeans on a nail protruding from the hardwood floor in Stanley's bedroom, (c) and still could not find the source of the smell.

It was only after I'd showered, changed into a fresh pair of pants, and opened the freezer to get some ice for my head that Jillily deigned to make an appearance, winding her way in and out of my legs and making enough eye contact to guilt me into a little snack of Ritz Crackers and cheese. And if you think that's an odd treat for a cat, consider Midge's favorite snack in his vegan home—curried cauliflower and broccoli—not to mention the Fiskes' long-departed Moggy's preference for Gwennie's spinach omelets.

It was when Jillily was cleaning off every lick of cheddar with gourmandish gusto that I heard the key in the lock.

Gwennie called out, "Halloooo?"

I found her in the living room, reaching a plump arm toward the bent shoulders of an odd incarnation of Stanley, one with a frantically winking eye and what looked like a giant white shower cap clamped against his jaw.

When he saw me, Stanley tried to smile, his face looking more froggish than ever. "Hawawa ma soro," he garbled.

Gwennie laughed, and then inclined her head toward him in apology. "Poor dear," she explained. "Emergency root canal went south. The tooth turned out to be rotten through and through. They had to pull it right away." Gwennie's face was a mask of worry. "I think it took the stuffing out of him." She led him to his favorite chair and helped him into it. Stanley stunned the both of us, I think, by commencing to cry.

"Ish the damned painkillers," Stanley managed to get out between sobs. "They futz with the brainsh executive function."

Fighting hard against the impulse to flap, I forced out a panicky, "What can I do?" I *knew* what I could do: spare them seeing me fall into a full-out fit of pinching and banging. I adored Stanley H. Fiske and could not bear seeing him in such pain.

"There's a love," Gwennie said, laying her battered black purse and a sheaf of papers onto the sofa. "Fetch us some fresh ice, will you? I'll get Stanley into bed and we can prop the ice pack against his face and see if he can sleep. It'll be the best thing. The endodontist said that, by tomorrow, he'll be right as rain."

I didn't know what rain had to do with it, but I rushed off to the kitchen, happy to fend off the void by doing something useful. It was only then that it occurred to me that I hadn't managed to ice my own aching head, but given how Stanley looked, I'd merely been a tourist in the ice-needing department.

Stanley conked out as soon as Gwennie tucked him in, his face propped against the ice pack and his body curved into a long cocoon. As luck would have it, the phone rang as soon as Gwennie and I were settled into our favorite perches in the den, feet overlapping from opposite ends of the sofa and Jillily stretched luxuriously across my belly and chest.

"Oh, shit," hissed Gwennie. "And he just got to sleep."

I leapt from the couch, displacing an indignant Jillily, who was forced to vault with me. Snatching up the phone, I heard Mother's voice, a little breathless. "You'll be happy to know he's on his way back." I froze. Mother began to giggle, sounding a little unsteady. "The thing is, I had to get off the phone with Abeba before she could tell me when he'll arrive."

I quickly tiptoed down the hall to the kitchen and pulled the door closed. "Why in the world did you get off the phone?" My heart was thudding a mile a minute.

"Well, the thing is …." Why was Mother dawdling? "How could I have known? I hate call waiting. It was one of those annoying political calls. I suppose I could have called Abeba back, but I thought that letting you know was the first priority? It's wonderful, isn't it—you two lovebirds reunited."

I was speechless. Looking down, I saw that Jillily had spied the ball of Christmas ribbon. Her ears lay flat against her head, and her mouth had that puffy expression that signified she was in touch with her inner murderer. She pounced on the ribbon and, with a low growl, held it in her front paws while her back legs scrabbled fiercely against it.

I lay the phone down on the kitchen table next to a nearly dead vaseful of the unnaturally early-blooming Austins and left the room, barely aware that Mother was still speaking.

As I stumbled up the hall, Stanley poked a head out of his bedroom. His remaining hair stood straight up from his scalp like Bob's had after sex.

There was nothing for it. I backed up against the wall, slid down, and began banging my head until Gwennie rushed over and shouted at me to stop. She pulled me up and hugged me as Mack-truckishly as Nana would in the old days, and, just as it had then, it did the trick.

Stanley insisted on joining Gwen and me at the kitchen table. Over a cup of chamomile tea, I ended up spilling the beans about everything—Assefa, Bob, Mother's call. I had to hand it to Stanley. He took the news about me sleeping with his newest assistant without batting an eye. Of course, the fact that he was grimacing in horrible pain and had an ice pack covering half his face might have masked his true feelings. Then again, he'd been the one who'd handled the job of taking me back to New York to inform my anti-abortionist father that I was pregnant at thirteen. Forget Bob Ballantine; Hector Hernandez had managed to seduce me with two words, "Beautiful dove."

I wasn't feeling so doveish right now. More like clumsy and crowy. But thirteen again, for sure.

It didn't help that Gwennie was managing to be a bit clumsy herself. "Sweetheart," she said, sliding a hand across the table to take mine, "You know, not everything is solved by ... getting physical."

Stanley flung his ice pack onto the table and jumped out of his chair, stretching his froggish figure to full height. "Gwennie Fiske. You sound like a god damned old maid. Give the girl a break. She needed to know she's still desirable."

I stared at him and only shut my mouth when I realized my jaw was hanging open. Stanley was right. That was exactly what had happened. I felt both mortified and relieved and more than a little guilty that I'd used Bob Ballantine to salve my silly vanity. But then I remembered how triumphant Bob had looked after we'd slept together and wondered who'd used whom.

Of course, by now Gwennie was filled with remorse and had to make more amends than a roomful of Bill W's.

Feeling a post-banging headache coming on, I fled to my room, averting my eyes from the wall mirror while stripping naked, and slid gratefully under the covers. Well, actually, what I slid under was Nana's old cave-scented robe that I'd rescued when Sister Flatulencia was cleaning out her belongings after the accident. Jillily rewarded my efforts not to pinch by spooning tightly next to me, motoring like a house afire. As if I were channeling Nana, I gave her a thousand little chicken peck kisses all over her sleek black head. To which Jillily responded with enough rough-tongued face washings to rival the best facialist in L.A.

At last I could have my nice, long cry. But the tears refused to come. So Assefa was coming back. For what? *To* what—a lover who'd layered sex over the shock of rejection like a cat sweeping litter on its poop? What finally loosened the floodgates wasn't the shame of having had intercourse with someone I didn't love, nor the confusing loss of the one I did, let alone his imminent return. When the void sucks you in, every bit of the world's misery dives in with you. Old hurts and current dreads swirl amidst stories of child abuse, oil spills, women across the globe being treated as chattel. Ultimately, my tears released themselves over the lonely end of the pelican on the beach—the grotesquery of its plastic-entwined entrails being treated with the averted eyes of all but a few Bob Ballantines of this world and a flurrying business of flies.

I fell asleep praying there *was* a parallel universe, one where humans were kind and rational and uncomplicated and life was actually fair.

Chapter Fourteen
Fleur

THE EMBRYONIC HUMAN heart begins beating about 21 days after conception, which is generally about five weeks after the last normal menstrual period. But what was normal if you tended to be irregular, couldn't recall when your last period had been, and hence had no idea when your window of fertility had been left wide open?

One thing I *did* know: I still hadn't bled by the time I finally decided to return Assefa's calls.

I'd managed to avoid him for a week and a half, telling myself I was too busy with my team's debate over what direction to take after the idiots in Congress—consistent with their penchant for fiddling while our planet burned—killed all possibility of pursuing P.D. in the coming year by a measly majority of one vote.

Far from fading from memory, the dead pelican on the beach that I'd come to think of as Pelican X had become a kind of totem, reminding me that every day our project was stalled, the more likely it was that we humans would take millions of species with us into oblivion. My team continued to be split between pursuing research that would feed into P.D. when the time came and exploring new territory entirely. It all came to a head during one of our Skype sessions with Adam.

Gunther started it this time, rubbing his pale, slender hands with an unaccustomed glee, his wandering eye having a field day. "I'm for investigating Eridanus. You never know what the implications of parallel universes might mean for our understanding of the exchange of matter in C-Voids."

Tom shot him a withering look, which I prayed Gunther's strabismus prevented him from seeing. "Oh, come on. Let's get real. By the time we make useful connections between Eridanus and C-Voids, the planet'll be fried." As if he'd realized he was being a bit harsh, he turned to Gunther and laid a hand on his arm, "Listen, bro. If we're going in the direction of supervoids, we might as well go whole hog and see where Nikodem Poplawski's idea that the universe exists within a giant black hole takes us. You've got to admit that his idea that we're sharing a Darth Vader condo with a bunch of other universes is pretty cool." It was intriguing, and for a few minutes the group spun into an excited hive of speculation, until Stanley hopped a few times and held up a hand.

"Okay, I like Nick's idea as much as the rest of you, but let's face it: it's too theoretical and still beyond our current capabilities to verify or confirm." He grinned. "We're consigned to the fate of a tuna. Nobody's blinder to the existence of the ocean than the fish."

That was when Katrina broke in, her eyes alight and her shiny brown ponytail swinging as she spoke with some vehemence, "That's why I like keeping it simple and staying with quantum entanglement. We were going to include it in our project, anyway, since it feeds right in to C-Voids and Congress has no idea how relevant it is for P.D. The more we learn, the readier we are to apply it next year if the elections go our way."

That, of course, led to one more round of ranting about the Know Nothing party that had a grip on Congress, until Adam piped up—speaking of tuna, his face disturbingly flattened into a narrow fish-face shape by the Skype camera. "I think Katrina's right. Nothing has a greater potential to make a dent in the amount of CO_2 in the atmosphere than P.D. That's why Fleur got the Nobel for it and why the Cacklers and Big Oil and their congressional minions are determined to kill it. We've got virtually all the scientific community and every major environmental organization behind us, and with any luck the mid-term elections'll get us the votes next year. I say we focus on entanglement, stay the course, and kick carbon ass next year."

Amir weighed in with a quick, "I'm with Adam. We'd be stupid to get off track from what we're about."

Amir's support was a nice surprise, but I already knew I could count on Adam. Sammie liked to say that Adam and I had a "history with a capital S-E-X." Which was a typical Sammie-ism, one that distorted objective reality for the sake of emphasizing an emotional element that I preferred to sweep into a distant corner of my mind. Over the years Adam had been my comforter, my tutor, my friend, and one of the most essential members of my physics team. However many mini-explosions I'd given myself in response to his perceptive green eyes and distinctive Campbell's Chicken Soup B.O., my feelings for him were far more complicated than S-E-X.

Before Adam there had been only the void and the small-c-catholic collection of methods I employed to fill it. Those methods included pinching the loose skin under my arm, banging my head, whirling, flapping, screaming, list-compiling, voracious reading, making Jillily's motor whirr, sniffing roses and armpits, watching my favorite sycamore with Grandfather, noting the patterns of the birds landing on its branches, insinuating myself inside one of Nana's Mack truck grips and feeling goose bumps spread across my scalp while she delivered little chicken peck kisses across my head.

Adam and I had met under what I would forever think of as the Very Worst Circumstances of My First Incarnation. My favorite person in the world (Grandfather) had died, and I'd tried to resurrect him in the spirit of the one I'd been taught to worship (Jesus), but had been stopped midstream by the man who made a political career out of saving babies from the devil abortionists (Father), who'd been squeezing me with his pincer-fingers to near-fainting point while we stood by Grandfather's casket until my father was caught by his arch rival (Senator Manus), whose son had actually cried along with me amid the tombstones of Eden Rest Memorial Park, where I first learned where dead people whom we love really go (filling the holes in our hearts). My sweet savior was Adam.

Needless to say, the first feeling that attached to my new friend was gratitude, though I didn't learn how to name that sensation, nor any other emotion for that matter, until Mother hired him to be my tutor after she left Father and the Main Line behind over the pincer incident. With patience and compassion for my odd-duck-ish quirks, Adam had filled my thirsty mind with history, literature, and what

Sammie would later call "the three fuffs": philosophy, physics, and feelings.

Which I suppose was why, several days following our team's last confab, I reached out to Adam by cellphone, rattling on about such topics as the likelihood of the CERN team finding the Higgs Boson (or, as the mainstream media liked to call it, "the God particle") and the potential for epigenetic consequences in the application of P.D. "I know I'm not the only one dying to see the Higgs field proven at last," I'd confessed the previous morning. "I mean, think about it, Adam. Our gooey universe held together by elementary boson superglue like a crowd piling into a phone booth with infinite room for more and more and more."

I have to confess that my enthusiasm wasn't exactly unambivalent. Yes, like most physicists, I was fascinated with the Higg's Boson, but my heart wasn't really in it. Instead, it longed to engage full tilt in the application of C-Voids to dematerialization and the revolutionary diminishment of our reliance on fossil fuels that was likely to be its outcome. Sammie liked to say that, when she was at an impasse with one of her paintings, she'd just move on to another for a while. I was discovering that my mind simply wasn't constructed like that. While my tweeter seemed intent on proving Freud's speculations about polymorphous perversity, my scientific imagination was stuck on one beloved project and couldn't so easily pencil another into my dance card.

"Wait," Adam said, wading through the squid ink of my defenses. "You're sounding like Sammie—you're talking too fast. What's wrong?"

Or, as Sammie would have said, "You're so busted."

He waited.

Have I mentioned Adam was particularly patient? I used to think that his twisted leg had something to do with it. But now I suspected it had more to do with growing up virtually alone in his own father's Main Line mansion, without even a wing full of saved babies or invisible beds of David Austins to distract him.

It occurred to me then that we should both thank God for physics, home for odd ducks with odd brains. (Though it was questionable which god we should be thanking. The baboon-headed Egyptian Thoth? Japan's scarecrow deity Kuebico? The Norse god Odin, who sacrificed an eye and hung from the world tree to achieve wisdom and frequently took advice from the decapitated head of the water spirit Mímir? Dhani once told me that, in her native town of Delhi, you can approach any stranger on the street and ask, "Will you be the incarnation of God for me?" If they say yes, you're free to set up an altar with their photograph, light candles and incense, and literally pray to their image as the soother of all your sorrows and grantor of your deepest wishes.)

Adam was so patient that all these thoughts were free to meander unhurriedly through my mind before he repeated his question. "What is it, Fleur?"

"It's Assefa. He's back."

"And?"

Somehow, this time around I was feeling uncomfortable talking to Adam about Assefa. It almost felt like a betrayal of each of them, even though Adam had no idea I thought of him as my first love (understandable on his part, since we'd never flirted, let alone kissed) and even though I'd had to witness his smittenness over a series of beauties from Stephanie Seidenfeld to his fiancée Lisa Trooly—she of the ecstatically-grinning Bird of Paradise yoga pose on her Facebook profile. (And yes, I sneaked more looks at her timeline than I cared to count. I couldn't be blamed if she chose to make it public, could I? You'd expect a Harvard T.A. to know a thing or two about security settings.)

Anyway, Adam had no compunctions about probing into my own private life, especially when he sensed I was unhappy or in danger. "Out with it, Fleur," he insisted. "You know you'll feel better when you've gotten it off your chest."

The only thing I'd ever really wanted to get off my chest were my breasts, which I had to use no end of postural exercise to keep from dragging me forward like the red-faced, baby-blue-robed young woman who lived next door to our Manhattan penthouse, who used to shuffle up and down the block scrutinizing the sidewalk for clues to something. Undoubtedly her lost mind. That fruitless ritual of hers had given me nightmares for weeks. Was there a cosmic Lost and Found located at the bottom of a particularly empty-ish void, where minds and lovers might be rediscovered?

I burst out, "I lost Assefa, and Makeda found him. I'm sure she filled his void in ways I can't imagine. I'll bet she's never flapped in her life. He dumped me like a plastic bag inside a bird. Like a giant garbage patch. He didn't want me anymore, but now he's home and keeps calling me, but I can't bring myself to call him back."

"I'm coming over," Adam said. Whatever was he talking about? The phone went dead. I couldn't believe he'd cut off our connection.

Sloping up the hallway like a vagrant ghost, I stared at myself dolefully in my bathroom mirror, treating my outer thigh like a twist tie. Things were getting precariously close to a Grade One. It was Sammie Time. I washed my face, grabbed my purse, and flung open the front door only to find Adam standing a few inches from my nose. I jumped, and not just because he was supposed to be in Boston. He looked awful. And strange. He was sporting a new soul patch that might have been sexy if it weren't accentuating an unfamiliar pair of dark half moons under his wide green eyes.

He gave me a rueful smile. "It was supposed to be a surprise."

"It is that," I squeaked, before he enveloped me in a comforting hug.

I felt grateful that neither Stanley nor Gwennie was home. Gwennie had insisted that Stanley owed her something for faithfully nursing him during the nasty infection that followed the loss of his tooth. Ushering him out the door for her weekly "C the Big Picture" meeting, she'd commented, "Somebody's got to make sure we get your project back on the docket for next year's appropriations. Lord knows Our Man in Washington isn't doing anything about it."

To the dismay of the rest of us, Gwennie and her activist friends had nothing but contempt for Barack Obama these days, her own current mantra being, "We knew he was going to sell us down the river as soon as he put Summers and Geithner on his economic team. Talk about putting the foxes in charge of the chickens." I'd thought it a pretty interesting analogy, since, if you believed Sammie, Barack Obama was the foxiest president ever. She should know. She'd actually met the man. She and Jacob had sat next to him at a North American Federation of Temple Youth luncheon, and he'd gripped her shoulder excitedly when she mentioned she was in Jungian analysis. They actually carried on a conversation about the collective unconscious and synchronicity before he got up to make his speech about the covenant between Israel and the American people.

But, as usual, I digress. The current silence of the Fiske house gave Adam and me a chance to bask quietly in each other's presence. If the enjoyment of shared silence and shared secrets are the measure of comfort in a relationship, then Adam was my alpha and omega. I'd been more disappointed than I'd cared to confess that we'd spent the holidays and my birthday apart for the first time since Mother and Nana and Dhani and Ignacio and Cook and Sister Flatulencia and Fayga and Ignacio and even Father and I had moved to New York from the Main Line. But I knew it would be hypocritical to criticize his intention to travel to Florida to finally meet Lisa Trooly's family when I myself had gotten engaged first.

As we shared a nice long stare from either end of the sofa, I worried about those dark circles under his eyes. I would personally wring Lisa Trooly's neck if she'd contributed to them. I decided I quite fancied the new facial hair below his bottom lip and just managed to stifle the impulse to reach across the couch to touch it. Instead, I rolled off the sofa, landing with the elegance of an elephant, and offered to brew us some Peet's Major Dickason's blend. Adam followed me out of the room and companionably leaned against the kitchen counter as I fetched coffee beans from the freezer and turned out half of Gwennie's cabinets to find a fresh filter. While the water heated in the coffee maker, I led him out to the backyard to say hello to the Austins, who dropped pink and apricot petals right and left in little bursts of exhibitionism. Jillily soon found her way outside and, seeing I was with one of her oldest friends, wove in and out of Adam's legs, purring like a house afire as he extolled her beauty. Actually, it was pretty embarrassing, watching her lap up his praise in her most vulnerable Charlotte the Harlot pose, flat on her back with her legs spread wide and paws aloft. I waited for Adam to explain why he'd come out west, but he said nothing. I decided to let him take his time.

"Sooo," I said, "now that Assefa's back in town, he keeps calling me. But why should I talk to him? He broke my heart."

Adam's voice crunched like tires on gravel. "I know what you mean."

I dropped the basket onto the ground. "She didn't."

He hung his head. "She did."

"Oh, Adam." For once, I was the one to comfort him. We sprawled together on the dewy grass, his head in my lap, and I stroked his perfect forehead while he cried, the sound of it harsh and juddering. Was it wrong that I felt terribly grown up returning the kindness he'd shown me, a stranger in a cemetery, nine years and fifty-six days ago?

How ironic that it was Adam who ultimately convinced me to call Assefa back. He delivered it as an afterthought once his tears had petered out and we'd ingested enough caffeine to power a couple of 747s. (And if you're curious, as I was, where the phrase "petered out" originated, I can happily direct you to the French word *péter*, which refers both to breaking wind and exploding—in Sister Flatulencia's case, virtually identical—culminating in *péter dans la main*, or coming to nothing.)

At any rate, in the manner of scientists the world over, Adam shifted from the fickleness of Lisa Trooly to the impossibility of taking on Eridanus without skipping much of a beat, until finally, when he realized he was going to be late for a scheduled lunch date with Tom and Amir, he took his coffee mug to the sink, rinsed it out, and turned to deliver the following advice: "Call him. Look at whatever he says as just so much more data. You've got to meet whatever reality brings, Fleur. Denial's as ludicrous as a cat with a feather in its mouth, saying, 'Bird? What bird?'"

My hand automatically went to my belly. Like those treacherous chutes in the game Chutes and Ladders, Adam's words sent me right back in time to my pregnancy at thirteen years of age, which I'd barely terminated within the legal limit, thanks to my denial that Mr. Heavyflow had gone missing.

As it had now. And really, I didn't know which was worse: the thought that I might have incurred yet another unwanted pregnancy or that, if it proved to be so, I wouldn't know for certain without a DNA test if the father was Assefa or Bob Ballantine.

Chapter Fifteen
Assefa

I DIDN'T BLAME Fleur for not responding to my messages. Why was I even calling her? What could I possibly say that would compensate for the hurt I had caused? The first time I pressed the starred key that would select her number from my contacts, I told myself that I did so because of our mothers' connection, that it would be damnably awkward for the two of us to be on non-speaking terms. But the truth was that this Hanging Man had returned to Los Angeles still hanging: suspended now between two yawning pits of loss—an existential doubling of what Fleur might have called the void.

Clamoring within me were sorrow, self-blame, and guilt over what would befall Makeda with only an aging ex-priest as her comrade, along with the sensation of an iron gate closing with an inexorable fixity against hope and desire. I'd known at the time that Makeda's plea to forget her was sheer folly—really, a bad joke. While her physical proximity had receded into that other universe that was Ethiopia, I knew I would grieve her forever, along with the eviscerating second loss of my native land. Tikil Dingay's vast skies and animal cries, its vibrantly colored buildings, even the tongue-daring taste of toasted *injera* soaked in *shirro* all conspired to urge me inward. Proust had known exactly what he was talking about. Each way I turned in my suddenly much-too-large duplex, in the food aisles of Ralph's, on my daily walk from the parking lot to the Ronald Reagan U.C.L.A. Medical Center, I was overcome by the sensation of being lost, the feeling that something was missing. Where were the aromatic teff fields, burning eucalyptus leaves, pervasive tang of *bunna*, and the permeating ubiquity of jasmine, frankincense, animal dung? The musk exuded by Ethiopian skin?

But to be perfectly honest—not the easiest thing for a Hanging Man—it was on my ride in the passenger seat of Enat's gray Acura from the Tom Bradley International Terminal to my parents' home that it dawned on me that Los Angeles presented a hopelessly dull palette without the crooked grin, penetrating blue eyes, luscious alabaster curves, and tantalizing honey scent of Fleur. And so, robbed of rhyme or reason or passion, I went about my business, inwardly disengaged and listless.

But my state of suspension gave way to a more turbulent twisting and writhing on the morning Abat and Enat interrupted my preparations for my shower by knocking on my bedroom door and leading me wordlessly into Medr's room. Dear God, I wondered, had my grandfather died? But no, here he was, sitting propped up in his bed, wearing his best turquoise silk pajamas with a colorful Lion of Judah emblazoned over his heart. A trio of our wooden dining chairs had been arranged in a semi-circle facing him, and Medr gestured authoritatively with his wizened old hand for the three of us to sit down. Which we did, as promptly as students in a classroom, the sound of our chair legs scraping the wood floor like fingernails against chalkboard. I darted glances at my parents, but they kept their eyes averted from me and doggedly faced my father's father.

I found myself wanting to leave the room, but knew that it was not possible. When I'd first alighted from my plane, Enat had greeted me as if she'd thought I had died and had only just learned I was among the living. Her tears were so copious that I tasted the salt of them long after she'd showered my face with a thousand kisses. She'd come to pick me up alone. I only saw Abat once we returned home. Leaning back in his favorite plush chair, he watched me carry in three heavy suitcases filled to near overflowing with gifts I'd brought home for family and friends. Before my journey (and his), he would have leapt up to help me. Now his unsmiling immobility told me I had not been forgiven for my rash words at the orphanage. He expressed no curiosity about what had led me to change my mind and return.

I presumed he hadn't mentioned our angry conversation to Enat, who busied herself for days joyously unpacking the *shammas* I'd brought back for her, running into my room at all hours to extol this or that particularly vivid border. I'd felt especially pleased to see the broad smiles on her face; I'd chosen each *shamma* with care, this one because its rich orange and sienna diamond design reminded me of the ornamental combs I'd seen displayed across the top of an old dresser in Makeda's humble room, that one because its bright reds and purples were like the red-hot poker flowers and hagenias that grew from the rich soil of Tikil Dingay.

But something serious had clearly taken place between then and now. Both Mother and Father were avoiding not only my eyes, but each other's, and Medr's face displayed, if possible, even more grief than it habitually wore. To my astonishment, my grandfather opened his mouth and began to speak. The sound of his voice was initially as faint as a dying kudu, but after a few scratchy words and a tinny cough or two, I could hear him just fine. Once it became clear what he was saying, I wished I couldn't.

He spoke in Amharic, but I was able to follow him fairly well. Too well. "My son," he said, rubbing his creased forehead repetitively with his thumb, "this life is never what we expect and often requires of us what we do not want. Your *abat* has confessed to me something I only suspected when he first informed me that we would all be coming to this new land. It concerns things we should not have to speak about, but I have convinced him and your mother that, if this family is to bring forward the fruit of further generations, speak of them we must." His voice was growing more faint again, as if flagging from the strain of underuse. He managed a final, "Your *abat* has something to tell you. *My son* has something to tell you." Then the room fell silent but for the soft sobbing of Enat, who rocked from side to side like a caged animal.

For the first time since I'd returned, my father looked me full in the face, but his voice was flat. "We were not honest with you." My mother sat up and flashed him a sharp look. Abat nodded, as if responding to an unspoken command. "*I* was not honest." His voice took on a pleading tone, and I found myself disliking him for it. "When I told you that you must not stay in Ethiopia with Makeda, I did not tell you why." He stood abruptly and began pacing the room behind our chairs. I had to skew around in my seat to see him.

"When we are young, we can lack … wisdom. Sometimes we behave stupidly. I was more stupid than most." He cleared his throat. "As I know you recall, the Geteye family next door was like family to us. Rede was my best friend." My father's face now streamed with tears, but from his voice you would never know that he was crying. "Genet—" He stopped himself. "His wife was your mother's dear friend. We, I … well …." He shot a look at Medr, as if begging him to intervene, but my grandfather was sitting absolutely still with his eyes firmly closed, only his right hand pleating the gold border of his left sleeve betraying that he was awake. I saw the fabric quiver, as if responding to a slight tremor. "The two women became pregnant very close to the same time."

My mother cried out, "I was so excited to be with child in unison with that woman. She was like my *sister*."

My father reached into his pocket for a handkerchief and swabbed his face. "Assefa, you and Genet's daughter were born only months apart. I tried not to think about the fact that you might in fact be … related."

It was at that moment that the Hanging Man went airborne. It was with absolute dispassion, as if I were miles and miles away, that I heard Abat say, "Of course, the two of you became inseparable. And at some point, Genet began to worry—"

"She told me," Enat interrupted. "It was the day before Christmas, and we were fasting. We observed the ancient rituals in those days. She confided in me that she was pregnant again and wanted to reassure me that, at least with this one, she was sure it was Rede's. I had no idea at first what she was talking about, but then suddenly the truth came upon me, and I knew."

My father sat down and tried to get hold of my mother's hand, but she shook him off. "It was only a few times," he pleaded, and I couldn't tell if he was addressing her, me, or his father, whose hands were still now and lowered by his sides. Medr showed not a sign that he'd heard any of this. Now he really did look as if he could be dead. I worried that this actually might kill him.

Somehow I found myself back inside my body. The room was stifling, my heart raced, and sweat had sprung up like a geyser across my forehead and cheeks.

"Of course," said Abat, "your mother confronted me immediately." He looked blindly across the room, as if he were seeing something we couldn't. "I remember watching you through the kitchen window playing *ganna* with Bekele and Iskinder while we struggled to talk it through. Your mother was—well, I'd hurt her terribly. I hated myself for it and knew that I owed her everything. I'd never stopped loving her. The other was only ... and God bless your mother, I realized that despite my ... lapse, she still loved me." He tried smiling at her, but she ignored him. I sensed that the events of the past days had re-opened old and terrible wounds. "By the time we entered *Timkat*, our plans were made." He shook his head sorrowfully. "By then, Genet had miscarried Rede's child. Your mother and I never mentioned the ... circumstances ... again. Until you spoke to her about Makeda. About my daughter."

I shot him a searching look. Returning my gaze with a hapless shrug, he said, "Yes, if I'd had any doubts before, I was certain it was true as soon as we bumped into her at the airport. I saw my own mother in her face." I heard a groan from Medr's bed. "The woman is your sister. Half-sister. So you see why I ...."

I reached out and slapped him, hard, across the face.

Medr stunned us all by flinging back his sheet and flying out of bed like a napping cat springing for a bird.

In this case, I was the prey. My thin-as-a-rail grandfather took both my hands in his and held them over my head, pushing his pointed chin into my face. "Never do that. You must not do such a thing. This is your father."

Father was in the corner, holding my mother away from the two of us. Wailing like a woman at a funeral, Mother fled the room, but not before Medr turned to my father and unloaded a series of curses. "This is what happens when you disrespect your family. The next generation learns to disrespect *you*." Then his lower lip began to tremble and I watched in horror as he slowly sunk to the floor, gripping a chair leg to break his fall.

I dropped down next to him and pulled his trunk toward me. As I hugged him, he sobbed. His chest was terribly narrow and his arms felt like sticks. My God, what had I done to him? What had the Hanging Man done to us all? Had my father been a Hanging Man, too?

But the next thing I knew, strong arms had encircled me from behind. I smelled the *bunna* of my father's breath, moist and warm against my neck. We three swayed, and I recalled the moment only a few weeks ago when Makeda and Father Wendimu and I had listened to Seyfou Yohannes singing his version of *Tizita* in Father Wendimu's tiny closet.

Wordlessly, my father let me go and came around to help his father onto his feet and into his bed.

I heard my parent's phone ring, and the next thing I knew Enat was kneeling beside me, handing me the phone. I nearly mistook my mother's voice for a stranger's. It was strained and tight, and I realized she was struggling to stop a torrent of tears.

"Here," she said, urging the phone on me. "It is Fleur on the telephone. She said your phone has been disconnected."

It occurred to me that I might not have paid my Verizon bill before I left for Ethiopia. I accepted the phone from my mother and, pushing myself up from the floor, took it with me into the next room. There was so much I needed to take care of.

Chapter Sixteen
Fleur

IT WASN'T UNTIL Adam left for Boston that I plucked up the courage to contact Assefa. But when I did, he failed to return my call. Or should I say calls? I must have tried his cellphone ten times over three days. Which is why I finally swallowed my pride and phoned Abeba to ask her to have him call me. I didn't know whether to feel lucky or not when she told me—rather tensely, I thought—that he was at her house and that she'd fetch him.

From the moment Assefa's voice came on the line, he sounded distressed. "Fleur," he sputtered, "I really do need to talk with you, but I'm …. How about if I call you back a little later?" Then, as if he was trying to gather himself, he added, "We can have a nice, long talk."

A nice, long talk sounded terrible. My body curled in on itself like a touch-me-not. I dreaded the thought of some protracted phone conversation that would hide all the visual cues I'd need to see if I believed anything he said. After countless little sighs and bitings of my lower lip I suggested we meet in person, and we wrangled over when like a couple of Mideast peace negotiators.

Our original plan was to meet the following Thursday evening, when Assefa would be finished with his rounds and I'd be done with the small, select group of first year Caltech students I was tutoring on worm holes, C-Voids, and superstring theory. But Fate intervened rather rudely in the person of a sweaty and distortedly muscular man in an ill-fitting suit pushing past my departing students, getting close enough to shove an envelope into my hand. He hissed rather threateningly, "Fleur Robins, you've been served," disappearing just as quickly, leaving behind a miasma of a particularly odious cologne.

The summons was a shocker in more ways than one. The closest I'd ever gotten to the legal system had been during my ill-fated incident with the Boy Who Called Me Beautiful, when I'd had a policeman's gun pointed at my naked breasts before being locked in a jail cell.

Leaving the last vestiges of my late lunch of Gwennie's vegan lasagna in the Lauritsen lab (which was a damned shame, since I doubted I'd ever be able to eat it again), I left a guilty message for Assefa, then called home and read aloud to Gwen the demand that I appear to testify in the civil suit of Fidel Marquetti vs. Kun-wu Kang.

"I can't believe it!" exclaimed Gwen. "He kills the poor man's dog and then has the gall to sue him?"

It struck me that Gwennie was omitting the little fact that Chin-Hwa had bitten Fidel Marquetti in the butt, but nonetheless I wailed, "Why does he want *me* to testify?"

"I don't know, love, but I'm calling our lawyer. I'll be damned if we'll let you be bullied by some idiot racist's attorney in a fishing expedition."

I'll save the deposition for another day. Suffice it to say it's a great mystery to me how it's possible to be so intimidated by what Stanley H. Fiske likes to call iguanid inferiors, men in jackets and ties with limited imaginations and too little heart.

As it happens, the Idiot Racist's Attorney didn't get to cross-examine me a second time, since Plaintiff Fidel Marquetti and Defendant Kun-wu Kang ended up settling out of court. I learned of that on the day I finally met up with Assefa. Mrs. Kang ran up to me as I was leaving Mother's, where I'd had a ridiculously yummy breakfast of *Uttapam* (a pancake-ish rice and lentils thingy topped with chopped vegetables and spices guaranteed to murder my butt the next day), rustled up by Dhani for Mother, me, and herself on— thank God—Abeba's day off. Mrs. Kang told me that she and her husband were moving, having sold their house to a realtor, who, Gwennie later grumbled, was sure to "flip it and pocket a small fortune." Mrs. Kang hastened to assure me that it wasn't as if she and her husband had been bankrupted or anything by the settlement, but that they'd decided they'd feel more comfortable living in Los Angeles, in what Stanley later informed me was Koreatown. When he told me that, I felt almost as voidish as when I'd seen Chin-Hwa's dead body. It struck me as tragic that an immigrant family had been pushed into a kind of ghetto by another immigrant, one who kidded himself that he wasn't viewed by many people as an outsider himself.

This phenomenon was something Sammie amplified for me when I related to her the dismissal of my second summons to appear in court. She and I were lounging on her unmade bed with Midge plopped down between us, creating a regular racket of purring and snoring. Sammie commented unhappily, "This whole Marquetti-Kang affair brings back all those times I was called 'nigger' by poor white kids when mum and I stayed with my bubbie and zayde in Orange County. Not to mention the little wannabe gangsters mumbling, '*Cocolo*,' under their breaths the year I taught art to middle schoolers in the *barrio*. It's a divide and conquer sort of thing," she muttered bitterly, petting Midge so exuberantly that he pushed his fat belly up from his cushy mound of duvet and waddled to the foot of the bed. "Actually," she added, her voice rising ominously, "the history of the South is rife with it. And now? Getting poor whites to identify with those who exploit them by encouraging them to feel superior to blacks and immigrants segues so nicely into convincing idiots to look down on intellectuals." She hesitated. "What was *that*?" *That* was Midge catapulting his bulging body off the bed in response to Sammie's increasing stridency. The good news was that it managed to at least persuade her to turn down the volume of her rant.

Sammie was in what she confessed was a "shit mood" because she'd had, for the umpteenth time, another row with Jacob. When I related to her my conversation with Assefa, she seemed more than happy to extend her rage to him. "Girl, the guy's a player. Can't you see it?" And as if that weren't enough, she emphatically raised one perfectly shaped black eyebrow and threw in, "Fuck the sod. Actually, don't." Then, after the slightest pause, she shifted her tone. "Why don't you give Adam a whirl?" she asked, as if he were an amusement park ride.

"Don't be ridiculous," I snorted. I didn't mention that, when I'd driven Adam to the airport, he'd leaned over to kiss me goodbye and somehow our lips had accidentally touched. Had it been my imagination that we'd lingered just the teensiest bit before breaking away?

The reason Sammie was going after me so fiercely was that I'd confessed to her I was still vulnerable to Assefa's charms.

He and I had met at last at the Huntington Gardens. He'd explained on the phone that he was going to be having dinner with his parents and would be in my part of town. There was no way I could handle the intensity of meeting him at their house. Or at the Fiskes.

Things did get intense, nonetheless, right from the beginning. Not in the way I'd imagined, not with me tempted to scream in anger or whirl and flap in distress, but with my heart cracking open like a glacier as I saw Assefa approach, tentatively padding toward the crowd convened in front of the ticket booth, gathering speed once his eyes picked me out.

Instead of shouting, I simpered. And instead of holding myself aloof, I rushed into his embrace. I felt his heart thudding rapidly—or was it my own?—as he whispered into my hair, "Fleur, Fleur. *Kiber le geta*. My God, I've missed you."

We aimed for an unoccupied bench overlooking a perfectly manicured, broad sloping lawn. Our hands found their way to each other, and Assefa broke our prolonged silence with a contrite, "I am sorry, my *dukula*. You have no idea how sorry I am." He shook his head mournfully. "And how wrong I was."

I really shouldn't have let him call me his "my" anything. Could I be elevated so easily from *discarded* to *dukula*? But the heart has little use for the head when love comes to call. Burying my nose into his neck and letting him nuzzle me back, nothing else mattered.

We ended up having what I felt at the time was a cleansing heart-to-heart. Warily skirting the topic of Makeda, I asked Assefa why he'd wanted to stay in Ethiopia.

He replied, "Even before I left the States, Fleur, I'd begun to think of myself as a potted plant, someone who would never become the man he was supposed to be in the soil of a foreign land."

His words took me aback. I'd had no idea that he didn't feel at home here in SoCal. Did I feel foreign to him? With his familiar smells and tender touch, he hardly felt foreign to me.

But he did get me thinking. Where were *my* roots, where was *my* natural soil? Here I was, nearly three thousand miles from where I'd been born, several incarnations beyond my months in Mother's Manhattan penthouse, a far cry from my cramped summer digs as a post-grad at the Sorbonne, a world away from the quaintly dilapidated Oxford lodgings where I'd researched macroscopic dissipative systems with fellow Nobel laureate Sir Anthony James Leggett's team. The fact was, I'd been uprooted more times than Assefa, though I'd never had to travel so far. No wonder I'd found it physically impossible to leave Stanley and Gwennie's even after Mother followed me to Pasadena.

But perhaps more importantly, what kind of plant was I? Notwithstanding Abeba's insistence on our floral kinship, I was unquestionably less a flower than a weed: hardy, determined, and not infrequently (at least in the case of Big Oil, the Cacklers, my father, and Congress) despised.

That particular train of thought made me sufficiently melancholic that I came out with the question that had been lurking at the back of my mind ever since I'd coaxed Makeda's name from a sleepy Assefa's lips. Rising with him to walk toward the main building's restrooms—I was peeing like a waterfall lately—I asked (in a fake casual tone), "How much did Makeda have to do with you flying to Ethiopia?

I could have sworn Assefa's eyes shifted guiltily as he replied, much too quickly, "You know why I went. To look for Abat."

"Okay," I reluctantly gave him. "But coming home after you said you weren't going to? Returning to the ... pot?"

I thought I saw a shaft of anger rise up in his eyes, but his voice was controlled. "It was not to be." Reading my lack of satisfaction from my crossed arms, he hastily added, "I came to understand that we could not be together." His pace quickened and I had to skip a few times to keep up with him. "We really couldn't."

I stopped in my tracks, forcing him to stop with me. "Did she reject you?" I flung at him, my own anger unmasked.

Assefa groaned, and in that sound I heard great pain. A vast, conical void presented itself before me, and I had to stifle the impulse to flap.

"Ah, *dukula*," Assefa said, coming closer, "you are looking for simplicity in something complex. Isn't it enough that I am choosing you, to be here in this country with you?"

I let him take me in his arms, let him rub his chin across the top of my head.

But making love a few days later was another story. Mother had gone to a Friends of Bill W. conference, leaving Cesar with Dhani and Ignacio, and Assefa and I took advantage of their absence by enjoying her pool. We swam like two seals, streaking wavery lines of light in the water. When we finally emerged, we collapsed onto twin *chaises lounges*, drying ourselves off with Mother's ultra-soft Missoni towels. I closed my eyes, stinging a little from chlorine, and saw a brilliant red film give way to a light show of cloudy gold, yellow, and pale cream phosphenes. I had to force myself not to get up to find a pencil and paper to diagram their patterns.

I wondered about the patterns in my own life. If Gerardus 't Hooft was right, I was a tiny beam of the cosmic holograph. Bob had informed me that pufferfish males created complex and beautiful circles in the seabed to attract females, whom they guided to shore for egg release when the time came. The females were pretty much the passive ones in the process, and I wondered if I saw a reflection of myself in their compliance. I certainly seemed a sucker for any man who showed the slightest interest in my body.

As if to prove my point, here was Assefa, laying a light hand on my arm as a prelude to tracing feathery spirals toward my breasts. He let his fingers inside my bikini top, pinching my nipple just enough to raise gooseflesh up and down my arms, amplified even more by a slight breeze. Suddenly I felt very cold, but now Assefa was sliding one hand under my butt and the other beneath my neck. He lifted me like a baby and took me upstairs into Mother's bedroom, where he stood me in front of her antiqued silver framed dressing mirror. With a deft touch, he urged me out of my bathing suit and then swiftly removed his trunks.

With Assefa by my side my insecurities dissolved. I had to admit we *were* a stunning pair, his skullcap of short black coils glistening beside my long wet waves. His erect *washela* was seconded by my aroused nipples.

There we were again, staring at ourselves in a mirror. But this time, the bed that Assefa led me to was my mother's, which failed to diminish the sensation of fireflies flitting madly inside my belly.

Our foreplay was as I'd remembered and dreamed about almost every night since his departure, his tongue a quick serpent slipping into the folds of my dark mystery, his member's Roquefort cheese and cinnamon smell pungent and beguiling as I circled it with my lips. But when he inserted his *washela* into me, it was as if he'd stabbed me with a knife. I screamed at the unexpected pain.

"What is it?" he cried, pulling away.

"I don't know," I whimpered, stunned. "It hurt." Without thinking, I curled up and rolled to the other side of the bed. "This has never happened before," I said wonderingly. "It felt awful."

There was no way I was going to try it again to see if my tweeter really meant it. Instead, we cuddled awkwardly for a while before rising to dress in an imperfect silence. I let him plant a kiss on my cheek before he drove away.

I fled Mother's house, but abruptly interrupted my drive to pull to the side of the road and put in a call to my gynecologist Dr. Elspeth Hurdly. She fit me in that very afternoon (pathetic pun unintended), for which I was intensely grateful. I was sure I had a raging bladder infection. But after testing my urine in a variety of ways, she pronounced that infection wasn't an issue. She also, with a simple blood test, ruled out pregnancy, at which point I nearly fainted with relief and something else that I determined only later was grief. There is no accounting for the folly of the human heart.

Once I regained my equilibrium, she had me climb onto the examining table and felt around—gently, but nonetheless excruciatingly—inside my tweeter and even my butt, patiently tolerating the yelps and table-bangings she was familiar with from my previous pelvic exams.

None too soon, she let me get down. While I recovered my breath, wiping glops of examining gel from my tweeter and hurriedly throwing my clothes back on, she busied herself washing her hands. Turning from the stainless steel sink to face me, she said cautiously, "I'm trying to decide whether I should do a further diagnostic test." Seeing my eyes widen, she signaled me to relax. "Let's not do anything precipitous. Why don't we give your body a few days to calm down and see if it doesn't right itself? Actually, let's have a chat in my office, shall we? I'll have my assistant Delvy bring us some tea." As she led the way out the door, she looked back. "Will chamomile do?"

Sitting in her consulting room, its walls covered with photos of her skydiving, windsurfing, white water rafting, and climbing what was undoubtedly Mt. Everest, I wondered if all that astounding athleticism helped her to be strong when she had to be the bearer of bad news.

But as she looked up at me from the computer she'd been fiddling with, she seemed anything but tough. "Here," she said softly, scooting our teacups to the side and sliding her iMac around so I could see the screen.

"There's a slight chance you might have the beginnings of I.C. Here's a little graph I often find helpful. Interstitial Cystitis is a condition that mostly women get that can produce pelvic pressure and pain. It's not dangerous. It doesn't affect lifespan. But it can be uncomfortable. One way to rule it out would be a potassium sensitivity test, where I place two solutions—water and potassium chloride—into your bladder, one at a time. If you feel noticeably more pain or urgency with the potassium solution than with the water, it's generally interstitial cystitis. People with normal bladders can't tell the difference between the two solutions."

Needless to say, this was a Grade One emergency. I reached for my cell as soon as I left the office. Sammie's voice was like a salve. "Oh, Fleur Beurre. Of course, you're scared. The test sounds miserable. I'm home. Do you want to come over? I hate to sound like a cheerleader, but I just can't believe you've got some disease. Why did you go to the doctor in the first place? I try to avoid them like the plague myself, but I suppose that's not exactly comforting to you just now."

"Well, I've been peeing a lot. But, listen, I'll be there in ten minutes and then we can …." I got off the phone as quickly as I could, having the honest excuse of needing to dig into my purse to give my ticket to the parking lot attendant, whose stunning face looked suspiciously Ethiopian. But the truth was that I'd suddenly realized I was going to have to confess to Sammie how I'd discovered I had a problem.

How many times would it take me to learn that best friends— not unlike the dog lovers Adam had teased me about—might judge you, but they don't *judge* you. Sammie gave me a Nana-worthy hug as soon as she opened the door. She led me through the incense-redolent hall into the modest kitchen, where she'd already begun to prepare us a can of Campbell's Chicken Noodle Soup. Which, needless to say, made me think immediately of Adam.

I'd never told Sammie how much I adored the smell of him—there are some things not to be shared with even a best friend. But we'd discovered early on that, despite growing up in the disparate worlds of London and Pennsylvania, we had in common memories of having been comforted when we were sick by Campbell's signature soup. Despite its dubious nutritional value, we were both still suckers for its vaguely tinny taste and gooey texture.

"So," she said, as we tucked our bare feet around the kitchen's two kitchen stools (much as I'd done on the Main Line, watching Dhani concoct the spicy dishes that wreaked havoc on my belly and butt a decade ago). "Is this something to do with a bladder infection? I hate the bloody things."

"Noooo," I replied cautiously, blowing on my spoon before taking a sip of the salty broth.

Sammie wasn't stupid. She carefully placed her own spoon down in her antique ceramic bowl. I noticed that hers had a pink rose design while mine bore a horizontal twining of what looked like purple and blue morning glories. "Okay. Out with it."

"You're going to hate me."

"There's only one thing I'd hate you for, and that's having sex with Assefa." I blanched. "Oh shit. You did." She put a hand on my forearm. I noticed it was tanned to an even richer chocolate by our current faux-summer. Patting me rather forcefully with each word, she emphasized, "Of course, I don't hate you. I love you more than anyone, except p'raps my mum." I noticed she'd left Jacob out of the equation. I think she realized it herself, for she pulled back her hand to hit her head with it theatrically. "Criminy. *I* should talk."

"He's really not a bad man."

"Jacob?" I shook my head. "Oh right. Assefa. I know, I know—they never are, are they? Except when they are." God, I loved her. Even when she was trying to be cynical she merely sounded sad.

She stepped down to retrieve the pot from the stove and poured us each some more soup, slopping it a bit over the edges of our bowls. As she returned with a paper towel to wipe away the overflow, I couldn't help but notice the contrast between the new stainless steel cookware Aadita had excitedly purchased on sale at Williams-Sonoma and the china soup bowls she'd inherited from her British husband's mother. Different eras, different sensibilities. Granny Schwartz might have forgiven the sleekness of the pot, but she would surely have pursed her lips when Sammie's cell burst forth with Jacob's *Acid Thunder* ringtone.

I gestured for her to go ahead and take the call.

"Really?" she asked. "I don't have to." But I nodded emphatically. It occurred to me that we were both way too preoccupied with the men in our lives.

As she greeted Jacob with a tense, "Please tell me you didn't mean it," I let myself down from my stool, grabbed my purse, and motioned to her that I'd be fine, mouthing, "I just remembered I've got to get to the lab. I'll call you later. I'm okay now."

None of which was true. It was a good thing I'd gotten Riku of Riku's Righteous Tattoos to remove the *No Bullshit* emblem from my lower back. (No matter that he'd misheard my original request for a tattoo to read *Nobelist*.) But I did tell myself that no thirty-minute potassium sensitivity test could equal the ongoing torture Sammie was undergoing with Jacob. I just prayed she'd come to her senses before actually marrying him.

I felt mortified that I'd fibbed to Sammie, but I knew I had to drive somewhere. I could hardly march across the street to the Fiskes and leave my car out in front. On automatic pilot, I let the Prius take over. Who knew why it drove me to Sister Flatulencia's apartment in South Pasadena, except that I'd been feeling guilty that I hadn't visited her there since the accident. When the door opened, I had to take a few steps back before rallying and entering. Mother's erstwhile companion greeted me in an effluvium equal in impact to an overspraying of Patchouli. Poor woman, she'd developed an allergy to Beano, and her original condition had returned in full force. As usual, her frizzy hair was peeking out from her signature bandana like pubic hair from a bathing suit.

I burst into tears.

"Dear girl, what is it?"

She watched in dismay as I fell into the old green velour sofa she'd only last year shared with the woman who'd more or less raised me. "She's really gone, isn't she?" I bawled. "And there's nothing we can do about it. People just go. We're so helpless about anything that matters. And I'm going to have a horrible test because of this pain in my tweeter. I've had bladder infections before, but this was so much worse." I kept babbling along those lines, vaguely aware that it was a kind of sacrilege to equate my little miseries with Nana dying. Despite myself, I blurted out, "It all started when Assefa tried to insert his member."

Sister Flatulencia paled but said nothing, instead marching over in her mannish brown shoes to stroke my head, making odd little clucking sounds that were surprisingly soothing. Nonetheless, I berated myself. Why had I brought up Nana's death in front of the woman who'd traumatically witnessed it, and why in the world had I chosen to tell an ex-nun about my sex life?

It took both of us a moment to register that she'd inadvertently released several bursts of wind. Full of apology, she fled to the bathroom. I walked over to the window and lifted the sash to air out the room. Outside, two noisy crows were on the ground harrying a third, who lifted off and flapped right past the window before lighting in raucous retort onto a branch of a nearby sycamore. My heart ached for the old days on the Main Line, when all my angels were still alive and Grandfather and I would sit together for hours considering the changing patterns of birds in our favorite tree. What kind of father would cut down such a glorious living thing out of spite? I felt sick. I had to get out of there.

Emerging from the bathroom, Sister Flatulencia was kind enough not to fuss when I said I had to go. I wondered if it had been part of the novitiate to learn when to be silent and when to intervene.

Needless to say, Gwennie wasn't nearly so restrained when I arrived home revealingly red-nosed. In the end, I was no match for what Stanley liked to call Gwennie's third degree. (I'd of course been compelled to look that one up the first time he'd used it, which had in turn acquainted me with the Freemasons, whose oral third degree of training led to a mastery of building and heaven knew what secrets pertaining to the Great Architect of the Universe, all of which struck me as an ingenious system for filling the void. I'd come away from entering this particular metaphor into my *Diary of the Origins of Phrases* with a renewed respect for how daunting it is to be human and subject to powers beyond ourselves.)

I ended up going through the drill all over again with Gwennie, who kept on interrupting my attempts to rush through the details with such questions as, "Were you sufficiently lubricated?" and "Do you think you could've just been tense and tightened up before he tried to penetrate you?" All this from the woman Sammie liked to describe, more lovingly than you might assume, as "a modern day Vestal Virgin."

As if she'd had the same thought, Gwen asked, "Have you spoken to your mother about this?"

I clapped a hand to my forehead, rose up from the couch and grabbed my car keys. I couldn't believe it. I'd left Mother's house without making her bed. The bed Assefa and I had disarranged with our abortive lovemaking. Making my excuses to Gwennie, I raced to my car and arrived just in time to see Abeba letting herself into Mother's house. Really, this was too much. I'd managed to avoid Abeba since calling the house looking for her son. What did she know about Assefa's time in Ethiopia? Of Makeda? Of what had transpired between him and me? I certainly wasn't about to ask. I drove away, praying she hadn't seen me.

As for Assefa, I met up with him again after I'd completed the potassium sensitivity test. The last thing I want to be in my life is a complainer, but the test itself had to be one of the lowest circles of hell. The only thing to be thankful for was that I couldn't tell the difference between the two solutions my gynecologist flushed through my tweeter, so I didn't have interstitial cystitis after all.

Alas, hell seems to come in a variety of shapes and sizes. When Assefa came to see me, only Jillily and I were home. Stanley was out with his old Harvard cronies and Gwennie was leading a MoveOn.org planning meeting over the hill. We sat in a living room littered with Stanley's sunflower seed shells and petted my cat. Assefa covered the front half, scratching Jillily's neck as she bent her head back for him, and I took care of raking my nails across her back toward her tail. Her rear was raised like a cat in heat, and she was motoring like a house afire.

The discussion went something like this:

Me: "Well, I think my tweeter was telling me I need to take things very slowly."

Assefa (frowning and letting his hand fall away from Jillily, who jumped off the couch and turned her back to us, her tail thumping resentfully against the floor): "Ah. What are the stats?"

Me: "My urethra, bladder, and ureters are normal, and I don't have any polyps, swelling, bleeding, or strictures. She doesn't think it's I.C. and is betting that, whatever it is, it'll go away. She wants me to avoid acidic foods for a few weeks … and sex, too."

Assefa (the expression on his face uncommonly stony): "Oh, God. "

Me: (Silent. Worried.)

Assefa (taking me into his arms so stiffly, it ended up being more awkward than comforting): "I feel very badly about this, Fleur."

Me: (Silent. Wondering if he was thinking what I was thinking. What if this doesn't get better? What if I'm never able to have sex again? Will pain keep my tweeter off-limits forever?)

Assefa: (Well, actually, Assefa said nothing now, but his stomach did make a series of rather alarming sounds. Loosening his arms from me, he clutched his belly. And then, finally, he muttered a bit, as if he were speaking to himself and not to me.) "Dear God, the irony. I have brought a curse back here with me. What foolishness to think that one world can be kept separate from another, or that betrayal only affects the betrayer and not the betrayed."

Me (very nervous at this point): "Assefa, what do you mean?"

Assefa (rising up and crying out): "It is a sign, *dukula*. I must go."

And then He Has Increased Our Family By Coming Into the World walked out the door.

The shame that washed over me was hot and prickly. It felt an apt accompaniment for the pain in my tweeter, which suddenly felt like it had been raked by a cheese grater. Assefa was leaving me a second time because I could not please him.

The void opened before me, and I leapt in.

But then it spat me out again.

No! I could not let him do this to me. Not again. I rushed to the door and caught him just before his car pulled away from the curb. Actually, I stood in front of the Honda, daring him to hit me.

I managed to convince him to come back in. Tightly holding his hand, I brought him into my bedroom. I gestured with my eyes and he obediently lay back on my bed, his head on my pillow, his expression a mix of confusion and something else I couldn't read. I proceeded to light the orange spice candle he'd given me last Christmas before reaching over to dim the ceiling fixture almost completely, leaving just enough light for him to watch me slowly remove everything but my lace bra and panties. I was about to approach the bed when I had a thought, swerved over to my iPod, and found the song I wanted. As the haunting strains of Teddy Afro's *Tizita* filled the room, I climbed onto the bed and approached Assefa on my knees. He grabbed me with an unfamiliar ferocity and set me under him, and before my tweeter even had a chance to get wet, he unzipped his fly, pulled aside my panties and was pushing himself inside me.

I screamed, "No! Stop!" I was hurting with that same stabbing pain. Hurting terribly and crying. But Assefa was not stopping. If anything, he was holding me down roughly as I struggled to get out from under him.

And then the door to my room was flung open and Stanley H. Fiske was grabbing Assefa and shouting, "You black son of a bitch! Oh no, you don't! I'm not going to let this happen again!"

Somehow Assefa ended up standing in the middle of my room with his pants pooled at his knees. I managed to persuade Stanley to leave us, and Assefa hastily pulled up his jeans and unceremoniously zipped them. His eyes darted to my iPod, where the final strains of *Tizita* were playing. He laughed a little maniacally, and his voice was thick with emotion. "So that's it, is it? The black beast? It all comes down to that?" I blanched, mortified. How *could* Stanley have *said* that? How could Assefa have *done* that?

As if he could read my mind, Assefa added in a choked voice, "I hope you can forgive me, Fleur. I don't know who I am anymore."

I was still breathing very hard, and my words came out in little disconnected bursts. "That was a terrible thing. What Stanley said." But the warring sides in my head weren't very satisfied. They pushed past politeness. I was shouting now. And flapping, too. "But you hurt me, Assefa. How could you? You hurt me! I told you to stop, and you didn't! You need to get out of here. Just go."

As soon as he left the room, I could hear yelling from Stanley, but not a word from Assefa. The living room door slammed so hard that my bed actually shook. Footsteps up the hall and then Stanley knocking on the door. I cried out, "Stanley, I know you want to help, but please go away. I need to be alone."

I went into my closet and fetched Nana's cave scented robe, stuffing a piece of it up my nose. I slunk down into the narrow space behind my hanging clothes so that I was sitting with my back pressed hard against the wall, wishing this were Nana's old closet, instead, with its handy old nail head sticking out. The air was close and thick with orange spice scent and something bitter that might have been my own B.O.

I tucked a hand between my thighs. What had just happened? Assefa had scared me. Really scared me. And hurt me. Who *was* he?

But who was I? The scientist in me knew that nothing ever happened in a vacuum. Really, it was my fault. I should never have behaved so seductively with him when things weren't right with us. When my body was still sore. When my own doctor, for heaven's sake, had warned me off sex!

As for Stanley, whatever had possessed him to say such a thing? Nonetheless, I felt grateful to him. Assefa had been hurting me, and he'd stopped him. I'd never been so confused. I wasn't exactly a stranger to people's peculiar feelings about race, but I was a latecomer to the territory. I suppose that was one of the few good things of having had so little adult guidance as a child. I hadn't been taught how to hate. At least not in that way.

What came back to me then was an encounter I'd had the day after my engagement with a rather worn-looking woman working the deli counter at Ralph's. Simply *having* to brag to anyone who'd listen, I'd flourished my ring as I reached for the package of turkey she'd sliced for me, announcing that my fiancé was ridiculously handsome, was training to become a doctor, and had actually been born across the globe in Ethiopia. She'd thrown me a confused look and sniffed, "Ethiopia? Isn't that one of those Arab countries?" And when I'd patiently explained, "Actually, it's on the Horn of Africa and shares borders with Eritrea, Kenya, Djibouti, Somalia, and Sudan," she'd responded, her baggy brown eyes suddenly skinny little slits, "Do you mean he's an *African?*"

It struck me then—as it did now—as an odd sort of question. It would have made so much more sense to ask, "Is he kind to you? Do you like his family? Can he carry on a stimulating conversation? Do you laugh at the same things?" Even, "I hope you feel perfectly comfortable with him the morning after you've had sex." Or, "Do you feel he really sees you and do you trust that you know him?"

Know him? My thoughts grew dark wings. No matter where he lived, what soil he treaded, what sky rained down on his perfectly shaped head, he'd crossed into some universe completely unfamiliar to me. Did I imagine the whole thing? Was he actually ever here at all? I was at least slightly aware that I was banging the back of my head against the closet wall, but I didn't care.

But as these things tended to go, the comforting blankness of mind that accompanied pain began filling itself up with memory. I saw the two of us on Assefa's bed, laughing at some silliness that I couldn't recall, our limbs twined around each other, me wanting to keep them that way forever. Had he wanted that, too?

I felt a gently insistent pushing against my leg, and Jillily leapt onto my lap, coming close enough to my face to touch noses with me. I hadn't even realized she was in my room. Had she been under the bed the whole time? *Poor thing, she must have been terrified.* But at the very moment I wrapped my arms around her vibrating body, something uncanny happened. Stanley would kill me if I called it a ghost, so I will call it an accident, perhaps Jillily brushing against the iPod on her way to the closet. Nonetheless, it felt eerie when *Tizita* began to play again.

I pulled Jillily even closer to my breasts and swayed with her in our cramped space to the melody that had once seemed so exotic, so sensual, but was now filled with disquiet and dread.

Chapter Seventeen
Fleur

SAMMIE WAS HUGGING me so tightly I could feel her heartbeat. I could have sworn it was synchronized with my own. We were outside a government building so overbearingly top-heavy that it seemed intentionally designed to crush the human spirit. I *really* didn't want to go in.

Having our hearts beat in tune didn't surprise me. As best friends who lived right across the street from each other, our periods had been aligned for years. How astonished we'd both felt when she'd confessed to me that hers, too, had come late this month, and that she, too, had both dreaded and longed to hear of a pregnancy.

I'd turned down Mother's offer to accompany me to court. I'd turned down Gwennie and Stanley, too. I knew it was Sammie's bright chatter that would be the most comforting as soon as I learned that some mischief of misaligned cultures had made the deal between Mr. Kang and Fidel Marquetti fall through. The compassion of the older people in my life would only magnify my misery at having to recall the shooting of Chin-Hwa. Especially since I was already in a state of torment over what had happened with Assefa.

Speaking of which, here are some of the people I spoke to after the awful incident:

1. Sammie (whose disgust soon enough blended in with her anger with Jacob—I was getting ready to lay money she'd break up with him by the summer);

2. Sister Flatulencia (who might have been an ex-nun, but had become accustomed by now to sordid tales of my sex life);

3. Dhani (who shocked me by insisting Not-a-Baby-Anymore-Angelina be present so that she could learn what not to do with boys—which, as you can imagine, did nothing for any fantasies I may have had about being a role model for the baby I'd witnessed being born);

4. Gwennie (who didn't know what to do with herself over the equal parts rage and gratitude she was feeling toward her brother).

Of course, I'd had multiple conversations with Stanley, who seemed as inclined toward jumping out of his skin as I'd felt after pinching Jillily as a child when my cat had suddenly struck me as downright pinchable. Shame is one of those emotions universally guaranteed to spiral us down the steepest whorls of the void. Having the most elegant brain on the planet evidently hadn't spared Stanley one of the vilest variations of the human condition. He didn't understand how he could possibly have said such a thing, and I didn't, either, except that we humans will do almost anything to vanquish heartache, terror, and the void.

I came home one afternoon to find him going through the kitchen junk drawer, the kind just about everyone has—except Father, of course, who insisted on a place for everything and everything in its place, especially children and their unwelcome smells and noises. The one at the Fiskes' was right below the tinfoil and paper bag drawer and contained at any one time approximately sixteen objects, including:

1. Tall kitchen matches;

2. A tangle of obsolete and current cellphone chargers;

3. Appliance touch-up paint;

4. A heavy steel tape measure that inexplicably terrified Jillily whenever I pulled out the tape;

5. An assortment of organic mints and chewing gum;

6. Felt surface protectors in graduating sizes;

7. Rose clippers;

8. An oven thermometer;

9. Packs of colored toothpicks;

10. Birthday candles.

I never found out what Stanley was looking for, because when he registered my presence he cried plaintively, "I don't know why I said it."

"You were angry," I offered.

"I still am. The bastard was hurting you. But why throw in the 'black'?"

"Because you wanted to hurt him as much as he was hurting me?"

"Well. Maybe." He sounded doubtful.

"Do you remember that when you yelled at Assefa, you said something about not letting it happen again?"

"Did I?"

"You did. Stanley, you know, don't you, that it wasn't your fault I got pregnant by Hector?"

"That's how you might see it, but I was in *loco parentis*. I fooled myself that you were more aware than you were because of that mind of yours. But now—you nearly getting raped a second time. I can't imagine what your mother thinks of me."

"Oh, Stanley," I said in a muffled voice as I buried my face in his brown pullover. Was what had happened with Hector really rape? Sammie thought so. At least date rape. I wasn't so sure. And Assefa? I couldn't possibly associate that word with him. Actually, I couldn't bear to think of him at all right now. The sense of betrayal was simply too great. I brought myself back to the moment. "Mother always thinks of you with gratitude."

Actually, Mother didn't know anything about it yet. When I'd shared the whole thing with Sammie, she'd declared that Stanley needed to get into analysis to "become more aware of his shadow."

Gwennie had her own theories, mostly to do with him "needing to do some work" on his pain over having been left by his Afro-Cuban wife Doris ten years before. As for Stanley himself, he didn't seem to know what he needed besides self-flagellation, but it was clear to us all that an apology was where he had to begin.

As it turned out, Assefa refused to meet with him or even speak directly by phone, but replied to Stanley's abject cellphone message with one in return that consisted of a wooden, "I have received your message. Don't worry—I will speak of this to no one. But I prefer never to see you or your ... family ever again."

Stanley insisted on playing the message for us over and over, which was something I could happily have done without, but like Stanley himself, I was struggling to digest what had happened. When I told him I'd been subpoenaed to appear in court in the renewed case of *Marquetti vs. Kang*, his first response was a bitter, "I might as well join whatever Stupid Club Fidel Marquetti belongs to, with his pathetic chinks and '*Buddha Hades*' bullshit." I realized nothing I could say would comfort him.

The person who had the most unusual response to my heartache was Serena McKenna. I'd emailed her in the middle of one of my worst nights, and from Jane Goodall's chimp reserve in Tanzania she'd responded almost immediately: "Fleur, dear, I've never known the love of a man, but if it's anything like the attachment one forms to chimps, you must feel nearly destroyed. When I first went to work for Jane, she spoke of her profound sorrow when David Greybeard died of pneumonia. Since then, I've lost two chimps that meant the world to me, John Lennonheart and Flossie. Each time, Jane had to spoonfeed me oatmeal and honey to keep me from joining them on the other side."

Not for the first time, I wondered whether the face-blindness that Jane Goodall and Serena shared applied to their perception of chimps, as well, and if so, how did they tell one from another?

But Serena evidently had more to say. My computer pinged and I found another email from her in my inbox. She wrote, "I've had a thought. Sometimes it helps to have a change of scenery. Would you care to come visit us at Gombe? Jane's joining us here toward the end of the month, and she'd be thrilled to finally meet you. She's always felt grateful that you're working to make our world habitable for generations to come. And needless to say, it would do my own heart good. How many years since I saw you receive your award? I nearly burst my buttons with pride for you."

Even at such long distance, I blushed. Pride? I myself felt nothing but shame for the speech I gave at the award ceremony. Who wouldn't over something that began, "Maybe it all would have happened differently if the bird on the front lawn hadn't given me my idea about my grandfather's balls?"

But something about Serena's openhearted acceptance soothed me, and I was able to sleep after that, roused only by the alarm clock that reminded me that today was Court Day. I was going to have to testify about the death of a dog.

A courthouse has to be one of the coldest, most mechanistic organizations of matter and energy known to humankind. With the power to preserve life or dictate death, it swerves far from the orbit of systems with similar capabilities, such as the human body, where warm and wet pulsing organs slosh around in their assigned areas to the beat of an equally wet and sloshy heart. Nor does it resemble the explosive tension of our solar system, where a sphere of red-hot plasma capable of annihilating anything too close to it makes life possible in a planet ninety-three million miles away.

Actually, anyone entering the unimaginative Stanley Mosk Courthouse, its cinderblockish ceramic veneer panels impervious to sun and wind, was pretty much on notice to leave all thought of body and spirit behind. Add to its imperturbable façade an improbable trio of terra cotta reliefs of an English knight, Thomas Jefferson, and Moses with his Ten Commandments (which took my thoughts you know where), and mouths are guaranteed to sag, shoulders to hunch, and feet to shuffle across the gray-floored hallways leading to mostly beige rooms absent of pictures (though I did spy a giant signed photograph of Harrison Ford on one of the larger courtroom's walls).

That this world was fueled by an archaic notion of justice became apparent as soon as I was seated in an astonishingly uncomfortable chair in a much smaller room than had evidently once been occupied by Mr. Ford. My tailbone already objecting, my eyes sought Sammie, who had found a seat behind an unsmiling, beetle-eyed man in a shiny gray suit who officiously rustled a pile of papers. On the way into the courtroom, we'd passed the disputants on opposite benches. Fidel Marquetti's habitual red face had transmuted into a shockingly Day-Glo vermillion, and Mr. and Mrs. Kang, who looked everywhere but at me, appeared several shades paler than usual. So I was happy to see now that Sammie's skin had retained its bronze glow.

But my heart sank when the man I soon began to think of as Nouveau-Javert arose and approached a little too closely, throwing a question at me in a condescending tone about what I'd seen when we'd all piled out the door on Christmas.

"I saw the water sprinkler running," I carefully replied. "It was making everyone wet. *Had* made everyone wet. The Kangs were standing to the right. I could see the outlines of their bodies under their wet clothes. Excuse me for saying so,"—I slid a look toward Sammie, as if for confirmation—"but it occurred to me that Mrs. Kang has a lovely body, with a—"

"Yes, well," Nouveau-Javert interrupted. "I'm sure it's very nice, but that's not exactly what we're here to do today, is it?"

"I'm not sure. What *are* we here to do?"

Nouveau-Javert waved a dismissive hand. "Actually, that's not your concern. What you're here to do is describe exactly what you saw on the night the Kangs' negligence allowed their vicious dog to take a giant bite out of Mr. Marquetti's posterior, causing him grievous bodily harm."

The Kangs' attorney popped up, but the judge forestalled her.

"Counselor." The judge's voice was as unpleasant as the dragging of a fingernail across a blackboard. But I knew I was biased; the fact that we'd all had to rise and stay risen until the judge sat down reminded me a little too much of Father, who habitually spoke to me and all the children he'd saved from the devil abortionists from his towering height, never considering it might be a little less intimidating if he'd only bend down just a little and refrain from complaining how much he hated having children underfoot.

But Nouveau-Javert was sending the judge a phony-granny grin, which he clipped into a tight little grimace when the judge instructed him, "Please resume examining the witness."

Well, you can imagine where my mind went with that one. I couldn't even comment on Mrs. Kang's beautiful body, and now this creep was being given permission to examine me?

"Miss Robins, what did you see Mr. Marquetti doing when you opened that door?"

"I saw him running around in circles, yelling. I also saw Chin-Hwa on the ground with blood running out of his—"

"Miss Robins! Please stay with the question. I only asked you about Mr. Marquetti."

"But all truth is contextual, and in the world of quanta, further altered by the fact of being observed."

Fidel Marquetti's attorney reached into his pocket to retrieve a handkerchief to mop his face, and no wonder. The thermostat in this building must have been set years ago and never been changed. Hot air was pumping into the courtroom as if SoCal were experiencing normal February weather, rather than this heat wave that global warming hath wrought.

I sneaked another peek at Sammie. She looked like she was about to dissolve in laughter, and I managed a weak grin back. I was all too aware that the man before me was regarding me as if it had been I who'd pooped on Fidel Marquetti's pansies. And the judge was eyeing me edgily as if I were about to let loose with a Sister Flatulencia-style wet one.

Eventually, Nouveau-Javert and I managed to bump our way to the end of our dance, and then the Kang's slightly-less-shiny-suited attorney had her turn. I was relieved that they'd chosen a soft-spoken woman with an endearing lisp to represent them. Her questions were few, but (I thought, anyway) to the point. Here is a representative sampling of them:

1. "Miss Robins, before the unfortunate episode on Christmas, did you ever observe Mr. and Mrs. Kang institute measures to keep their dog away from Mr. Marquetti's yard?"

2. "Miss Robins, did you ever see any public signs on Mr. Marquetti's property that might have been aggressively directed toward Mr. and Mrs. Kang?"

3. "Miss Robins, given that Mr. Marquetti was obviously proud of his rather unusual garden, did you ever see any evidence—such as installing a hedge or a fence—that he'd tried to protect it from animals in general?"

I knew that the latter line of questioning wasn't going to get too far. There was no way around it. The Kangs had been remiss in failing to effectively control Chin-Hwa. But the question remained: who became violent first—Fidel Marquetti with his gun or Chin-Hwa with his teeth?

Fortunately, my testimony wasn't required to resolve that one, since I'd only seen the tragic aftermath, but I left knowing that justice in this situation was more complex than this building was likely to offer. Whether or not the Kangs had controlled their dog, they were the ones who'd suffered the greater loss. Fidel Marquetti still had a butt to sit on, but they had no Chin-Hwa to fill their voids. If only the three of them had found a way to take on the problem as a team, who knows what the outcome might have been? What if Fidel hadn't been so garden-proud or so uncontrollably angry? What if the Kangs has been a little less helplessly doting on their dog? What if poor Fidel hadn't already been tormented by his inflammatory skin condition? And the Kangs—might they have taken a little pleasure in Chin-Hwa pooping in the garden of the man who'd put up such an offensive sign?

I must confess I didn't linger overlong on my reflections. Once dismissed, I nearly skipped with Sammie out of the courthouse. It was then, and only then, with Moses staring down at me from the façade of the building, that I checked my iPhone and saw I'd missed six calls from Mother and at least as many from Gwen. My fingers couldn't punch in Home fast enough. Gwennie's voice sounded ghastly. Sammie managed to grab me before I went down.

Chapter Eighteen
Assefa

I DID NOT tell Abat. Nor did I tell Enat. I certainly could not tell my grandfather. While I hadn't entirely created the catastrophe on my own, I was sufficiently responsible for it that I dared not share my shame.

I cannot say I was not angry with my father, though I was hardly the one to judge him for being untrue to one woman with another. I was also angry with my mother for keeping their secret from me and for the fact that it had happened in the first place. That one was just as irrational, but nonetheless true. What is it about a son that he blames his mother when life is terrible? I had no one to ask if that were true for daughters, too.

Nor did I need to ask myself if I was filled with rage toward Stanley H. Fiske. The man was a fraud. Oh, yes, he was undoubtedly as brilliant as my Fleur, but his pretensions to be a good man were as much of a lie as my family's story of coming to America to avoid war. If they did, the war was personal and had nothing to do with Somalia or Eritrea.

I was a fraud myself, of course, and a fool for thinking of Fleur as "my" Fleur. I myself was a scoundrel, and she—well, the girl might as well have come from another universe. She would never understand the Hanging Man.

Makeda might, but she could not be bothered by him.

I awoke on this particular Monday morning determined to redeem myself by pouring my energies more conscientiously into my work. Showering, I resisted the temptation put forward by some demon to touch my *washela*. I turned off the hot water tap and laughed. The old saw was true. In the icy shower, my *washela* contracted like a withered old man.

I rubbed my body roughly with a bath towel, avoiding looking at myself in the mirror. There was no one there I wanted to see.

The street was still quiet as I walked out to my car, although the sun shone like a devil already. How could this be February? In Tikil Dingay, it would be hot, too. Had God decided to visit this heat wave upon Los Angeles to taunt me? I brushed the thought aside as soon as it arose, embarrassed that I would take the weather personally. *You are not the center of the universe, Assefa Berhanu.*

I was calm but also aware that I was driving faster than usual. Much faster. I should not have been surprised when the creature came out of nowhere to present itself to the front fender of my car. I felt the impact and saw it go flying. My heart racing, I pulled to the curb and ran back. A white cat with black markings and a red leather collar. Someone's pet. Though its jaw was smashed, its pregnant belly was intact. But the babies would not survive.

And then I remembered. I had never asked. Surely she would have told me.

I shouted at the dead animal. "Why did you do that? You stupid creature! You did not have to die!"

I sensed people coming out of their houses. I lifted the still-warm carcass with my bare hands and laid it at the side of the road. Avoiding censorious stares, I returned to my car and drove off.

The animal's blank eyes stayed with me. They merged with those of the young kudu I'd seen die as a boy. Struggling to clear my head, I found Bezaworqu Asfaw's *Tizita* on my IPod and played it. I was rewarded with a greater clarity than I'd had for some time.

It was good I was going to a hospital.

Entering the elevator, I said hello to three nurses I recognized from cardiology. One of them made some private joke that only they understood, and the other two laughed, eyeing me nervously.

I got off before them and took the steps two at a time back down to the floor I wanted. I found my way to the physical therapy storage room. Pulleys of various sizes were leaning against the wall. I managed to cut the rope free from one of them and was gratified that it seemed long enough.

I held the nylon rope at arm's length, letting it suspend itself, testing it. It wasn't thick, but I knew it was strong. Removing papers to make room for it, I tucked it into my valise.

Finding a vacant room was difficult. One after another was occupied by staff. The patient rooms were all full of cotton-gowned men and women captive to the world of illness, in bed or out, some of them with their gowns untied and their back ends revealed.

My heart rate was elevated. A pressure was building inside me that I knew I must relieve. The inability to find a room filled me with outrage. Not one empty room in a hospital of over five hundred beds? Emergency Medicine, in particular, was like a scene from a battle zone. Had the town gone crazy with murders and accidents the night before?

I found a vacant room on the oncology ward. It suited my needs perfectly. The staff had tougher hides here, watching patients they'd grown fond of lose their wars.

Stretching the rope over the television support arm and locking it in place was easy, getting the rope adjusted properly a little harder. It took patience, and it was difficult to have patience now, with this wild buzzing in my ears and my fingers suddenly like rubber.

I prayed no one would enter before I was done.

The thought flashed by, what a strange thing to pray for, but the tension released itself in an instant. I had no more need of prayer.

Chapter Nineteen
Fleur

AS A CHILD I'd seen abusive welts and bruises on the skin of my ailing grandfather, been pinched to the point of fainting by a Father who hated having children underfoot, and heard the hollow sound of my own small fists banging on the locked door of my intoxicated mother's bedroom. More recently I'd been flattened to the point of despair by photos of pelicans transformed by the Gulf oil spill into beasts slouching toward Bethlehem to be born. But this was an entirely new kind of horror.

Stanley H. Fiske was like a madman. In a living room crowded with leaden-limbed people who were mute with shock and sadness, he couldn't stay still. Gwennie, Mother, Aadita, Sammie, Jacob, Amir, and I watched with red-rimmed eyes as he flitted like a firefly out of the room and back, stopping only to pound his head against a wall or cry out some version of, "God, it should have been me, instead!"

I had never seen anyone else cause themselves pain, but right now it struck me as something strange and awful for a human being to turn against himself as Stanley was doing. As I liked to do.

As Assefa had done.

At some point—I can't tell when, it all blended into itself like a pulsing *moiré*—I slid down to the carpet from my perch on a sofa littered with crumpled tissues and sunflower seed shells. I wanted to scrape my fingernails across the insides of my arms, twist the skin of my inner thighs, hit my head against the floor, but I couldn't.

Mother landed like a sack of coal beside me and pulled my head to her breast. Someone, I don't know who, was at my other side, stroking my back. And still, I knew Stanley was flitting. I could hear him, an uncomforted ghost seeking penance for the unforgivable—and unforgiven—thing he'd said.

I have no idea how I got through that day. How any of us did. Our own lives had been hijacked by Assefa's attempt to leave this world. We'd heard nothing since Dr. Sitota's call to Mother, so we sat together for comfort. Except for Stanley, who could not. At least some of us shared with him a similar torment. Assefa was in the ICU. Would he live or would he die? Would he suffer permanent paralysis or brain damage? What could we have done to prevent this? Was it our fault?

Make no mistake, John Donne was right. If I'd had any previous delusion that I was alone on this earth, I'd been wrong. As a physicist, I should have realized how much we matter to each other. Our deaths (or, please God, our near-deaths) don't just ripple outward like stones thrown across a river; they shake and splinter the ground for those standing at the shore.

If Assefa had been seeking revenge, he'd gotten it. But somehow, I didn't think he'd been seeking revenge. It was something far worse than that, but I didn't know what. Even though I hated what he'd done to his family, to me, to Stanley H. Fiske, I ached for him. I knew his act spoke of an intolerable confrontation with the void. But still, why?

I kept adding up everything I knew that might have led to him trying to take his own life. Gwennie had called what had happened between us "rape." It had been awful, but the word still felt too strong. What about the vicious appellation, "black son of a bitch?" Words associated with humiliation, lynching, dehumanization. What Stanley had said was astonishingly ugly, but Assefa was not a weak man, nor a stupid one. Surely he wouldn't have taken in what Stanley had said as true.

I'd heard that suicide attempts were often cries for help. Had he counted on being saved? I'd also heard that taking one's life was a hostile act. If so, why take his rage out on his parents, who, as much as I ached all the way to my bones, would surely be destroyed if their only child died by his own hand? In my feeble attempts to understand, I was like a fish flapping frantically on the deck of a ship. And the ship was at risk of going down.

By midnight, there was still no word from the hospital, where Assefa's family was keeping their own vigil. Dhani had brought over an aromatic array of *paneer tikka masala, aloo gobi*, mushroom *mutter*, and Kerala shrimp curry. To avoid offending her, I'd pushed my food around my plate, but really, who among us had an appetite? Eventually, she and Ignacio, then Amir, Sammie, Jacob, and Aadita had peeled away with promises all around to call one another if we heard anything during the night. It was down to the Fiskes, Mother, and me. Stanley's body finally registered the ten milligrams of Ativan Gwennie had made him swallow; we could hear him snoring like a bear from his bedroom. Mother offered to sleep with me in my bed, but I so visibly shuddered that Gwennie gave her an afghan to cover herself on the couch.

My body felt like a pincushion, with sharp little electric jabs pricking my skin. Thoughts paced my mind like pent-up animals. How could such a blissful connection between two people go so irreparably out of whack? Assefa had become a mystery to me as soon as I'd succeeded in cajoling the name "Makeda" from his lips.

I must have fallen asleep at some point, because I woke up crying. I ran out to the kitchen to be greeted by Gwennie shaking her head. "No word so far." A spatula in one hand, she came over and pulled me to her bosom. Repositioning my head so that I could hear her heartbeat, I counted along with it.

A toilet flushed; I presumed it was Mother, since I'd seen through the arched doorway that the living room was empty, a bed pillow and Gwennie's afghan flung carelessly on the floor.

I pulled away from Gwennie's embrace and went out to the living room. I lifted the blanket from the floor and began to fold it. Stanley shuffled past like a blind man. He wore plaid blue and green pajama bottoms and, improbably, a red Caltech Beaver hoodie over his head. He was pacing again, albeit much slower this morning, as if some hyped up inner clock was winding down. Mother appeared, running a hand through her tousled, graying hair. We hugged, and then she and Gwennie and I struggled to do at least partial justice to Gwennie's spinach and mushroom frittata.

After a few minutes, Gwennie called out, "Stan, come on and get some breakfast. It'll help settle you," but he kept moving. At one point, she had to physically restrain him from calling the Berhanus and "confessing." She got him to sit at the table with us, though he pushed away his plate and tapped the edge of the table frenetically. "Stanley," Gwennie said, "if you tell the Berhanus what you saw when you went into Fleur's room, you'll kill them. I want you to promise never to tell them. Ever."

I saw Mother turn sheet-white, but Stanley merely looked bewildered. "But I—I have to make—how are they ever going to understand why he—"

"Stop it!" Gwennie abruptly pushed herself out of her chair and stood over Stanley like a storm cloud. "How dare you presume you're important enough to make Assefa want to die!" I pinched my thigh to stop myself from fainting. I could barely see through my tears. "Yes, what you said was astoundingly disgusting. Someday, you're going to have to figure that one out. But none of us know what was going on inside that poor boy. Right now, we have to focus all our energy on hoping he survives this thing. And helping Fleur get through it."

Stanley stared up at her, open-mouthed. I think I did, too. I realized that Mother had taken my hand. She squeezed it unusually hard, and I felt a rush of gratitude toward her. But—I don't know why, probably sheer habit—I loosened my hand from hers and reached for a napkin to blow my nose.

Stanley skewed in his chair to face me. "Sweetheart," he pled, a thin gob of snot dangling from his left nostril. "I can't bear that you had to go through what you did and now this." I couldn't concentrate on what he was saying, fascinated by how the snot ball trembled with each syllable. He continued, "Don't you remember South Africa's Truth and Reconciliation do dahs? I just think—"

"Don't think," Gwennie horned in, and I nearly laughed. Telling a physicist not to think was pretty funny. Gwennie went on. "This is one case where less truth is best for those who are suffering the most."

Me, I wasn't so sure. Even debating the question felt a little like playing God. But if God in any of His, Her, or Its manifold incarnations hadn't managed to stop Assefa from trying to kill himself, maybe it was foolish to think of God as a useful concept.

I escaped across the street to Sammie's as soon as I could. Seeing Stanley struggle to inhabit his own body again was simply too much to bear. After offering to stay, Mother had seemed only too happy to accept my solemn vow to call her if I needed her.

But it was she who phoned me a little after 3:00. I discovered I'd missed her call when I checked my messages in the Schwartz's bathroom. Mr. Heavyflow was rubbing it in that I wasn't pregnant. I'd soaked through a tampon *and* a Maxi pad. I ran back to Sammie's room, shouting to her and Jacob, "He's alive! And awake! Dr. Sitota called Mother about five minutes ago. Of course, he's in no end of pain. He's been on transfusions of—hell, I can't remember, something like vecuronium and midazolen. He's got a cervical collar, but he's not paralyzed. They managed to take a chest CT and a cervical spine X-ray with him in a seated position, and Dr. Sitota told her that the results look clear. He's still kind of out of it, though. We won't know for a while if he's suffered brain damage."

All three of us fell silent at that one, and I realized the enormity of what I'd said. Sammie and Jacob were sitting shoulder to shoulder on her bed with their backs pillowed against the wall. They'd grown closer over the past twenty-four hours, holding hands and exchanging meaningful looks. Would it last? Probably not, but I was awfully glad she had him right now.

I sat on the edge of the bed, realizing at some point that tears were rolling down my face. I'd never known before that you could weep without even knowing you were crying. As if sensing my distress, Midge waddled over and collapsed onto my lap. Actually, my lap was too small to contain him, but he did a good job of melting his large body across my folded legs, with his head dangling over one knee and his eyes heavy-lidded in ecstasy.

"Fleur Beurre," Sammie said.

"Don't," I replied. "I really don't have the strength to fall apart again."

It was then that Jacob interjected, "Has anybody actually spoken to Assefa's parents?"

"No," I said. "I'm sure they've been by his side ever since they found out."

"So we don't know exactly how they heard? Or who found him?"

Sammie jumped in, shooting Jacob a warning look, "Do we really need to be talking about this right now?"

"No, no," I said. "It's okay. I've been wondering myself. Since it was a … hanging, I'd presume someone cut him down almost immediately."

The room went quiet enough to hear Sammie's alarm clock ticking. The ghastly reality of what Assefa had done thrummed inside my head.

Sammie murmured, "It's a blessing he's been spared."

"I hope so," Jacob responded. "What if he's brain damaged?" This time, Sammie looked as if she could hang him.

But Jacob seemed oblivious. "Do you think his folks know what he did to you? What Stanley said to him?"

"Oh, God, I hope not. Stanley actually wanted to tell them everything. To 'confess.' Gwennie convinced him not to, at least for now, but what if Assefa told them himself?" I could hear a gathering hysteria in my voice. "Will they even want to speak to us? What could we say that would possibly …?" Howling, I flipped over onto my belly, displacing Midge, whose claws left a track of blood across my arm. I barely noticed. I wanted to join Assefa in whatever bottomless pit had claimed him.

As if she could read my mind, Sammie slid down and aligned her body next to mine, stroking my head and whispering comfortingly, "My poor Fleur Beurre. It's too much, isn't it, my darling dear?"

I turned my head toward her so that we were nearly nose-to-nose. A long worry line was bisecting her forehead. Her breath on my face was like warm milk. God, I loved her. I tried to smile. "It's a little redundant, isn't it? 'Darling dear'?"

We both sat up, and I kissed her forehead.

I heard Jacob's voice as if from a long distance. "It makes me think about the wisdom of Solomon."

Sammie looked as puzzled as I felt. "Huh?"

Jacob raised his eyebrows. "Hell-*oh*. Solomon, the Jewish epitome of wisdom?"

I knew the *Book of Wisdom* well, having read it on my own at the age of four. Instinctively, the words flew out of my mouth: "The breath in our nostrils is like smoke, and conversation sends out sparks from the stirring of our heart …."

Jacob muttered, "Actually, I was thinking of 'The Judgment of Solomon.'" Sammie and I stared at him. "You know, King Solomon being asked to judge which of two women claiming a certain baby was hers was actually its mother. Have you ever heard of the *bat kol*?" I shook my head. "It translates from Hebrew as 'the daughter of the voice.' It's not quite 'the voice of God,' which we wouldn't be able to hear, anyway, but of God's wisdom. It's what came to King Solomon when he was asked to rule in favor of one of the women. Jewish scholars agree it was *bat kol* that suggested he propose that a sword be brought to him so that he could divide the child in half. The true mother revealed herself when she begged Solomon to give the baby to the other woman rather than cut him in half."

I knew it well, of course. "Pretty clever," I commented.

"No," objected Jacob, sliding off the bed to stand in the middle of the room, gesticulating. "It wasn't just cleverness. In one of the few, but significant, dreams in the Old Testament, Solomon had already asked God to give him 'a hearing heart.' One that would listen to God."

I frowned. "But what does that have to do with what we say to the Berhanus?"

"I'm not sure," Jacob said, "but we *all* love Assefa." I opened my mouth to respond, but Jacob waved a hand in the air. "I know, I know. He's treated you like crap lately; Stanley called him something really shitty; Sammie was ready to kill him for breaking up with you—" The three of us exchanged a shocked glance. "Sorry. But no. Listen. Bascially, he's a bright, decent guy. We all love him. Hell, I'm an asshole, and *I* love him."

Did all assholes know they were assholes?

Jacob continued, "Whatever any of us say to the Berhanus, that's really all that matters. We're never going to fathom why he did what he did. Hell, for all we know, he has a brain tumor."

You had to hand it to Jacob. He was absolutely right. He was an asshole.

I had to get out of there. I felt certain Sammie knew why I had to go. I also knew they were going to have a hell of a fight once I'd gone. But there was simply no more room in my head to worry about it.

I ran across the street and let myself in the front door to find Stanley sitting on the living room couch. The drapes were drawn. I sat down close to him, my eyes still adjusting to the lack of light. I could tell he'd barely registered my presence. "Stanley, I don't care what you said, anymore. You weren't in your right mind when you said those things, and Assefa wasn't in his right mind when you came in. Honestly, I wasn't in my right mind, either." *Was that true?* "I keep hoping I'll wake up and this will all have been a bad dream. There's a part of me that still can't believe that Assefa's fighting for his life, or at least his beautiful mind. Well, I hope he's fighting. It's as if we're all puppets in some play, manipulated by invisible strings." And then, like some idiot, I added, "A new kind of string theory." Stanley didn't laugh. I didn't blame him.

In the dim light emanating from the hallway, it looked as if Stanley was wearing an oddly positioned skull cap over the top right quadrant of his salt-and-pepper head. First the hoodie, now this? Was his guilt driving him to Judaism? I turned on the coffee table lamp and did a double take. What I'd assumed was a cap was actually an oddly-shaped, five-inch island of bare scalp where hair had most definitely been the day before.

I knew his hair had been thinning; just a few days earlier Gwen had complained that he was leaving it to her to clean out strands of his hair from the shower. But this? My first thought was that he'd pulled it out as some sort of penance, but then I remembered that stress could sometimes exacerbate an out of whack immune system condition called alopecia areata. This I knew from a bored moment at Mother's, when I'd read a confession by Viola Davis in *Elle* magazine that she'd suffered from the disorder. "Oh, Stanley," I whispered. I leaned over and pulled him to me.

Eventually he spoke, his voice muffled against my chest. "All my life I've wanted to help young people. I actually took pride that I did. Now, I've failed all of you. Especially Assefa, but you, too, Fleur. I've never loved anyone on this earth as much as you, and now—what must you think of me?"

That one stopped me in my tracks. I shoved it to the back of my mind for later contemplation. It was odd to be sitting with him like this, both of us blubbering, and his nose butted up sharply against my collarbone.

Only a few days ago, the bored-as-hell God with his immense void had spoken to Assefa through the fiercely protective lips of my mentor. Not as a calming "daughter of the voice" pronouncement from the lips of a bearded Jewish patriarch, but a smiting eruption of primitive rage from a man who looked like a frog.

As much as I wanted to reassure him, I had no words for Stanley. Instead, I rocked him, rocked myself, as we both continued to cry.

Chapter Twenty
Fleur

IT TOOK THREE days for the doctors to determine that Assefa had likely not incurred any serious brain damage. Mother phoned me with the news.

"Abeba just called. Isn't it wonderful? A miracle, really."

"How did she sound?"

"Exhausted. Teary. Relieved. And disturbingly apologetic."

"Apologetic! For what?"

"For putting us through so much distress."

"Mother!"

"I know."

"Do you think I can call her?"

"I think that would be a lovely idea."

Without allowing myself to think, I did.

Abeba answered the phone on the first ring, and I realized she must be on perpetual tenterhooks. "Yes?" Her voice cracked a little. I let my body down into a kitchen chair.

"Abeba, it's Fleur."

She started to cry. Which, needless to say, set me off, too.

"I'm so sorry," she finally said.

"Abeba, please," I remonstrated. Then, of all people, Jacob came to me. "We're all in this with you. Me, Mother, Stanley, Gwennie, all of Assefa's friends. Everyone loves him and has been praying for him."

"Does he still have friends, Fleur?" Her voice had a slight edge, and for a second I thought, *He's told them*. But then she went on, "I am so afraid he has lost everything by doing this. How could he, Fleur? How could he? I knew he was … unsettled. But this?" She broke into sobbing again. I hated myself for having phoned her. "I am so glad you called," she said.

"Abeba, I didn't want to add to your burden. I just wanted to tell you how grateful I am that he's okay. Well, maybe okay is the wrong word. I know he's got to be in a lot of pain. But at least he's here, Abeba. At least he's here."

This was stupid. We were both sobbing now, speechless.

I heard the clatter of her phone being put down; in an obvious attempt to gather herself, Abeba was blowing her nose. She came on the line again. "He is sitting up and eating and even talking a little." She gave a faint laugh. "Enough to tell us to go home. He is such a good boy, Fleur. Always thinking about others. You will visit him today? I know he will want to see you."

"Of course," I said, panicking.

Which is how I ended up entering the labyrinthine complex where Assefa had morphed from healer to patient. The place was a zoo. Well, not really, but from the point of exiting the packed elevator at his floor it took me ten minutes to find Room 515.

The door to the room was open, but a nurse was blocking the threshold, her back to me as she peered inside. Tall and thin, she'd captured her fiery red hair in a tight rubber band. I tapped her shoulder. She wheeled around and flashed me a wide grin. "He's asleep," she said, stepping away from the door, presumably so as not to wake him. I followed suit. "No, no," she said, "I was just looking in on him. I try to come by at least once a day. But, please. Go on in."

"Are you a friend? Do you work with him?" I asked—anything to delay the moment of actually seeing Assefa.

She threw me a shrewd look. "Are you his fiancée Fleur?" I instinctually nodded, then decided not to correct myself as she went on, "His mother speaks so highly of you. What a sweet family," she said, a doubtful look in her eyes. I could tell she would have liked to ask a million questions, but I certainly wasn't going to encourage her. I had a few, myself.

Then she threw me for a loop, no awful pun intended. "Actually, I work in oncology. I'm Evelyn McDermott." She held out a surprisingly strong hand. I shook it. "I was the one who found him. I can't tell you what it's meant to me that he's survived."

I stared at her. "You saved him." I reached out to shake her hand again, this time with feeling.

We walked down the hall, distancing ourselves further from Assefa's room. "Well, I suppose I did, but somehow I felt the whole time that something was moving through me, if you know what I mean."

She clearly wanted to tell me. I nodded for her to go on. "I'd actually had a dream the night before. It was an awful dream, a real nightmare. Someone had to make a life or death decision. It was a man with his son—the kid was in terrible pain, and the father was about to spare him any more suffering by killing him. With an axe. I woke myself up screaming at one a.m., and I thought to myself, 'Well, something's not right.' I actually texted my son in the middle of the night and scared him to death. The thing is, my son has no father." Her speech had become increasingly rushed. Now she paused for breath. This woman had been traumatized, too, by what Assefa had done.

"I don't know, when I saw this man—your fiancé—slumped over with that ... thing ... around his neck, his face grotesque— such a terrible shade of purple and a horrifying gurgle coming from his throat, I knew I had to get it off him. Thank God he had the knife he'd cut the rope with right there. It had fallen onto the floor. Still, it was almost impossible to cut through. It was a pulley rope, and they're meant to bear hundreds of pounds of weight." The expression in her eyes seemed both stunned and triumphant, like a runner who'd come from way behind to win the marathon.

When I told the story later to Sammie, she'd commented, "Good lord. How horrid. And how lucky. Just like stinging nettles, with the mugwort plant that heals their sting growing right next to them."

My own body itched with invisible hives as I said yet another thank you to Evelyn McDermott and hesitantly entered Assefa's hospital room. He was awake and struggled to sit up as I came in.

"Don't," I said. "Please. I'm just ...."

But he managed to pull himself into a quasi-seated position, his face ashy and gaunt above his white cervical collar, the arms that poked out of his flimsy, cornflower blue gown angular and listless. "Hello, Fleur." His voice was unrecognizably hoarse.

Determined not to break down, I pulled a chair next to his bed. *But not too close.*

"It's okay," he said. "You can cry."

But I daren't. I barely managed a halting, "Assefa."

"I'm here," he whispered, giving what sounded like an attempted laugh. "Like it or not."

"Oh, Assefa." This was no time for real conversation. He was far too weak and there were too many elephants crowded into the room. "I'm glad you are," I said.

"Are you?"

"I am," I said, more emphatically.

"Well, that's good," he said, closing his eyes. At some point it dawned on me that he'd fallen asleep. I gave him a long look before leaving. His eyelashes were thick with gunk, the outer creases of his lips chalky with dried spittle. Staring at him without any semblance of desire, it occurred to me that I'd never loved him properly. I'd wanted him, yes. Madly. Who wouldn't? I'd never seen a man more beautiful. And certainly, I'd admired him. But I had never felt the kind of sadness for him that I felt now. The kind of tenderness that his mother undoubtedly experienced every minute she sat here at his bedside.

I felt small and more than a little ugly as I tiptoed out of the room.

Chapter Twenty-one
Fleur

I MET WITH Assefa a few weeks after his release from the hospital. It had nothing to do with getting back together. Without either of us explicitly saying so, we knew we were beyond that. On my side, I'd concluded that I'd had enough of desire. My own was too dangerous. Ever since puberty it had been like some out-of-whack pinball machine, creating disasters at every flip and ping. I didn't know which was worse—my contribution to the wreckage of Assefa's life or what he'd done to my own trust in love.

I didn't speak much about the latter, but surprisingly, it was Mother I most longed to confide in. Given Stanley's moral lapse, the Fiskes were out of the question; Sammie's hands were full with the inevitable return of Bad Jacob after a brief appearance of the nicer one; and Jillily didn't count.

When I let spill that I'd actually met up with Assefa the previous morning at the Huntington Gardens, Mother gently asked me if we were patching things up. "Do you think you might still get married?" she asked hopefully.

I told her it was out of the question. "Mother, I can't believe we were engaged when I knew him so little. I thought nothing could faze him. I had no idea he was so ... complicated."

Mother eyed me oddly. "Most people are, Fleur."

The two of us were sitting on her bed, the very same one where my tweeter had set Satan's proclivity for disaster in motion. The bed covers were different, though, thanks to Mother's weakness for shopping therapy. The silky duvet we spread ourselves across, propped up on our elbows, was a new find from Barney's, appliquéd with satisfying patterns of butterflies, morning glories, and bees in dusty rose, sage, and a buttery yellow.

"Well, maybe working through what happened might be a prelude to a deeper love."

"No," I said firmly.

She sighed. "Well, I guess that's why they call it first love. It's because it's usually followed by a second. At least a second."

I didn't dare tell her that Assefa had been the second. But perhaps she'd argue that Adam didn't count, since he knew nothing about it.

Without warning, Mother pushed herself off the bed and began removing her black cashmere V-neck and honey-colored crepe slacks, groaning slightly with the pleasure of removing the constriction from her skin. I saw that her black lace bra barely contained her bulging breasts, and her belly and behind made cellulite moons around the elastic of her matching black bikini panties.

The only other time I'd seen Mother unclothed was when I'd stolen into her closet as a child for a pinch-fest and spied her through the crack in the closet door posing with her naked body in the mirror. Then, my eyes had fixed on her every-which-way pubic hair, which had contrasted so starkly with her alternating cool and fragile demeanor in the fearsome house of my father.

She'd always been a beauty, with classic features and a long, lean figure perfectly complimented by her signature sleek skirts and silk blouses, pearl necklaces and Chanel No. 5 perfume. But with the approach of middle age, she'd widened and sagged and grayed, and I'd ceased to think of her as particularly attractive, certainly not sexual. Until now. The matter-of-fact ease with which she'd flung off her clothes to get more comfortable in her royal blue sweat suit, the earthy musk that wafted from her naked flesh, the frank smile she threw me when she saw me staring at her, all spoke of a mysterious comfort with her body that I suddenly envied.

Breaking the spell, she asked, "So, what did you two talk about?" before climbing back onto the bed, giving me a quick peck on the forehead, and plumping up a few large pillows to nestle against.

Her question took me by surprise. I wasn't sure I wanted to share everything Assefa had confided in me. He was still so raw that it would feel like a betrayal. One of the harder things to hear had been his apology for hurting me. But the worst was his halting, but nonetheless detailed, description of his Hanging Man and his obsession with Makeda.

Assefa had confessed when I picked up the phone that he was calling on the spur of the moment. He was still staying at his parents' house—"on suicide watch," he'd muttered bitterly—and they were only too happy to relinquish him to my care. It had been a shock to see him, looking somehow smaller than before, and he seemed a bit wary to see me, but we'd resolutely pushed through the clusters of young families milling around the Huntington's ticket kiosk and walked past a museum shop displaying posters of their collection of incunabula, including a rare vellum Gutenberg Bible that I promised myself to return to peruse properly one day. We made our way toward the vast Australian garden, where we settled ourselves under one of the taller eucalyptus trees. The air was thick with its honeyed, minty scent, and only the occasional *chwirk* of a Red-tailed Hawk or a lone Black Phoebe's *tee-hee too-hoo* punctuated the stillness. Our exchange went like this:

Me: "How's your neck? (He was still wearing his cervical collar, so it was a pretty natural question, but still loaded. My voice had been, accordingly, a bit wavery.)

Assefa: (With a rueful smile, his hand flowing up to inch two fingers under the bottom of the collar.) "Oh, not too bad, really. Considering."

Me: (Leaping in like an idiot, but there you have it. Nothing in life happens without a leap or two.) "Oh, Assefa, was it what Stanley said?"

Assefa: (Giving a slight grimace before offering a non sequiturish) "Fleur, can you ever forgive me?"

Me: "I do. I will. Well, anyway, I want to." I paused. "But I really wouldn't have forgiven you if you'd succeeded. Assefa, how could you?"

Assefa: (putting up a hand.) "Stop. Please. My parents are already driving me mad with their questions. But I have to admit, I feel strangely relieved. And not just to be alive." I shoved that one into a cupboard in my mind. One not too far back, since I knew I'd want to pull it out and examine it as soon as I was alone. "But, listen, Fleur," Assefa went on, "there is one weight still heavy on me. I am ashamed for what I, how I ... treated you that last night."

Me: "It was my fault. I should never have—"

Assefa: (Interrupting) "No. It is not your fault. We must be truthful with each other, or we have nothing. I nearly raped you. Maybe more than nearly. I don't know what I— That music. I just—"

Me: (Totally confused.) "The music? What are you talking about?"

Which is when he really began to talk, and I really shut up and listened. I was able to bear it only because I was secretly pinching my outer thigh the whole time. He told me he couldn't remember his childhood without thinking about Makeda. He admitted that he remembered more about her than Bekele and Iskinder, more than even his mother and father. The expression on his face when he spoke her name nearly killed me, but it also filled me, strangely, with a kind of desire. Not for Assefa himself—that seemed to have been swallowed by a particularly dense department of the void—but for Makeda. As if I'd caught an invisible virus from Assefa. I wanted to see her, touch her, get inside her skin. Better yet, *be* her.

But Assefa was saying, "Fleur, the worst of it was—well, not the worst, but when I was there in Ethiopia, I thought about you. Some devil had decreed I would never be satisfied. Never be a whole man. I could not have her, and—"

This was what I was dying to know: "But why couldn't you? Did she reject you?"

"No. She didn't. She didn't have to." A shadow came into his eyes. "She'd had a botched genital mutilation as a girl." Then he whispered, "As if any of them aren't." A terrible dizziness overtook me, but, relentlessly, Assefa continued. "It was done to her during the war that my family escaped by having left. She was captured. By our own people." He gave a bark of laugh that made me want to get up and run away. "It ... ruined her capacity for pleasure. Or at least her desire for it. Here I'd been imagining that the country my parents had ripped me from was some kind of Eden." Assefa's voice grew hard. "Instead, it is a shit pile of poverty, ignorance, violence."

It must have been his sorrow speaking. I was far too ignorant about Ethiopia, but I knew that the home of the Blue Nile was brimming with richness and beauty. There was no way such a large and diverse land could be encapsulated in a few bitter words. Whether or not the Ark of the Covenant was actually kept at Aksum, Ethiopia was where the oldest human fossils remains had been discovered. It was the birthplace of our species. I'd never been there, but I sensed—no, *knew*—it was something special. I knew it from the graciousness of Assefa's parents, from the streaks of shiny color woven into Abeba's white *netelas*, from the bitter-fruit taste of *bunna* and the longing in *tizita* and the way Teddy Afro's "Aydenegetim Lebie" made me feel. I knew it from Assefa's seriousness of purpose and his wry wit. But still. "Genital mutilation?"

Assefa took pity on me. "I'm sorry. That was cruel. But you wanted to know."

"I do. Well, I think so, anyway." I'd also thought I must be mutilating my outer thigh, but no matter. "But I—"

"What, Fleur?"

" Assefa, we never had a chance, did we?"

"Because of my neurosis?"

"Neurosis? No. Because neither of us have any idea who we are yet."

When I told Mother at least that part of it, she laughed. "Oh, my sweet, sweet girl. By the time you get to my age, you realize that we keep thinking we know who we are and discovering we're something else. The damned thing won't stay still, no matter how much we want it to."

I wasn't so sure I agreed with her. Mother was Mother, and Gwennie was Gwennie, and Stanley was ... well, maybe Mother was right. But I didn't like it. It made the void even more voidish. I didn't like it one bit.

Chapter Twenty-two
Fleur

MOTHER WAS CONVINCED that a weekend together at Two Bunch Palms was just what I needed to conquer my unyielding blues. Built by gangster Al Capone in the 1920s (and with bullet holes in its walls to prove it) and memorialized in the Hollywood send-up film *The Player*, the resort was everything the rest of the country derided and envied about SoCal. During our two hour and forty-one minute drive there, we saw more freeways than any human should be subjected to, opening thankfully into vast expanses of desert dotted with sagebrush, arrestingly shaped cacti, and dazzling splashes of orange ezperanza, purple lupins, and sweet-faced monkeyflowers.

Nearing our destination on Two Bunch Trail, we passed a woman with way too much make-up walking a calico cat on a leash. The animal looked terrified. When I shared my observation with Mother, she nodded. "I don't doubt it. I'm all too familiar myself with the terror of being saddled with something, or"—her eyes raked over the woman with the too-plump lips—"*someone* you can't bear." With Mother, the purgatory of her years in a miserable marriage was never far from her mind.

Over the next few days, we kept ourselves occupied perusing copious quantities of mindless magazines, taking Tai Chi classes in the Yoga Dome, chatting about nothing and everything during long walks amid the spectacular rock piles of Joshua Tree, and tracing a path in Big Morongo Canyon alongside a creek created by a major earthquake fault. Mother was sensitive enough to let me fall into long, meditative silences as we floated in the resort's mineral water grotto. On our last night, we splurged on an unbelievably yummy dinner at Tinto's in Palm Springs.

But a life avoided is a life unlived. I returned to the Fiskes' with relaxed muscles, pampered pores, and an actual suntan, determined to pour my energies into quantum entanglement. Even a particularly unsettling phone conversation with Assefa didn't deter me from my resolve. On Monday morning, I leapt out bed, cooked up an omelet seasoned with fresh basil and thyme gifted to me by Two Bunch's friendly head chef, and sped off to Caltech, eager to dive in.

But my heart sank as soon as I arrived. It *would* have to be Bob Ballantine who was there to greet me. The room was empty but for him, the sun shooting a shaft of light through the window blinds, which someone had opened at enough of a skewed angle to be annoying. He looked up with a surprised smile, which he quickly adjusted into an expression of sympathy.

There was nothing for it. I had to approach and be subjected to what I made sure was a brief hug, pulling away with an embarrassed little laugh. In recent bouts of torturing myself over my shameful lack of interest in Assefa's original Ethiopian incarnation, the void had used the face of Bob to punish me for the faithlessness of my desire. Now, with the actual man right before me—and despite the fact that he'd shown me nothing but kindness (well, that and a rather determined concupiscence)—I struggled to understand how I'd gotten myself into bed with him. I couldn't help but notice that he had the usual glob of lox fat between his teeth, this time between the two front ones. Did he never breakfast on anything but smoked fish? Or brush his teeth? I saw, as well, that he'd evidently given up on the gel he'd been using in his hair. It was longer now, edging toward the shoulders of his navy pullover, upon which his ubiquitous dusting of dandruff was hitching a ride.

"I'm so sorry, Fleur," he murmured, his eye tic seconding the motion. But my ears were attuned to what sounded like Stanley and the gang coming up the hall.

I turned to see my mentor burst into the room with his old verve, moving forward with something just short of a serious hop. I'd returned from Two Bunch to discover that Stanley had secretly been conspiring to arrange Assefa's transfer from UCLA to New York-Presbyterian University Hospital of Columbia and Cornell. The favor had clearly gone at least a little way in assuaging my mentor's gargantuan guilt. According to Stanley, Assefa had submitted to sitting down with him this past weekend and, while he hadn't exactly forgiven him for his atrocious lapse of decency, he'd heard him out, eking out in return a terse acknowledgment of Stanley's sincere regret.

I'd called Assefa as soon as I heard, gingerly broaching the topic and getting a reply that pretty much skirted his encounter with Stanley. He delivered the relieving news that his doctor had removed his cervical collar, and he actually sounded a little enthusiastic about moving to Manhattan, where his parents had a few friends among the city's large Ethiopian contingent. He'd stressed how grateful he was to be able to continue his training at one of the top-rated cardiac wards in the country. "Even better than UCLA, Fleur," he'd said, and I told myself it was an awfully good sign that such things were starting to matter to him again.

I had no idea how Abeba and Achamyalesh were going to bear letting him go. Mother had speculated that the fact that Achamyalesh had actually been hired to teach two classes at Pasadena City College would go some ways in filling the empty nest. But this was from the same woman who'd moved halfway across the country to live near a daughter she'd never been terribly close with. I worried about them. I'd said as much to Assefa.

Which led to a surprising outburst. "They're not saints, you know!"

"I didn't think they were."

"I mean, really."

"I don't ... Assefa, what are you saying?"

"I'm saying that you should probably let your pal Stanley off the hook."

I'd sat heavily onto my bed then, displacing Jillily, who quickly rearranged herself by my side, kneading the bedclothes and purring ecstatically. Given my sense of dread, her pleasure felt discordant. I nudged her off the bed, and she set herself hunched in the middle of the room with her back to me, her tail angrily slapping the floor.

"The truth is that if anything sent me over the edge, it was my father telling me that Makeda was conceived from him fucking her mother."

I think my heart actually skipped a few beats. "What!"

"You heard me. I came back from Ethiopia to learn that she is my sister, Fleur. My fucking sister."

"Half sister," I'd murmured.

"Does it really matter?"

I had to admit that it didn't. And I have to admit now that I simply could not take in his disclosure. The pain he had to have felt was unfathomable.

Then he'd cried out, "Oh, God, I should not have told you this! I don't know what's wrong with me. It is a private family matter. You have to swear to me that you will never tell another soul."

"Assefa, I promise. But listen, you've been through way too much. I hope you can meet this new incarnation with an open heart."

"Is there such a thing, Fleur?"

"I used to think so," I'd replied.

I could have sworn he was crying, too, when we ended our call.

I'd rolled over and lain across my bed, pressing the edge of my pillow against my mouth as I sobbed over what felt like a particularly dark instance of the Butterfly Effect. To think that the event of an Ethiopian anthropologist having sex with another man's wife would ripple across continents and time to prompt a moral crisis for a froggish American Nobelist and settle a secret weight inside another Nobelist's soul.

How could Assefa and I live separate destinies when we knew so much about each other? Could he ever find relief from his obsession with Makeda? His passion for *me* seemed to have evaporated entirely. I have to confess that it hurt.

Had I lost mine for him? If it was there, it had gone into hiding. But the beautiful god who'd chosen me and me alone to love, whose naked skin was satin and whose voice a velvet whisper ("Come, *dukula*, let me see you"), who'd teased me with his humor and his hands and his quicksilver mind, offering endless avenues of surprise? I knew the strains of "Aydenegetem Lebie" would haunt me forever, reminding me of something exceedingly precious that I would never know again.

Meanwhile, here was my team, looking at me with so much love and worry that I choked on my own spittle. Fighting for breath, tears rolling down my cheeks, I gestured that I was okay. Katrina put a hand on my arm, and Amir proffered a handkerchief. It definitely helped to blow my nose. I offered his hanky back to him. Eyeing it distastefully, he refused to take it. Everyone laughed.

"She'll be fine," Stanley pronounced, and for some reason, I started to choke all over again.

Never one for tact, Gunther rolled his good eye, muttering, "This is the one who's going to convince Congress to fund our work?"

At that, my choking morphed into giggles. Stanley gave a few silly hops, and I started waving the handkerchief in Amir's direction. He backed away, and I went after him, weaving around desks and chairs. When we came to a breathless stop, he panted, "Reminds me of Lord Hanuman," which got everyone jabbering over the time the chimp had thrown volleys of turd balls in this very room, with us scurrying frantically for cover.

"Wait," I said, still breathing hard.

"What?" asked Amir.

"I can't believe I forgot. Serena McKenna's invited me to come visit Lord Hanuman at Gombe. Jane Goodall's actually going to be there."

Amir's eyes widened. He grabbed me and demanded, "When?"

I did a quick mental computation, realizing that in the midst of Assefa's crisis, I'd not gotten back to Serena. "Oh, God, soon. Like maybe next week."

"Call her," Amir said urgently. "I'll come with you." His expression was intense. I could sense everyone watching us. Amir was usually the happy-go-lucky one of our team, wearing a peace sign *bindi* when the mood struck him, teaching Katrina Bollywood dance routines, cheering madly for Naduparambil Pappachen Pradeep, no matter which Indian football team he was playing for. But about two things he was always serious: our work on P.D. and his love for Lord Hanuman. The chimp, that is. He'd cared for Lord Hanuman ever since a friend had liberated him from a lab that no longer needed him, and he'd relinquished him with great sadness to Jane Goodall's Gombe Stream Chimpanzee Reserve when it was clear the creature needed more wilderness for his wildness than could be provided by the environs of Pasadena.

I mentally kicked myself. It should have occurred to me that Amir would give half a leg to see his simian friend again.

Stanley H. Fiske caught my eye. He nodded slightly, silently mouthing the words, "Say yes."

Gunther looked lost in thought. I knew he was aching to get back to our work on dematerialization. I also knew that Congress was in no mood to hear testimony from me while they were busy shutting down the government for the umpteenth time.

Katrina and Tom were holding hands and grinning at me encouragingly. They were the physics team members Amir was closest to, besides Adam and myself, of course. Which I suppose is a roundabout way of saying that Gunther, our team Eeyore, had a rather hard time getting close to anyone.

"Okay," I said. "I'll email her as soon as I get home."

But when I got back to the Fiskes', things were in disarray, throw pillows littering the living room floor as if Lord Hanuman himself had tossed them. It turned out that Gwen had gone to her ENT Dr. Nastarti, who'd confirmed what she'd secretly been suspecting. She was slowly going deaf in her good ear. It wasn't too bad yet, but it would likely be in the not too distant future. Needless to say, she was pretty distraught, sobbing on my shoulder, "Fleur! I don't want to get old! I hate this!" I couldn't imagine what it was like to feel your body failing, piece by piece, but I did know I was terrified of losing either of the Fiskes. I was relieved to hear Stanley's keys rattling at the front door. Sensing my distress as soon as he entered the room—it might have been the moans coming out of my mouth and the little mini-flaps of my hands—he took hold of the situation, telling his sister in a gruff tone (which I knew belied a deep filial devotion), "Gwen, get a grip; there *are* such things as hearing aids." And then he turned to me. "You'd better get online quick and see if you can find a flight for yourself and Amir."

At which point Gwennie shifted gears, demanding, "Flight? With Amir? What's going on?"

I let them sort it out and retreated to my bedroom, grabbing my laptop before flopping onto the old Liberty fabric covered armchair that Mother had bought during our New York incarnation and which Jillily had managed over the years to shred into a tattered version of its previous glory. But just as I located a website detailing which airlines flew to Tanzania, I heard my meowing cat ringtone. I got up from my desk chair and frantically fished around in my purse for my cell. As soon as I answered, Assefa burst out excitedly that he'd firmed up his own travel plans. In four days, he'd be leaving for a two-week seminar offered by the American College of Cardiology in D.C. before flying directly to New York to begin his new incarnation.

Four days. I dropped heavily onto my bed and stared bleakly at the Einstein poster on the opposite wall, for once unamused at one of our species' most brilliant men sticking out a tongue that had to be longer than Miley Cyrus'. Scratch any delusion I'd had that I was even partially over Assefa.

I tried to sound enthusiastic. A few months ago, he might have picked up my distress. But now he was full of details of the apartment he'd be sharing with a couple of med students and a U.N. staff member—one from the U.S., one from Addis Ababa, and another born in the Omo Valley. I knew about the Omo tribes, had seen videos of how they celebrated themselves with ornate body and face decorations. They were an unusually beautiful people. I resisted the temptation to ask Assefa what gender his roommates were.

Assefa deserved a little unfettered happiness. I'd actually caught sight of him the previous Wednesday seated at the Starbucks near his parents' home and he'd looked like a man with a Do Not Disturb sign on his face. It would be stupid and selfish for me to spoil his pleasure.

Instead, I told him about my intention to visit Gombe. I could hear the catch in his voice. "Ah. Africa." *Oh dear.* I just couldn't seem to cure myself of foot-in-mouth disease.

A beep signaled that another call was coming in. "Assefa, can I call you right back? I hate that damned call waiting feature."

With an abrupt, "No worries," he was gone.

It was Adam on the other line. "Hey."

I took a deep breath. "Hey."

Unlike Assefa, he noticed immediately that my voice sounded strained. "What is it, Fleur?"

"Oh, God—I was just telling Assefa that Amir and I are going to visit Serena at the Reserve, and—"

"What!"

"She invited me for when Jane Goodall will be there. I'll have a chance to meet her, and Amir will get to see Lord Hanuman again after all these years."

I sensed his mental gears whirring. "Fleur, do you really want to do this?"

"Yes. Jane Goodall comes right after Einstein and Feynman and Stanley and Frank Wilczek in my list of living heroes."

Adam chuckled. "You and your lists."

He wouldn't let me off the phone until I promised about a hundred times to take good care of myself.

Four days later, I didn't know if it was taking good care of myself or not that I persuaded Stanley to drive me to the Berhanus for the closest thing I could get to seeing Assefa off. Stanley told me that (a) I was nuts and (b) there was no way he'd expose himself to Assefa's parents after all the misery he'd caused.

Cringing with the knowledge of what I knew that he didn't, I'd replied that (a) it was about time he pushed back against his shaming inner bully, and (b) since I hadn't been able to take Assefa to the airport the last time he left me, the least Stanley could do was help me get some sort of closure now. Watching my mentor struggle with my request, I tucked away inside my Sly Soldier cupboard the discovery that guilt could be a marvelous motivator. But once we got to the Berhanus' neighborhood, Stanley insisted on parking halfway up the block on Yolo Street so he couldn't be spotted. The most I managed to persuade him to do was inch his car forward so I could watch Assefa follow his parents out of their house carrying a couple of suitcases. We were too far away to discern any of their facial expressions—actually, Stanley could see nothing at all, as he'd compressed his tall frame downward and buried his head into his neck like a tortoise below the bottom of the windshied. But refusing to shrink Uncle Bobishly myself, I watched Abeba and Achamyalesh bump along like rag dolls whose stuffing had been stripped. I thought I detected in their slumped shoulders their sadness at having to say goodbye. As for Assefa, once he'd deposited his bags and an overcoat in the trunk of his father's yellow cab, he walked around the car with the deliberate grace of a panther, not pausing once to look back at the house he'd lived in before opening the rear passenger door and disappearing inside.

Stanley and I ended up back at the house, sprawling on the living room sofa, his newly bald head up against his grease spot, though he kept sitting forward to throw another handful of sunflower seeds into his mouth. I'd brought them out from the kitchen at his request, noticing for the first time that the package of David's Original Sunflower Seeds actually read, "Eat. Spit. Be Happy!" Which I pointed out to Stanley, who gave a comic croak, "I like it. The atheist's answer to *Eat, Pray, Love*."

But his mood darkened just as quickly. He ate and spat as he conveyed its cause. "It seems I've turned into a Class-A Asshole lately. I can't help but observe that I've been giving Gwen a hard time over her deafness. Well, more accurately, over her fear of it." He gave a quick, froggish lick of what must have been pretty salty lips and slid me a sideways glance.

I waited. I'd noticed the phenomenon he was describing and had wondered about it.

"The thing is, I'm bone tired. I've been sleeping poorly ever since … well, the whole damned thing. You have to admit it's been an awful year. That horrible accident on New Year's Day, our God damned know-nothing excuse for a Congress tying up our work, Achamyalesh going missing, the Kangs, the crap with your … with me … oh, you know what I mean. Seeing my sister suffer on top of that." He leaned forward to clank his stainless steel bowl of shells onto the glass coffee table, then commenced picking little pieces of shell off the sofa, his pants and shirt. "I remember her when she was a little pipsqueak. You know, one of those irritating younger sisters who trailed after you wherever you go. Probably why I started burying myself in books. Somewhere she couldn't follow me. Cute as a button, but I never would've admitted it. Didn't even notice it till much later. Not too many guys her age did, either, as I recall. And the ones who did—well, they treated her pretty badly. Poor Gwen." He gave a strangled sort of laugh. "Turns out we were both pretty hopeless at relationships."

"Are you referring to Doris?"

He looked surprised and gave a grudging nod. "You remembered. A good-looking woman, and she knew her science. But she was inconsistent in other ways." Then he made a face. "And yes, she was black. I suppose Gwennie told you. And if she's been feeding you some armchair psychology about how my feelings about her transferred over to Assefa, then all I can tell you is phooey! The truth is, I'll probably never understand why those words came out of me, besides the fact that we all probably soak in some of that crap from the world around us. I don't know about your Sammie's Jung, but I think the human mind seems pretty capable of keeping secrets from itself. And others, of course." My belly rumbled in voidish agreement. "I remember when our father died, my first thought was good riddance, but I never voiced it to another soul. Didn't even remember it until now. Maybe I shoved it into some parallel universe." He grinned. "See what sleep starvation does to you?" He paused and scratched his head. "The thing is, at my age, going to sleep isn't the simple thing it used to be. It's a practice run for the big one. The hours leading up to bedtime are as melancholy as a Sunday night for a school kid. The party's about to be over."

"Over? Don't say that! You won't even be sixty-five until June."

"Yeah, and my doc tells me I'd better start exercising or I won't get a hell of a lot older."

"Well, then, let's take a walk. It'll do us both good."

After locking up, I purposely led us to the left so we wouldn't have to look at the mega-renovation taking place at the Kang's. I wondered if we'd always call it the Kang's, even if for the rest of our lives it would stay in the hands of its new residents: a family of redheads named—don't laugh—Daniel, Dara, Dylan, Darren and Daisey Delahaney.

Actually, the first thing I did when we hit the sidewalk *was* laugh. Besides their ludicrous attachment to the letter "D," the Delahaneys shared a penchant for political proselytization and had chosen to celebrate their moving-in day by passing out flyers headed, "Stop the Invasion! Illegal Immigrants are Invaders of the U.S.A.!" The fact that Fidel had only become a citizen thanks to a previous amnesty for illegal immigrants probably accounted for Chin-Hwa's killer's markedly low profile these days.

Neither Stanley nor I felt like skipping. If anything, the continued unseasonal heat was enervating. As we drifted past a neighbor's Tudor-style house with a front yard full of drought-resistant yellow yarrow, curly onion, chamomile, and several varieties of manzanita, Stanley heaved a sigh.

"What?"

"They call these years the age of wisdom, but I've turned out to be an old jackass. Spent my whole life trying to forward the cause of human progress and in a split second I'm channeling Rush Limbaugh."

I squinted up at him. "Now you know how I felt after talking about Grandfather's balls in my Nobel speech."

"Yeah, but yours wasn't cruel."

"Maybe not, but only because he wasn't alive. It was still a betrayal."

I was relieved that he didn't try to rebut me. "What can I tell you, Fleur? Look at it like this: life is very fair; it breaks everyone's heart." He gave me a bleak excuse for a grin, but oddly, his words were actually comforting.

Part II

Place me like a seal over your heart, like a seal on your arm;
for love is as strong as death, its jealousy unyielding as the grave.
It burns like blazing fire, like a mighty flame.

(Song of Songs 8:6)

Chapter Twenty-three
Fleur

OUR JOURNEY FROM Los Angeles to Gombe National Park was uneventful, if you don't count having to endure four plane flights (to Dubai, Dar Es Salaam, Mwanza, and Kigoma) comprised of a descending number of hours (equaling in total 30 hours and 35 minutes) and a logarithmic ascension of discomforts ranging from economy seats designed for miniature Uncle Bobs to an airliner loo minus toilet paper *and* seat covers, capped by a boat ride from hell overcrowded with fifty voluble Tanzanians, sizable nets full of smelly fish, and an assortment of cumbersome cargo.

By the time we arrived at Gombe, Amir was a wreck and I was bruised from anxious pinching, scratched on the face by spiky plants overhanging the banks of Lake Tanganyika, and beset with leg cramps—probably from dehydration. I disembarked from our boat with only one further mishap: the leather travel journal Mother had pressed into my hands at LAX somehow leapt out of my purse and into the water, promptly sinking as if it weighed five hundred pounds. But who was complaining? We'd arrived at the Research Center established by Jane Goodall that had revolutionized how we humans view our nearest relatives.

Amir and I hauled our carefully packed and by now thoroughly battered hiking packs onto the steps of a wide wooden porch fronting a tin-roofed building where the whippet-thin Serena stood, her black hair silver now, but her inky eyes in their dark-framed glasses as buggish-looking as ever. She stepped toward us and hugged a surprised Amir, greeting him with an enthusiastic, "It's so good to see you again, Fleur." I thought Amir made a damned fine job of transferring her over to me, given that he'd been suffering horrible stomach pains ever since consuming what I personally thought were some dubious-looking fried plantains from a stand outside Mwanza Airport.

Not exactly in the mood for company, poor Amir spent his first evening alone in the little tented cabin Serena had reserved for him, his tired brown eyes signaling a deep gratitude when informed there was a decently maintained outhouse nearby.

For me, there was the heretofore unimaginable relief of peeing in a real toilet, bathing in a small but serviceable tub, sitting cross-legged with Serena on a comfortable mat in the bedroom she would share with me, and being plied with chai tea and cinnamon flavored pancake "cookies" that our server, a young blond ponytailed volunteer named Nikka, told me were called *chapatti majis*. I realized right then that I had so much to learn about, not the least of which were the origins of the sonance I was hearing from the wilderness surrounding us.

I said as much to Serena, and she replied enthusiastically, "Oh, yes, of course. I barely register them anymore. A pity. Like you, I was so taken with the cries when I first arrived." She paused a moment. "Okay, did you hear that? The low crescendo leading up to high-pitched screams?" I nodded. "Those are the chimps' long distance pant-hoot calls. Each one has a different signature call, and they know each other by them. Sort of like cats or dogs; no two sound exactly alike." Well, that was true enough. Jillily's sweet chirrups were a far cry from Midge's low-pitched moans. Serena gave an impish grin. "You may have noticed that I have a bit of trouble recognizing faces. I know each one of our chimps by the sounds they make and, of course, their smells."

But it wasn't just pant-hoots I was hearing. After a particularly piercing *weee-ah-hyo-hyo-hyo*, I cried, "What was that?"

Serena was daintily inserting a forkful of *chapatti maji* into her mouth. Finishing it, she replied, "It's a fish eagle. They're fearsome hunters, though they actually only seek food for about ten minutes a day. They terrorize the red colobus monkeys around here, who are, alas, also prey to our chimps. But you won't see any of that going on now. The chimps hunt most of their meat in the dry season we get in August and September."

I frowned. "I didn't think chimpanzees were meat eaters."

"Oh, but they are. Well, they mostly like fruit, but they hunt the colobus like crazy. Wild pigs and antelopes, too. When Jane first reported her observations of their hunting forays, many anthropologists at the time were skeptical, but as usual, Jane was right." I registered the reverence in Serena's voice and silently concurred. I couldn't wait to meet the world's preeminent primatologist. "Actually," Serena continued, pushing back a stray lock of her enviably shiny, silver-white hair, "there's some debate about why chimps hunt at all, since meat accounts for such a very small part of their diet. Some think it's for social reasons, perhaps providing the males an opportunity to prove their virility to the females—who are often in estrus. A young man from your own neck of the woods, Dr. Craig Stanford from USC, comes out here regularly to study their hunting patterns. He's written a book about it. Actually, I believe he's written scads of scholarly texts about our chimps. You can't chew on one topic here at Gombe without biting off a load of others."

Nikka padded in quietly and offered us more tea, but Serena shook her head. "Alfred, the poor girl needs to get some sleep tonight or she'll be tortured by jet lag the whole time she's here."

A grinning Nikka threw me a complicit look before tiptoeing back out again. Serena finished off the last of her pancake and, with a few crumbs lingering at the corner of her mouth, said with a twinkle, "The fish eagles are noisy, but the most ubiquitous birds here are the Peter's Twinspots—little red-throated finches that hop around us like old friends. You'll see plenty of them tomorrow morning, but you won't hear them now; their buzzy chirps don't stand a chance against the more robust calls."

Soon enough, Serena pushed herself up to standing with an impressive alacrity for a woman in her sixties and excused herself from the small room so I could wash up and be helped into my sleeping hammock by the attentive Nikka, who fastened a mosquito net around me while explaining that this was a space-saving way for Serena to entertain guests. I'd never slept in a hammock and never under netting, and it was undoubtedly due to that and an imagination heightened by the newness of this environment that I fell into a deep sleep in which I dreamed I was a white butterfly wrapped in its cocoon. I woke but once in the night, wanting to pee, saw where I was and decided I didn't really have to. Thank God whatever had irritated my bladder seemed to have slunk off to wherever it had come from. I had no idea how I'd get out of this thing and back in again. But no matter. The soft snoring of Serena sleeping nearby was like a lullaby. All the uncertainties of the past few months had made the earth feel more than a little Swiss cheesy, so I was surprised to feel so safe and cozy suspended mid air, supported by the strong crisscrossed roping beneath me and the solid, reassuring presence of the face-blind but creature-wise Serena.

I woke to sun and cacophonous sound. Gombe was alive with it, and it had nothing to do with leaf blowers and traffic. Somehow, I managed to disentangle my legs from my cocoon, and still wearing my pajamas, went outside and saw the adorable little Peter's Twinspots Serena had mentioned the night before. They were busily hopping around the porch in a variety of interesting patterns. I heard lots of pant-hoots and a cascade of cries I couldn't possibly identify. I left the porch and walked with interest toward a mixed woodland scrub, covered in winding vines and thorny plants and patches of tall, coarse grasses. The air was filled with pungent green smells and splashing sounds coming from the lake. Even the bees seemed to buzz louder here. But the vista looked surprisingly familiar, not unlike the Santa Monica Mountains, where Adam and I used to hike and debate the merits of the Higgs particle and superstring theory back in the old days.

I heard a voice coming from behind, startling me. "So you're finally up. I thought you'd never come out. I'm dyin' here."

I turned to see Amir, dressed and obviously raring to go, eagerly clutching the straps of his backpack. I laughed, but took pity on him, hurrying back to the building and assuring him I'd be ready to go in fifteen minutes if someone could manage to scramble up some coffee and a little something for me to eat. Though I'd slept like a baby, I was a little groggy with jet lag and absolutely ravenous.

As if she'd been summoned by my imagination, Serena appeared out of nowhere, along with the real Alfred, who bore a tray of just what the doctor ordered: Chai tea with sweet, hot milk and an array of tasty fried treats that Serena identified as *half keki* and *andazi*, along with two hard-boiled eggs and a fruit basket of bananas, watermelon slices, and generously swollen papayas. Well aware that Amir was nearly out of his mind with longing to see Lord Hanuman, I did faint justice to the spread, quickly stuffing my mouth with a delectable pastry and shoving two bananas into my backpack with which I fantasized I might befriend a chimp or two.

Soon enough, Serena was leading the way into the bush. She'd explained before we set out that we needed to defer conversation for later and to observe her example when we encountered any chimps. After about ten minutes of the three of us carefully padding through the dense brush, I was very excited to see a chimpanzee pop out to greet Serena, who assumed a somewhat bent, submissive posture, making soft grunts. The chimp, much larger than I'd imagined, reached out to pat her silver head, at which point she took a few steps forward and actually embraced him. Amir and I exchanged a quick look before the chimp ambled over to my friend and touched his arm and his cheek before turning away. As he disappeared into the brush, I could hear Amir exhale and realized he'd felt as scared as I had that the chimp might take aggressive affront at our presence. Serena looked at the two of us, gave a little grin, and motioned with her head to follow her.

Again, she made intermittent little grunt sounds. The bottom of my right foot began to itch horribly, but it didn't seem right to ask to stop so I could remove my shoe and scratch it. By some miracle, the sensation disappeared several minutes later and I was free to stop pinching my thigh. Just inches above my head, two gorgeous dark brown butterflies swept by, displaying uneven white circles on their wings. The air was thick here, as if with the exhalations of hundreds of hidden creatures. We walked long enough that I began to lose faith that we'd find Lord Hanuman, though I knew I'd never regret coming here. I was mesmerized by a symphony of pant-hoots, grinding cicadas, the bubbling calls of cuckoos, and what I speculated might be the crunch of bushpigs trampling dry leaves. I had to duck my head with some frequency to avoid long clusters of grape-like fruits suspended from eight-foot tall, scrubby trees and nearly got caught a few times by treacherous nooses of leafy vines. I could only imagine what sort of spiders and snakes lived in this dense wood. Adrenaline surged through my body with an enlivening blend of fascination, curiosity, and fear. I decided that—alongside mini-explosions, petting Jillily, and my discovery that dark and light matter are continually exchanged in the cells of the human body—this wild land was a Grade A void filler.

Suddenly Serena stopped. Amir and I looked around, but saw nothing. We traded a confused glance. Then Serena meaningfully cupped her ear. Listening more intently now, I detected a rustling in the brush and an echoing response to her grunts from somewhere to our left. *Pant, pant, pant, grunt.*

This chimp was smaller than the first, and I had to restrain myself from running in the other direction as he wildly flung himself out from behind a stand of vine-entwined trees like a Halloween goblin. Seeing Amir and me standing hesitantly behind Serena, he halted and beheld us with a comical tilt of his head. Then something came over his face that spoke simultaneously of joy and grief. Before we knew it—forget the ritual of bowing and patting—he was all over Amir, vocalizing like the poop-flinging maniac we'd known so long ago. Hanuman gripped his old friend in an exuberant series of hugs and screeches, soft punches and lippy kisses. Tears were streaming down Amir's face, and I was so overcome I had to look away. But then I sensed a panting at my ear, and soon enough Lord Hanuman was patting the top of my head. I let him hug me tightly, nuzzling my neck, and I felt every bone in my body relax. I guess I shouldn't have been so surprised he'd remembered me. He had, after all, groomed my scalp innumerable times back in the day, despite his bouts of jealousy when I diverted Amir's attention by talking too much about the space-time continuum and emergent five-dimensional black holes.

There wasn't much danger of that now. Soon enough it became apparent that Lord Hanuman would attempt to remedy his previous loss of Amir by sticking to him like Velcro. It reminded me of what Assefa had once described to me during his psych rotation as an anxious attachment.

From that moment forward, Lord Hanuman and Amir communed in the bush, communed in Amir's tent, and communed everywhere else. Amir reported that Lord Hanuman actually waited beside the outhouse in the middle of the night until Amir emerged from having his pee. As the days wore on, I think we all started to dread the moment Amir would need to leave. And Amir worried constantly over how Lord Hanuman would cope with his loss a second time around.

I was contending with preoccupations of my own. Despite insisting to myself that I was over Assefa, I wondered how he was getting along in Manhattan, whether his new digs were to his liking, and—especially—what his new roommates were like. Did he ever think of me? I had to confess I hoped so. I really didn't want to be with him, but missed the ecstatic feeling of being in love with him and the glorious confidence—unwarranted, as it turned out—that he was in love with me and me alone.

I expressed some of this to Serena on the third day, right after she informed me that Jane Goodall had been forced to postpone her visit to Gombe, having been invited to participate in an urgent symposium on the worldwide threat posed by Monsanto's genetically modified seeds. I was terribly disappointed at first, but now—sitting side-by-side with Serena on a pair of conveniently flat, reddish-brown rocks facing the lake, while a few hundred yards away a young water-slicked otter navigated onto the shore to sun himself on the narrow, lightly-pebbled beach—I found myself relishing the extra time with her. The two of us had enjoyed a long hike that morning, stopping to observe small groups of chimps climbing amid croppings of low trees and vines, happily feasting on the little grapelike fruits of what I'd learned were called lamb's tail trees. Later, we'd come upon a clearing where a large group of lip-smacking olive baboons, including several nursing mothers, barely bothered issuing a few nervous cough-barks as they ensured we were actually detouring around them. With their doggish faces, broken-looking tails, and rings of yellow-brown and black hairs on their backs, I found them impressive creatures, and said as much to Serena, as we sat hugging ourselves for warmth, a cool wind suddenly coming off the lake to riffle our hair.

"They *are* pretty regal," she replied, bending over to pick out a small stone and then weighing it in her hand before standing to fling it across the lake, where it bounced elegantly on the water three times before sinking. "It's no accident they're also known as Anubis baboons."

"As in the Egyptian god of the dead?"

"The very same."

"I think I need his services now."

Serena turned to inspect my face as if it were that of a stranger's. "Whatever for? Assefa is alive, Fleur."

249

I picked up a stone in an attempt to mimic what Serena had just done. It flipped clumsily onto the beach just a few feet away. We both laughed.

But I sobered quickly enough. "He is, but I guess my selfishness is so severe that I've already moved on to me." My voice caught a little. "I have to say I feel a little dead inside. I really don't think I'll ever love anyone—ever trust anyone—again."

"Dear girl, you mustn't think in such absolutes. It is a quality of the young that is best outgrown sooner rather than later. I'm sure you have people in your life whose affection has proven to be steady."

I thought long and hard about it. There was Mother, of course, but I wasn't sure mothers counted. Sammie claimed it was because mothering was an archetype, but I'm sure Jane Goodall would have more simply summarized it as instinct, ensuring the survival of the species.

Sammie I felt sure of, but I myself had been at times a seriously faithless friend to her. Stanley had been solid, but what he'd said to Assefa had rocked my sense of him and made me wonder what might someday pop out of his mouth at me. Really, was it that I couldn't trust others or that I set everyone an impossibly high bar?

I turned to Serena. "Who do you trust?"

She looked surprised. "Me?" She squinched up her eyes. "Well, let's see. My mother and father were terrific people and were unhesitating in their support of their only child's unorthodox wish to leave comfortable Cirencester for the African wilds. Jane, certainly— she's like the sister I never had. Chimps. They aren't saint-like. Or non-violent." Serena nodded several times, as if in remembrance. "We learned that in the seventies, during the Four Year War."

That sounded ominous. "What was that?"

"Well, starting in nineteen seventy-four, the main group we were studying, the Kasekela community, conducted a series of bloody raids against a smaller group. The Kasekela literally annihilated the Kahama sub-group in order to annex its territory. I'm afraid that over the years we've learned it was hardly an oddity. The ancestral roots," she commented dryly, "of genocide." Seeing the horror on my face, she added, "But they are exactly who they are, the chimps. No dissemination. No beating around the bush." She laughed. "No pun intended. There's something about the honesty of animals that I find very comforting. But still, I have to say that I trust, ultimately, the human race. Despite all the danger we pose to our planet, I see such tremendous goodness in people every day. It's an advantage of living here at Gombe."

I mulled that one over. I knew that Serena was a central figure in Jane Goodall's campaign against bushmeat. I'd cringed when she'd explained to me that people pay a small fortune to eat more great apes every year than currently inhabit all the zoos and labs of the world. How could she trust our species?

Serena put a hand on my arm. "I know what you're thinking. But during my interview all those years ago with Jane, when I was a dewy-eyed Cambridge post-doc, she admonished me not to expect any creature to behave better than I do in my worst fantasies. She emphasized that reality is far more cruel than we'd like, but if we accept it, we have a much better shot at meeting it with intelligence and compassion. Her words have stood me in good stead for over thirty years. Even," Serena gave a wry grin, "when the two of us have fought like a couple of she devils over administrative details."

We both fell silent now. I heard the *whoo-whoo-whee* of a Black Cuckoo, and then a flash of something moving across the beach caught my eye. I squinted and focused in time to see an otter slither back into the water toward a waiting raft of them before they swam away. The lake glistened in the waning sun, and a sudden drop in temperature sprouted gooseflesh across my arms. "I always wanted a sister," I murmured.

"Pretty typical for an only child. One thing I've learned from the people of Gombe—we are truly one family. In this community, even when a man leaves one woman for another, hurt and all, the two women stay friends. If anything, they even become closer." She grinned. "The way they tell it, nothing brings women together better than complaining about the foibles of their men. And if it's the same man, well then, all the better." She hesitated. "Don't you want to meet her?"

Startled, I echoed her words a bit loudly. "Meet her? Meet who?"

"Oh, please. You know who I mean. Makeda. Meet the one at the other end of Assefa's wobbling scales. Wouldn't you just love to see what she's like?" I couldn't believe Serena was stirring that particular pot. She went on, "Ethiopia is only a couple of hours away from here by air, you know."

Hastily pushing up from my rock to stand and dust off my hiking pants, I told her I couldn't possibly consider it.

The following morning, Amir delivered his big news. We were sitting on Serena's covered porch, a sudden rain clattering vigorously against the tin roof. It was evidently odd that it hadn't poured until now. Serena commented with a frown that the rainy season at Gombe generally lasted until April, but they'd had an exceptionally dry winter.

"The same with us," I replied bleakly. "We've been having a heat wave since last Christmas. But God forbid we mention climate change."

Serena, Amir, and I were taking advantage of the torrent to linger over our late breakfast of creamy sorghum porridge topped with yogurt and sugar, fried plantains, and generous chunks of sweet potato. Amir kept pausing to slice pieces of ripe banana for Lord Hanuman, and at first I thought he was speaking to the chimp, so he had to repeat himself. "I'm not coming back with you, Fleur. Not right now, anyway. I can't leave him." He allowed the happy chimp to touch lips with him and grabbed him in a tickly hug. Wresting free, Lord Hanuman sneakily snatched the rest of the banana and ran across the porch with it, victoriously holding it over his head with a grunty chimp laugh. Amir grinned at him, calling him his favorite nickname for him, "You little *barstard*," before turning back to us with an earnest, "Truthfully, it's not just Lord H. I can't leave this place." He paused. "You know I'll return in a heartbeat once Congress gives us the go ahead."

I pretended to be shocked, but I'd discovered the pull of this place myself. I'd been giving little prayers of thanks that Stanley had encouraged me to come. Here in Gombe, it was as if a brokenness in me was beginning to heal, as if the tightly coiled energy in my cells was loosening, light matter replacing its dark counterpart. How could I quarrel with Amir's decision to linger at Gombe, when I could imagine myself growing fat on *maandazi* and the spinach and peanut curry called *mchicha*, and growing happy among these knuckle-walking chimps, who were incessantly goofing around, grooming, and climbing vitex trees with nonchalant alacrity to feast themselves on their favorite purple-black berries.

The volunteers here comprised a real community. At home, I had my physics team, joined in a common purpose to transform transportation on this planet by manipulating the cellular black holes I'd discovered at fourteen. Given my admittedly rotten managerial skills—I was, after all, only twenty-one now and most of my team nearly a decade older—I'd relied on Stanley to keep us united during this endless political impasse. But Stanley was hardly a miracle worker. We were a socially diverse bunch—Amir with his fixations on soccer and Bollywood dancing, Tom and Katrina with their glued-at-the-hip obsession with each other, Bob with his passion for the ocean, Gunther moping at home most of the time, and Adam 2,983 miles away (but who was counting?). We differed on what to do while Congress twiddled their bigoted thumbs, and we differed on how we liked to spend our now over-abundant spare time.

But here at Gombe, and despite their obviously self-reliant natures, volunteers and staff gathered together every evening for shared dinners of fish stew, manioc, pumpkin, various *masalas* and spicy rice dishes—often enjoyed with the gin-like Konyaki or Burundi's finest Primus beer. Jane herself was a vegetarian, so there was always a fine assortment of beans and greens, producing the inevitable flatulence that everyone good-naturedly ribbed each other about. I loved that the ones who didn't cook automatically cleared up. Everyone competed at telling the funniest or most original or even the most heartbreaking stories of the day's observations and mishaps, but underneath all the crowing and teasing, this was a tribe rooted in a mutual love of animals and a reverence for the beauty and wellbeing of our planet.

In the five days we'd been here, Serena—besides listening to my moaning about Assefa and Makeda and my broken heart—had taken me on a grand tour of the reserve's twenty or so mud and cement buildings. The rest of the group was just as generous with their time. Fred Tambliss, who hailed, he told me, from Baltimore, took me deep enough into the thick forest beyond the beach to see the famous Sparrow, Gremlin, Samwise, and Siri, along with a host of other chimp family groups grooming and nursing and foraging. His video camera forever at the ready to document the displays and distances of some of the hundred or so chimps of Gombe, Fred was kind enough to avert his aim from me as I clumsily struggled to climb over fallen branches, slipping and sliding on the wet leaves now that the daily rains had finally come.

Nikka introduced me to the hills above Kahama, where the chimps took delight in tossing orangey-red Mshashai berries into their wide mouths like popcorn. Nikka was the one who gave me a peek at the infamous Frodo, who she swore had calmed considerably since the day he'd killed a human baby in 2002. Needless to say, I preferred to give him a very wide berth and was glad to come back down to the grassy valley. Much more pleasurable were my swims in the soft waves of Lake Tanganyika with Nikka and her two best pals Audrey and Lilia, both of them potty-mouthed girls from Australia who spoke with surprising tenderness of pulling on yellow latex gloves and using plastic scoops to transfer the thick olive dung of chimps suspected of carrying SIV into specimen tubes, hoping against hope that their favorites wouldn't come back positive, which would make them vulnerable to all sorts of autoimmune disorders.

It was actually Audrey who'd pointed out to me my first Livingston's Turaco, a gloriously iridescent green bird hiding in the wide canopy of a tree, its almost pointy comb reminding me of Bob in his hair product days, though its reddish beak and red eye markings were more like Mother's Chanel Infrarouge lipstick.

Perhaps my favorite of the young women was a very bright undergrad from Harvard, who told me she'd carried a placard next to Adam at the March Against Monsanto in Boston the previous year. Her name was Desoto Delumbre. She'd been born the oldest child in a large Spanish family, had studied at Harvard, and was here to do volunteer teaching at the one-room schoolhouse in the next village, accompanying the children of Gombe there by boat each morning, where she was learning enough Swahili to help their overtaxed primary teacher. She'd actually invited me to join her one day. Though I'm typically a bit wary with children in groups, I had to admit these kids were adorable, and I laughed myself silly watching them play an African version of Duck, Duck, Goose after their lessons. I helped Desoto cook the children's lunch, a giant batch of porridge, on a charcoal stove outside the schoolhouse, and with aching arms I swore to myself I'd bring Dhani some sort of gift when I got home again to thank her for all those huge and hugely complicated Indian dishes she'd made in bulk for our family over the years.

It was on the boat trip back that Desoto confided in me about her conversation with Adam on the march. "I happened to mention that I'd first gotten interested in anthropology when I was a middle school student in the Independent Honors Program at Reed."

I turned to her excitedly. "You're joking."

She smiled shyly. "I'm not. Actually, that's exactly what Adam said. When he asked me if I knew you, I told him I didn't, but I'd seen you play Jennyanydots in the school play and thought you were the prettiest girl I'd ever seen." I felt my cheeks go hot. She gave me a surprisingly penetrating look. "He couldn't stop talking about you. I assumed he was your boyfriend?"

I knew the latter was a question, rather than a comment, and I responded with a hearty, "No. Never." But now I felt a stab of guilt that I hadn't made contact with him once we'd safely arrived here. But surely he would have contacted Stanley, with whom I had, albeit grudgingly. I'd felt a certain reluctance to connect with anyone back home since we'd boarded our first plane.

That night I had a dream that I was cradling the pelvic bones of the early hominid Lucy before carefully passing them over to the waiting arms of a woman wearing a *shama*, as well as a thick, black veil that completely hid her face. I awoke with a sense of profound loss and wondered immediately what Sammie's analyst might have said about the dream. I knew only that it was haunting, and I found myself fantasizing as I climbed into my hammock the following night that the dream would continue when I fell asleep. But it didn't.

On the seventh night, I was already hanging suspended in my cocoon, and Serena had just slid under her own covers when I offered a tentative, "Serena?"

Her voice was sleepy. Life at Gombe was very physical and though she was a hardy woman, she was quick to point out she was hardly a spring chicken. "Yes, dear?"

"Well, I was just wondering. How would I go about switching my flight to Addis Ababa?"

She turned on her little bedside lamp, and I saw her direct a gratified grin up at me.

It didn't take Serena long to come up with a plan, though she swore it was Jane's idea. The two of them had evidently been conspiring by phone. I learned about it when I shuffled out of the bathroom rather late the next morning, having had a nice long soak in the little tub. Serena was on a purple mat doing her morning yoga stretch routine, which she'd informed me had been taught to her by one of Gombe's previous volunteers, "a blithe spirit named Alison—fantastic energy; I love that girl! She saved me from myself after I fell out of a tree observing Freud and his sister Flirt."

It was a little odd watching the not-so-spring-chickeny Serena easily contort herself into a series of complicated yoga positions while she prattled on as if the two of us were chatting on a couch. For the first time since my arrival at Gombe, I found myself missing Siri Sajan, and the only thing that stopped me from getting down on the floor and joining in was that I'd be crowding Serena. As Nana would have put it, her little house wasn't exactly the Ritz.

As soon as Serena informed me that Jane Goodall had suggested that their friend Melkamu Berhe would be the perfect guide to get me from Addis Ababa to Tikil Dingay, I flopped onto Serena's cot and objected that this was asking too much—of Jane *and* Melkamu.

Lying on her back with one bent leg and then reaching both arms above her head with fingers outstretched like stars, Serena rejoined, "Don't even think about it. On Jane's part, she's been following your career with great interest ever since the initial brouhaha about your father and his Cacklers. As for Melkamu, Jane was good enough to intervene when the university seemed inclined to refuse him admission because of a—well, a rebellious adolescence." She paused, both arms midair on their way back to her sides, and looked past me, her expression pensive. "It was his time as a volunteer at Gombe that turned his life around. Like your Amir, he made a connection with one of our chimps. Kanoodle." Her arms landed and then floated up again for another reach over her head. "Who I'm afraid fell victim to the simian immunodeficiency virus." She turned her head toward me, and I saw a tear travel across her pale cheek. "I hate to tell you this, Fleur, but the chimps are dying at younger and younger ages, too much of it thanks to that bloody SIV. Which you probably know crossed the species barrier to become HIV thanks in great part to the hunt for bushmeat."

I nodded sadly. Now that I'd seen the chimps at Gombe, watched them feed and groom their families and play with their young, eating bushmeat struck me as just this side of cannibalism.

But Serena was moving on. "In his grief, Melkamu couldn't bear to attach to another chimp, so he transferred his attentions to the terrible deforestation around the park. The human birth rate in this part of the world is way too high, and Gombe absorbed a tremendous number of refugees from wars in Burundi and the Democratic Republic of the Congo. As soon as he graduated, Melkamu became a part of TACARE, our community-centered conservation program, and now he teaches other young people who are preparing to join us." She lay with her knees bent and touching at an angle, her hands on her belly. "He's also on the Board of Roots and Shoots."

"Roots and Shoots?"

"Yes," Serena effused, rolling to her side to rise gracefully. She sat beside me on the bed, brushing a silver lock back from her eyes. "A part of Jane's determination to bring crucial environmental, animal, and humanitarian issues into public consciousness. This one's really wonderful—aimed at engaging young people in activities that are both fun and meaningful."

I felt a sharp twinge of regret. "Serena," I said, gripping her arm urgently, "you've got to promise me we'll figure out some way for me to meet her, either here at Gombe or if she ever comes to SoCal."

She smiled slyly. "Hooked, eh? Of course, you will, dear. Though I'd much, much rather you return to us, Jane does come to Los Angeles from time to time." She rose to extract a pair of colorful shorts and a T-shirt from her little bamboo dresser. "Did you know there's a Jane Goodall Research Center at USC? Actually, Craig Stanford, the man I mentioned who's doing that work on chimp predatory ecology, is co-director there." Seeing the light in my eyes, she added, "Make sure I give you Jane's personal email address before you leave. That way, you can begin to know her yourself."

I could almost hear the wheels whirring in Serena's brain. I was beginning to learn about the power of politics in scientific endeavors—a case in point, P.D.'s entrapment in the web of Congress' venality. Though Jane herself was a well-deserved superstar, I had to acknowledge it probably wouldn't hurt to have the youngest Nobelist ever lend her name to one of her projects.

Two days later, and thanks to the concerted efforts of Serena and half the volunteers at Gombe, as well as an environmental science colleague at the University of Dar es Salaam who'd generously offered to meet me at Julius Nayerere Airport to make sure I made my final flight to Addis Ababa, I stood on Serena's porch and said a series of teary goodbyes. Only Lord Hanuman seemed oblivious to my departure. He was circling around one of the porch posts making a series of raspberry sounds until even Amir became annoyed, shouting, "Oh, give it a rest, you noisy *barstard*!"

Then turning back to me, and for the fifth time that morning, Amir asked, "You sure you've got your passport?"

"I'm sure."

"And my letter to Stanley?"

"In my backpack. You could have emailed him, you know."

"Yeah," responded Amir dubiously, "but if you hand it to him, you can, you know, smooth his feathers a little. You know how he is with you."

But now Desoto Delumbre came up and shyly offered me a photo she'd taken of me with the village schoolchildren. I looked like a white ghost amid the vital and impish dark faces gathered against a backdrop of bottle green trees. I comforted myself that I was at least a happy looking ghost, my sideways grin even more crooked than usual and my long blond hair skewed every which way.

Nikka was next to step forward and, before I knew it, she'd looped a Masai beaded necklace over my head. I looked down to see its multi-colored beads perched nearly horizontally over my breasts. "Oh, how beautiful!" I exclaimed. She and I exchanged heartfelt kisses on each cheek.

Fred proceeded to stuff a packed lunch into my backpack, and then Serena grabbed me, looking intensely into my face as if she were going to try very hard to remember it. She let me go only to whisper ticklishly in my ear, "You're going to have to write me all about it. About *her*. I've got a feeling that everything is going to change for you in Ethiopia." I felt the hairs on my head and arms rise up like tiny soldiers.

Serena let me go and stepped back. I saw Audrey give Lilia a dramatic nudge in the ribs with her elbow, and Lilia pressed something into my palm. I opened my hand to see a tiny wood carving of a naked woman emerging backwards from the rear end of a chicken. The two women burst into bawdy giggles, and I couldn't help laughing myself. Shaking my head, I said, "I don't even want to think about what that could be a metaphor for."

So it was with laughter, rather than tears, that I left Serena's little house in Gombe, shrieking pant-hoots and hoarse turaco calls chiming in from every side.

My friends walked me to the lake without speaking. Like a visiting dignitary, I was allowed to board the boat first. As the other travelers piled in, I kept moving around the crowd to keep my eyes on my friends. Once the boat began pulling away from the shore, I saw Desoto emphatically pointing toward a couple of women just to the right of where she and the others stood. They were washing dishes in the lake.

As I waved at Desoto and Serena and Amir and all my new friends lined up like schoolchildren at the shore, the dishwashing ladies waved, too, their dresses billowing out like bright yellow and purple and red balloons in the strong breeze.

Chapter Twenty-four
Fleur

IF I THOUGHT getting to Gombe was difficult, finding my way from Addis Ababa to the orphanage at Tikil Dingay was like Theseus navigating the labyrinth. Thank goodness I had my own Ariadne, the extraordinarily kind Melkamu Berhe.

One thing Serena hadn't told me about Melkamu was that he was in every way a big man. Not fat, but solid, and as tall as a basketball player. His spirit proved to be just as robust as his size, and his good cheer was infectious. Meeting a very relieved me at baggage claim, he shoved into his shirt pocket the hand-lettered piece of paper with the words "The Esteemed Miss Robins" with which he'd sought me out. Adjusting his round wire-rimmed glasses, he scooped up the boxes of gifts for the folks back home that I'd accumulated at my longish layover at Dar es Salaam International Airport, but only after enveloping me in something that gave palpable credence to the expression "bear hug."

Both his strength and the hug turned out to be just what the doctor ordered. With its overwhelmingly crowded chaos and spiky (and spooky) modernistic concrete "trees," Dar es Salaam's airport had flung me precariously close to the edge of a particularly terrifying void. As soon as I'd spotted its shops, I'd taken refuge in my mother's favorite form of therapy and had the two bulging boxes to show for it. Stuffed inside were:

1. A violet-blue tanzanite ring for Mother;

2. A Batik painting of women carrying baskets of fruits on their heads for Sammie;

3. Brilliantly colored Masai blankets for Dhani and Ignacio;

4. Carved wooden bowls and spoons for Gwennie;

5. A riotously fantastical Tinga Tinga painting for Stanley;

6. A turquoise and iridescent green men's bead necklace for Adam that would bring out his beautiful owl eyes;

7. A red and white flora Kanga cloth for me to wear that was inscribed with a Swahili proverb that, according to a little piece of paper under its plastic cover, translated as, "The intoxication of love is the ultimate disease."

Bole Airport was as spiky and modern as Dar es Salaam's, but much grander, all steel and glass with pyramid-shaped sculptures and a geometrically patterned marble floor. Still, I was only too glad to be led away from the loud and incomprehensible public address announcements and the louder crowds of people to the parking structure, following Melkamu Berhe like a baby duckling.

I may have mentioned that, at sixty-eight inches, I'm considered rather tall. Melkamu Berhe was at least half a head taller. After easily hefting my two cumbersome boxes onto a cart, Melkamu told me to call him Melky—"All my friends do."—and led me to a car that was so small I couldn't imagine how he was going to stow himself inside. But, after he'd methodically shoehorned my boxes and backpack into what he called the boot and ushered me into the passenger seat, he performed the requisite acrobatic maneuver, throwing me a broad grin that showed he knew just what I'd been thinking.

I couldn't wait to get out of Addis Ababa, which was as smoggy and exhaust-filled a city as I'd ever seen. We got lost seven times on our long and winding drive to Tikil Dingay, each time reduced to stopping and asking for directions, mostly from people walking in sandal-clad feet alongside the poorly paved roads. Our roadside advisers (male) wore knee-length shirts with white collars or (female) gaily colored loose dresses and shirts. Some of them also wore *netelas*, and one young woman balanced a cloth-wrapped package on her shawl-covered head. They invariably answered Melky's requests in Amharic accompanied by lots of broad smiles, expansive gestures, and curious glances at me. Each time, I intentionally grinned what I hoped were friendly but bland grins, determined to show that Americans were a good sort, really, and that I wasn't being kidnapped by Melkamu. I'd heard that western women could be vulnerable in Ethiopia, since they had a bit of a reputation for promiscuity. (Well, that certainly fitted, but I resisted the voidish urge to go there.)

As we passed lush fields of maize and wheat, I battled the desire to ask my garrulous host to stop and let me walk out to the grazing sheep, cattle, and goats to make their acquaintance. Melky seemed politely determined to pepper me with questions, insisting I share with him every detail of my trip to Gombe and each step toward the discovery that won me the Nobel Prize. When I described how I'd first met Serena at a Christmas party at the Fiskes', opening the door to a big-eyed woman who'd said, "How good to see you again, Stanley," Melky laughed so hard, thumping his thigh with his free hand, that I worried we'd go off the road.

Instead, we beetled along at a bumpy 50 miles an hour, stopping once at a small town with a dilapidated café that nonetheless served a yummy lentils and yam dish plentifully flavored with ginger. Before leaving, Melky had our waitress fill two silver flasks of his with *bunna*—"sweetened," he assured me, "with *tinish sickwar*, a little sugar"—and we sipped it as we drove under what had to be the biggest sky in the world. White clouds drifted across it in constantly-changing patterns, and I fell into a powerful longing for Grandfather, with whom I'd identified the patterns made by the birds in our favorite sycamore, the one that Father had cut down.

Despite the caffeine and sugar in our *bunna*, we fell into a postprandial quiet. The road veered into a landscape of tall teff grasses, crimson-flowered hills, tiny mud-built houses, and lower-slung clouds looming heavily across a particularly sharp-peaked gray mountain. Melky pointed out a small sign covered in the stick-figureish glyphs of Amharic. He ran his hands excitedly over the steering wheel. "Getting close now. We've crossed into Tikil Dingay."

Two sets of directions and only one wrong turn later, we came upon a paint-peeling building with a tattered old fashioned gold, green, and red flag of Ethiopia, a lion of Judah at its center, suspended from a rusty iron post pointing diagonally toward the sky. The dilapidated gate to what looked to be a rather dusty front yard bore a placard that someone had hung with the hand-printed words *As-Salāmu ʿAlaykum. Peace be upon you.*

"We've arrived!" crowed Melky.

Oh, God, I thought, adjusting my face to give him the grateful grin he deserved. I'd tried rehearsing it a million times, but I had no idea what I was going to say to Makeda Geteye.

To make it worse, lifting my suitcase from the boot, Melky casually announced, "I hope you don't mind, Fleur, but I'll be leaving you here for a few days. I explained to Serena that I've got a group of students arriving from England, and it would be rude of me not to greet them. But I promise I'll be back to fetch you from your friends in good time to make your flight home. And I'll keep your boxes safely at my place; we can pick them up on the way to Bole." He set down the suitcase, stuck a hand into his shirt pocket, extracted the little greeting sign he'd made for me and shoved it back again, then fished around in his trousers pocket until he pulled out a computer print-out of my flight itinerary. He had me look it over. I nodded miserably, barely noting what I saw.

Desperate now, I asked, "Wait, I didn't …. Isn't there a hotel?"

Melky looked a little surprised. "This is hardly Addis. Not exactly a vacation spot."

I blushed. "But I can't just invite myself. What if they have no room for me?"

He laughed. "Don't worry. This is Ethiopia. There is always more room." And then he lifted my suitcase and motioned with his head to follow him into the lion's den.

I was happy to let Melky go first. The rusty gate croaked like a corvid, and a gaggle of small children quickly greeted us, jostling to be in front of the haphazard queue and flinging their most winning smiles at what they undoubtedly assumed to be potential adoptive parents.

A short-statured man sporting a rather wrinkled *netela* and a slightly bow-legged walk pushed through the children, issuing exasperated directives. "Get back, Lebna. Hagos, Girma—leave Kanchi alone." Soon enough, I had two rough hands clasping one of my own and a pair of almond-shaped eyes inspecting my face, then Melky's. I realized he was trying to assess what the relationship between the two of us was. He gave a nod to Melky. *"Tena yistilign. Endemin-neh?"* And to me: "Father Wendimu, at your service. Nominally executive director, but in truth All Around Dogsbody. We run a professional show, in that we'd give our lives for these beautiful imps, but we all pitch in as needs arise. In this case, we're a bit short staffed. Our director, and the one who actually makes sure the trains run on time, is on a much-needed run for antiretrovirals."

He paused for a moment, pulling his *netela* more securely around what I now saw was an ugly scar on his neck, then resumed, "Not that all the children are HIV positive; far from it." He flicked another glance specifically in my direction. Why did I feel like his last words were a test? "But forgive me," he murmured. "You are?"

Noting my deer-in-the-headlights expression, Melky took pity on me. "She is Miss Fleur Robins. From California. A friend of Jane Goodall, who is my mentor. She is here to visit one of your staff."

I could see Father Wendimu recalibrate. The children had fallen exceptionally quiet, quizzically looking from one to the other of us. It dawned on me that they'd barely understood a word that had been said. I found my voice. "I'm so sorry to disturb you. I'm here to pay a visit to Makeda Geteye, but if she's not here ...." I bent to reach for my bag.

Father Wendimu and Melky simultaneously put hands out to stop me. "No, no," said the priest. "She will be here shortly, I can assure you."

The children had grown bored. By twos and threes, they straggled off to play in a yard that looked even dustier up close, but offered a few benches covered with peeling paint, some wheelie toys and Coke cans, and a soccer ball. Father Wendimu shot me a canny look. "You are from California. Might I ask if you know our friend Assefa Berhanu? I see you have brought luggage with you. Perhaps you have come to spend a bit of time with us?"

I sighed. "Yes, I do know Assefa." Then, cringing a little, "I'm so embarrassed. I should have written first. It was so last minute .... But really, I don't know what I ... I thought I could stay at a ... I'm sure this is an imposition. You have so much to do."

At this point, Melky interrupted with an, "Excuse me," to me in English and a torrent of words in Amharic to Father Wendimu.

265

"*Awo*," Father Wendimu, replied. Then turning to me, he said emphatically, "Of course you can stay for a few days. It will be our pleasure. Any friend of Assefa's is truly a friend of ours."

Before I knew it, Melky—with a departing, "*Dehna hun*," to Father Wendimu and a, "See you soon," to me—was gone. He'd taken my boxes with him, as well as my nerve. I stood staring helplessly at Father Wendimu until the man lifted my bag, took me gently by the arm, and with a reassuring smile said, "Let's see if we can scare us up some *bunna*, shall we?"

As he led me toward a small, thatch-roofed building, Father Wendimu attracted children to his side like a magnet. They were a noisy bunch, each one skinnier than the next, but as kinetic as cats covered in fleas. Father Wendimu barely seemed to take notice of them, but for a mock punch in the arm here and his lined brown hand rubbing a coiled head of hair there.

Expecting an interior as shabby as the fading and peeling paint on the outside, I ducked my head through the low doorway only to discover a beautiful blaze of geometrically patterned purple and green and red and turquoise hourglass-shaped basketry. The smaller sized ones, flat-topped, were placed in circles around the larger ones, all of which had domed lids. Father Wendimu beamed. "I still can't get over it myself," he said. "Until a week ago, we ate at the kind of benches you passed in the playground. But a couple of our adoptive parents chipped in for this, and we're all so happy." He motioned me to sit on one of the shorter baskets, woven in an intricate green and red pyramid design. "We call the stools *barchumas* and the tables *mesobs*."

I'd encountered just such furniture when Assefa and I had grabbed a quick dinner at Addis Restaurant on a patch of Fairfax Avenue known as Little Ethiopia, just a few blocks away from his Carthay duplex. But I let Father Wendimu show me how the basket tables had lids that could be removed to allow pancake-like "trays" of spongy sourdough *injera* to be placed on top, upon which would be ladled chicken or lamb *wat* to be eaten by hand, using torn-off pieces of *injera* to scoop up the stew.

As if she'd known I'd be coming, a woman wearing her *shama* in what I knew from Abeba was *medegdeg*-style shuffled in with a tray bearing steaming cups of *bunna* and a little bowl of sugar with two spoons.

"Ah, Adey, aren't you just the one? Fleur, this is both my right and left hand woman, Adey Gatimo. She's been here longer than I have, and we'd be literally lost without her." Now he broke into Amharic, and I understood only the words, *Fleur*, *Assefa*, and *Makeda*.

At this point, Adey directed a much more curious gaze at me, and I could only imagine what she was thinking. She said nothing more than a brief, "*Siletewaweqin dess bilognal*," before leaving the room, and I knew by the empty pang in my belly that she already disliked me.

"Sugar?" Father Wendimu asked. I shook my head, and he proceeded to spoon a surprising amount into his own cup. I took advantage of his distraction to glance around the room. It was gleaming with cleanliness, despite its faded yellow walls. Someone had placed a chipped sage-colored vase on the *mesob* to the right of me, and I leaned over to examine its arrangement of what had to be the largest red roses I'd ever seen. They were perfect, each petal layering over its inner counterpart in a seamless pattern. But one sniff told me that they weren't nearly as fragrant as David Austin's Falstaff or even William Shakespeare. And I couldn't help but note that these were the more standard roses, not the cabbagy, almost peony-like blooms of the Austins.

Lest Father Wendimu's flowers feel insulted, I stroked one of them tenderly, and found myself appreciating its velvety, but sturdy feel. As Nana might have said, definitely not a delicate flower.

I sensed Father Wendimu staring at my back and skewed around to return his gaze. I was feeling voidishly vulnerable, sitting here in this foreign land with an utter stranger.

He gestured with his head toward the vase. "Makeda tries to pick a bunch nearly every morning. To cheer the children. Well, to be honest—us, too. They grow along a nearby hillside. We don't know who planted the bushes to begin with. These are obviously not wild."

"They're beautiful," I said, ashamed of my previous comparisons. I was dreading meeting Makeda more than ever, now that her world had assumed a reality that included the friendly Father Wendimu, gaggles of boisterous children, and the cultivation of roses.

Suddenly, I felt rather than heard the rustle of beads behind me, and I picked up the scent of something cinnamony. Father Wendimu pushed up from his *barchuma*. "Speak of the devil," he said.

I rose and turned around, nearly bumping right up against the perfect breasts of a copper-colored woman with a wild frizz of black hair escaping her *shama* and the most attractive lips I'd ever seen, upturned over the faintest of feminine moustaches. Her dimpled grin was infectious. She stepped back to give me more space and put out a hand. "Are you here for one of our babies?" Except she pronounced it *bébés*.

I blanched.

Father Wendimu didn't wait. "Makeda, this is Fleur Robins from Los Angeles. She's a friend of Assefa's, come to pay us a visit. Now isn't that nice?"

I had to give it to Makeda. After a nearly imperceptible flicker of dismay, she summoned up a generous, "What a lovely surprise." Without warning, she leaned forward to kiss me on each cheek, enveloping me in that intoxicating cinnamon smell, accompanied by a low note of something rich and green, like freshly mown grass. I wondered if it was teff.

Father Wendimu cleared his throat loudly and began moving toward the door. "Well, I'll leave you two to it then," he said. "I know you'll have so much to talk about."

Makeda and I stared at each other haplessly. Then—as if we'd orchestrated it—we slid onto *barchumas* at the very same second. We burst into laughter. "Twins!" Makeda cried. "We are twins."

Of course, we weren't. But, unlikely as it was, we seemed to take to each other. I was impressed by how perfect her English was and told her so.

She made a wry face. "People in the west think Ethiopians are ignorant because we are poor. But many of us learn several languages in school if we are lucky enough to go. My family and Assefa's were intellectuals. Achamyalesh was offered his first teaching post at Addis Ababa University the year before they moved away, and he was gone—commuting—most of the time. My mother told me he needed to save up his money by staying in the students' dormitories in the city, but he was here over the whole three months of summer vacation. When they left for America, my mother tried consoling me that they were going to leave our village anyway, but that is no consolation to a child." For a moment I saw her as the girl she must have been, losing her best friend. I wondered what I'd do if Sammie picked up and moved back to London or Delhi. It took me a moment to catch up with where Makeda was going. "For me, it was very sudden," she said. Without skipping a beat, she added, "How is he?"

Playing for time, I repeated, "How is he?"

"Don't toy with me, Fleur. There is a reason you are here."

If I'd gotten virtually no guidance during my formative first incarnation, at least Adam had taught me well in my second. "He's fine now. He really is."

She said nothing and sat as still as a statue. I realized this was torturing her. I took a deep breath. Then another. *I know I'm breathing in, I know I'm breathing out.* "I don't know if he told you we were engaged?"

"Engaged," she said flatly. "Not exactly. But I knew someone was waiting for him to return." She paused. "What do you mean by 'he is fine now'?" Her dark eyes were penetrating, as if they were testing me for the veracity of my words.

"Well, we're not engaged anymore. We fell out. It was ... complicated. I didn't speak with him after that, and then I got a call that ...."

"That what?"

I think I stunned us both by bursting into tears. "He tried, he tried ...."

Makeda was gripping my arm, mercilessly pushing past my sobbing. "What did he try?"

In response to her commanding voice, and with tears continuing to cascade down my cheeks, I offered a garbled, "He tried to hang himself. He very nearly succeeded. At his own hospital. A nurse saved him. She had red hair. And a dream. He was very lucky—no permanent damage. But I'd never seen him so ... frail. He's gone now." I saw her eyes widen. "No, no, not that. Gone from SoCal. Just before I left for Gombe. He transferred to an internship at a university hospital in New York." I knew I should stop talking. I had just met this woman. *How do you do? Your true love tried to kill himself.* What was wrong with me? Makeda was visibly trembling. And still I went on. "It was only after ... his episode that he told me about you. I mean *really* told me." And then—I couldn't help it: "Did he tell you about me?"

"You?" she asked. But her mind was clearly somewhere else. "I cannot believe it of him," she said, not so much to me as articulating her own thought process. "When he saved Father Wendimu I thought, how strong he has become."

"He saved Father Wendimu?"

She seemed to recall herself to the present. The eyes looking into mine were confused. "Yes. One of our more troubled kids attacked Father Wendimu, trying to steal his *khat*."

I frowned. I'd learned about *khat* from a National Geographic special. "Father Wendimu takes *khat*?"

Makeda brushed away my surprise with an impatient, "Don't judge him. Don't judge *us*. Your Assefa liked it just fine."

Now it was my turn to look away. Was it a different Assefa who'd inhabited this Ethiopian universe? Perhaps if I'd known that to begin with, something entirely different would have played out. Would it now? Just last month, I'd read a paper by Yakir Aharonov of Tel-Aviv University suggesting that the quantum world preserves the illusion of causality by masking the influence of future choices upon the past until those choices have actually been made.

Makeda coughed. I looked up. "What happened?" I asked. She stared at me blankly. "What did he save Father Wendimu from?"

She flushed. "Sorry, I'm just a little …. It was Dawit," she said. "Foolish boy. Never meant for a good end. He slit open Father Wendimu's neck with a knife and cut Assefa's hand and ended up with a broken nose himself." She smiled slyly, undoubtedly sensing I'd be shocked. "Assefa broke it for him."

Shocked I was. I tried to re-sort Assefa in my mind. I'd seen Father Wendimu's wound. This Dawit hadn't been kidding.

But Makeda was just picking up steam. "Assefa operated on Father Wendimu right here in this room. Adey and I assisted. Father Wendimu would have bled out without him. Assefa will forever be a hero to the children. Sometimes they ask me to tell them the story before bedtime. They love hearing about something turning out well for a change." She stood. Asked if I was finished with my *bunna*. I nodded. She took the dirty cups and began to walk with them toward the door. Just before exiting the room, she turned back, her expression grimly set. "Dawit wasn't so lucky. He got into a fight with a local boy over a girl and was knifed to death on the road to Sar Midir. His cousin found him the next morning. Father Wendimu wept like a baby at the news." And then, just like that, Makeda walked out.

She hadn't asked why Assefa had tried to hang himself. Perhaps I'd be saved from that one. Instead, I'd been dismissed. Rightfully so. So much for wearing out the welcome mat.

The room felt eerie as soon as she left. There were ghosts here with me, and I wasn't at all sure they were friendly. I hastily made my way out to the yard. The children were playing in teams, kicking and running after soda cans. Dust swirled everywhere they ran. It covered their worn sneakers, the bottoms of their pant legs. I kept my distance. Watching children play had made me a little anxious ever since my abortive Sunday school days, when I'd ruined any chances I'd had to join the other kids with my whirling and flapping.

I found a bench and sat down, closing my eyes. The children's excited cries pierced the void in interesting patterns. I sat for what felt like an eternity, sat long after the sounds diminished and the sun grew warm enough to bead my upper lip with sweat. So lost was I in trying to fathom the reality of strangers who'd been no stranger to Assefa, of Assefa himself, who'd become even more of a stranger to me, that when Father Wendimu came to sit beside me, he had to poke my shoulder to get my attention.

"Penny for your thoughts."

Opening my eyes, I sighed. "I thought I'd understand him better if I came here. But now ...."

"Listen, dear, Makeda is shaken, too. She begged me to extend her apologies for leaving you like that. She is too proud a woman to cry in front of you." Thinking back to my own tears, I wondered if I suffered a deficit of pride. He cleared his throat. "I, too, was distressed to hear about Assefa. I have met many broken souls in my life, but I can't recall any one of them who tried to take his own life."

"No," I said urgently, turning to face him. "Please don't think of him like that. I was terribly angry with him, but he'd fallen into the abyss."

"Whatever do you mean?"

What an idiot I was. How could I imagine anyone normal would understand what I meant? "He—I think he was torn between two worlds."

Father Wendimu sat with that a bit, rubbing his forehead. "Ah. Yes. I can imagine that. Do you think he is going to be okay?"

Words began tumbling out of my mouth. "I hope so. He's a good man, really he is. He just got caught in something that he couldn't … he didn't know how to … if I thought for a moment he wouldn't be okay, I couldn't stand it. I'm just hoping that a change of scene will help. I know sometimes it can. I felt ever so much better after I moved to SoCal. I'm sure it will take him time. He'll probably have to take it slowly, but …."

Father Wendimu stared at me curiously. I flushed. "There was a reason he loved you, wasn't there?"

I hung my head. "I don't know about that. I did a lousy job at loving him. It was a selfish kind of love, really. I loved him for how he made me feel."

Father Wendimu raised an eyebrow. "Oh that. Excuse me for blundering into territory I know nothing about. Isn't that how all love begins?"

"I don't know," I whispered, pleating the hem of my blouse. "I've never gotten to the middle."

The next morning I woke to the sound of a cock crowing outside Makeda's window. I was in her room. In her bed. She'd insisted on sleeping on an unsuitably narrow cot with one of the children and hadn't listened to my objections. I'd gotten a sense right then of how stubborn she could be. I'd gone to sleep enveloped in the cinnamon scent of her, dreaming amaranthine butterflies with flecks of black and gold on their wings. Now she poked her head into my room, a purple and black *shama* flowing over her shoulders. "Would you like to take a walk with me?" she said, awfully cheerily, I thought, for the stroke of dawn, and an odd contrast to her saturnine mood of the night before.

I threw on a pair of jeans and an orange Caltech Beavers hoodie and met her in the yard. The sun was barely rising, and a heavy dew gave the handles of the childrens' tricycles an iridescent glow. I closed the rusty iron gate behind me, wincing as it creaked, and breathed in the scents of burning fires, animal dung, and the balsamic hint of what I later learned was wild hagenia nearby.

The dirt road felt soft and forgiving under my sandaled feet as I paced myself to match the swaying gait of my hiking partner. We said very little, with Makeda pointing out the spot where she picked her roses. The elegance of their display was in sharp contrast to the wayward shrubs surrounding them. A small red bird with a blue beak swept past, just inches from my nose. I gasped, and Makeda cried out, "A firefinch," her laughter like wind chimes. We approached a field of maize where sheep and cattle stood like stolid sentries. I could hardly contain myself. Navigating the tall, scratchy plants, I made my way to a particularly appealing brown and white cow, but ended up edging away from her implacable brown gaze, deciding she hated me for eating spicy beef *wat* just the night before. But when I backed away toward the road, a lamb appeared out of nowhere, full of ridiculous exuberance. I could sense Makeda watching in amusement as I matched its frolicking, my breasts bouncing as I ran after it until it disappeared around a curve in the road.

Panting, I resumed my place by Makeda's side. She mused aloud, "I don't believe I've ever seen a grown woman with such play in her. If you would stay with us, the children would fall in love with you."

We both fell silent at her unlucky choice of words. We walked more quickly now and soon approached the bank of a shallow-running river. Water spilled with a pleasing splash over gray and cream and salmon-colored rocks. Spreading trees with flaming red flowers lined the bank. Makeda waded into the soft soil and plucked one of the flowers. Climbing back up with infinite grace, she handed it to me. "We call it the tree of Dire Dawa."

"What does that mean?" I asked.

"That it comes from Dire Dawa."

We shared a laugh.

On our way back to the orphanage, we detoured through a small farmers' market spread out before a line of little shops on a haphazardly paved street. Makeda stopped to speak to one of the vendors, a young man with flashing eyes and acne scars and a narrow beard that nearly came to a point. I noticed a couple of old men seated on faded stools. They were playing a game that involved the metal tops of beer bottles and a rough piece of cardboard with checkers drawn onto it.

One of the men, skinny and wrinkled and with skin a mottle of copper and dark chocolate, grinned a partly toothless smile at me and gestured across the board. "*Dama.*"

I repeated after him like a young child. "*Dama.*"

He nodded with pleasure.

Makeda joined us. The musical clicks and slides of Amharic flew around me like the chattering of blue jays. She turned to me at one point and translated, "They would invite us to join them, but one is happily beating the other for the first time in his life."

I grinned and motioned for them to continue. Makeda and I left the market carrying creased, old brown paper bags filled with bananas and prickly pears and two bottles of Coke that Makeda had bought at one of the little shops.

We ended up gorging on the fruit at the edge of a teff field, waving away bees and wasps that tried to horn in on our feast. Gwennie Fiske would have fainted if she'd seen me take long gulps of sugary soda after each mouthful of the slightly biting raspberry-ish cactus fruit, but Gwennie Fiske was nine thousand miles away.

We made a little ceremony of burying the thorny skins of our fruit, lest someone come by and step on them. As I was patting my own mound, Makeda murmured in such a soft voice I had to go over it in my mind to register what she'd said, "Isn't he beautiful?"

"Yes," I whispered. "Yes, he is."

I think we were both stunned by the sudden intimacy.

"What happened?" she asked. "Please, I need to know why he tried to hurt himself. You can't come out here, tell me half of it and just leave me hanging." She realized as soon as she said it that the word choice was terrible. A vagrant coil of shiny black hair had sprung free from her *shama*. She tucked it back with trembling fingers.

"You don't want to know."

But she was implacable. "You must tell me."

So I told her about Assefa's violation of me and Stanley's shocking intervention.

She looked at me as if I'd let loose one of Sister Flatulencia's silent but deadlies. Her words crawled out thickly, as if each one cost her everything she had. "Sometimes I cannot sleep. Particularly when something very evil has happened that day. And sometimes I have to face the evil in my own heart. I wished you ill even before I knew you. I begrudged that you could have what I could not. But now— that teacher of yours is a very evil man to have driven such a good one to nearly cut his life short."

I felt that my heart would burst from my chest. "But Assefa isn't just good. He was cruel to me. Forcing me."

I saw a shudder work its way from her head to her shoulders to her hands. She grabbed hold of her *netela* as if to stop it. I knew she was recalling being forced herself. Violated. Cut.

"Do you ever think of the mantis? Is the act of eating her mate pleasurable to her? Does she enjoy it even more seeing the suffering of her prey?"

I buried my face in my hands. "Stop! Can't you see I—"

But without ceremony, she'd pushed up from the ground and was walking away from me. Her predilection for walking off was starting to resemble Sammie's penchant for hanging up on me whenever we argued back in the early days.

I rose and stumbled after her, cursing myself for saying too much.

"Oh," she cried, turning back to face me, "what a fool I am. I thought I understood you. I looked you up on my computer last night after you went to sleep. You are the one who kept going when the others thought you were wrong. You have an idea that might save our species. I tell myself, 'This woman has come here to see if there is a claim on the man she wants to marry.' Now I see you have come here to assuage your guilt. Yours and that of the ugly man you call your mentor. Why should I believe what you say? That Assefa tried to rape you? Please. He could have any woman. Why would he ...?"

I lashed out, "He couldn't have *you*."

And then she threw her head back and laughed. Her laughter was harsh, so low-pitched it sounded almost masculine. It was not an infectious laugh. It did not welcome me to join in.

As we marched along, her bark-laugh turned into tears And then she stopped, her face goopy with snot. I wanted her to say something, but she just stared at me.

"What?" I pleaded.

"Do you have any idea what I would have given to bear Assefa's child? To lie with him?"

Without thinking, the words popped out. "But you couldn't. It wouldn't have been good at all. It would have been incest."

I didn't see it coming. Before I could move, she'd pulled her arm back and brought it forward with ferocity, slapping me in the face. The force of it threw me back a few steps. "How dare you!" she cried. And then, "What do you *mean*?"

My face stung so hard that I couldn't stop blinking, but that wasn't what hurt the most. I couldn't believe what I'd just done. I'd promised Assefa I'd never tell anyone. And then to tell *her*? There was something terribly wrong with me. First my Nobel speech about my grandfather's balls. Now all this.

How dishonest I'd been to judge Stanley H. Fiske. What was it Jane Goodall had told Serena? *She admonished me not to expect any creature to behave better than I do in my worst fantasies.*

"What do you mean?" Makeda insisted, arms akimbo, her *shama* completely askew.

I bowed my head. "Forgive me. That was terrible. I had no right."

"You had better damned well finish what you began."

I shook my head. I'd dug myself a grave; I might as well jump into it. "Assefa only found out when he came back to the States. He didn't tell *me* until after he …. His family was afraid he'd return here. To you."

She stared at me, her face a map of anguish.

"His father. Your mother. His father swore it was only a few times."

"Who are you?" she cried. "The devil? You come here—why? To rip my heart from me?" And then she crumpled, reaching out helplessly toward my arm and taking me down with her. We knelt awkwardly on our knees, and I held her as she sobbed. I was weeping myself. Her body felt so much lighter than I would have imagined. My own felt like something I wished I could crawl out of.

Plato was wrong. The truth is not an abstraction. Jesus was wrong, too. It will not necessarily set you free.

Stanley had once told me that he couldn't possibly believe in any God who'd create a world where absolute innocence and absolute cruelty co-exist. But wasn't that what the universe itself was?

In sharing what I'd heard from Assefa in confidence, I'd turned another woman's world inside out and bound myself to her in a way I wouldn't have imagined. I've heard it said that saving someone's life makes you responsible for him or her forever, but no one had told me about the impact of wrecking one. I cried inconsolably alongside Makeda over the terrible thing I'd done.

The remainder of our walk back to the orphanage took place in silence, with me having to run to keep up with her. But when we reached the rusty gate with its hopeful flag, I mumbled that I'd be back in a while. She nodded without looking at me, and I kept going. I trudged long enough that my feet began to hurt and nothing was recognizable. I stopped to dig pebbles from my shoes and rose to find an elderly couple approaching, she bearing a bright green and orange basket of bananas on her head and he leaning heavily on a gnarled stick. Very dark in visage and, seemingly, mood, they exchange not one word with each other as they walked, nor did they acknowledge my presence as they plodded past me. I imagined them as an eternally unhappy married couple. I knew that many marriages in rural Ethiopia were arranged. It was sobering how much the quality of our relationships depended on chemical connections with one another. Put two human substances together and you'd get either a caustic or magic. With Assefa I thought it had been one, but it had turned out to be the other.

It wasn't long before I found myself in an informal enclave of roughly built huts surrounded by trees and forming a horseshoe-shaped clearing of hesitant grass. Someone had lit a fire nearby. I couldn't see it, but I took in with a deep breath the sharp aroma of burning teff. It smelled wonderful, but stung my eyes. Pointed gray-thatched roofs topped the huts here, and I saw a woman smiling at me from one of the doorways. She wore a *netela* with a blue-toned border in an intricate diamond design.

"*Sälam*," she called out, and I responded in kind. Then she tilted her head and rattled off a long series of words in Amharic, which I of course failed to understand.

I shrugged helplessly back at her, asking, "Do you speak English?" though I doubted she did. In turn, she shrugged, held up a finger, then disappeared, only to emerge a moment later bearing a somewhat battered silver tray with two steaming cups of *bunna*. I hardly needed much encouragement to sit down with her on the scrabbled earth. We had our own little coffee klatch, she speaking to me, gesturing excitedly, in Amharic, and me speaking to her, equally animated, in English. I obviously had no idea what she was saying, nor she me, but we had a jolly time, her generosity washing away, at least momentarily, my awareness of my awfulness.

She wasn't a particularly attractive woman, her nose rather beaky for an Ethiopian and her teeth so large they looked liable to bite through her lips at any moment, but her honey-toned skin was flawlessly smooth, her gesticulating hands as graceful as a ballerina's, and her smile a winsome child's. After I downed the last of my cup, a white goat approached us and butted its head against my cheek until the woman shushed it away, clapping her perfect hands so sharply that the sound of it rent the air like thunder. The goat skipped off awkwardly, and I guffawed. The woman looked at me in surprise, and I wondered whether such a loud laugh was impolite in this part of the world.

But I couldn't avoid Makeda forever. I was going to have to return to the orphanage. Thanking the woman profusely—at least I knew how to pronounce *Betam ashmesugenalew*—I knelt and reached toward the tray, but she gestured for me to stop, instead planting a kiss on each of my cheeks and whispering, "*Minem Aydelem.*" Her hair smelled of *bunna* and frankincense underneath its white *shama*. I left her without looking back, her kindness a warming cloak across my shoulders.

The gate to the orphanage was wide open when I returned. Beside it stood a cab with its motor running. Its driver appeared suddenly in front of me and walked hastily past, the whites of his eyes so bloodshot I wondered what was wrong with him.

Entering the yard, I saw Makeda sitting on one of the colored benches, dandling a baby I learned was named Eldina on her lap.

I approached with sagging shoulders. "Makeda, I .... How are you doing?"

She replied without expression, "I am doing what I was born to do." She cupped a hand around a drooling Eldina's chin.

"But ...." I felt inhibited by the presence of the little girl. "I'm so sorry .... You must feel—"

She interrupted, waving an impatient hand, "Feel? You Americans with your feelings! I have learned from these *bébés* that it is a conceit to believe that my suffering is worse than anyone else's." I involuntarily took a step back. But now she was gesturing with her head toward the main building, her voice as smooth and cold as stone, "You have a visitor."

Oh, God. Had Melky come already to fetch me? Though a part of me wished I'd left twenty-four hours ago, the timing felt stark and terrible.

The feet that took me into the building moved as if stuck in molasses, my heart as heavy as lead. That—and the human mind's dependency on context—delayed my response time. Father Wendimu was seated facing me, and opposite him was the back of a man with light chestnut hair. That man turned and rose as he

278

undoubtedly noted Father Wendimu looking up toward me. It took me several seconds to register that it was Adam limping around *barchumas* and *mesobs* to get to me.

His arms wrapped around me as tightly as they had when I was a girl of twelve, whirling and flapping over my failure to understand Sartre or Rousseau. I let myself collapse into his embrace and took a nice long whiff of his Campbell's Chicken Soup B.O.

I was laughing and crying at the same time. Father Wendimu had left the room. I knew, because when I pushed away finally from Adam's warm hug, only a second cup of *bunna* on the nearest *mesob*— alongside a worn black and white photo—remained as evidence that he'd been here.

"Adam, what in the world are you doing here?"

He shook his head. "I could ask you the same question. When Stanley called Serena to see how you were doing and she told him you were traveling on your own to Ethiopia, we were all worried sick. While everyone else dithered, I bought a ticket." He spread his hands in frustration, reminding me of the old days. "Fleur, what got into you? Don't you realize how dangerous it can be to travel around as a single, young American woman in Africa?"

Evading his accusing eyes, I reached instinctively for the photograph, took one look, and collapsed onto the nearest *barchuma*. Assefa and Makeda must have been about five or six when the photo was taken—it was surely they; I fancied I saw a similarity in their grins. They were standing in front of a twisty-trunked olive tree, holding hands and smiling impishly at whoever had held the camera.

"Fleur, what is it?"

"Adam, you're right. I am a stupid, stupid person. I hate myself! I really do."

Chapter Twenty-five
Fleur

THE DINNER THAT Adey Gatimo served us that evening was unusually delicious, but that might not have been the only reason I was behaving like such a bellygod at the meal, nervously scooping up so many mouthfuls of *wat* with my little rolls of *injera* that I could sense Father Wendimu and the three children perched around our *mesob* eying me with no little astonishment.

Once we'd all seated ourselves in the dining room, we set about rhapsodizing over the sunset we'd observed before we came inside. Unfettered by intrusive cityscapes, the vast sky of Tikil Dingay was free to reveal its treasures without restraint. I knew that many of the world's people worshiped sky gods and goddesses. In my teens I'd developed a particular fondness for the Sumerian Inanna, also known as the Queen of Heaven, an appellation that was later extended to the mother of Jesus. The image of Inanna being stripped naked in her descent to the Underworld and then managing to come back up again had helped me no end after I'd made such a fool of myself in my Nobel speech. I needed her now.

Tikil Dingay's sunset was like a celebration of the Queen of Heaven's re-emergence with a brilliant display of raspberry, amaranth, and heliotrope fireworks. As if preparing for her comely brown head, pale pink clouds were plumped across the sky like royal pillows, each dramatically outlined in near-blinding white light.

As we regretfully went inside, Father Wendimu had commented, "I think of a sky like that as a God sky. Reminds me that I inhabit a mystery I will never comprehend."

I had an urge to bring up Inanna's story right then, but thought better of it. Instead, as we settled onto our *barchumas*, I set about explaining that an intense sunset like this one required at least a few high clouds, since the sun's rays are less dissipated by the lower atmosphere, where the air has more particles.

"Of course, pure sunlight is seen by us as white, encompassing all the visible colors of the electromagnetic spectrum. The dissipation of light as it enters the earth's atmosphere is called 'Rayleigh scattering,' discovered by a Nobel physicist who was born John William Strutt, but was later called Lord Rayleigh. Go figure. Anyway, call him Strutt or call him Rayleigh, he found that amazing sunsets like this are the result of photons penetrating objects with much smaller particles than their own wavelengths. It's amazing what can happen when something large encounters something smaller."

Maybe I should have brought up Inanna after all. My scientific comments were met with a uniformly blank stare. By all but Adam, who was seemingly more interested in smiling at Makeda than paying attention to anything I'd said. Unsurprisingly, Makeda herself had made the most perfunctory of eye contact with me. As the conversation shifted to what the children had learned that day, I contended with a large force of my own. Why was I so overly conscious of Adam sitting at the next *barchuma*? On his lap sat young Elfenesh, who kept reaching over to tickle the tummy of Kanchi, who was sitting on the lap of Makeda. With each tickle, Makeda and Adam laughed just as enthusiastically as the little ones, but their laughter was much saltier.

My mind slipped down mossy steps into a dank grotto, where a familiar beast with bulging green eyes emerged from the shadows and sank its teeth into me.

Adam wasn't just anyone. He was my oldest friend. Everything that came before him was prehistory. When we first met, I was intellectually precocious but emotionally illiterate, confined to expressing myself by pinching, whirling, screaming, and flapping. Hired by Mother to tutor me in philosophy, art, and physics, he had the sensitivity to understand I also needing tutelage in the language of feelings. It was no wonder it was his face I imagined when I first learned how to make mini-explosions in my tweeter after my episode with The Boy Who Called Me Beautiful.

But now I sensed Father Wendimu's eyes on me. I realized I was shoveling food into my mouth at a speed that should be illegal. Slipping off my *barchuma*, I turned to Adam. "I need to talk to you. Outside." Looking back, I'm embarrassed by my rudeness, which the considerably more gracious Makeda leapt to excuse with a hasty, "No, no, you are guests—please," on the heels of Adam's flustered, "Fleur, we really should help clean up."

He vented his irritation with me as soon as we cleared the doorway, the shadows of benches and tricycles eerie now in the light of an orange half moon. The sound effects of a ranting hyena didn't help. Adam barked at me, "What the hell was that about?"

"I couldn't stand it."

"Couldn't stand what?"

"You making goo-goo eyes at Makeda."

"Goo-goo eyes? Are you kidding? We were laughing at the kids. They're so cute."

"It was Makeda you thought was cute."

I could see Adam's eyebrows lift in the moonlight. "Oh, for heaven's sake, Fleur. If I didn't know better, I'd think you were jealous."

I fidgeted with a button on my sweater.

He looked puzzled. "Wait—what's going on?"

I didn't dare respond. I was grappling with confusion myself.

Adam took hold of my arm then, rather roughly, I thought. "Fleur, were you intending to come here all along when you flew to Tanzania with Amir?"

"No! I told you it was Serena who suggested it. She said it would be so easy to stop over here and satisfy my curiosity."

"And you do everything someone tells you to do?"

"No. I .... Well, I guess I did want to see ...."

"See what?"

"See why he preferred her to me."

He let go of my arm, and his voice flattened. "Of course. Makes sense. You're still in love with him."

"I'm not," I replied hotly. Which I realized right then was true. "I'm not, you know. I'm just missing—"

"Him."

"Oh, stop it! Why do I feel like I'm being cross-examined? I just miss how it was before. I know there's no going back. But I miss that feeling, just as I miss how I felt when ...."

"When what?"

Oops. There are some things that simply can't be spoken. "Nothing."

"Oh, I give up." He limped away.

But I knew he'd gotten into bed before I did. I hated being out of sync with my oldest friend and purposely walked past the goat shed where he slept, only to hear the sounds of a man sobbing. It was a harsh and guttural sound, and I felt it deep inside my belly. Not knowing what to think, I tiptoed back to my own bed, nearly knocking over the vase on the side table with its solitary rose.

Still later that night, Makeda came into the bedroom where I lay under her own thin sheets, sleepless.

"Excuse me," she said hesitantly, and I felt mortified. *What must she think of me? I come here from out of the blue and destroy almost everything she's believed in. And now, here I am, sleeping in her bed, and she's apologetic?*

I started to get up, but she stopped me. She sat down at the foot of the bed, which creaked rather gratingly.

"Why did you come here, Fleur?"

Not again. I replied dully, "That's what we all want to know, isn't it? Adam. You." I gave a wry shrug. "Me."

She cocked her head. "Do you really not know?"

"Really. I mean, sure, I can tell you it was jealousy, confusion about why Assefa did what he did. Curiosity."

"About?"

"You." I spread my arms. "But also, Ethiopia. We'd talked for ages about visiting where he was born. I'd listen to Teddy Afro and picture the compound where Assefa lived, his school, the cousins he grew up with." I realized that, for a moment anyway, I'd become animated. "I even had "Aydenegetem Lebie" on my ringtone."

"On your ringtone?"

"Of my cell," I answered lamely.

"Ah." She paused, shot me a piercing look. "We exotic people— we entertain you?"

"No!" I replied hotly. "It wasn't like that at all. I may not know you, but you don't know me, either. Before I met Assefa, I felt like a specimen in a petri dish to any male who wasn't a physicist. Assefa came along and he was actually interested in *me*. He was kind. He was brilliant. He was beautiful." I began to cry. "And he wasn't put off by my oddness. I don't know, maybe it was because people thought he was odd, too. But I certainly never saw him like that. We had a similar sense of humor. And we loved the same music. Not just Teddy Afro. Kate Bush. Jennah Bell. Rokia Traore."

She threw me a blank look. I realized how defensive I sounded. I'd loved Assefa because of his protectiveness of his grandfather, his elegant language, his sense of mission to be useful as a cardiologist, his goofy humor, his catlike walk. It occurred to me that I hadn't been fair to myself when I'd told Father Wendimu that I loved him solely for how he made me feel, though that was certainly a part of it. He felt like family—but also decidedly not. And anyway, since when was finding someone exotic so terrible? Throughout our species' history, tribes that adhered to rituals of exogamy were healthier, lived longer, and benefitted culturally and economically from the exchange.

But I didn't say any of that. Instead, I added, rather idiotically, "I mean, you think Adam's adorable, don't you?"

She eyed me warily. "Adorable? I don't know. He is your teacher."

"Yes, and he's also a man. You can't tell me you weren't flirting with him tonight."

Her long lashes batted slowly a few times, and she looked as shy as a young girl. "Flirting?" I couldn't believe it. Was I worse off than I'd thought? She actually sounded surprised.

And then she burst into a broad laugh. "Do you know, I didn't realize it. But I think I was."

Her admission made her feel simultaneously safer to me and more dangerous. I found myself remembering how tortured I'd been all those years ago by the very existence of Stephanie Seidenfeld. I was clearly a sick person. I was threatened by the appeal of this beautiful woman to a man who'd nearly raped me and to one who was in many ways like my older brother.

But Makeda was still laughing. "He is a nice looking man, your teacher. A little pale, but …."

It took me a moment to realize she was teasing me. I forced a laugh.

"You two worked together on your discovery, yes?" I nodded. "When you go back, are you confident your research will accomplish what you wish?"

I replied quickly, "I really believe it can."

"Then I wish you success with it."

When she left the room, my mind was reeling dangerously toward the lip of a lurking void. Had all that been a signal she'd forgiven me? I distracted myself with the strident shrieks of an African fish eagle, the bleating of one particularly persistent goat, and a serious bout of pinching a particularly soft patch of my inner right thigh.

I woke the next morning feeling famished. As if I hadn't consumed mass quantities of food the night before. My mouth watered at the prospect of Adey's *bula* for breakfast, spiced with its chili-heavy *berbere*. I threw on some clothes and sailed toward the dining room just as Makeda and a few of the children were piling in. She threw me an unreadable look, but before she could speak, a sobbing young boy burst into the room, crying, "Makeda! *Tolo bäl!*"

We all rushed after him to see Father Wendimu sitting cross-legged at the farthest corner of the dusty yard. The sun had broken free from the branches of a wanza tree to spotlight a melancholy tableau. Father Wendimu was stroking the forehead of a flaccid-limbed child who lay across his lap. I recognized him as one of the older boys at the orphanage who was a bit of a leader of the younger kids. He looked as if he'd melted across Father Wendimu's legs.

Makeda ran toward them, screaming. "Zeki! Zeki!" She flung herself down to kneel beside the two of them.

Tears were streaming silently down Father Wendimu's face. It was shocking to see the sturdy man so distraught. My fingers slipped under my blouse to take hold of the skin at the outside of my ribcage. Father Wendimu kept repeating, "*Yiqirta, yiqirta. Yiqirta,* Zeki. *Yiqirta,* Makeda." I knew what *yiqirta* meant. He was saying, "I am sorry." Makeda's face was a mask of horror.

So much for hunger. I turned away from the children in front of me just in time to eliminate the previous night's chicken *wat*. The pain of it was welcome. The inside of my nose and throat were fire.

Turning back, I fought back the impulse to retch again as I watched Makeda bend over the lifeless body to cover it with chicken-peck kisses. She let her head fall back, cupped her palm by the side of her chin, and loosened a sound I'd only heard in films or on TV. Her ululation split the air. The children surrounding me were all crying without restraint, the babies held by the older ones were crying, too. Adam had appeared by my side and seemed as transfixed as I was. He gripped me tightly to hold me up. I knew I must smell awful. *Nice one, Fleur.*

After a mere minute or two, and as if on some sort of invisible cue, Makeda ceased her wailing, exchanged a look with Father Wendimu, and the two of them shifted into an entirely different gear. It was jarring. One moment they were overcome, and the next as competent as an E.R. team, with Father Wendimu setting his burden aside with heartbreaking tenderness so he could rise up, lift the rag doll that was now Zeki's body, and carry it away. Makeda and Adey moved into action as if they'd done it a hundred times before, organizing the children into a small circle to sing a song with such purity of voice I had to work especially hard to stifle the impulse to flap. I saw Adam's eyes stray to the disgusting mess behind me. "Do you want to shower?" he asked tactfully.

"Yes," I said, mortified. "Yes, I do."

The rest of the day was mostly a blur. At some point, Makeda told me they'd be burying Zeki the next day. "We like to do it quickly, so that the other children can return to their normal routines." Routines? I myself had now seen a dead grandfather, a dead dog, and a dead child. I never wanted to see death again. I couldn't imagine how these children, let alone their caregivers, could stand its ghastly pall constantly hovering over them.

I said as much to Makeda. She shrugged. "What can we do? We cope as best we can. We try to direct them toward celebrating those they've lost. Remember, they've all lost their mothers, their fathers, their families. In Zeki's case …." She gave a small shudder before launching into an explanation of how he'd suffered a medication-resistant form of epilepsy since before he'd come to them. I sensed she was struggling with a sense of guilt and wished I could ease it for her, but of course I could do no such thing. "We knew it was why his family had decided they could not care for him. He was so young, he barely knew how to walk when we saw him coming in through the gate, clutching a blanket his mother had made for him so tightly we had to let him shower with it for a while." She got up and went off, returning a minute later to hand me a multi-colored little fringed blanket. I stifled the impulse to rub it against my cheek. It was so threadbare it felt as smooth beneath my fingers as Jillily's fur when she was a tiny kitten. Suddenly I missed my cat desperately, though her coat tended to be more matted than silky these days, as if she was so old she simply didn't have the energy to bother cleaning it. My heart thudded. *Don't go there. Just. Don't.*

"Soft, isn't it?" Makeda smiled. "The women of Tikil Dingay perform miracles with cheap wool and waste cotton. I've been keeping it for him. He was a strong boy and helped very much with the younger children. He was so proud when he felt ready to let his blanket go. It will surely give him comfort in his grave." Her voice broke.

I wanted to comfort her, but what could I say? I'd nearly done her in the day before. I felt the void sucking me toward it like a giant vacuum.

Makeda went on, speaking as much to herself as to me. "There really was nothing we could do. And he … he knew his hold on life was precarious. It didn't stop him. That is how these children are. You see how it is, don't you? If they can be so courageous, it would be self-indulgent of us to capitulate to despair." And then she shot me a look, as if something had just occurred to her. "He will be buried before breakfast tomorrow. It will be just us three—these children have no one else, and we don't let the other children see their friends put into the ground. But if you would like to come …." And then she paused. "You should not feel obligated." And then, from out of nowhere "Someday you will have a *bébé?*"

My heart fluttered crazily.

"Oh, gosh, I …."

I think I astonished us both by bursting into tears.

She put a hand on my cheek and with the other began stroking my hair. I closed my eyes and eventually let myself lean into her ample breasts. Her scent of cinnamon and frankincense was extremely soothing. Though I was several inches taller, she took my weight without effort. I hadn't had anyone comfort me this tenderly since Grandfather died.

When I finally stepped back, she nodded and excused herself, reappearing a few minutes later with two small cups of *bunna*. She handed me one of them and sat down beside me. I realized that the circles under her eyes were particularly dark this morning.

I felt split open, raw. "I don't think it's hit me until just now. In all the insanity over Assefa's ... crisis, I don't think I fully comprehended what I'd lost. Really, it was like a whole universe had dissolved."

Makeda's eyes filled. "I am sorry for your pain, *ihite*."

I froze. *Ihite.* She'd called me her sister. I reached up and pulled her face to mine, so that we were nearly nose-to-nose. "You are better than I am. You need to know that. After everything I told you, I don't know if I can ever forgive myself. I'm a terrible—"

She broke in, "No, Fleur. I needed to know the truth. It hurts very much now, and it made me very angry, but it will pass. At least now I will be able to let Assefa go." Her frown belied her words.

"Why don't I believe you?"

"It's not that," she insisted. "It's only, well, to tell you the truth, I was very disappointed and angry to learn how weak and dishonest my mother was. But I can see now that she was human." She stared out the window. "That is not a bad thing to know."

"Well, that's something I can relate to. Up until a few years ago, my mother was often ... human, too."

Makeda directed her gaze back to me. It took her a moment, and then she chuckled. "It guess it is the same the world over," she said dryly.

"I guess it is."

She set her cup down on the small iron bedside table and stood, stretching and shaking off her tension. "What is it you told Father Wendimu the other night? The universe is in us? Do you think the stars are as crazy as we are?"

Now that was a thought. "Not as crazy as I am, that's for sure. How you can trust me enough to—"

"Trust?" she asked wonderingly, as if the concept hadn't even occurred to her.

"Let's face it," I interrupted. "I don't trust myself. I'm like a pinball in an arcade game. Every time I make contact with someone, I do more damage."

"Pinball?"

I had to explain it to her.

She shook her head. "Damage? I believe we are all damaged. Father Wendimu says we are all the abused children of God. It has not been lost on me that if terrible things had not happened to

Kanshi and Elfenesh and all the others, they would not be here with me. I do not think you are evil. Just very naïve and very young."

I sensed she didn't mean it unkindly, but I felt suffused with shame.

When we emerged, Adam was standing nearby, looking more than a little awkward. His face was wreathed in worry. I sensed Makeda slipping back into the building. Suddenly, I felt very shy. Adam had officially seen me throwing up in an Italian restaurant, making a fool of myself in front of the King of Sweden, and now puking my guts out in the Ethiopian countryside.

The smell of burning teff stung my nostrils. I nearly jumped at the outboard-motor sound of a warthog somewhere nearby. Could anything be more surreal than standing here with Adam in the middle of Africa? He'd asked me why I'd come, but why had *he*? He'd said he'd felt worried about me traveling all alone, but a ticket to Ethiopia on his Assistant Professor salary? That had to have been a whole lot of worry.

Adam, for once, was speechless, but he watched attentively as I knelt to scrape at the dry dirt by my feet until I had half a handful of it, which I stuffed into my shorts pocket.

Only then, did he break the spell by articulating what was on his mind. "Listen. I know the timing's terrible, but I've checked my emails on Father W's computer. I had a whole slew of them from the team. There's been an election to fill the office of that asshole who campaigned so hard against gay marriage and then turned out to have molested the young son of his campaign manager. Creep." When I failed to chime in, he went on. "The long and the short of it is that the Dems have got a majority in the Senate again. Stanley thinks we'll have a bill giving us the go ahead in our research within the month. I don't know when your ticket's for—mine's open—but I'm thinking it's about time to be heading home." It took me a minute to even register what he was talking about. The lunacies of American democracy and even our work on the application of P.D. felt foreign, unreal.

"But Zeki will be buried tomorrow."

Adam sighed heavily. "Fleur, I'm not saying we should leave right this second. Just that we should probably be making plans. I don't even know when your flight back home's booked for. I'd like to see if we could fly back together."

I would, too. I explained to him about Melky and my luggage, and we agreed to call both him and the airline right away.

But before we parted, I asked him, "I know it's just email, but how did Stanley seem?"

"Seem?" He snorted. "Actually, his words just about jumped out of the computer. I haven't gotten so many messages marked URGENT! since you won the Prize."

I was flooded with relief. I hadn't realized how worried I'd been about my mentor. I should have known. As long as there were theories begging for application, there was no keeping a scientist down.

When I finally made contact with Melky, the connection was crackly, but he was his typically enthusiastic self. "Right. Glad you were able to change your flight. It can be a bear sometimes. And a friend, too? The more the merrier." I remembered how tiny his car was. How in the world would we stuff ourselves in? "I think I can get out to you first thing the day after tomorrow. Will that do?"

It would, but Zeki's funeral had to be navigated before then. Makeda shook me awake at 5 a.m. the next morning, then padded quickly out of the room. My inner thigh ached so badly that I peeled off my pajama bottoms to scrutinize it for open sores. But my skin merely bore the all-too-familiar blue and yellow of bruising. Some habits die hard, and some don't die at all.

For a brief moment, I felt myself shrinking into a miniature facsimile of myself, like the version of Uncle Bob that likes to stuff itself into my pocket. In the next, I was expanding Alice-in-Wonderlandishly to the point where I could see the tops of the trees outside the orphanage. And then, just as quickly, I was myself again. I looked around, opened and shut my eyes a few times. It was as if I'd been momentarily subjected to a passing gravity wave. My legs and arms were goose fleshed, and not only with dread. It was just possible I'd been given the final key to activating the process of dematerialization, and, call me crazy, I was convinced it had come to me from Zeki.

I peeked through Makeda's curtains and saw that a thick mist had completely obscured everything but the nose of Menelik the goat butted up broadly against the window. The raggedy *baa* that came out of him was so wetly rude that I couldn't help but laugh. I could hear Makeda and Father Wendimu talking somewhere nearby, but couldn't quite make out what they were saying. I gathered up what I needed and rushed past them with a towel around my middle to subject my body to the spiky jets of the outdoor shower, which stung my sore thigh like a thousand wasps.

Back in the room and fully dressed, I rustled through my suitcase for the turquoise floral Hermes scarf Mother had given me for Christmas. She'd been quick to point out that she'd chosen its pattern of red butterflies against a background of turquoise-stemmed flowers in honor of my fascination with the Butterfly Effect. Finding it at the very bottom of my bag, folded carefully under a copy of Camus' *The First Man* that I'd foolishly planned to read on my trip, I hastily secured it over my head.

I found Makeda and Adey clutching each other in the yard. Father Wendimu stood by them, his hands clasped as if he was about to deliver a sermon, but he was silent, acknowledging me with a quick nod.

Hearing footsteps, I turned and nearly tripped on my own feet, only to fall into the arms of Adam.

"Fleur," he murmured, clasping me as tightly to him as was humanly possible without crushing me to death. As if finally realizing that we couldn't stay like that forever, he pulled away, his owl eyes conveying naked concern. It was what Amir liked to call "déjà vu all over again."

I'd met Adam just like this ten years ago, my grandfather's body laid out in his casket, the water I'd tried to resurrect him with drying fruitlessly on the crotch of his suit. No returning from the dead then. There would be no return for Zeki now. But there *was* a crack of thunder. It shattered the sky and loosened shards of liquid light over our heads.

We walked at full speed in the downpour. No one suggested returning to the compound for umbrellas. We just walked. Our shoes squished in rhythm, and our wet clothes clung like anxious children to our bodies. As we cleared the last of the goat sheds behind the building, the rain subsided as quickly as it had come.

We passed a rangy row of shifara trees to see a clearing up ahead, dotted with heartbreakingly small mounds of earth marked by little piles of stone pyramids and wooden markers. A tall man clad in a sopping white shirt and *netela* stood unperturbed with his shovel beside the hole he'd just dug. As we approached, he sang several bars of a hauntingly beautiful lament. As we got closer, I was able to look into the chasm to see how snugly the diminutive casket fit against its earthen walls. Makeda and Adey's ululation rent the air in eerie waves. The tall man passed his shovel to Father Wendimu, who began to fill the grave from the adjacent mound of what was, thanks to the rain, a deep brown sludge. It felt like it took forever. When the coffin was fully covered, the tall man tamped the broad side of his shovel what seemed like hundreds of times against the earth to secure it, then bent his lean frame down to pat it and shape it more subtly with his bare hands. Makeda and Adey stepped forward and knelt in unison to arrange a pile of stones in the shape of a pyramid on top. Their flowing white *habeshas* were mottled with mud. Somewhere in the distance, a Hadada Ibis croaked loudly, as if it were laughing at our solemnity, reminding us that nature was nothing if not cruel.

I felt like a voyeur. I had not known Zeki, had not raised him from a starved babyhood to an earnestly responsible boy with rangy limbs and a winning smile. I wanted to run back to Makeda's room and grab the dirt I'd scraped from the yard the day before to throw onto his grave. But instead, I would take that handful of Ethiopian grit back to SoCal with me to remind me of Kanshi and Elfenesh and all the other friends of Zeki whose lives Makeda and Adey and Father Wendimu were sacrificing and fighting for.

Only after we'd returned to the compound, cleaned ourselves up as best we could, and had a meal with the heedlessly laughing and larking children was I able to grab a much-needed hour alone with Adam. Serenaded by the deep-throated calls of a pair of Dusky Turtle Doves, we trudged up the hillside to the place where Makeda picked her morning roses. I knelt on the grass to take a nice long whiff of a perfectly formed flower whose deep crimson rivaled David Austin's Velvet Cherry Red Peony variety. Only then did I allow myself to cry.

I sensed rather than saw Adam fight back his own tears.

"I'm so glad we're going back!" I whispered.

"Too much for you?" he asked.

"Too much? No, that's not it. Adam, I don't know what I've been thinking. I've got so much work to do! And I think—I can't explain it yet, but I think I may have just gotten the key to the whole thing. And I hope to God it's true. Bob was right. Not caring—*that's* the real void." By now, I was shouting. I knew my nose was overflowing with snot, but I couldn't be bothered. "I've been pursuing my scientific research like a fascinating diversion, like a game. But our work on P.D.—it might actually make the difference between whether the children alive now—and their children's children—will live or die."

For once, he didn't try to calm me down or comfort me. Instead, he said, "Bingo. You finally get it. That Nobel prize of yours, fame, turning twenty-one. Even falling in love. They're nice." He gave a little grin. "Well, actually, they're very nice. But this is the real rite of passage, Fleur. Even more so, for someone as gifted as you."

We walked back to the orphanage in silence.

Melky arrived at the crack of dawn the following day. He'd insisted on the phone that we allow time for a detour. "How can you come to my country without seeing something so much at its heart? I would feel remiss if I did not take you to Aksum." Adam and I agreed, though I could hardly escape the irony that Achamyalesh's attempt to do just that was what started all the trouble in the first place.

But first, we had to say our goodbyes.

Makeda had refused to come out of her room that morning. I sought her out while Adam conveyed his thanks to Father Wendimu.

"Knock, knock," I said, pushing past the colorful bead curtain in her doorway.

She was sitting on her narrow bed, eyes streaming, her uncovered hair an aureole of glistening sable curls. She smiled wanly and honked into a handkerchief. "I did not cry when Assefa left, but you ...."

I sat beside her, hip to hip, resisting the urge to flap. It felt like an infinitely vast amount of energy was passing back and forth between our two bodies. There wasn't much either one of us had left to say. I knew it was unlikely we'd ever see each other again.

Chapter Twenty-six
Assefa

LIKE A LION in the bush, the past stalks us wherever we go.

After an uneventful flight from Ronald Reagan National Airport to JFK, I collected my luggage and was directed toward the taxi stand outside the American Airlines terminal. A blast of hot air hit me, and I broke into a heavy sweat. The man who inserted my luggage into the trunk of his yellow Nissan looked so familiar he could have been a relative, but I would learn soon enough that he was Eritrean, hailing from Asmara. As I slid into the back seat, he reached over to shake my hand. His own was rough and dry, and I felt unusually long fingernails graze my palm. "I am Adonay Gevreselassie," he smiled, and I introduced myself to him.

"Ethiopian?" he asked, and I nodded, a little nervous. But he kept on grinning, and as soon as he started up the engine, a languorous melody filled the interior of the cab. It took me captive.

I shouted excitedly, "But who is this singing?"

He called out, "Qorchach!" His eyes flashed at me from the rearview mirror. He turned down the volume to add, "He is called Qorchach, but his *Habesha* name is Tesfalem Arefaine. The song is *Ztegefe Aymlesen Eyu*. It is in my native language, Tigrina. It is *tizita* music, one of many things in common between our people. It reminds me of home. I myself sometimes play the *krar*." That explained the long fingernails.

I liked the song very much and felt well-disposed to Adonay Gevreselassie as we compared notes regarding his own experiences of driving a cab and the stories my father would share at the dinner table. The only discordant note during our cab ride came from a niggling voice that reminded me that my grandmother had died at the hands of Adonay Gevreselassie's kinsmen.

Adonay had the devil of a time getting me to the glass and brick Riverwalk building on Roosevelt Island, cursing and calling in to his dispatch office many times before finding his way to the bridge that brought us to the front of a massive complex where I would somehow have to find my new home. I had known ahead of time that the hospital's staff housing was shared with measured proportions of the rich and the poor, but I had not been prepared for a building so imposing and prosperous. I shook hands with the Eritrean after he deposited my luggage on the sidewalk, and I watched with a surprising pang of regret as his cab pulled away from the curb. Before lifting up my bags, I fished around in my wallet until I found a dog-eared old business card from someone named Theosophus Kelly—I had no idea who he was. I hastily penciled "Adonay Gevreselassie" on the back and replaced it in my wallet, in case I wished to look him up sometime.

The lobby of this architectural landmark was what one might expect: large view windows, subdued modern lighting, shiny parquet floors. The medical center must be incredibly well endowed to subsidize such princely accommodations for its Heart Institute staff. But this complex looked too much like the tall buildings lining Westwood's Wilshire Blvd. for comfort. Despite being stuck inside the handle of my heavy suitcase, my hand automatically wanted to reach up to finger the scar that remained on the left side of my neck. It had become something of a habit, a confirmation, I suppose, that it had not all been a dream. For a brief moment, I saw the faces of the nurses who'd been leaving the elevator as I entered with nothing but death on my mind.

In accepting Stanley H. Fiske's offer to secure me a residency in New York, I had harbored a secret hope that in working among heart patients fighting for their lives, I might once again discover an appetite for my own. But would it prove true? I set down my bags and raised a hand to ring the doorbell to Apartment 553A, where I knew only that two cardiac medicine residents were sharing their rooms with a staff member of the United Nations and, now, me.

The barefoot, bare-chested fellow who answered the door with a quick, "Hey, you must be Assefa. I'm Samuel. Hang on a mo', brother," disappeared as soon as he'd opened it, leaving me to move my bags into a sun-splashed room with the same parquet flooring as the lobby's, but furnished with much cheaper furniture. I heard the telltale sounds of a shower being turned on. Still sweating despite the unmistakable air-conditioning, I pulled off my light jacket and stuffed it in the crook of my arm as I took in the two mismatched upholstered chairs—one an ugly mustard color, another a liberally stained beige—opposite a stainless steel wheeled stand supporting a large flat-screen TV that had some kind of zombie movie playing. At the far end of the room stood a tiled coffee table missing a few of its tiles. Just behind it was a newer-looking Ikea-style navy sofa. And there my eyes came to a full stop. On the sofa was perched a goddess with midnight skin.

Her slender legs were slung like a lazy smile from sofa to table. I couldn't help but notice the little square bottle of nail polish on the table, nor the brush in her long-fingered hand, nor that she'd already painted all but two of her perfect toes a glittery green. I saw now that at its far end, the sofa was companioned by a diamond-patterned *mesob* of bright yellow, red, pale blue, cream, purple. Across its knobby lid was strewn a *shama* with a gold and silver fringe. Was it hers? I tried to imagine the *shama* struggling with her curly explosion of obviously dyed, brilliant red hair. The truth was, I couldn't imagine *anything* different, or better, than the insouciant stare with which she regarded me, the way her rolled-up jeans and cropped red T-shirt hugged her boyish chest with its sharp little nipples, nor the way her hair rose from her round forehead in a crown of flaming waves. She threw back her head, and a fountain of laughter gushed from her throat, betraying a beguiling gap between her front teeth. I saw now that she had a thin gold band curling around her right nostril. She looked like no one I'd ever seen, a strange blend that was extremely satisfying.

"Cat caught your tongue, Assefa Berhanu? I'm one of your crazy new flat mates. Don't worry. I don't bite." She patted the space beside her on the sofa. "Come sit and keep me company." I complied, my limbs moving slowly, as if soaked in honey. I set my jacket down next to a book splayed open on the sofa. I saw it was Toni Morrison's *Song of Solomon*. I had always meant to read it. The woman turned away from me to methodically dab polish on her two bare toenails, but she kept speaking. Her voice had a distinctive skip to it, alternately husky and light. "Dumb to do this right now. They're going to take forever to dry, and we've got somewhere to be." She threw me a quick glance. "All of us. I hope you don't mind that we've already made plans for you. Really—it's amazing: they're actually opening a little *bunna* bar a couple of blocks away. Right here on Roosevelt Island. And we've invited some members of the community to join us there to meet you at the grand opening."

As if sensing me staring at the tattoo stitched across her anklebone, an Amharic rendering of the word "woman," ፆማን, she skewed around, leaned back against a throw cushion on her side of the sofa, and—astonishingly—stretched out her other leg straight across my knees. "You're supposed to read this one first," she chided. Her other ankle bore the script ብሉእ ኔለ. "Blue Nile." Which I knew was, for at least some of my people, the holy river called Gihon that flowed from the Biblical Eden.

I tried to subtly slide my jacket over my erection, and she hastily retracted her leg, as if only now realizing the audacity of what she had done.

But her laughter was light, teasing. "You must forgive me. I haven't even introduced myself. My benefactor always told me, 'Lemlem Skibba, you are a terrible girl.'"

It was obvious from her comfortable laugh that whoever had said that hadn't meant it. But I was curious. "Benefactor?"

"I am 'tooth *mingi*.'" She gestured toward the gap in her teeth. "My tribe is Kara. They only stopped sacrificing girls like me a few years ago. Bad luck. They thought we were bad luck."

I could not speak. Was there no end to the cruelty of my people?

As if reading my mind, Lemlem Skibba said with no little heat, "Don't even go there. It was Kara people who saved me. At significant personal sacrifice. Ignorance and cruelty are equal opportunity cultural phenomena. We at the U.N. have that lesson beaten into us every day."

"Actually," I said slowly, "We might have more than you'd imagine in common. I am bad luck, too."

I listened to the *shhh* of the air conditioner as she considered me more carefully. Suddenly, she pushed up from the sofa and deftly slid her feet into a pair of flip-flops. She called out toward the rooms I hadn't yet seen (including, presumably, my own), "Samuel Zerezghi, are you done admiring yourself in the mirror? Let's go!" I stood myself, and she slipped her arm into mine and began walking us toward the front door, commenting in a slightly surprised tone, "You know, I do believe you and I are going to become very good friends."

Wondering whether the past need necessarily determine the future, I submitted to the electric sensation of her arm touching mine.

"If you say so," I replied.

The ride back down to the lobby was far different from the one going up. Samuel made up for his rather cavalier initial greeting by offering up a surprisingly strong hug, after which he and Lemlem rapid-fired questions at me about the quality of my internship at UCLA, the number of Ethiopian restaurants in Los Angeles, how much racial discrimination I'd experienced at school, and which movie stars I'd met. To his credit, Samuel didn't ask one question about why I'd transferred from one of the top heart hospitals in the country to another. Instead, he filled me in about our missing fourth roommate, Sisay Mulugeta, who was born in New York to Ethiopian parents. As we were happily marching off to a café opening, Sisay was evidently assisting at his first coronary bypass, which reminded me that I'd left L.A. determined to bury my sorrows in work.

We passed a series of small community gardens. The streets of Roosevelt Island seemed extraordinarily clean for Manhattan, and I ventured a comment to that effect. Lemlem snorted, "Bloomberg likes to take all the credit for it, but people here have taken pride in their community long before he was even elected." It went unsaid that Samuel and Lemlem were once lovers, but I knew it had to be true. There was something about their easy familiarity. Or was this how roommates behaved? I did not know that I could ever achieve that.

There was a yellow and green banner displayed across the shop front of the Bunna Head Café. The crowd waiting to get in was boisterous and friendly and dressed as casually as Lemlem and Samuel. They seemed to be mostly Ethiopians, many of whom I was introduced to (with me knowing I'd never remember their names), but I saw some white faces, too, including a blond-haired girl with a crooked grin who I mistook—for one agonized moment—for Fleur. The ache that swept over me was physical, and I bent over as if stricken. Samuel asked, "Hey, man, you okay?" But as quickly as it came, it was gone.

I straightened and reassured him. "Not to worry. Just a little cramp. Bloody airlines treat you like sardines." When the café's doors opened, I let myself be carried along by the crowd, whose voices automatically rose to compete with the refrain of *Sawa Sawa Sawale* blasting from the sound system until some of them gave up and joined in, singing along with Ziggy Zagga and dancing in place, shimmying and shoulder shrugging. I was convinced I could smell Lemlem's nail polish behind me. I knew I could not even imagine what was to come in this new life of mine. Fired with adrenaline, I raised my own voice to sing along with the crowd.

Yet even in that moment of release, with Lemlem tapping me on the shoulder and me inching around in the crowd to face her so closely I could smell the peppermint of her breath escaping from her gap-toothed grin, there in my heart was *tizita*. Some part of me would remain forever betrothed to the memory of my *dukula*. Would it be the same for her? It shouldn't matter, but I knew it did.

As people found their seats, the chaos began to sort itself. The group of men and women who'd surrounded the booth where Lemlem had slid in beside me moved aside to allow our waiter to approach our table. His glistening dreadlocks reached down to touch the shoulders of his Lion of Judah T-shirt. When I gave him my order, he asked, "Do you want your *bunna 'tinish sickwar'?*"

I'd never taken sugar in my *bunna* before, but without a moment's thought, I heard myself answering, "Yes."

Chapter Twenty-seven
Fleur

I STILL DON'T know how we survived the road to Aksum. To say the paving was uneven would be a serious understatement. My bum felt like a sadistic masseur was pounding it. We bounced and jiggled and, I hate to say, skidded around narrow hairpin turns pitched precariously at the edges of verdant, misty mountains. The scenery was stunning, but who cared? My relief when we reached flatter ground was momentary. Now we convulsed across tire-threatening stony roads lined with brilliant red hot poker plants and giant lobelias, captive to the limitations of Melky's little machine and the contrasts of extreme poverty and extreme beauty we observed through its insect-smudged windows.

These are some of the things I saw:

1. Crude thatched houses painted the most vibrant hues of turquoise, coral, and purple—many of them embellished with murals of streaky clouds and sandy beaches;

2. Boys wearing impossibly threadbare clothes and ornately-designed basket hats;

3. Long lines of blasé-looking camels, bearing tall piles of vivid baskets and woolen blankets that towered over the

inevitable dented and dusty auto rickshaws crawling alongside them.

But Ethiopia, rich in just about everything but literal cash, offered its own bountiful brand of comic relief. A case in point: after an hour of my thirsty whining, Melky agreed to adjust his ambitious timetable by stopping at a wind-whipped roadside diner, where we sat at the one inside table, throwing bottles of Coke down our throats while a troop of about twenty gelada baboons ambled across the road to what must have been a lusher grazing spot than the one they'd left behind. They scratched their behinds, the babies comfortably clutching their mothers' backs, and stared at us curiously as if we were zoo animals. If this had happened in Pasadena, someone would have called the local animal shelter, but here, the notion of animal control seemed inflated and ludicrous.

I think I annoyed Adam and Melky by interrupting their rather passionate conversation to ask for Melky's key so I could tiptoe out to the car to retrieve my camera from my suitcase. Melky had managed to fit our luggage into the miniature boot of his car—thank God the bulk of my boxes were waiting for me in his flat in Addis Ababa. He and Adam had hit it off like a house afire, and I could barely keep up once they discovered they were both fans of what was also Dhani's favorite football team, Arsenal. As we sat at the funky-smelling café, they couldn't stop rhapsodizing over the player they agreed was the best Arsenal member ever, France's top goal-scorer Thierry Henry.

Managing to catch a humorous shot of the rear-guard of the straggling band of primates, my mind traveled along an odd associative loop from baboons (which I have to confess I found, despite their signature bleeding heart markings, rather ugly) to Amir (whom I realized I was missing rather badly, along with the whole gang back home) to Lord Hanuman. It occurred to me that Amir loved that chimp as much as I'd thought I'd loved Assefa, though admittedly in a far different way. My mind then wended its way to the chimp-championing Jane Goodall (who I couldn't miss or love, because I still hadn't met her) and took a final incomprehensible leap to the *Lamed Vav*.

"The *Lamed Vav*?" you might ask. Or, as Nana might have put it, "What's that when it's home?"

The thing is: the *Lamed Vav* are never home. I'd first learned of them from Jacob—with whom I prayed Sammie had had the guts to break up while I was away. In one of his less obnoxious moments, Jacob had spoken of a Kabbalistic belief that, at any moment in time, there are thirty-six good men who, by virtue of their decency and good deeds, make the continuance of the world possible. Hearing about that sacred thirty-six from the mouth of one of the least admirable people I knew didn't exactly incline me to credit the idea, but then I'd thought about Jane Goodall, who would surely be one of them if they existed at all, and I'd decided that the important thing was to behave as much like that as possible. Oh, those good intentions. Yours truly was hardly succeeding in the High Moral Aspirations Department, what with failing to resurrect Grandfather, nearly ruining the chances of P.D. by babbling about his bulbous balls during my Nobel speech, murdering Baby X, driving Assefa to near-suicide, and most recently ruining Makeda's belief in almost everything she'd held dear.

Of course, the notion that only thirty-six people could manage to keep the world going was a bit, well, ambitious, but then again, people had thought that dematerialization was impossible until my award for P.D. and recent experiments with our mossy little sister-species, the water bears.

The other thing about the legendary *Lamed Vav* was that, not only did no one else know who they were, they themselves didn't know. It seemed like that would screen out a whole slew of characters, like Father, who were rather terrifyingly certain they were directly channeling the wishes of God.

Then again, what if there were another thirty-six people out there, sort of anti-Vavs, hell-bent on destroying our world? (Actually, if you asked Gwennie, I'm pretty sure she'd insist there were many more than that, and every one of them either a global capitalist or a Tea Partier.) Perhaps, as with the asymmetry of matter and anti-matter, there were only thirty-five of the anti's, which is why I still existed and could actually visit the supposed home of the Ark of the Covenant, through which, according to the Jews, God had pretty much conveyed to our species that what we do actually matters.

All of this was to say that I had more than one way to fill my void while Adam and Melky dissected every Arsenal match known to mankind.

I'm happy to report that my mind's peregrinations lasted me the rest of the way to Aksum, the onetime capitol of an empire known alternately as Abyssinia, Ethiopia, and India. When I unfolded my cramped limbs from Melky's car and hobbled toward our penultimate destination, here is what I saw:

1. A gray cement block Chapel of the Tablet that was far humbler than I'd imagined, sandwiched between the old St. Mary of Zion Cathedral (which didn't allow women, so we'll say no more about it) and the newer, Neo-Byzantine one, built—along with the Chapel—by Haile Selassie in gratitude for Ethiopia's liberation from fascism. All this I learned from a couple of pamphlets thrust at me by a man with a wart the size of a quarter and shaped like a water bear above his upper right lip.

2. An iron gate surrounding the Chapel that was painted a particularly pleasing matching blue to the decorative iron grates behind its white, cross-shaped window frames.

3. Pretty, if hodge-podgy touches of decorative stonework embellishing the chapel, along with a circular window and a square-cross design above the doorway, which was completely covered by a rather unevenly suspended, long, red drape, out of which my errant mind imagined the bogus Wizard of Oz shamefacedly emerging.

4. A rather dull turquoise-tiled dome crowning the Chapel that was marred by numerous missing tiles, but redeemed by a lovely Ethiopian cross at its top.

Behind the Chapel, a low rocky hill dotted with a few trees and an equally humble small yard of craggy grass, a few struggling bushes, and no pilgrims, which was notable, since there were hordes of them everywhere else, looking more than a little awed. While their garb was mostly the same, variations on the theme of enwrapping white *netelas*, their faces bore the features of many of the eighty ethnic groups that made up Ethiopia. I could have studied them—undoubtedly, quite rudely—for hours. Instead, we quickly circumambulated the building complex and made our way back to Melky's little car.

We were pressed for time. Thanks to Thierry Henry, our journey here had taken longer than anticipated. And it wasn't as if we were missing much. Melky had already warned us that we couldn't enter the Chapel, nor set our eyes on the Ark. In fact, I knew that no one could, save a lone guardian monk who served as Keeper of the Ark for his lifetime.

Nonetheless, something about the simplicity of the setting touched me. I took a moment to kneel and surreptitiously swept a small fistful of dirt into my windbreaker pocket. As I rose, a young girl of eight or so standing beside a rather restless little lamb caught my eye. The child was assiduously attempting to place postcards into the hands of passing pilgrims, most of whom met her efforts with utter indifference, looking right through her as they rushed toward their goal at the crowded blue gates. I say assiduously, but she couldn't help but giggle from time to time at her wooly companion, whose four-footed frolicking was nothing if not endearing and put my skipping with Uncle Bob and Stanley to shame.

The lamb's haphazard black and white markings were a striking contrast to the girl's *habesha*, woven with what appeared to be threads of every color of the rainbow. But it was the child's deep dimples and sweetness of countenance that took hold of my heart. I left Adam's side to run to her, holding out my hand.

"*Sälam*," she said, overjoyed to be able to place in someone's palm one of her little cards, which at a glance seemed to bear directions to the Church of Debrie Birhan Selassie in Gondar, as well as photographs of its exterior and interior. Hoping to cheer her even further, I studied the card and pointed to the image of a church ceiling covered with row upon row of round, brown-skinned faces. "*Mekonnen?*" I guessed.

She nodded emphatically, her smile lighting up the universe. "*Mekonnen!*"

Of course, I thought. Angels.

I thought of all the people who'd saved me during my first incarnation under Father's devilish dominion. Nana. Sister Flatulencia. Fayga. Cook. Dhani. Ignacio. Not to mention those of my second, third, and fourth incarnations: Adam, Stanley, Gwennie, Amir, Katrina, Tom, Gunther, Sammie, Aadita, Serena. I imagined all their faces lined up in rows, interspersed with the Mekonnen of

Gondar, and wished for a moment that I had Sammie's skills at portraiture.

But the girl who'd given me the postcard was tapping my shoulder, bringing me back to the moment. She pointed to the lamb, who'd ventured out a little to gambol amid the pilgrims, a little spark of unacknowledged, animate joy. The girl winked at me.

"*Mekonnen?*" I responded.

She grinned back. "*Mekonnen.*"

I planted a kiss on her cheek and we silently beamed at each other. With a little wave, I ran back to a waiting Adam and Melky with the feeling that, here in this place where, 2500 years ago, the Ark had supposedly ended its diaspora from Mt. Sinai, a very different sort of covenant had been made between this child and myself.

Buckling up next to Adam, who threw me a curious look but then got caught up in a discussion with Melky about Haile Selaissee, I thought about what our Ethiopian friend had told us about the Ark: that there were replicas of the tablets in all of Ethiopia's churches; that the sole monk who's ever allowed to set his eyes on the supposed original burns incense before it and recites to it all day from the Book of Psalms.

I myself had memorized the Book of Psalms at the age of four, the Bible having been my primary means of trying to comprehend what grownups made of being alive—well, that and *Elle* and *Vogue* magazines and Charmin toilet paper packaging, with its emphasis on the importance of feeling "fresh and clean," with softness being a particular premium, emphasized by a rather astonished looking bear proffering a six-pack roll to the reader. Nana later informed me that not everyone reads toilet paper packaging, and I was astonished, since someone had clearly taken considerable care to festoon Father's preferred brand with words of all sizes set in eye-catching designs.

The truth was, if the powers-that-be of the Ethiopian Orthodox Church ever decided to join the twenty-first century and have a woman monk for a change, I'd be a natural to recite the Psalms by heart to the Ark and anyone else who needed to hear it. Though why the Ark needed such constant recitation was beyond me and might have something in common with its originator, the Old Testament Yahweh, who really did seem to require a rather constant stream of praise and affirmation that he was a good God, a just God, and, in fact, the only God, as if he was perhaps more than a little, well, insecure.

As Melky pulled our tiny car away, I skewed around for one last look at the dimple-cheeked girl, a forlorn little lighthouse in a roiling sea of pious people. *Children are a heritage from the LORD.* I prayed this child wouldn't always be cursed with the cross of invisibility. Such a sweet humor as hers deserved its own crowned dome.

Before saying our final goodbyes to Ethiopia, we needed to stop at Melky's apartment in the heart of Addis Ababa, and I was surprised, as we unfolded ourselves from his cramped car, to see that he lived in a rather luxurious-looking, multi-storied terraced building with a façade of alternating orange and gray blocks, flanked by a pair of redolent eucalyptus trees and fronted by a deep flower bed filled with prolific climbing roses and majestic, white calla lilies. He grinned at my expression, cried out, "All hail to Cambridge University for its generous grant money," and then quickly appended, "It's not nearly so posh as it looks," which became quite apparent as we laboriously mounted five sets of stairs—"Bloody lift's always broken"—whose once-white paint was chipped and scarred.

Melky's scantily furnished apartment (worn brown leather couch, piles of books on a thin beige carpet generously daubed with stains, small kitchen table and two straight backed chairs) would have been characterless without the large framed photos lining the walls depicting scenes from Gombe: wide stands of lush vegetation surrounding pristine, sandy beaches on Lake Tanganyika; fields of deep-green coffee plants bearing flowering white blossoms and bright red coffee berries; chimps in every configuration imaginable, some tapping knuckles with Serena, Jane Goodall, and Melky himself.

Despite Adam's objections, he and I were ordered to sit at a small tile table on Melky's patio and take in the view of the city. Adam objected fruitlessly as our host carried my boxes from a room beyond our sightline, through the living room and down the stairs, his heavy footfalls like a herd of elephants in the echo chamber of the stairwell. I wondered how in the world we'd all fit in the car with the boxes in it, but somehow had faith that Melky would figure it out. He was that sort of man.

Melky had plied us with bottles of Ambo mineral water and little packets of Kolo. Adam tore his packet open with his teeth, threw a fistful of Kolo into his mouth, and flushed when I commented, "Man overboard." He quickly brushed the vagrant roasted grain of barley from his lower lip and asked, "All gone?"

I nodded, assuring him, "Handsome as ever." He blushed an even brighter shade of crimson, and I could feel my own face heat up. *Really, Fleur?* What was wrong with me?

We quietly surveyed the vista Melky's balcony afforded us. Adam was the one to break the silence. "Pretty amazing, isn't it? Such extremes—modern freeways looping over all those unpaved roads. Everywhere you look, skyscrapers going up next to tin-roofed huts and tiny *souks*. Makes you wonder if the rich'll push the poor right out of the city or raise their level of existence by employing them at all these bank headquarters and hotels."

"What do *you* think?" I replied, and then chuckled, pointing out a man blocking traffic as he herded a small tribe of goats across a wide street.

Adam laughed with me. "Oh, man, that is ca-razy."

I was pleased to note that Melky's part of town had plenty of trees, including the beautiful specimens out front, but then I caught a glimpse of quick movement and was anything but pleased.

"Oh no!" I shouted, pushing up from my chair and running out of the apartment, nearly tumbling head first down the stairs.

I could hear Adam behind me, screaming, "Wait! Fleur! What is it?" But I had no time.

Shooting out of the building, I nearly careened into Melky, who was just slamming shut the boot. I slowed myself like a cartoon character as I neared the end point of the scene I'd spied from above. It was, as I'd feared, a baby bird, feverishly flapping its little wings, which were circumscribed by the intersecting branches of a thickly thorned white rose bush.

I sensed rather than saw the two men arriving on either side of me as, without thought, I knelt and carefully teased one sharply thorned branch away from the bird. It made no sound, but its chestnut wings and gray head and shoulders suggested it was some sort of sparrow. The poor creature was so small I was afraid it wouldn't be able to fly, but as soon as it perceived it had clearance, it took off, making it to the bent antenna of an ancient, pale blue Cadillac before succeeding at a longer ascent to a limb of a peach tree. Then it winged out of sight.

"Fleur," Adam whispered. "Oh, Fleur." Sucking my bleeding finger, I could barely breathe.

"Good God, woman," Melky boomed, "that was a hell of a feat. You must have the best vision on the planet." Realizing I was currently beyond reach, he turned to Adam. "She's got a surgeon's hands. Glad she's doing some important work, or I'd suggest she change professions."

"She's got vision, all right, in more ways than one. Plus, she's the sweetest soul I know," is how Adam replied. But I barely noticed. I was in shock, trembling.

After that, our ride to Bole was pretty anticlimactic. Once he'd made sure a porter was doing the right thing with our luggage, Melky offered us warm bear hugs followed by a brotherly pat on Adam's shoulder with a solemn, "Let's keep up the energy for Arsenal." Then, making some poor excuse that he needed to convey a message to me from Jane, he pulled me aside and murmured in an uncharacteristically soft voice, "So. Makeda. Do you happen to know if she has a boyfriend?"

I stared and then bumbled, "Well, as a matter of fact, I do. I mean, no. No, she doesn't."

He hesitated. "Do you think it would be amiss if I called on her?"

This big man's voice was actually shaking. Was it like this for all of us? Poor us. "Why not?"

Afterward, Adam asked me what he'd said. It shouldn't have been hard to explain, but I felt a strange reluctance to tell him. "Oh, nothing," I said.

And I knew it would most likely end up being nothing. Then again, I couldn't help but imagine.

Chapter Twenty-eight
Fleur

IT TOOK US twenty-four hours and thirty-five minutes to get back to L.A. On the first leg of our journey, we shared a row with a white-collared Anglican priest, who insisted we call him Bertie and who was on his way to a conference in New York after what sounded like a failed assignment in Addis Ababa. He seemed eager to convince us of the primitivity of Ethiopian religious life, pursing his thin, pink lips to resemble a cat's butt. Adam and I rolled our eyes at each other when he wasn't looking. Remembering the angel goat of the young girl at Aksum and the generous humanity of Father Wendimu, "Bertie's" comments hardly endeared him to me.

Somewhere between Bole Airport and JFK, I fell asleep and was wakened by the voice of a stewardess asking, "Do you think she wants lunch?" I opened my eyes and realized I'd slept with my head on Adam's shoulder. I felt a reluctance to move, but did as soon as I sensed his and the stewardess' eyes upon me. Her glance was friendly, but impersonal; his was warm and melty. Was I reading too much into it? I told myself to stop being so fanciful. Adam was my first and oldest friend, and if he still possessed an uncanny gift for bringing tingly feelings to my tweeter, I needed, as Nana might have said, to put a lid on it. Actually, it wouldn't hurt to send my desire on hiatus for a nice long time. Nothing good seemed to ever come of it.

I distracted myself by recalling the little sparrow in the rose bush, how quickly it had taken flight once its way had been cleared. So different from the baby bird on Father's lawn. I'd tried so desperately to revive that one's barely beating heart with my makeshift dropper filled with warm milk, but I hadn't done anything but accelerate its death. I knew Sammie would say it was some sort of sign once I told her about my success this time around, but a sign of what?

Adam excused himself to go to the bathroom, and I noticed that his limp was more pronounced than usual, undoubtedly thanks to sitting in a sardine box much too long. I felt a pang of guilt that he hadn't been able to move about sooner with me snoring and drooling on his shoulder.

It occurred to me that I hadn't heard a peep out of Bertie and allowed my eyes to drift to his seat. He was dead to the world, which I decided was just fine by me.

Right about then, I also realized the couple in the row behind me were having a rather muted argument, but an argument nonetheless. The man hissed, "So who do you think you're punishing more, me or you?"

For some reason, it struck me as funny, and I had to clamp my lips shut not to laugh. When I saw Adam coming up the aisle, I was dying to tell him, but he was busy doing a do-si-do with the stewardess approaching from the other direction, who placed plates of astonishingly yummy smelling food on our hastily assembled trays as soon as he sat down. I devoured my chicken teriyaki, mushroom risotto with green beans and rolls and butter and coconut cheesecake at a record pace and capped it off with a burp, for which I immediately apologized, mortified.

Adam grinned. "I think it's the Chinese who feel there's no better way for thanking the host for a great meal than a noisy belch."

I clapped a hand to my mouth. "Was it that loud?"

He shook his head emphatically. "No, no. Nothing like that. More like a little hiccup."

I looked down at my dishes, where barely a crumb reposed. "God, I might as well have licked the plates clean. I've been eating like there's no tomorrow." Which immediately sent me down a mental Chutes and Ladders to Bob's conviction that our species was busily ensuring there would be no tomorrow. I grabbed Adam's arm and with some urgency said, "Adam, do you really think P.D. can rid us of our dependence on fossil fuels?"

And like scientists the world over, he took a long a pause and responded in a considered tone, "I think we have some reason to be optimistic that we can make a meaningful dent. But you know as well as I do that there are untold numbers of variables at play."

"But what about the Precautionary Principle?"

"What's that?"

"It's something Bob told me about." I blushed, but forged on. "He's very ecologically-minded. They made it part of the Kyoto Protocol. It's the idea that scientific advances that might harm people or the environment should have the burden of proof that they'll do no real harm before they're applied, rather than afterward."

Adam frowned a bit, then slapped his knee. "Oh course. I heard about it recently on *Science Friday*. Great show. Real science. Cutting edge stuff. Ever listen to it?"

But I wasn't ready to go there. "Adam, we're going to have to be very careful how we use C-Voids to facilitate dematerialization and rematerialization. When we get home, I want to make sure the team agrees that we aim for a result that isn't harmful."

Adam sighed. "They'll agree, Fleur, but can we anticipate its long-term impact? Don't foget the Butterfly Effect."

"I know, I know, but I don't want to be an Einstein, regretting the mass destruction coming out of his discovery of the equation of matter and energy."

"Sweetheart," Adam said, "I'm right there with you, and it's to your credit that we're not accepting any funding from oil companies, but I'm afraid that once an idea becomes public, we lose control over its application. We just have to hope that P.D. will result in significantly more good than harm."

The name Sweetheart only intensified my feelings. "Oh, God," I moaned. "Maybe Sammie's right. She's always quoting that line of Jung's that the fate of the world hangs on the fragile thread of the individual human psyche."

Adam's eyes strayed to Bertie, and he made a face. "Well, let's hope he didn't mean just any psyche, because in that case, we're fucked."

We had a two-hour layover at JFK that we quickly learned was more likely to be at least five, thanks to a hurricane called Frank heading for North Carolina and lousing up air traffic everywhere. Hoping it wouldn't prove to be as destructive as its namesake (my father), I persuaded Adam to take a cab ride with me to visit some of our old haunts in Manhattan. The gate agent was confident we'd be fine if we made it back to JFK in a few hours.

We were nearing Mother's penthouse when I spied the Italianate townhouse where, as an eleven-year-old girl, I'd naively agreed to meet the older boy who'd called me Beautiful. I shouted, "Stop!" to our cabbie and was out of the taxi as soon as he pulled to the curb. Adam flew after me. Furtively looking around and seeing no one peering down from the dark green shuttered windows, I let myself into the familiar garden filled with giant ferns and tropical flowers. Adam was quickly at my side, hissing into my ear, "Fleur, this is private property. You can't do this."

I hissed back, "Do you know where we are?"

He cocked his head, and I told him. He knew the story, but he'd never seen the place where I'd met up in the middle of the night with the stranger who'd dared me to jump, stark naked, into the icy pond—this pond—my nipples jutting erectly from my newly sprouting breasts and the older boy masturbating, though I didn't understand it at the time, and then the whole scene being lit up like a movie set with a policeman's gun pointing right in my face.

What a child I'd been! I started to cry. "Do you think this is why I ended up becoming such a slut?"

Adam looked as though he wanted to punch me. He took me by the shoulders and marched me out of the garden, stopping only to latch the scrolling wrought iron gate behind us. "That's just plain dumb, Fleur. Stop punishing yourself. First of all, you were a babe in the woods when that juvenile delinquent preyed on you. Second, you are hardly a slut." As an aside, he murmured, "It's a sexist word, anyway."

I could sense the cabbie's brown eyes boring into me, and I think Adam did, too. He ran over, paid him some money and the cab took off with a squeal. Adam ushered me around the corner to a bus bench, actually the bench Uncle Bob had hid behind when the Boy Who Called Me Beautiful had first approached. When I'd embarked on my first lone foray exploring the city streets of Manhattan after Mother moved us here from Father's Main Line estate, I'd felt safer when my shrinkable Uncle Bob had offered to skip along with me. A fat lot of good my imaginary friend had been.

"How old are you?" Adam was asking me.

"Twenty-one."

"How many guys have you slept with?"

"Three."

"Do you think that makes you promiscuous?"

"Well, probably not, but I shouldn't have slept with Hector Hernandez, shouldn't have killed Baby X, and shouldn't have had sex with Bob."

"Sex with Bob? Bob who?"

I squirmed.

"Surely not Bob Ballantine."

I'd done it again. "It was only the one time. And Sammie said it was just a rebound shag."

For one long moment Adam looked absolutely stricken, and then he started to laugh. And laugh. And laugh. I felt mortified, but then he seemed to realize what his laughter was doing to me, and he abruptly stopped.

He shook his head. "Oh, hell. I didn't mean it that way. It's myself I'm laughing at, not you."

Confused and more than a little hurt, I waited for him to explain, but he looked down at his watch, exclaimed, "Holy shit, we're going to miss our plane," and stood up, waving his hand until another cabbie stopped for us.

We had to dash inside the United terminal as soon as Adam paid our driver, stopping only to check the board for our departure gate and begging to be allowed to go right to the front of the security checkpoint. We got no end of dirty looks for holding up our flight, and, suffused with guilt, I was soaked in sweat by the time we took off. Adam was unaccountably quiet during most of the flight. I fell asleep again, but this time turned away from him with my face plowed into my folded up hoodie.

As soon as we landed, Adam seemed rushed as he grabbed my hand, led me out of the plane, and pulled me toward the baggage carousel. But we needn't have hurried. After fruitlessly waiting for our bags and my boxes to slide down the chute, we spent a miserable forty-five minutes haggling with a harassed clerk before it was finally pinned down that our luggage had been removed from our plane for security reasons when it had seemed we wouldn't show for our scheduled flight. The clerk promised she'd make sure it would be put on the next flight to L.A. and that it would be delivered to us within the next twenty-four hours. Disheartened, we turned away from the counter. We were both beyond exhausted.

Luckily, we were able to catch a cab immediately, and our driver turned out to be a friendly and garrulous expat Scot with exuberant bright red eyebrows and a faceful of freckles. He insisted on shaking hands with both of us, introducing himself as Donald Mackenzie, and when he turned on his CD player, he loudly sang along with a catchy tune about walking five hundred miles that I'd never heard before.

We'd realized as soon as we'd exited the terminal that SoCal was suffering yet another heat wave. I could actually see waves of heat shimmering over the asphalt once we broke free of LAX. The cab's air conditioning wasn't working all that well, and we rolled down our windows. Blasts of hot air hit our weary faces.

"Hotter'n hell, ain't it?" editorialized Donald. "You two have a pool where you're heading?"

I shook my head, but Adam leaned forward suddenly and said, "Hey, listen, Donald, it's still soon enough to take PCH north. Would you mind heading for Santa Monica beach instead?"

I saw Donald's eyes seek mine in the rearview mirror. I turned to Adam. "What—"

He interrupted hastily, lowering his voice now so that I had to lean closer to hear him. "Listen, Fleur, I know we're both knackered, but it really is such a perfect beach day. Admit it, we're going to be working our asses off in no time. Let's extend the holiday for a few more hours. Will you come to the beach with me?"

"Come to the beach? Are you crazy?"

He laughed. "Maybe. C'mon, it'll be fun."

"But we've just flown for more than twenty-four hours and people are waiting for us and we're not even dressed for—"

"If we stop at Shutters, we can buy bathing suits and towels and be on the beach in no time."

He fastened his gaze on me, his green eyes expectant despite the fact that they were red-rimmed with fatigue. I was aware of Donald following our conversation. He actually turned off the music and contributed, "*Ach*, girl, the man's offering you a swim in that gorgeous ocean on a day like this? If I didn't have to earn my scran and scoop, I'd be joining you two myself."

I laughed and commented drily, "Oh, all right. I see I'm outnumbered. I'll do it, Adam, but we'd better call Gwennie and Mother or there'll be hell to pay."

Chapter Twenty-nine
Fleur

IN MY POST-FLIGHT haze, I'd forgotten that Shutters was virtually next door to Casa del Mar. Was it really only a few months ago that I'd toasted my 21st birthday with Sammie and Jacob and Assefa?

Oh, Assefa, where are you now? Will your Hanging Man find his peace? Will I ever be less haunted by the memory of you? Dukula. You called me your Dukula. Will I always be tied to people who name me?

Adam was fiddling in his wallet for his credit card. I knew it would be useless to offer to pay half. Shutters was quieter than usual, probably because this heat wave had struck far from the normal tourist season. I speculated as much to Donald, adding, "Thanks to climate change, travel agents could probably make a fortune exploiting the shifting weather patterns." I was rewarded with the sort of empty expression people assume when reminded of what we're doing to our planet.

Instead, he wrote down his cell number on a card and handed it to Adam. I wouldn't be surprised if Adam took him up on his invitation to go out sometime for a pint. I could hear him singing loudly as the cab pulled away.

Adam seemed to have picked up steam at the prospect of a swim, and I had to admit I felt a little excited by our impromptu detour from the expected road of going home to share a few brief highlights of our journey with the Fiskes before passing out from jetlag. Adam went over to the check-in desk to speak with a pair of toothy clerks behind the counter and returned a few minutes later reporting our clothes would be safe while we swam. We proceeded down a burnished wood hallway to find a gift shop as upscale as the beach-clubbish hotel itself, where the labels on most of the items proclaimed James Perse had designed them exclusively for Shutters.

I selected the cheapest pair of flip-flops they had, a plain white beach towel, and a turquoise bathing suit that left the largest amount possible (not much) to the imagination. Changing in a lemon-scented restroom that was roomy enough for a small homeless encampment, I emerged to pass to a waiting Adam the clothes I'd flown in, all balled up around my stinky tennis shoes. He delivered them along with his own to the concierge. I was impressed by the generosity of the hotel staff to store our gear like this until it occurred to me that he might have offered them a tip.

When he returned to me, grinning lopsidedly in his new red and white, floral Hawaiian trunks and a pair of flip-flops, his towel flung rakishly over one shoulder, I noted that he was more fit than I remembered, his torso lean and long with a virile blanket of chestnut chest hair. Though he had to be as weary as I was, his limp was barely noticeable. I have to confess that my tweeter was moist enough to make me worry I'd make an audible little swish with each step as we crossed the skaters on the boardwalk. We passed a hundred Stephanie Seidenfelds as we trudged across the broad stretch of sand, but Adam didn't seem to notice. As we neared the sea, its roar made conversation impossible, but who cared? We were enveloped by the sound, each muscle of our airplane-compressed bodies releasing to the salty, serenading wind.

Closer to the shore, we cased out the crowded sand for a vacant spot to lay down our towels. There were people everywhere, their shouting voices joining the tumult of the waves. Flitting past sand castles and seaweed were various species of shorebirds—here a Snowy Plover, there a Sanderling, and everywhere the ubiquitous seagulls with their lonesome, echoing cries.

Adam thought he'd found a good place, but I caught sight of a cloud of flies hovering over something suspiciously visceral on the wet sand nearby and, immediately averting my eyes—*I know I'm breathing in, I know I'm breathing out*—I enjoined him to keep walking.

We had to go a bit further afield before we found a place to settle, squeezed between a family with a handful of kids who were happily spread out across a couple of overlapping blankets, mariachi music blaring from their radio, and two couples dead asleep on their towels, their pale pink backs looking uniformly about to burn.

Adam wasted no time. Shouting, "Beat you into the water," he ran. Shaking my head at the craziness of it all, I took off after him.

The sea was rough, but we were both strong swimmers. We dove in nearly simultaneously and came up for air, gasping for breath. We managed to get out beyond the breakers and swam and dog-paddled around each other, making fun of each other's strokes, shaking water from our heads like puppies, pointing out the boats farther out. He disappeared into the rolling water and the next thing I knew, his hands were pulling me underwater by my feet. Kicking myself free and rising up sputtering, I furiously splashed him in the face. He dove to get away and came up with his hair covered in a caul of seaweed. He flung it off without ceremony and trailed his hands in the water, letting the ocean wash them.

"Ew," I cried, teasing. But instead of teasing me back, he swam closer and grabbed me by the waist and pulled me tightly to him. What was this? As I frantically dog-paddled to stay up, his hardness pushed against my pubic bone. But his whisper in my ear was as soft as the whirr of a hummingbird's wing.

"Let's go back to the hotel, Fleur. I want to take you to bed."

"What?" I swam away, but he came after me again.

His voice was huskier than I could have imagined. "You heard me. I want to take you to bed."

"Adam, what are you talking about? We can't just …. Where?"

"I rented us a room." My dog paddling became considerably jerkier as I began to take in what he was saying.

"Wait. You planned this?"

The expression on his wet face was steady and earnest. "Actually, yes. I did."

"Why you … you sneaky Pete."

He laughed. I laughed. I was terrified.

"Will you?" he asked.

"Yes." I couldn't believe he'd asked. I couldn't believe I'd agreed.

If I've learned anything by now, it's that some things must stay veiled. Suffice it to say that when the night was nearly over and we were groggy with jetlag and soaked with sweat, Adam felt around on the bedside table for one of the floating gardenias the hotel staff had thoughtfully placed in a shallow Japanese bowl. He tucked it behind my ear so tenderly I might have been a baby and he my mother. Or I a mother and he my child, bringing me the sweetest flower. Or, or, or. Really, there never had been a category for what he meant to me, and there wasn't one now. I drifted into a floral-scented dream world.

But I woke the next morning thinking, not of flowers or sex or love, but of Zeki. Did you think I could forget him? I would make sure the world knew all about him once I found a way to utilize his parting gift to me of the instrumentality of gravity waves in the application of P.D.

I thought, too, of Makeda, my *ihite*—her haunting ululations, her courage to stay where death loomed so close. I'd seen too many deaths, myself. I was constitutionally unsuited to it. As a child, I'd cried when Mother's David Austins dropped their petals into my hands and was despondent for days when her Anne Boleyn shriveled up, a victim of root rot. I wasn't getting any better with practice. I hated the economy of the natural world, hated that the price of nothing being wasted was life feeding on life, eternally dependent upon death. For all I knew, I'd pursued P.D. to at least momentarily bring things back from the abyss.

Adam stirred from his sleep and smiled. He had a crust of dried spittle at the side of his mouth. He stretched like a great cat. "Good morning, glory."

I gave a half-hearted grin.

"What is it?" he asked in a cautious tone.

"Oh, Adam, I'm afraid I'm not so glorious."

He sat up, reflexively covering his chest with the sheet. "Oh, God. Was I wrong? Are you regretting what we—"

I shook my head emphatically. "No! It's just ... I'd make a crummy Buddhist. I don't think I'll ever make my peace with life being suffering."

Looking relieved, he leaned forward and brushed his lips against my cheek. He smelled of something besides Campbell's Chicken Soup B.O. He smelled of me. "It's not all suffering."

But melancholy had sunk its teeth in me. "No, really. I'm always a little sad inside. That can't be normal."

He threw up his hands. "Oh, come on. You've got some cockamamie idea that you're weird. Unusual, sure. You're a quantum physicist, for Christ's sake. You want to be average, too? Fleur, that sensitivity in you, even that sadness, is precisely why I love you." He paused, then put a finger on my nipple and traced a circle on it that made it stand at attention. "Well, that and a few other things," he murmured, licking it now.

I felt my tweeter get wet, but still, I didn't succumb. Something was holding me back.

Adam stopped, looking stricken. "It's not Assefa, is it? Do you still love him?"

I really pulled away now. "Adam, you can't ask me that."

His face flushed. "Why not?" he said gruffly. "You had sex with me last night. Don't you think I have a right to know?"

There was a fire flickering in his green eyes that I'd never seen before. This was a new Adam. I told him so.

"Fleur, I just …. Listen, I don't think you know your power. That's dangerous for a woman. You need to know it or you'll end up doing harm. Harm you don't intend."

"Did I hurt Assefa?"

"This isn't about Assefa, damn it, but no, I don't think you had anything to do with what happened to him. He had his own demons." Adam fell silent, and my heart ached for him. "So do I."

"What are yours?"

"I'm too fucking nice."

"No, you're not."

"Yes, I am."

I repeated, "No, you're not."

"Am."

"Not."

And then we both laughed.

Looking relieved, Adam gave my arm a squeeze. "I don't know about you, but I could kill for a cup of coffee." I nodded. He leaned over toward the bedside table and put in a call for room service, then rose from the bed like a careless god, flung open the drapes to flood the room with sunlight, and grabbed the box of donuts we'd left unfinished the night before. Only after our lovemaking had he confessed that, when he'd given Donald Mackenzie our cab fare, he'd taken a chance and paid the all-too-willing Scot an extravagant tip to buy a box of Krispy Kremes and leave it for him at the front desk. And only in L.A. would a hotel employee tie the familiar polka dot box in rose and sage ribbon before setting it on a small table for us like a hospitality gift. After Africa, the sheer indulgence of it fairly took my breath away. I knew it would probably take Adam half a year to pay for all this.

Room service arrived with a knock on our door just as I was stepping from the shower into the thick white bath sheet Adam was holding out for me. He gestured with his head and left the bathroom, shutting the door behind him. I heard him cheerily wishing the waiter a good morning. Suddenly, I found myself fighting for breath. *How would I ever survive if he went away?*

I opened the door as soon as I sensed the coast was clear. Adam sat naked on the bed, his white hotel robe flung across the foot of the rumpled duvet. He was dipping a donut into his coffee with the bemused air of a man who'd just won the lottery. I was still in shock myself. I shuffled across the creamy Persian carpet and sat beside him, my damp body liking the warm feel of his skin. At least that part of me was uncomplicated.

I wanted time to stop, but of course it wouldn't. From a cupboard in my mind tumbled something Stanley had once said about the nature of being human: that we were each one brief nanosecond in a vast cosmic wave, the void oozing itself into shape and color and sound, then sucking it all back into blankness again.

I knew it was true. The matter, energy, and yes, information that briefly coalesced into the life of one discrete individual was just that—fleeting. And beautiful and cruel. There was no inalienable right to happiness, liberty, or even a vote for life or death except for the suicidal souls of this world. Everyone I'd ever met would be ripped away from this incarnation by a force with all the impersonality of a man running late for work, dashing out his front door oblivious to the ant he's crushing underfoot.

But in this moment, the dew was falling from the lip of the leaf. Adam put a hand on my thigh and kissed me. His mouth was moist and tasted of coffee, tasted even more strongly of Krispy Kreme Dulce de Leche. He set down his cup and we entered the dark, melting together into its crevices. A musical refrain played inside my head. What was it? Surely not Daft Punk's *Get Lucky*? A little giggle burbled up from my throat and, even as he proceeded to kiss the hollow of my neck, the curved shell of my ear, Adam chuckled with me despite having no idea why I'd laughed.

But that was the point, wasn't it? We were just two loose-limbed kids who'd thrust ourselves blindly beyond the shoreline, all gooseflesh and manic jumpiness in the icy water, screaming as an impossibly big wave rushed toward us. At its crest the water hesitated, as if momentarily surveying what it was about to consume.

I dove with Adam into the belly of it. My heart beat crazily with nearly equal parts hope and fear, with the tiniest advantage to hope.

Acknowledgements

In writing this leg of Fleur's journey, I found myself more than once needing to borrow cupfuls of the courage displayed during their lifetimes by my bubbie and zayda, Bessie and Chaim Wodlinger, and my parents, Ethel and Charlie Karson. And while it was the genius of C.G. Jung that opened the door to my imagination, my stamina for writing fiction in tandem with maintaining a vibrant analytic practice would have flagged without the soul centering afforded by my precious Heath, Noble, and Karson kin, as well as certain humorously inclined British beloveds and a circle of extraordinary friends who take our world seriously, laugh loud, and live large. My social media tribe continues to remind me of the living fabric of interconnection, and I'm especially grateful to Carolyn Raffensperger and the Apache and Arikara healers whose generous efforts helped keep the circle of life intact at a critical moment.

The beating heart of music played a seminal role in the unfolding of this story. The richness of Ethiopia and, in particular, the characters of Assefa and Makeda quickened to life inside me in response to the *tizita* songs of Seyfu Yohannes and Teddy Afro, whose "Aydenegetim Lebie" never fails to make me cry. A shout out to Deborah Howell and Neil Baylis for egging me on just enough to get me dancing with the Krar Collective onstage at the Getty, and grateful kudos to Claire Noble for finding the perfect Ethiopian necklace, fashioned from the recycled bullet casings of war, to remind me that creativity and love can transform even the most terrible suffering. Many thanks to Chris Heath, Janet Muff, Constance Crosby, Judie Harte, Pamela Kirst, and Elizabeth Trupin-Pulli, who read earlier drafts of the novel and offered helpful and encouraging feedback. Dr. Craig Stanford kindly shared with me the physical characteristics of the actual Gombe; my yoga teacher and dear friend Alison Crowley kept this old body of mine fairly fluid despite way too many hours at the computer; and Smoky Zeidel and Malcolm Campbell were warm-hearted advocates in bringing me into the Thomas-Jacob family of authors. I've been enormously inspired by the work of Jane Goodall and hope I've not been too presumptuous in my fictional rendering of her and the Gombe Stream Chimpanzee

Reserve. My publisher Melinda Clayton's can-do approach and collaborative spirit have made the physical incarnation of this book more of a joy than I could ever have imagined.

This novel had its inception in repeated visitations by a strong and supple African woman who saved my sanity during the dark nights of a serious illness. She moved the two of us through dense brush, crawling on hands and knees, with me suspended beneath her ample belly like a baby sloth. She felt to me like the first woman who'd ever lived, a magnificent personal image of the mitochondrial Eve, whose strength of spirit and DNA have stood us all in good stead for thousands of generations. May we as a species find in ourselves the wisdom to do justice to her and all our ancestors and to this exquisite earth that is our home.

Also by Sharon Heath

The History of My Body, The Fleur Trilogy, Book 1

About the Author

Sharon Heath writes fiction and non-fiction exploring the interplay of science and spirit, politics and pop culture. A certified Jungian Analyst in private practice and faculty member of the C.G. Jung Institute of Los Angeles, she served as guest editor of the special issue of *Psychological Perspectives*, "The Child Within/The Child Without." Her chapter "The Church of Her Body" appears in the anthology *Marked by Fire: Stories of the Jungian Way*, and her chapter "A Jungian Alice in Social Media Land: Some Reflections on Solastalgia, Kinship Libido, and Tribes Formed on Facebook" is included in *Depth Psychology and the Digital Age*. She has blogged for *The Huffington Post* and *TerraSpheres* and has given talks in the United States and Canada on topics ranging from the place of soul in social media to gossip, envy, secrecy, and belonging. She maintains her own blog at www.sharonheath.com.

93187925R00187

Made in the USA
Columbia, SC
05 April 2018